"MY TWO NOTES MUST HAVE BEEN SWAPPED," KAILEY SAID.

"And if you got the market list . . ." She turned her bright eyes on Simon in rueful wonder. "I wonder what Brother Claremont thought of the note *he* got?" She began laughing, hard enough to have to sit down.

"And the other note, madam? What was the subject?" Simon demanded.

She blushed. "That I hoped you would come home for a fine supper tonight . . ."

A harmless enough sentiment, he thought, but now she was trying to stifle her giggling but failing miserably. "Go on."

"I . . . intimated in my note to you that after supper . . . Simon, I wanted you to understand that—it was acceptable to me if we acquainted ourselves more intimately with . . ." Simon couldn't imagine what she was reaching for. "With what, wife?"

Her eyes were enormous. "With our marriage bed—my lord," she said quickly.

"And you put that down in ink, wife? In a missive read by a monk?" he roared.

"It wasn't meant for Brother Claremont's eyes."

"Damn his eyes! That note was for *me*!" Simon had never felt so madly jealous in all his life.

HER SECRET GUARDIAN

LINDA NEEDHAM

AVON BOOKS  NEW YORK

This is a work of fiction. Names, characters, places, and incidents either are the product of the author's imagination or are used fictitiously. Any resemblance to actual events, locales, organizations, or persons, living or dead, is entirely coincidental and beyond the intent of either the author or the publisher.

AVON BOOKS
A division of
The Hearst Corporation
1350 Avenue of the Americas
New York, New York 10019

Copyright © 1998 by Linda Needham
Inside cover author photo by Expressly Portraits
Published by arrangement with the author
Visit our website at http://www.AvonBooks.com
Library of Congress Catalog Card Number: 97-94325
ISBN: 0-380-79634-1

First Avon Books Printing: April 1998

AVON TRADEMARK REG. U.S. PAT. OFF. AND IN OTHER COUNTRIES, MARCA REGISTRADA, HECHO EN U.S.A.

Printed in the U.S.A.

WCD 10 9 8 7 6 5 4 3 2 1

To Damaris,
for her unflagging faith and encouragement

HER SECRET
GUARDIAN

Chapter 1

Chestershire, England
August 1174

"**C**ome quick, my lady!"
Kailey Hewett looked up from the fragrant patch of lavender and brushed a drop of cool rain off her forehead.

"What is it, Davie?"

Sir Robert's young squire was on the battlements above the kitchen gardens, waving his boy-thin arms as if to scatter the heavy clouds from the sky.

"Please, my lady! He's called for you!"

A cold fist closed around her heart. *Sir Robert!*

"And he's called for a priest!"

"A priest!" Dread washed over her, battered against her knees as she stood.

"Did you hear me, my lady?"

Aye, his reedy voice sounded in her chest like the darkest thunder. "Hurry to the village, Davie! Find Father Carigg!"

She raced her panic through the rows of boxed herbs toward the gate in the castle wall, cursing herself for having left Sir Robert's bedside. She'd been gone not a quarter hour, and then only to

1

gather fresh medicines for him before the storm broke.

"Please, my Lord, don't take him yet!" A roundly selfish prayer, but Kailey wasn't ready to lose him, would never be. He was family to her, as loving and gracious as any true father could have ever been. They'd had but eight short years together, and now he was dying, slipping through her fingers in the course of a week.

"Not yet. Please!" Kailey hurried through the great hall and up the narrow winding of stairs toward Sir Robert's rooms. She let herself into the deserted solar, trying to calm herself and not come raging into his chamber. He deserved her comfort, her peace at the end of his life—not the storm of grief and weeping that seethed inside her.

Sir Robert had already put his house in order, had confessed to Father Carigg and eaten of the Bread of Life, and only this morning had been given Extreme Unction to speed his soul to heaven. Though she knew that something still preyed upon his spirit, making him melancholy and restive, he did seem at peace with his dying—and so she must be.

But how can I possibly bid him good-bye?

Kailey snuffled back her tears, wiped her eyes, and then slipped past the thick curtains into his chamber, into an eerie darkness that clung to the stone walls and to her heart as well.

The coming storm spilled its watery light over the deep sill of the casement window, barely reaching the rush-strewn floor, leaving only the dying hearth and a single candle to illuminate the large room.

Even as her eyes adjusted to the dimness, something seemed wrong, the world out of sorts. The shadows between Kailey and the huge tester bed were moving, were dense when they should have been only a gossamer veil that softened the figure of the withered old warrior huddled beneath his counterpane.

But Sir Robert wasn't in the bed at all—he was sprawled backward against the low chest at the foot of the tester, his breathing a ragged, terrifying thread.

And there in the towering shadows above him was a darker presence—a vast, empty place where sunlight must surely go to die.

Kailey had always imagined the Angel of Death to be a wispy delusion of the dying, no more real than a night terror.

But there the phantom stood, faceless and huge and fully formed.

And now he was grasping Sir Robert by the throat!

"Let him go!" With no more thought than to pull Sir Robert from the brink, Kailey launched herself at the intruder.

She might as well have thrown herself against a stone gargoyle, for all the damage she did. The giant shrugged his granite shoulder and Kailey landed in a hard sprawl across the room, the breath struck from her and stars pricking the insides of her eyes.

"He's finally come, lass, just as he said he would!" Sir Robert's tottering voice rose up like an evensong when he ought to be frightened for his life. The front of his nightshirt was still wound up in that great, gauntleted fist, but he was gazing up at his tormentor with a face incandescent with bliss. "As blessed as the bright angels!"

Mother of mercies! He'd called for a priest because he thought the angels had come for him!

"Sir Robert, you've mistaken a brute for an angel!" Kailey scrambled to her feet and swallowed her terror as she picked up the nearest candlestick and advanced on Sir Robert's demon. "And you, sir, will back away and leave this chamber, else I'll be forced to crack this over your head!"

"He won't hurt me, love." Sir Robert's voice was as wispy as his breathing, but his adoring eyes were on the stranger and he clutched a small, unfamiliar box to his chest as though it were the dearest thing in the world. "Please, Kailey. Do welcome him."

"Kailey."

Her name seemed to rumble out of the sky, echoing sharply in the thunder just beyond the casement.

Sir Robert touched the stranger's sleeve. "Aye," he whispered. " 'Tis *her*."

The stranger hissed and let go of Sir Robert's nightshirt as though it burned him. He straightened to the fullness of his soaring height, stepped away from Sir Robert, and turned his ice-bound gaze on Kailey.

His eyes were clear and gray and drew her dangerously, as though to the edge of a stark cliff, as expertly probing as the sleek-bladed dagger that gleamed in its silver-webbed sheath against the folds of his cloak. Sir Robert's dark angel should have smelled of cinder and gall, but the cool trace of mountain-stirred clouds hung about him, making her draw in another breath of him, though she expelled it in a fury.

"I don't know your commerce, sir, but we are full up with heartache here." Kailey rushed to Sir Robert and gathered his slack-boned frailness into her arms, felt his feeble pulse and wanted to weep. He'd grown light of limb, as though his hasty spirit was working its way through his skin. "Whatever your business with Sir Robert, my lord, speak it quickly, and then be gone."

"Nay, Kailey! He mustn't leave. He's come all this way." Sir Robert touched his unsteady hand to her cheek and raised his lake-blue eyes to a place beyond and above her, to the intruder and his chilling silence.

"But Sir Robert—"

"He's brought me such peace this day, Kailey. You'll see. Someday you'll see."

Kailey heard the man's curse, felt his heavy footfalls on the planking as he moved sharply away from them, far across the chamber to the dampened hearth.

Sir Robert's eyes misted as they followed him. She saw a dreadful longing there, and the cold ashes of hope. An eddy of uneasiness brushed against her heart. This man was no ordinary stranger, no rogue intruder.

"Your name, sir?" Kailey meant to sound commanding as she wrapped a blanket around Sir Robert's shoulders and stood up to face the man full on, to let him know that she was no coward where Sir Robert's life was concerned. But her words tumbled out in a whispered rush, hardly a threat to this too-real figment of Sir Robert's imagination.

The man's gaze swept the length of her as he turned toward her, ruffling her hair and the edges of her gown—like the cool, down-drawn current of a falcon's flight.

"I am Baron Simon de Marchand." His voice was tethered in restraint, its resonance so immeasurably deep that it seemed to shake the stone walls and rattle the rushes beneath Kailey's shoes. "I am sheriff of this shire."

"Nay, sir, Lord *Fletchard* is sheriff of Chestershire."

"He *was.*" The surety of Marchand's words snapped at Kailey's courage like a howling winter wind.

"What do you mean, my lord? What's happened to him?"

"Fletchard was hanged two days ago in the bailey at Chester."

Hanged. Not that! Not Anson Fletchard! Kailey had to force a breath before she could speak again. "What was the charge against him?"

Marchand watched her from beneath his starkly shadowed brow, his distaste for whatever he saw clear in the iron planes of his jaw, in the ice glinting from his eyes.

"Treason," he said finally, flatly.

Kailey caught the felling word in her throat before it became a gasp; she couldn't speak it for the heat and the bitterness that stirred in her chest. Fletchard wasn't capable of such a coward's crime; he wouldn't have risked his home—his family.

Aye, but her own father had, and he'd paid the price with his life, as Kailey paid for it still. Lord Fletchard's children would suffer dearly, if Marchand's word could be believed.

"How do you know so quickly of Fletchard's execution? Were you there as witness?"

"As the king's justiciar," Marchand said coolly. "I heard Fletchard's plea in my court."

"Sheriff *and* judge; how wickedly convenient, my lord."

Marchand took a step toward her, bringing him into the pale light from the window. His brow sharpened and shaded his eyes more deeply. His face was clean-shaved and roughly angular; his midnight hair was shot through with fine steel threads at the temple.

"I judged only the merit of the Crown's plea against Fletchard's treason, madam. I care not of his guilt or innocence. God alone can judge the intent of a man's heart. And in the king's court, that judgment is left strictly to the Almighty."

"With a few falsehoods mixed in to help prove the king's plea?" She'd never seen eyes so icy gray and distant, nor flecked at the edge with the golden yellow of an eagle's. His features hardened to flint. He bent to her, as close as a breath.

"No man speaks falsehoods in my court, madam," he said through his straight white teeth. "Truth is the way and the light of the law."

"Aye, and forgiveness is the way of the Lord. Isn't it?"

Marchand drew back sharply, as if she had struck his cheek soundly. "Think what you will, madam."

"As I always do, my lord sheriff. And if you'll tell me why you have come to High Stoneham—"

"He's come, lass, because I sent for him."

Kailey turned in amazement and found Sir Robert struggling to stand on his unsteady legs, still clutching the box against his chest.

"You, Sir Robert? How?" Fearing he'd fall, Kailey slipped her shoulder under his. "When could you have sent a message?"

"I whispered my wishes to Hinch."

"To Hinch?" The old jester had a memory like a sieve. "And he remembered?"

"Aye, Kailey. 'Tis a miracle." Sir Robert's craggy features had softened and the corners of his eyes were lit with expectation. "But there are miracles yet in the world, aren't there, Simon?"

"Don't, old man! We are finished." Marchand's voice hissed like low lightning across the chamber, seemed to strike Sir Robert in the chest, dropping the old man back onto the chest-lid with a startled grunt.

Kailey grabbed Sir Robert's hand and glared at Marchand. "If you harbor an ounce of compassion for this man—"

"Compassion, madam?"

Kailey stood her ground as Marchand approached, growing ever colder as he came, a threat to everything she loved.

"Guards!" she shouted, though the word came out in a useless croak, and she could only pray that someone was near enough to hear.

Marchand simply set her aside with a sweep of his huge paw. When Kailey swung back on him, he was bearing down on Sir Robert again.

"Where is this priest, old man?" he asked beneath his breath. "I haven't got all day. And, pray God, neither do you!"

"How dare you, Marchand!" Kailey yanked at his thick arm to dislodge him, but he didn't budge. She yanked again. "Summoned or not, you will leave here—"

"Ease yourself, Kailey." Sir Robert's throat sounded raspy and thick, distorting his words. "My feelings are not so easily damaged, love. And your anger is misspent, Simon—as it has always been."

So that was it: an old bitterness brought here to Sir Robert's deathbed. "Sir Robert, do you know this sheriff?"

"Aye, Kailey." He smiled tenderly into the hate-mottled face above him. "We once knew each other very well, didn't we, Simon?"

Marchand paused, then shoved angrily away from Sir Robert. "That was another lifetime, old man."

"Aye, it was, my boy." Sir Robert took Kailey's hand. His was as cold as the memory of winter, but his eyes were warm and tearing as they rested on Marchand's broad back.

"You see, Kailey—Simon and I were once father and son."

Kailey felt outrage blossoming on her cheeks in great blotches of crimson. "He is your son?"

"Aye, lass."

The shadow son, estranged since his youth—the great sorrow of Sir Robert's life—and now the cold-hearted justiciar, come to torment and abuse him in his last moments.

"You are a wicked man, Marchand! How dare you treat your father with such dishonor? How dare you abandon him?"

"He didn't, Kailey." Sir Robert touched her elbow. "The fault between us was mine alone. He knows that. Please—you must hear this from me now."

Still blazing with anger, Kailey knelt at Sir Robert's knee and gathered her peace about her. "Tell me, my lord. And then to your bed."

"Yes." He seemed to relax, smiled crookedly down at her. "I once gave a most solemn and sacred promise that I would care for you; that I would see you happy through all your days with me."

"And so you have, my lord." Kailey tried to memorize the bright goodness in his smile, for she would be long years without him—this father of her heart.

"Then be sure to tell him so, Kailey." His eyes were glassy and distant. "He must believe."

"He will." She hadn't the faintest idea of whom he spoke, but she would say anything to give him peace in his last hours.

"And when I'm gone, sweet . . . when I die, he'll do his best to keep you."

Then she knew: Sir Robert spoke of the Almighty. She'd always had an orphan's eager trust in His tenderness; had always felt deeply loved and looked after, as if a great benevolence had woven itself through her life.

"Aye, Sir Robert; though I am the most undeserving of creatures, He has always kept me kindly."

Marchand stirred on his nearby precipice and Sir Robert's eyes found him, unblinking. "You can't know how kindly, my girl. Or with what courageous devotion." Tears coursed down his leathery cheeks, and a sob nearly choked him.

"No one has been more loved than I, nor better cared for." She had made her family wherever she'd found one lacking, and loved with as much devotion as if they shared blood and sinew. "I shall be taken care of, and loved again."

"Always! Dear Kailey—" His breath now sounded as if it came through a faulty reed.

"To your bed, now. Please?"

He nodded. "Aye, it's time."

Stifling a sob that would surely fell her, Kailey slipped her arm around Sir Robert's frail ribcage as he tried to stand. But his legs wouldn't support him, and he dropped back onto the chest.

Shamed that she couldn't bear Sir Robert's

weight on her own, Kailey turned to Marchand.

"Will you help me?"

The hearthlight played accusing shadows across his face, layering its sharp planes and hollows with the restless ghosts of the men he'd sent to the gallows.

The moment dragged like a winter storm. She bit the inside of her cheek to keep from weeping. "Please."

Without a word, Marchand lifted Sir Robert into his arms as he would a sleep-weary child and carried him easily to the broad bed.

Kailey drew down the counterpane, but Marchand was still holding his dying father against his chest, an act of filial love perverted by the hatred that hardened the son's jaw. Kailey was seized by the sudden image of Marchand crushing the life out of Sir Robert.

"Put him down, sir! Can't you hear him struggling to breathe?"

Marchand settled Sir Robert against the bank of pillows, then moved like a wraith to the opposite side of the bed, an unrelenting sentinel of death.

Kailey straightened the covers and kissed Sir Robert's cheek.

"Kailey, love, you must . . ." Sir Robert's voice was little more than a vapor, his breath as cold and hollow as a cave wind.

She bent closer, her ear to his mouth, her eyes upon his son's unforgiving glower. "Again, please."

"Marry," he breathed.

Marry? She couldn't have heard right. She was not a true ward, was penniless, her family's name a pariah. Nay, he'd said something else.

"Do *what*, Sir Robert?"

"Damn it, woman! Do you not listen?" Marchand's vast shoulders were drawn back, his chest was high and wide, and his great gloved fist was wrapped around the hilt of his long-bladed dagger. "I've come here to take you to wife."

Kailey stood slowly on legs of applesauce. Her palms had gone clammy, and a roaring pounded in her ears. So this was Sir Robert's grand scheme for her welfare! He was truly feverish if he thought she could make a suitable wife for Simon de Marchand!

"I thank you, Sir Robert," she said, without glancing down at him, "but I need no husband."

"We will wed, madam," Marchand said, in a voice that he must use to frighten the life out of those who stood accused in his court. "And the deed will be done this day."

Blessed Mary, he had all the charm of a pit viper! To have no husband at all would be better than to marry this heartless justiciar. A husband meant family, and making a family out of Simon de Marchand and his arrogance would be near impossible.

"Please, Sir Robert, I know you mean well, but this marriage would be a grievous mistake."

" 'Tis my greatest wish, Kailey. For your happiness, and my son's."

"Damn it, woman!" Marchand came round the foot of the bed like a gale off the ocean. "It will be done as I say!"

What would this sheriff, this defender of the king's peace, think of this marriage if he knew who her father had been? *Aye, let him try to swallow that burr.*

"Do you know who I am, my lord?" She left Sir Robert's bedside and went to face this would-be husband. "I am the daughter of Neville Hewett, a man hanged for treason nearly twenty years ago. Did you know that?''

Marchand met her stare full on, but she could see that it cost him, in the rise and fall of his breathing, in the tiny beads of sweat that bristled in the stubble of his beard. He was a man ready to deny her, and in spite of herself, she felt the stir of loss deeply. A family never begun.

''I know of the charge against Hewett, madam.'' His admission startled her out of her next thought, left her to watch a paleness gather around his finely wrought mouth, as though he could taste the taint of treason and detested it. ''I know of his trial and his fate. I know of the newborn daughter that he left—''

''A penniless ward, orphaned the same day by a mother who died of her grief. Neville Hewett was my father; I've not abandoned him, and I never will. If his name offends your honor, you'd best not take me to wife.''

''Enough, woman!'' He clipped his words, left space between them.

''I have no dowry, my lord, but a family name that will surely haunt our marriage and your tenure as justiciar if the king discovers it. For all these reasons and more, this marriage makes no sense. Unless I'm a secret heiress, with a great treasure entombed somewhere?''

Sir Robert slid his hand across his heart, gave her a doting smile. ''You are my treasure, lass.''

Marchand made a derisive snort then leveled a gloved finger at her. ''You'll marry me, woman, because I say so.''

Chapter 2

$\mathcal{S}$ imon's mouth was limestone-dry, his nerves bound to this scrap of saffron-skirted arrogance who stood guard over the accursed old man's deathbed. The girl should have been long ago vanquished by the misfortunes of her father's house; she should have been weepy, clinging and crisply obedient to any man who would claim her, grateful to be gone from this stinking abyss. And yet here she was, fearlessly examining his motives for this marriage as if *he* were a village thief caught red-handed and *she* were the king's justiciar.

Damn the woman!

"Madam, my reasons for this marriage are beyond discussion."

"Then I am beyond wedding, my lord!" She crossed her arms and became a paralyzing work of contrary grace. Her eyes burned with the brilliance of the moon's afterlight.

They were Hewett's eyes, a singular, candid blue.

He'd heard from those who had watched her through the long years that she had grown from a spriggy-limbed girl-child into a fierce-hearted young woman of astounding beauty. He had learned that her hair was a hundred shades of

14

freshly hewn oak scattered with dark walnut, and that it coiled to her slender waist in cascading strands of silk. He'd been prepared for all that.

But it had been the unadorned melody of her name that had struck the breath from his lungs. Though spoken by that base old man, the sound of her name had ribboned itself round his heart and still clung there like an everlasting echo, like a bell not yet rung.

And a sizzling stone had dropped into his belly. *Kailey.*

"You need only know, madam, that when Robert of Stoneham dies, your wardship passes to me."

"Then should I not be your *ward*, my lord, instead of your wife?" The fine arcs of her mouth were drawn tightly in her irritation, her soft brow grown firm in the storm-gray sunlight.

"I have need of a wife, madam, not a ward." No one had told him of her stubbornness. Not that any part of her character, nor the accident of her comeliness, had any bearing on this marriage. It had been writ in blood many years ago. A pledge, a duty—and no more.

"Come," he said. Impatient to be quit of the smothering chamber and the withered form on the bed, Simon held aside the curtain for her to pass beneath his arm. "We will find this priest and do the deed in the chapel."

But she stood fast, her fists stuck against her fine hips. "First, sir, I will not leave Sir Robert's bedside. He is too ill. And I'll not move another step until you hear me out in the matter of this marriage."

He should have sent a rider to bring her to him. But even as he thought it, he knew she was *his* now, and he alone would have to contend with her and all her tempers.

"You will come with me now, madam, else I shall carry you."

"I'm quite sure you would try, sir." The girl positioned herself at the foot of the old man's bed as if she were poised for a bout of fisticuffs. "But mind your more tender localities, because I have the means and the motive to do you great mischief with my heel."

"Kailey—" The old man saved Simon from having to reply to such foolishness.

"I'm here, Sir Robert." She threw a skin-scraping scowl at Simon, then ran to Stoneham's side, took his sin-gnarled hands between her virgin-pale ones, and rubbed his fingers as though she had the power to revive a long-dead corpse. She whispered soothingly, her soft voice caught between the pair of them, the healer and the damned, the song of the angels wasted on defiled ground.

"Promise me, Kailey." Life was seeping out of the old man breath by stale breath. "Promise me you'll marry Simon."

"I won't even consider it, Sir Robert, unless he allows me a moment to speak."

Simon loathed the intimacy between them. It spoiled the air and scoured his stomach raw. His palms itched to yank her away. He strode roughly to the table instead, dragged his knuckle lightly along the aged grain of the smooth oak, unsettled by his envy.

He'd been numb for so many years he'd forgotten the metallic taste, the tilt of shifting emotions. The sooner he was away from here with the girl, the sooner he could steady the spinning.

"Speak then, girl, but quickly. And do not think to change my mind."

"Nor would I the course of the Thames, my lord sheriff." Her cadence made his title seem an ill-tasting oath instead of a royal honor. "I'm not a fool. I understand the sanctuary you offer. After twenty years of fostering, and three honorable foster fathers—"

"Honorable—" Simon nearly spat the word into the rushes. If the girl only knew from which sewer this honor had come, if she knew of the innocent blood that stained the hands she so fondly caressed—

Her father's blood, spilled in reckless greed. Would she be so eager to kiss the man's hoary cheek then?

"Aye, my lord, *honor*. These fine men and their goodness have taught me to appreciate a sound roof over my head and a warm bed at night. But I care naught for myself. 'Tis my family I have to think of—"

"Your *family*?" The word roared out of Simon's chest as he moved to stand above the girl. She was orphaned: family could mean only one thing, and the thought tore at his vitals.

"Christ, woman, have you born bastards to some village cur?"

"How dare you, sir?" Her frown was meant to wither him, but Simon grasped it and her denial gratefully. "You'll find me chaste when—and if—you take me to your bed."

His bed. He had never allowed himself to think it. Yet she would be his wife within the hour, and the stunning reality of it spread like a flush of guilt from his chest, through his gut, to lodge like an indictment in his loins.

The daughter of Neville Hewett.

He gathered a breath and spent it in a near-bellow. "Then what family do you mean, madam?"

"I'll go nowhere without them, my lord." She tucked Stoneham's hands beneath the counterpane, then stood and faced Simon, her mouth gone grim and determined. "We will take to the road and live off our wits if we must."

"Then you will surely starve. What family?"

She grasped his insult and knotted it into another of her death-dealing scowls. "There is Hinch, my lord. A jester."

He nearly laughed. "You have a jester?"

She tilted her head as if she dared him to disbelieve. "He's quite old. His memory has faltered, my lord, and he's no longer a true jester. He came with me to High Stoneham when FitzLandry died—Baron FitzLandry was the second of my foster fathers."

FitzLandry. He'd known the man.

"Who else?"

"A squire, my lord, Sir Telford's orphaned son. The man who was my first foster-father."

Telford de Broase. That name crawled up from a stinking grave, made Simon glance unwillingly at the frail old man dwarfed by the bed, weighted by the silken counterpane, no longer the formidable warrior, his heart and his flesh wasted by his sins.

Another hour perhaps, and Simon would be the last of the conspirators. It fell to him to keep her now, and in some distant future, to carry their profane secret to the grave.

"How many other outcasts have you collected, madam?"

"There are but two, and *I* make three." Her jaw was set. "I will agree to this marriage, Lord Simon, on the condition that my family travel with me, live with me always. What say you, sir?"

Family. The girl had a damaged sense of the word.

But Simon could quite easily imagine her leading a misfit band of vagabonds into some night-gloomy forest, there to become outlaws, to plague the roads with their incompetent banditry. He'd someday find her standing before him in his court, with a price on her head and rebellious intent in her heart—and she would soon after join her father on the gallows.

He couldn't have that particular blackness on his conscience; there was not room enough where the girl was concerned. And that tipped the scales dangerously in this marriage. He didn't like that at all.

He had kept his distance all these years; he had no plans to involve himself with her any more than he was forced to.

"Done," he said, surprised at his own calm. It was settled. She belonged to him, in fact as well as in trust. He wondered why his chest ached.

"Be a family to him, lass." The old man's impossible appeal crackled as it escaped him, like the dry echoes of a dying flame.

"Aye, my lord." She ran to kneel beside the old man, but Simon caught the skeptical glance the girl sliced toward him. "I will do my best."

"I failed the boy. But you, Kailey, you can give him your heart's peace."

She shook her head in confusion at the old man's rumbling, but Simon had recognized the plea—the longing for grace that could never be. The hope of peace found in secret penance. Simon had sought his redemption in the law, yet had discovered nothing there beyond his own judgment postponed.

"And forgive me, Kailey."

A pike-pointed fear stepped its way down Simon's spine, locked his knees. *Not now, old man. Take it to hell with you.*

"Forgive you, Sir Robert?" she asked, gazing down in her generosity at this man who had stolen her father, her birthright.

"Forgive my trespasses against you."

The old man's eyes were fastened on Simon, his quivering claw of a hand raised, beckoning him backward in time to his childhood. If he touched it, he would burn.

Simon stayed away.

"Forgive me, my son."

"Go to hell, old man." The words still came easily, like the canon they had become through the years.

"He's your father, Marchand!"

But the scurrying footfalls in the solar sent her glance to the passageway. A dark-draped priest rushed into the chamber, out of breath, a high pink flushing his young cheeks.

"My lady, Davie found me in the village, told me that I was needed here. Is it his lordship? Has he . . . ?" The priest peered fearfully down at Stoneham.

"Nay, Father Carigg, Sir Robert still lives, thank the blessed Lord." She flashed Simon an impeaching frown as she went to the priest's side. " 'Tis a wedding you've been summoned for."

Carigg raised his pale eyebrows when his gaze found Simon.

"And you will do it now, priest." Drained of patience, Simon clamped the man on the shoulder and dragged him to the center of the room.

There was blue-hot balefire in the girl's eyes. "Have a care, Marchand!"

"Come, woman." Simon ripped the gauntlet off his right hand, took her by the elbow, and led her to the priest. "You will wed us."

Carigg lifted his hands. "My lady?"

" 'Tis Sir Robert's wish, Father." Her sigh contained all the woes of the world—and condemned Simon as their creator.

"Very well."

"Please—" Stoneham had roused himself to a sitting position and was trying to open the box he'd carried to the bed.

"Sir Robert—"

Simon grabbed the girl's skirts when she would have deserted him again for Stoneham. Not again. *Never* again. "The priest will see to him."

Carigg shot over to the bedside and had the box open in a moment. Stoneham wheezed and muttered as he stirred and rattled the contents with his palsied fingers.

"Let me go to him, Marchand!" The girl wound her fingers in Simon's sleeve, nearly strong enough in her growing frenzy to drag him with her to the bed. "He needs me."

"You will stay here, madam." Simon drew her hard against him, fitting her proud back to his chest, the exquisite shape of her hip a shocking contact against his groin. He held his breath as she tried to wriggle free.

"Please, my lord!"

"Bless God and Mary, 'tis still here!" The old man wrapped his fingers around a bauble of some kind, then held his trembling fist out to the priest and whispered something.

"Aye, Sir Robert." The priest nodded, then scudded back across the room.

"Marry them well, Father," Stoneham whispered, as he settled himself into the bank of pillows, looking too much at peace for such an unredeemable sinner. "God keep you both."

"Hurry, please," the girl said, shrugging out of Simon's grasp, standing close, but fidgeting to be gone.

Carigg looked askance but nodded gravely. "Aye, my lady." He sped through the marriage rite, gaining first the girl's lightning quick vow and then Simon's more harshly spoken one. And soon it was done.

Simon contained the quaking of his hands by fisting one around the hilt of his dagger, saying nothing because he couldn't speak through the unwelcome stricture in his throat.

"You are married now, my lord, my lady. In God's eyes and in man's." The priest then lifted Simon's hand and dropped something weighty into his palm. "For your bride, my lord."

A ring. The old man's. A bolt of anger flared in Simon's chest. He'd be damned if he'd allow his wife to wear such a profane gift. He was about to fling it to the floor when he realized the golden band was quite small, not a man's ring at all. He opened his hand and the tiny circlet rolled into the valley of his palm, canting against his heartline and exposing its amethyst rose.

He knew the band then. He'd seen it only once, a very long time ago, adorning an exquisitely slender hand, a hand that had trembled in sorrow and grief. What would his bride think if she knew the ring had belonged to her mother?

But Neville Hewett's daughter had been told nothing of this connection between them, knew nothing of the guttural pledge made over her father's still-warm body. FitzLandry and de Broase, Stoneham and Simon, himself.

And the girl. *Kailey.*

He was the last. And now she was his.

He looked up then at Stoneham, resented the peace he saw in those ancient eyes as they fluttered closed, hated having been the source of his stolen contentment in these last seconds of his wicked life.

The withered chest stilled then, and didn't rise again.

May you burn in hell, old man.

It was finished. Bile rose from Simon's gut to sting his throat as sharply as salt stung the backs of his eyes.

He lifted his wife's hand, prepared to slip the band on her finger. Her palm was silken warmth and welcoming as he held it in his bare right hand, her eyes the softness of springtime as he slid the ring clumsily into place with the still-gauntleted fingers of his left. His hand was huge and hers was small. But the ring fit perfectly, as if it had always belonged there and was determined to stay.

Her eyes sparkled with welled-up tears—resentment or grief, he couldn't tell, nor could he let it matter in this marriage.

Distance mattered. It was safer that way.

"Now we are family, my lord."

Family. Simon swallowed back his heart and bowed curtly to her as he tugged his gauntlet back on.

"Pack your belongings, wife. We leave High Stoneham within the hour."

Her bright face paled to chalk. "Leave Sir Robert? To suffer and die on his own, without his family round him? I will not!"

He should have warned her, should have said something. But she was already on her knees and bending over the old man before she noticed the deathly stillness.

"Dear God, no!" She frantically gathered the raggedy man in her arms, brushed her cheek against his. "Sir Robert!"

Carigg was at her side, seeking signs of life. "He's gone, Kailey. He'll suffer no more."

"But I never said good-bye!" Her sobbing wail of stark grief stirred Simon to the pit of his dark soul. "I never thanked him enough."

Simon couldn't stay for the lies he would inflict, feared the unheralded rush of wildly misplaced grief that battered in the hollow of his chest.

"One hour, wife."

"An hour? But there are prayers to be offered—" Her eyes blazed with fury. "I will stay to see Sir Robert interred. Surely even you can understand!"

"I understand that you are my wife now, and that you will be in the courtyard in one hour."

Simon turned deliberately from the girl's outrage, from the corpse in the bed, and stalked from the chamber.

Kailey watched him leave, stunned that he was now her husband, that Sir Robert was his father, and that he was gone.

Married and grieving, all in one brief moment.

"Receive him in Your mercy, Lord." Father Carigg's measured voice slipped through her sorrow and settled in her weary shoulders.

"Dear Sir Robert." Kailey brushed her lips against his bristly cheek. "How can I be a family to a man like that?"

She wanted the comfort of Sir Robert's wisdom just now, and felt his loss so profoundly that she touched her chest where the hollowness ached, sure to find a hole. But he was at peace now, and she had to take her joy in that.

When Father Carigg was finished with his soothing prayer song, Kailey kissed Sir Robert's forehead one last time, certain that his soul had already been lifted to heaven, to that shining place of heroes and angels—and fathers. His shell was clay-cold and ready to become a part of the sweet earth again. She imagined a fine oak rising up from his chest in some century to come, bearing plump acorns and a canopy of sturdy green-leather leaves.

"Fare thee well, kind sir. I will miss you as greatly as I loved you. And I will do my best to ease your son's heart."

Brushing away her scalding tears, Kailey left Sir Robert's chamber to find Davie and Hinch. He had set her on this mission himself: he knew she wasn't one to take half-measures, that she would see this son of his molded into her family—even if she had to melt him down and recast him.

After breaking the news to Davie and Hinch, she packed her clothes and culled her herb closet for the irreplaceable items, for the things that would comfort her family in their travels. She had no notion of where Marchand was taking her, where home would be—or if she'd ever be allowed to return.

The minutes scattered like quicksilver, and in an hour, Marchand and two other men were mounted and waiting in the courtyard near the gatehouse.

He dropped from his horse and strode toward Kailey as she approached, his steady gaze fixed upon her as if to keep from looking elsewhere. The cloud-heavy afternoon darkened his skin to warrior bronze, even as it sharpened and lightened the icy gray of his eyes. She would almost think him handsome if it weren't for the coldness that seeped through from his heart.

If this husband of hers indeed had a heart.

Husband. Forever and always. Dear God, and dearest Sir Robert. *How shall I make a family of this distant man?*

"Well, madam?" Marchand was staring down at her, as thunderous as the sky.

"It is done, Lord Simon. Your father will be laid to rest two days from now in the churchyard at Stoneham Abbey."

He threw away the information with a toss of his shaggy mane. "So where is this *family* of yours, wife?"

Wife. The word was a coldly foreign echo in her chest, as empty there as it sounded coming from Marchand's lips.

"They're right here." Kailey thought they had been trailing her, but when she looked back, she found Davie halted, loaded down with saddlebags, and Hinch anchored behind him.

"Come, please!" she said. "We're leaving."

But they stood like graveyard statuary.

"They come now, wife, or you go without them."

"Patience, my lord." Kailey stomped away from him and took a lumpy bag from Davie.

"Hinch is afraid," Davie told her, staring warily at Marchand over her head. "Is that *him*, Kailey?"

"I don't like horses." Hinch was clutching Sir Robert's krummhorn to his chest, as he had been since he'd been given the gift two nights before. The old jester was built of lanky willow wands, and now hunched down from his teetering height to peer into Kailey's eyes. "And I should give this back to Sir Robert. He'll be missing it."

Davie rolled his eyes at Kailey. "I told him, Kailey."

"I did too, Davie. It'll take a while and then he'll remember." And then Hinch's soft old heart would break and break again. "Sir Robert wants you to keep the horn, Hinch."

"Does he? I don't play very well. It doesn't work at all like my old lute."

"Hinch, I know you don't like horses," Kailey said, as she looked back at Marchand, who seemed only seconds from claiming her by the scruff of her neck. "But you do like carts, and I think there is room for you with the baggage."

He cocked his head, jangling the rusty old bell that hung from the back of his cap. "Can I practice my horn then?"

Kailey knew without a doubt that Marchand would lack patience with Hinch's idea of music. She couldn't help her smile. Family was the sour notes as well as the sweet. Better her husband learned that sooner than later.

"Of course."

"Then all right. I'll play a tune for Sir Robert." Hinch smiled broadly and set off for the cart as Kailey returned to Marchand with Davie in tow.

"My lord, this is Davie—"

"David de Broase, my lord." Davie's bow was deep and innocently honoring, and his capricious voice had dropped precipitously in the last minute. "I was Sir Robert's squire."

Marchand narrowed his eyes and intensified his frown.

"You've made us late," he snapped. "Mount up."

Davie took off like a bird in its fledgling flight, all arms and spinning legs, his milk-spun hair whisked high off his forehead.

"That wasn't necessary, my lord. He's just a boy."

Marchand grunted.

But it had certainly gotten Davie mounted, and now he was admiring the dappled gelding that would pull the cart and Hinch.

Satisfied that her family was well settled, Kailey put her foot in the stirrup and was reaching for the pommel of the saddle when she felt herself lifted by a great force onto her horse. Before she could right herself, her husband was stalking away toward his own beast.

Husband! The realization had come again with the force of a blow to the midsection. Moment by moment he became more real, taller, his shoulders wider and his skull thicker. She belonged, body and soul, to this emotionless stranger who could do whatever he pleased with her and spare not a second of concern for the local authorities. He *was* the authority!

Sir Robert had been so easy to love. Simon de Marchand would be impossible. And yet he was part of her family now—her truly wedded husband, no matter how unthinkable his faults.

Give him your heart's peace, Sir Robert had said. *Make a family of him.*

But how?

Fostered three times in her life, and now she was married, handed from one man to the next with nary a breath between. The responsibilities of a wife would be far more complex than those of a foster daughter: care of the sick, keeper of the keys, kitchen supervisor, indeed, all the duties of running the lord sheriff's home. She ought at least to know where they would be living.

"My lord Marchand!" Kailey wheeled her mount to his side. "Where are we bound?"

He wound the reins in his leather-clad paw. "To Chester."

"Do you live there?"

"No." He gave a rude heel and his horse pranced through the gateway, its huge hooves racketing like thunder across the planks of the drawbridge.

Kailey bristled, and raced past him to the other side of the moat. "My lord—"

When he didn't stop for her, Kailey plowed forward to keep up with his impatience. She heard the others crossing in a clatter over the drawbridge.

"Why do we go to Chester, my lord, if it isn't your home?"

He kept his face in profile, not bothering to spare her even a glance. "I told you, wife, I am the king's justiciar. The court is in circuit there for another fortnight."

"Two weeks in Chester? And then home?"

"Nay, madam. The court is in circuit for three months more."

Three months chasing through the countryside on Marchand's quest to enforce the king's justice.

Not a terribly domestic beginning, is it, Sir Robert?

"Where then is home, Marchand?"

"In the north."

"North. Thank you."

Realizing that there would be no talking to the man, Kailey let it go for the moment. Time was on her side.

She stopped and let Davie catch up. He looked as if he were trying to remain somber, when he would rather have galloped down the road on his way to high adventure. He stole furtive, unreadable glances at Marchand. She hoped he wasn't looking for approval or kindness—that well seemed quite brackish and bitter.

As the cart came level with her, she saw that Hinch had laced up his shoes with the yellow ribbons she'd given him last Eastertide. He blew his first blat on the krummhorn, making her mare dance sideways a step.

Marchand's dark head lifted and she waited for his anger. But he merely kept up his pounding pace, even as they rode through the narrow, twisting lane that marked the edge of Stoneham village. Kailey waved her farewells to friends who came out to meet them, accepted hands and fervent embraces.

And in the midst of all the hurry, the sun dodged past the clouds and glinted sharply off the weighty wedding band. The sight of it made her heart race recklessly and quickened her breathing for no reason but that the band hugged her finger as if it had been fashioned for her.

Bright, pounded gold, stamped with roses—and in the center of one a simple violet stone. Sir Robert had struggled to his last breath to retrieve it from his treasure box, had rested only after he had found it.

A family ring, perhaps? One that he had hoped would bind Kailey to his lost son?

"Would you like to hear a tune, Kailey?" Hinch

grinned up at her from his cradle of stuffed bags, as happy as daybreak.

"I'd like that very much."

The chapel bell began its mourning peal. It clashed horribly with the tuneless melody from Hinch's krummhorn, but she knew that both sounds would find Sir Robert in the highest heavens.

Kailey lifted her gaze to Stoneham's keep, to the home she'd loved for the past eight years, and let her tears come freely.

"God keep you, Sir Robert."

But how in blazes am I to keep your son?

Chapter 3

⌒◦◦⌒

Marchand drove them relentlessly, as though a ghost sat upon his shoulder, urging him onward. He glanced backward rarely, but each time he looked to the diminishing hills, to the soft contours of High Stoneham, and a darkness came over him; he snapped his attention forward and redoubled his pace.

Aye, a ghost. She felt a moment's odd compassion for the man's flight. Her own father's spirit was persistent and not always welcome. But she had never hated him for leaving her to the mercy of the world. He was family and forgiveness.

Kailey was as grateful for the numbness of her grief as she was for Marchand's stony silence. She was proud of Davie; he hadn't voiced a single complaint or groan, even with Hinch and his everlasting horn tagging so closely behind.

Darkness was nearly on them when Kailey heard a bellow and glanced back down the lane of riders to find one of Marchand's men passing the others, slapping his way through the underbrush at the edge of the road.

"My lord sheriff!"

Marchand reined in his horse, waited for the man to catch up. "What is it, Allan?"

" 'Tis only that I am weary to the bone. So is Hopton."

"Another three hours and we will be in Chester."

"Another three minutes and I will be on the ground with my face in a rut, as Hopton nearly was a moment ago. The last any of us saw of our beds or a good meal was near two days ago."

Marchand gave Allan a sweeping assessment, as if he could gauge the truth through the man's skin. He grunted and shifted his gaze to Kailey. She raised her chin. Let him look. She wouldn't be his excuse to stop.

"A meal then, Allan, in Wrexham, just ahead. Then we ride on to Chester."

The evening was late and the alehouse yard nearly deserted when they arrived. Marchand used his title and his considerable size to bargain well for a late meal, then sat with his men and ignored Kailey completely. He looked impatient to be gone, straddling the bench with his thick-muscled thighs, watching the common room with a wary eye.

Married! And a wedding dinner served up at separate tables.

She hoped Sir Robert was seeing this.

Kailey rubbed at her temples, trying to force away the dry ache that had come from too many tears, and from trying not to imagine beyond the moment.

Hinch tapped her on the arm. " 'Tis very dull in this castle keep, my lamb."

"We're not in a castle, Hinch."

"Dull anyway. Shall I go fetch my krummhorn?"

"No!" Davie was on his feet behind him, pressing down on his shoulders. "One more note, Hinch," Davie said between his teeth, "and I shall

unfasten your lips from your mouth and feed them
to the nearest goose."

Hinch stood in all his jangling height, despite
Davie's best efforts, then raised a crooked finger
skyward and bumped the ceiling with it. "My lords
and ladies all, I shall recite from my memory for
the wonderment of sundry, the ballad of the Hay-
stockings."

" 'Battle of Hastings,' Hinch," Kailey said, able
to recite the thing herself—backward, probably.

Hinch cleared his throat as he always did. " 'For
it came to pass in the time of ogres and dragons
that a certain king named . . . that . . . ' I know the
fellow's name—"

"Harold . . ." Davie offered automatically.

Hinch didn't hear. As usual, he'd pinched at the
bridge of his nose to aid his memory—but now his
fingers had slipped and were closing off his nostrils, making him quack every word.

" 'That . . . that . . . that . . . ' "

Lord, how I do love them.

Kailey spared a glance at her husband and his
quirked brows, then at his grinning men, and
laughed into her hand. She almost felt sorry for the
lord sheriff. Almost.

Just as Hinch began to stutter the name of good
King Harold, a solid little man clomped through
the alehouse doorway, pulling a dark-haired young
woman by her torn sleeve.

"My son told me the sheriff's here," he an-
nounced.

Marchand rose imperiously, hand to his dagger,
his head nearly brushing the rafters. "I am the sheriff. State your business."

"This here's my business." The man gave the terrified girl an emphatic shove that sent her stum-

bling into the back of a chair. "She's a wicked, lying thief, my lord sheriff! And I will have my due."

Kailey was on her feet in the next breath, throwing herself between the girl and the snarling little troll.

"Leave off, sir! You have no cause to give injury."

The man made a grab past Kailey, but his plucky victim ducked to safety under the table.

"Stand aside, chit!"

As he batted Kailey away, she heard a roar from across the room, and then a pathway of chairs being shoved aside. Before she could get to the opposite side of the table to help the girl, Kailey felt Marchand's great looming presence at her back.

"That will be quite enough, madam," he said, so close that his breath heated the top of her head. He had a warm hand-hold of her skirts at her hip. "I'll take care of this."

She was quite sure that the rumbling sound coming from deep in his chest was a growl. He smelled of the moon-bright night, of tangy mead and horse-sweated leather.

Kailey braved Marchand's dark gaze but found it locked on the grimacing troll. "I was protecting her, my lord."

He grunted and gave a tug at her skirts, and then Kailey could no longer see the scene for the wall that was Simon de Marchand.

Unwilling to be dismissed in the midst of this unequal battle, Kailey stepped from behind him.

Marchand scraped aside a chair and motioned to the frightened girl, still hunched under the table. "You sit."

She looked near the same age as Kailey herself,

a year or two older, perhaps, and frightened to death as she clambered from beneath the table's protection. "Aye, my lord."

"I insist that you arrest this girl, sheriff. I demand my right to bring suit against her in the king's court."

"And you, sir," Marchand said, leveling a dangerous glare at the man, "will stand respectfully in the presence of the king's agent." Marchand lifted away another chair and stood towering over the suddenly fidgeting man. "You will quietly tell me your name and the girl's, and then you will tell me your complaint. I will determine whether it merits a plea in the king's court."

"My name is Pegshaw. I am Wrexham's thatcher. I am also a merchant and a very rich man. This girl—"

"My name is Julia!" Julia glanced between the two men, saw danger in any direction, then looked down at her broken fingernails.

Defeated so easily. Kailey felt her cheeks heating in outrage.

"Aye. It's Julia!" Pegshaw said with a sneer, "and she hired into my house only last week, to help my wife with the brewing and in the tavern of an evening. And now my best set of stamped tin cups is gone!"

Julia lifted pleading, doe-brown eyes to Marchand. "I know nothing of the missing cups, sir. I told him—"

"Don't trust the little chit, my lord. Whatever she tells you will be a lie." Pegshaw balled his thick fist and shook it at Julia. She cowered and lowered her chin to her chest.

Kailey wanted to thump the troll *and* her husband, as he took it all in with his distant scrutiny before he spoke in low, even tones.

"And your evidence against the girl, thatcher?"

Pegshaw folded his arms across his pillowy stomach. "The cups were there in the plate-chest only this morning. She was in and out of the buttery all day, and now the cups are gone. She took them."

Kailey wanted to laugh at the weakness of the thatcher's evidence. His word alone? A man who would toss around a young woman as if she were a dishclout? She patiently awaited Marchand's suspicion.

But he only turned his dispassionate inquiry on Julia. "And what is your defense against this claim, mistress?"

Julia flinched as if he would strike her, shook her head between her tension-hiked shoulders. "I . . . I didn't take the cups, my lord. I didn't."

His frown deepened. "And that is your sole defense? Have you no one to stand surety?"

"I speak the truth." She flicked a wary glance toward Pegshaw. "I know not what else to say, sir."

"I see."

Kailey stiffened at the direction of Marchand's logic. "But you don't see at all, my lord sheriff. It's Julia's word against Pegshaw's. A draw, by my account."

"Not by mine."

"Sir, you must let her go."

Marchand ignored Kailey and continued to stare down at Julia. "If you have no irrefutable proof of your innocence, girl, then I must arrest you, and bind you for trial in Chester."

"Arrest her? That's it?" Kailey sputtered in

astonishment. "Julia convicted on the word of that man?"

"I said nothing of conviction, madam." Marchand now turned his interest fully upon Kailey, a startlingly oppressive sensation—being looked through to the bone. "The thatcher has the right to bring his plea to be heard by the circuit judges."

"And what of Julia's defense? What of the truth?"

"The sworn jury of Wrexham's Hundred will present the suit, and then the judges will hear the pleas of both sides, along with their oath-givers. If the suit has true merit, we will let it proceed."

"It *has* merit, my lord." Pegshaw's pig-set eyes shifted to Julia, his palms relishing each other with a grinding zeal. "But should the girl see fit to return the cups—" The man's wicked pause said enough to make Kailey's skin crawl.

"I don't have them!"

Another snarl. "Do I bring the girl with me?"

"She will come with us," Marchand said. "And should you fail to appear at the king's inquest, sir, or if your plea has been brought unjustly, your fine will be far greater than the loss of a few tin cups."

"Mark me, I will be there. And the girl will pay for her sins against me. I will see her in Chester. My lord." Pegshaw made his exit with an excessive nod.

But Marchand had already dismissed the troll and angled his way back to his chair, no doubt to enjoy his plate of steaming pottage and a good laugh with his men-at-arms.

Kailey wasn't hungry at all. Nor could she fashion a single sensible word for what she'd just witnessed. Justice? There seemed little enough in the world for a girl like Julia.

Kailey sat down beside her and put a hand on the girl's thin, sagging shoulder. " 'Tis no moment what Marchand says or thinks, Julia. *I* believe you."

A sob escaped alongside a pitiful moan. "And I believe I will hang."

"You must never say that!" Kailey hated the monstrous images that came to her. Lord Fletchard no longer sheriff, his familiar grin twisted in his pain, her father's shadow-features hidden by a hood, his body hanging slack.

"But I *shall* hang, my lady. That's a certainty."

"It is no such thing. Please, tell me what happened."

Julia looked disgusted with herself, embarrassed. "Pegshaw thought he'd hired himself a cowering bed mate."

Kailey glanced at Marchand and his broad back, realizing for the first time that this husband of hers would make demands of her body. "Did he hurt you?"

"I gave him no chance." She dug a thumbnail crescent into the tabletop. "When he found that he couldn't steal his way into my pallet, he accused me of stealing his precious tin cups."

Such a grievous breach of trust. Sir Robert had been Kailey's friend and protector, never a predator. She would see Julia's wrong turned to rights.

"What of your family?"

She shook her head. "My *grandmère* died this spring. I do what I can to live."

"You'll not suffer for this man's sins against you, Julia." Kailey stood up, took a breath of smoke-stained air.

Julia grabbed her hand. "Where are you going, my lady?"

"To speak to his lordship, the high and almighty sheriff."

"Nay." She clutched at Kailey's forearm. "Don't risk yourself for me."

" 'Tis a risk I am most willing to take, Julia." Her husband had claimed that he forbid falsehoods in his court; here was a case that would test his integrity.

Kailey stood by Marchand's table, drawing the eyes of his men. She watched silently while he drained the last of his pottage.

"My lord sheriff, that vulgar little man who just left here is a great liar."

Marchand rose and fitted his sword to his belt as he gazed casually down his long, straight nose at her. "And how do you know this?"

"Julia told me that Pegshaw tried to force himself upon her, and when she resisted, he accused her of the theft, and now she has been arrested. That is the truth of the matter."

"It may be." The man wielded his cool detachment as other men wielded their broadaxes. "And I will happily hear it in my court—sometime in the next two weeks."

"Happily?"

Marchand clasped his cloak to his leather hauberk, seeming to find great interest in watching her words form on her mouth before she could say them—no doubt one of his foolproof tricks for ferreting out liars. His knuckles were callused and scarred, his fingers nimble for such broad, battle-bronzed hands.

"And in the meantime, Julia is arrested?"

"Theft is a felonious charge, madam. She must be held somewhere. If what she says of the thatcher is true, then isn't she safer as a guest of the king than with her accuser?"

He waited for her answer with one dark brow raised. Damn the man, he was right. "I—"

"There is nothing more to say on the subject. The thatcher will purchase his writ from the king's clerk and the suit will proceed. And that is all that matters to me."

"All?"

"Come, madam, 'tis time we left here."

Kailey stopped him with a hand to the center of his hard chest. Heat poured off him, past her nerve-cooled fingertips. He looked down at her hand, at the ring he'd so recently tucked there.

"Yes?" he asked, looking again into her eyes.

"Do you mean, Lord Simon, that the king seeks justice only as a means to fill his coffers?"

"Bind a man's plea for justice directly to his purse, and that man will keep the king's peace. I merely administer his laws per the Assize of Clarendon."

"What is this Assize?"

" 'Tis a charter agreed upon by the king eight years ago, with the assent of the archbishops, bishops, abbots, earls, and barons of all England. Damnation." Marchand caught himself and stepped impatiently around her. " 'Tis not a point to be challenged by such as you."

"Because I am a woman and not a baron?"

"Because you know nothing of the law." He'd gotten to the door and now stood blocking the moon's light from spilling in. "Do you come, my lady—or do I carry you?"

Kailey ignored his question as well as his threat, took Julia by the hand, then nodded to Davie and Hinch to follow.

"I may not know the law, my lord," she said, as she passed beneath his nose, towing Julia behind her. "But I do know what is right and honest in the eyes of a just God."

Kailey did her best to dismiss Marchand's silent glaring as she led Julia toward the horses. A righteous anger burned in her breast. Justice only for the mighty and the wealthy—she could not let this pass.

Their marriage would not be a simple one, no matter what Sir Robert's hopes for it were. She was well prepared to run Marchand's house, to plant his gardens, and to give him children, but keeping his court of law from ruining the lives of innocent people might prove a danger to this "heart's peace" that Sir Robert had so wanted her to grant to his son. She might as well try to serve him up the moon on a golden trencher.

"Fear not, Julia," she said. "I'll save you from the king's justice." *Or die trying.*

"I don't see how, my lady." Julia cast a doubtful sigh toward Marchand. "Though you seem to know the sheriff well enough."

Kailey laughed at that, unable to hear a speck of humor in the sound. "I know only that his name is Simon de Marchand. And that he's my husband."

"Your husband?" Julia gasped. "You're married to the sheriff?"

"Married only today. My reasons for such a marriage barely make sense to me, else I'd explain them to you. For now, I think it's best you ride with me. We can discuss our strategy against Marchand, the king, and the thatcher."

She hadn't the first idea where to begin. Marchand's laws seemed a tangled web; and if she didn't watch her step, she'd surely become bound up in them herself and be no help to Julia. The answer was to learn Marchand's ways, to glean all she could of the king's laws, and then construct a defense.

She was just about to mount behind her client when a large and familiar hand clamped around her elbow.

"You'll ride with me, wife."

"Why?"

Marchand said nothing as he hurried her past Davie, who was helping Hinch into the cart.

"My lord, there can't possibly be room for both of us in your saddle."

Marchand merely swung himself into place and waited with his hand outstretched as Allan gave her a foot up onto the lord sheriff's boot top, and then into his lap.

"There, you see, my lord?" Kailey said, straightening her skirts over her calves, feeling a flush creep out of the neck of her shift as she realized exactly where she was perched. "I told you there wouldn't be room enough."

But Marchand remained silent as he reached round the front of her to position the reins in his bare hands. His arms were bands of hard flame; his chest was an even hotter place. And yet it wasn't so bad here, not as disturbing as she had expected—except that her heart had taken to thrumming and she didn't quite know how or where to sit.

She tried a half-dozen ways, and each made Marchand grunt.

Simon wished to God that his wife would stop her squirming. And he wished that her voice wasn't quite so low and silk-wrapped, nor so close to his ear when she turned back to him and lifted her chin to speak.

"My lord sheriff, as long as I have your undivided attention, I've a few questions for you."

Fine. Simon reined his mount in a swift half-circle, away from the brush of her words, toward the confusion as the jester started up on his krummhorn again. He welcomed the grating on his nerves as a negating influence on the impossible craving that coursed through him.

"We ride!" he shouted. "Now!"

He motioned for the outrider to move ahead with his caged lantern, then he set his heel to his horse and led his straggling entourage into the Wrexham-Chester road.

"My family, Marchand! Do they come?" She peered over his shoulder, her slender backside grinding down his carefully crafted restraint.

He anchored her with a hand to her thigh and regretted the action in the next moment, for his imagination took root in the lean play of muscles beneath her woolen skirts.

"The others will follow. My men will see to it."

She sat upright and away from him, like the dragon prow of a Viking ship. "I think you would drown the lot of us, if you could find a convenient ditch."

"Don't tempt me." Her hair hung loose over her shoulders and down the front of her, had tangled itself in the reins and caught its silkiness between his fingers. For some reason beyond understanding, he had not donned his gloves as he always did when he rode, and now he could feel every strand as it sought purchase around his knuckles.

She ought to have tied it back, or plaited the mass with a ribbon—which made him think of the small offering he'd brought to appease her as a wedding gift: a thin length of brocade woven with silver. He'd thought she liked ribbons, but she had nary a one on her. It was for the best that he hadn't given it to her. The last he looked, the ribbon was a crinkled mess wadded into the bottom of his belt pouch, and he'd have felt the fool.

"Now that I think on it, you wouldn't drown us, my lord sheriff, because then you'd be breaking the king's precious peace. And if you broke the king's peace, then you'd have to arrest yourself, instead of wasting your time arresting innocent young women."

Now, there was a stunning concept that rattled old bones. He shook off the sound and the memory. "The law will decide the worth of the thatcher's suit. And that's the end of it."

"Then tell me, sir, of Fletchard's crime. The one that made you sheriff."

"The *king* made me sheriff, madam. Fletchard raised an army to ride against Henry in his son's rebellion and was caught in an ambush on his way with his column to raze the town of Newcastle. Treason."

"I still can't imagine him—" The rest of her denial was caught up in the quick rise of her chest. She was quiet then, pensive, and he wondered if she was thinking of her own father, as Simon did each time a charge of treason was raised against a man in his court.

Treason was too simple a charge to make in times of unrest: a whispered suspicion, a man's honor dragged through gutter slop. There was no better way to rid oneself of a rival.

"The admission came from Fletchard's own mouth, madam," he said quietly. "His confession is contained in the court pipe rolls if you wish to read them."

Simon had made certain Fletchard's guilt was beyond doubt. And still the sight of the man's slack body had sickened him, had yanked him backward nearly twenty years to that frosty morning when the world had darkened and Neville Hewett had been hanged.

"What are these pipe rolls, my lord?"

"The king's record of his court, set down on parchment by his clerks. Henry lets nothing escape his notice."

"Except the truth, when it pleases him."

He was tired of her inquest, irritated by the jaggedness of her naive conclusions. He'd devoted his life to the study of jurisprudence; he had no intention of debating its boundaries with so unskilled a practitioner.

" 'Tis late, wife. We have a few hours yet before we reach Chester."

"Will the king throw you into his dungeon if you're late to your judge's bench come morning?"

"The king is in France, still battling his sons."

"Then you have much in common with the Young King and his brothers. Sons rising up against their fathers: you do that right well."

But his rising up against Stoneham had lacked the sting of satisfaction. He'd waited long years to spend his righteous wrath against the man who had betrayed his youth. But that man had been a warrior then, not an enfeebled old man, and Simon had been proud, had loved him, had worshiped him beyond reason. Today he had merely worn his anger as a shield against his disabling memories. His anger had held firm, but he hadn't won.

"Ah, my lord, but those sons of Henry want their

father's lands, his title, and all his riches." She looked up and he felt her breath on his chin, the scent of lavender clinging to her temple. "You wanted nothing from Sir Robert."

Nothing but you, wife. The errant thought brushed past his heart, leaving a swath of warmth. Simon swallowed hard against it.

"The matter is dead, madam. Leave it."

She flinched from him and Simon knew that he had whispered too sharply, felt every bit the callous clod.

But she recovered with her stubborn chin raised. "I loved Sir Robert, my lord. When I speak of him I will do so out of reverence for his memory, and not to devil you." She was sitting upright again, and the night wind made his bones ache. "I am pledged to forge a family with you. It won't be easy."

It would be impossible.

"But I can't be stumbling over your temper every time I take a step. I know nothing of what passed between you and your father; I don't want to know. But he was a dear man who meant the world to me, and nothing that you say about him could ever change my love for him. Nothing."

Simon knew better, but he would never reveal the cause. No one would, for all the rest were dead. And the burden had passed to him. She was his now.

But then again, she had always been.

His wife had at long last fallen asleep against him, the top of her head tucked under his chin, her fingers twisted up in the front of his cloak. Even now, in the bobbing light of the outrider's lamp, her beauty was utter and stark, the sort of beauty that had fitted itself against his wildest dreams as perfectly as she'd fitted herself against him.

The quickening in his groin was a natural reaction to her nearness: she smelled of willful innocence and kitchen gardens; her hair caressed his hands and his neck; her ankles caught around the back of his calves, persistent and soft-edged. What man could deny the compelling call of such enticements?

But she was the daughter of Neville Hewett, passed from hand to hand to hand as though she were nothing more than a solitary, ill-fitting glove. She should have grown up bitter and bent, should have lived her life striking out at a world that had wronged her from the start. But she was love and hope and generosity of heart.

And she frightened the hell out of him.

Here, tucked away in his arms, was his phantom made flesh. Finally. The reason he had chosen to champion the law, the reason he had never married.

Kailey.

Yes, he should call her that now, would try his best. But he'd always thought of her as "the girl," as "Hewett's daughter." Distance had been his salvation, had preserved his sanity. The habit of years would be difficult to break.

Kailey.

A melody. A gathering of hearts.

His wife.

He'd stolen her family from her, and now she conspired with Stoneham to punish him with her enterprising goodwill, thinking she could make a family with him and these cast-off souls.

Family.

Simon cleared the thickness from his throat, then set his mind on the shadowed path before him— trying to restore the untroubled numbness.

Chapter 4

Kailey awoke with a start, sitting bolt upright in the saddle—or rather, in Marchand's lap. She'd had the oddest sensation of bobbing down a river in a wine barrel, but Blessed Lady, she'd been asleep, resting like a babe against the man's chest.

"Settle yourself, madam." His arms were invitingly warm as they tugged her back against him, a most sleep-shaking surprise.

"Davie? Hinch?" She twisted to look over his shoulder, but he righted her with hands that lingered warmly on her hips.

"They are with us. And the thief."

His voice was the gentle thrumming of her dreams. Had he been humming while she slept? Nay, an austere man like her husband couldn't possibly be the sort who would hum, let alone have a melody anywhere in his ice-thick head.

Her husband. Her family. *Dear Sir Robert, you've confounded me with your prayer for your son.*

Simon de Marchand wouldn't know his heart's peace if it bit him on the backside. Still, she'd better start learning how to talk civilly to him, else she'd surely fail Sir Robert completely.

"How far have we come, my lord?" It seemed a safe enough subject.

"We are passing through Handbridge," he said easily, his voice coming from above her head. "Not yet across the Dee."

"Handbridge?" Kailey carefully relaxed—a shoulder blade here, the back of her head there against his neck—and tried her best to accommodate Marchand's disorienting warmth. He wasn't selfish with that; he seemed to burn with a heat all his own.

"Aye, and there is Chester, across the river," he whispered, nodding toward the west.

The village of Handbridge had folded itself tightly against the night, but the walls of Chester and its castle-keep stood darkly alert across the Dee with its torchlit gates that ringed the city.

"I remember the city well, my lord. Walled completely, a handsome abbey church, a fine market square. I liked best attending the horse fairs with Sir Robert—"

Kailey closed her eyes against Marchand's coming indictment for the mention of his father's name, but he answered as though he hadn't heard, as though his father had never existed.

"You'll find little has changed in the town, madam. Except that with Earl Hugh taken prisoner, the king no longer shares the third penny in taxes with him."

"I do think Henry would fine his subjects for taking air from his sky, if he could manage it."

"Indeed he would, madam." Marchand's laughter surprised her as it rolled into her chest. "But I would keep your opinion to yourself, should you ever meet the man."

He led the procession over the planked bridge that spanned the Dee. A few words to the guard at the Welshgate and their party passed through without a toll; then Marchand led them west toward the shadow-faced castle and its squat, square tower. As Kailey was about to ask their destination, Marchand turned off the lane into a two-storied enclosed innyard.

The Cask and Coffer, the sign read.

A trio of caged lanterns burned from an ale-pole at the center of the yard, throwing meager light against the neatly trimmed, lime-washed walls. The windows were as dark as coal; not a soul stirred this long after midnight.

The rest of the entourage clattered behind them into the forecourt. First Davie and his creaking cartful of Hinch, then Julia, her head bowed, and last of all, Marchand's men—both of whom seemed much the worse for their two day's wear.

"Is this where you live, my lord, when you're sheriffing in Chester?"

"Aye, madam, and 'tis where you will live."

"With my family."

Marchand missed not a beat as he disengaged her from his lap, then dismounted onto the rain-puddled cobbles and lifted her from the saddle.

His huge hands spanned the breadth of her midriff; his thumbs formed casual husbandly arcs at the base of her breasts and left beneath them bands of palpable anticipation that made Kailey's knees wobbly. The searing heat of his gaze made her realize that this was her wedding night.

"You'll excuse me, my lady."

Wedding night!

Blessed Mother of mercy! That very powerful man striding from her, his fists clenched, his cloak tucked behind the sword at his hip, was her husband. And he would certainly demand his husbandly rights before the sun met the sky again.

A sweeping flush crept up her neck and surely lit the tips of her ears like beacons, dread mixed with a heady dose of wonder. Would he be as coldly uncaring toward his wife as he'd been toward his father? Would he be as abrupt in his lovemaking?

"My lady." Davie hobbled over to her, scratching at his backside, the need for sleep paling his high cheeks and drawing down the corners of his eyes. "Are we in Chester?"

"Aye, Davie." She tousled his hair into place and he tousled it askew again. "How did Hinch fare?"

"Still asleep, my lady." Davie yawned and talked at the same time. "As is his krummhorn. Thanks be to God."

"Your job, boy," Marchand said brusquely, coming on them as quietly as a cat and planting himself behind Kailey, "is to see that the horn stays silent until well after dawn. Do you understand me?"

Davie's eyes grew large. "Aye, my lord."

"Come, wife." Marchand took off toward the inn.

Kailey saw Julia then, or the flicker of her skirts, as she was led out of the innyard, away from the inn.

"Julia!" Kailey sped across the lantern-lit courtyard, dodging between the horses, Marchand close on her heels. She made it into the narrow street before he caught her around the waist.

"Leave her to the law, madam!"

"To the devil with the law!" She pummeled her elbows against his ribs, but he was a stone wall.

"This is not your affair, wife."

"Julia!" Kailey shouted to the figures retreating into the damp night. "You said she was to come with us. I thought she would be staying!"

"Quiet, woman!" Marchand said against her ear.

"Julia!" Kailey called again, louder this time. Surely the girl had heard, yet she only hung her head and obediently followed her captor. "Damn you, Marchand, she is innocent! Falsely accused by a lying, lecherous blackguard! And I shall prove it!"

Marchand banded her with his arms as if to quiet her from rousing the street. "The girl only goes to be presented—"

"And held against her will in the darkness!" Kailey knew all too well the course of pleas and trials and executions; her own life had turned upon one. "I want to go with her."

"No."

"Then I will see her, my lord. Tomorrow!"

"You will stay away from the king's prison."

"How can you—" Kailey closed her mouth abruptly, afraid that her anger would tell too much of her determination to circumvent his plans and put Julia's world aright as she had promised. "Very well, my lord."

He muttered a curse and turned her inside his furious embrace, holding her at a distance, clutching her upper arms and peering into her face. "Very well what?"

"Very well, I'll stop shouting."

"Madam, I trust your silence far less than I trust your shouting." His eyes gleamed like clear water over brook stones. "You'll keep away from my prisoner."

"But I'm afraid for her. She has no one to speak for her."

"The evidence will. As it will for the thatcher."

Kailey had never heard such a crock of pig droppings in all her life. A peasant girl's truth against a rich man's lies—ha!

"May I watch the jury's presentment against her?"

Marchand's jaw shifted as he seemed to weigh the worth of her question. He would find only her simple interest, no matter how deeply he searched her eyes.

"Presentments are public fare, wife. Anyone may watch."

"Even women?"

That seemed to amuse him. "Even women."

He must be trying to placate her. An impossible task, given his ruthlessness and the gravity of Julia's plight. But she would make him think he had made inroads into her confidence, while she set about changing his mind.

"Thank you, my lord." She yawned into her hand, hardly exaggerating her weariness.

"I have a room," he said abruptly. "Come."

A room.

He hooked her wrist with his fingers and started once again toward the inn. Kailey followed. Not out of fear of him, but to face the inevitable and be done with it. Courage would carry the night.

Would her introduction to marriage be this swift? Thrown down upon his bed, then a lift of her skirts so that he could do what ever it was that men did to women, and then . . . but her imagination stopped there for lack of information.

Sir Robert's wife had been dead for years by the time Kailey had arrived; FitzLandry's wife didn't live at the castle and he was gone to his estates in Brittany for most of the years of her fostering; and she'd been too young to remember much of Sir Telford and his wife.

She hadn't known a single married couple in all her life; didn't know how to conduct herself as a wife in the light of day, let alone in the marriage bed.

The tavern below the inn was a dark jumble of tables and benches and the leavings of the night's merriment; a recent fire still flicked spots of light from the hearth. The thick smell of roasted pig and ale must be denser still up there near the ceiling, where Marchand's great height forced him to stand between the beams.

"Odard!" he shouted—a name or a curse, impossible to tell which. He pounded his fist on the serving counter and in a bare moment a sleep-starved innkeeper stumbled down the narrow stairs, balancing off both walls.

"We're closed, damn it!" He stopped abruptly when he caught sight of Marchand. He gave an overly grand bow. "Oh! My lord sheriff! Welcome back—"

"What rooms have you free, Odard?"

The innkeeper looked stricken, clutched at his throat as though he remembered Marchand's fingers wrapped there.

"There are no extra rooms, my lord Marchand. Yours is the only one left unlet. The royal court of justice is in session, as you well know. And we have doubled up our lodgers. But surely you and the . . ." The man lifted a wild, wiry brow and nodded toward Kailey. "The lovely *lady*—"

"My wife."

"Makes no never you mind to me what you call h—" Odard seemed finally to register what Marchand had said. He smiled at Kailey with all his snaggled teeth in plain view. "Your wife? By the blood! Congratulations, sir!"

Only Kailey heard Marchand's grunt, and her stomach reeled. She spared a glance at him and was struck by the weariness etched into his brow and the corners of his eyes.

"She will have *my* room, Odard."

"Of course, my lord. After all, a new bride needs—"

"And you will make room enough for two more men in your stable—a boy and an elderly man."

"Immediately, my lord." Odard was already skittering out the doorway and across the innyard toward the stable.

"Well, Marchand, you certainly know how to wear your office in full view. Does it please you to see the man so fearful of you?"

"He fears his own thoughts. The law is no threat to him, unless he pours a short cup of ale or raises his rents during my session." He lit a rushlight from the lantern on the counter, handed Kailey the holder, then picked up the bags he'd brought in with him. "Come."

Marchand's chamber was as high-raftered and square-cornered as the rigid laws he revered. It was large and had a niche cut from the wall where the stairs outside in the corridor continued up to a third floor attic. Kailey set the light on a table chest, and her husband wordlessly dropped the bags onto the floor.

He stood for a moment studying the room, frowning at the chair and the shutters and the unlit brazier, until his gaze slipped off the bed and slid across her face, banked fire in his eyes.

A steamy kind of heat seeped into her limbs. She wondered about his large, capable hands: how their heat had blazed through layers of wool and linen; how they might feel brushing against her bare flesh.

" 'Tis our wedding night, my lord."

Mother of mercies! Why did she say that?

Now he was scowling with those ash gray eyes, measuring her from hairline to toes, until she felt thoroughly rummaged and her skin scrubbed luminous through her shift.

"Not tonight, madam."

Kailey's face went crimson. Rejected from his bed? How then, were they to start this family?

"When?" she asked.

There she went again—as bold as brass nails!

His conciliating sigh made her feel like a peasant lass newly come to London.

"In its season, wife."

He dragged his gaze away from her, rifled a small coffer. "You'll find coins in this bag, if you need them. I've posted Allan in the tavern below. He'll know where to find me."

"And where will that be?" Kailey tried to bite back the question but only caught the end of her tongue. She didn't want to know where he would sleep tonight.

"I will most likely find a cot at the abbey," he said, lifting his saddle bag to his shoulder, looking dreadfully tired as he started for the door.

The abbey! Kailey exhaled a wayward breath of jealousy and sat down on the edge of the bed. She felt suddenly quite charitable toward the contrary man.

"Sleep well, then, my lord."

Her husband stood for the longest time in the open doorway, his hand gripping the latch. He looked as though he might be thinking something significant, but merely said, "Good night, madam."

Then he was gone, leaving her shamelessly curious about her husband, still feeling his presence as though he'd just left his warmth trapped between the blankets and the mattress.

I am trying, Sir Robert, but your son is prickly in the best of his moments. 'Twas no wonder that she hadn't felt his loss as acutely as she ought to have: she'd spent all day conversing with him, as if he'd been in the same room and not gone to Paradise.

Her own father had become nearly as persistent; uninvited but undismissable, because she did love him, as she loved her mother. And if her mother were here, she'd ask her how to be a good wife, how to handle a husband.

Kailey slipped her arms around his pillow and settled her cheek into its hollows. She detested Marchand's treatment of his father, found little to respect in his politics, was still confused at this marriage and all its meanings.

But truth be told, she thought as she closed her eyes, *I do like the way the man smells.*

Chapter 5

"**T**hat to which the accused has sworn, my lords of the court, is true, so help me God."

"Thank you, Master Helsby. You may stand down." Simon leaned forward in his high-backed chair and scanned the great hall and the eager crowd of spectators who seemed to take a prurient interest in watching their fellows squirm under the piercing light of the law, when there was bear-baiting to be found just outside the bailey. "And the last man of the jury to swear to the verity of Martin of Davenham?"

"That would be me, my lord sheriff. Arngrim . . . of Davenham." The rugged little man nodded and flashed Simon and the other two judges a nervous smile.

Beside Simon, Abbot Wingate returned Arngrim's nod with an ecclesiastical patience that Simon had never been able to understand in all the years he'd known the elderly Benedictine. The third judge, Baron Cathmore, was new to the bench, and was forever deferring to Simon for his advice on the most elementary legal point.

Henry had made sure that his judge's bench was diverse.

The oath-giving came to a complete standstill while Arngrim waited for prompting—or waited, perhaps, for hell to freeze solid.

Simon rubbed at his right temple, where a small hammer seemed to be pounding out a strong, steady rhythm. "And do you, Arngrim of Davenham, swear . . ."

"Oh! Aye, my lord, my *lords*. That which the accused has sworn is true, *sohelpmeGod*." Arngrim finished his oath at blinding speed, then bowed a half-dozen times as he backed away from the judge's bench.

"Thank you, Master Arngrim." Simon took a deep breath, hoping to clear his head of the sticky cobwebs brought on by lack of sleep, cobwebs that had tangled themselves in a very distracting scent of lavender. "Judgment as to the ownership of the chicken in Martin's custody will be returned at the end of today's session. The next writ before us, Abbot Wingate?"

Wingate scratched at the fringe of silvery gray that served as a natural tonsure, then thwacked open the board-bound book of writs, the sound as sharp against Simon's temple as a stake.

Lord Cathmore leaned to over to Simon. "All this legal gamboling over the fate of a single chicken, Marchand?" he whispered, a huge grin hidden behind his hand. "I had taken the king's judicial appointment to be a great honor, and now I wonder if I shouldn't have stayed home with my new granddaughter."

Simon tried to be diplomatic, but sharing a judicial bench with men who knew nothing at all of the common and prescribed laws of the kingdom was the single most frustrating aspect of being an itinerant justiciar. It demeaned the precedents set down in the sessions, and diluted its outcomes.

Simon had devoted thirteen grueling years to the study of English law under the Earl of Leicester; had done a humbling stint as the Earl's clerk; spent three years learning Roman law at Canterbury under the great Lombard Master, Vacarius; had held a position of trust on the court of the Exchequer; and had undertaken two circuits as justiciar.

Cathmore had gained his seat on the bench because he'd raised an army for Henry against the rebellious barons.

"It's not the value of the property that matters, Cathmore," Simon stated, "but the point of law itself. The king's peace. A matter of order, based upon discovering the truth."

"I see." But Simon knew by Cathmore's folded brow that he didn't see at all, that he couldn't possibly because he wasn't trained.

Yet Simon tried again because he actually liked Cathmore, liked his brash sense of humor and his unremitting loyalty to the king. And besides, the man was far from stupid.

"With Earl Hugh in rebellion for most of the year, the pleas of the royal court in this shire have been sorely neglected—suits left unheard, thieves left in prison for these eighteen months. The great wheels must be kept oiled, else the process will break down. The court cares not a whit about the chicken; 'tis the process of discovering the rightful ownership that must prevail. The process, Cathmore."

"You'd do well to listen to Simon, Cathmore." Wingate leaned across the opposite arm of Simon's chair. "He knows the law as few others do. You'll see a case tomorrow that has been wandering through the courts more than three years."

"Three years? By the rood!"

"A great mess for all involved," the abbot said gravely.

"Most interesting." Cathmore nodded and stroked his chin as he sat back in his chair to reassemble his judicial bearing.

And so the next presentment continued. In the midst of the tedious but vastly important process of oath-taking, where falsehoods and truths would be uncovered by careful inquisition and the presenting of evidence, Simon found himself thinking again of his wife.

Kailey.

Simon heard his own voice and looked up, then around, to see if he'd actually spoken aloud. But all eyes were on the jury from Wirral Hundred.

Simon forced his attention back to the jumble of petitioners, but the moment he relaxed his guard, his wife slipped eagerly to the fore of his thoughts.

Aye, his wife—in name, if not in truth. He'd yet to claim her fully . . . as she'd prompted him last night. Her unmistakable invitation still rang in his head.

But he'd purposely left her to his bed at the inn; it would have been no kind of wedding night. He owed the girl more consideration than the quick possession of her virtue, which was all he could have managed last night. His very pulse had thrummed with the heat of her: he already knew the shape of her hips against his hands, and burned still with the memory. He'd have surely spent himself inside her like a rutting demon, then fallen into a stupor across her lovely, naked bosom. Nay, he could not risk any more of her ill will. She had plenty of that to last a lifetime.

And he needed to keep his distance, until he

could determine with a cool head exactly how she would fit into his life.

He had abandoned the idea of a cot in the abbey guest quarters and instead staggered to the great hall of the castle, hoping to find a spot to lay his head. But the hall had been piled to the walls with snoring bodies of clerks and freeloading petitioners. He'd managed to find his way across the floor to this very chair, where he had spent the next few hours trying to find sleep. And only three hours of sleep in two days' time was too little for a man of more than thirty. His bones ached, and his head buzzed.

She had been there in his restive dreams, not a phantom any longer, but a flesh-solid memory— the blow of her hair across his brow, and a wisp of lavender and moonlight as she teased past him, eyes that shamed the sky with their bright hues.

He wondered where she was at the moment. He'd heard nothing from his man, Allan. There was good news in that—or so he dared hope. She seemed to be full of opinions and was not to be trusted any farther than the span of his arm.

But she was probably still tucked into his bed, sleeping off the journey, that tumble of hair spread across his pillow, her mouth soft and dream-moist.

Yesterday his life had been so simple.

Yesterday he hadn't been married to Neville Hewett's remarkable daughter.

The first blast of Hinch's krummhorn yanked Kailey from her dreams and sent her rushing to the window. Hinch was standing in the yard just below her, his horn poised, his cheeks full to bursting.

"Hinch, please! No."

He looked up and smiled at her. "Cock-a-doodle-doo, my lamb!"

Kailey laughed and it felt like home. "Yes, good morning. Where is Davie?" She saw the lad then, hopping out of the stable on one boot, trying to pull the other on at the same time.

"Here, my lady!" He was grunting and grimacing. "Hinch, I told you to wake me!"

"I just did, didn't I?"

Davie stumbled and stopped, his boot still in his hand, his stockinged foot ankle-deep in a puddle.

"Yes, Hinch, yes, you did."

Kailey hid her smile and praised the boy for his patience. "Meet me below in a quarter hour. We'll see the castle."

She ducked back into her husbandless wedding chamber and wondered how she was going to keep track of Hinch and Davie in a city the size of Chester. At least it was walled and gated, and Hinch was nearly impossible to miss or to forget. She would think of something.

But first she had to find Julia.

Kailey washed off the road dust with water from the ewer, wishing dearly for the bathtub she had kept in her chamber at High Stoneham.

That made her think of her absent husband, and the sumptuous dreams she'd had on her solitary wedding night. Her bridegroom had been cranky and growling, but she had peeled him of his travel clothes, had bathed him in startling, heart-thumping detail, and had then taken him to her bed. She remembered his hands hot on her thighs and his mouth straying down the cleaving between her breasts, and all this had come untried out of her dreaming!

Her husband had probably dreamed of locking

his new bride in a tower and throwing away the key.

She dressed in a fresh shift, the same pale green linen that she had used to make a shirt for Sir Robert this last Twelfth Night. They had looked a splendid pair, leading the carol dances in their laurel-wreath crowns and the bright new ribbons that she'd found draped on her door latch. That had always been her favorite part of Christmastide: twelve ribbons, one for each of the twelve days, gifted to her by a spirit, it seemed, for she had never learned the name of her ribbon-giver.

But that was Twelfth Night, and everything was different now. Everything.

She wriggled into her russet over-kirtle, grabbed a few of her husband's generously offered coins, then hurried down to the common room.

Allan was gone, replaced by Hopton, who wrenched to his feet when he saw her and nodded.

Hinch and Davie were hunkered over a chessboard that had been crudely chiseled into the tabletop, the pieces mismatched and well worn. Hinch seemed to be winning.

"Come, gentlemen," Kailey said, kissing Hinch on a cheek that was three-day bristled. "To the castle."

They left the Cask and Coffer and joined the throngs of people who were streaming through the streets of Chester. They stopped once to laugh at the antics of three trained squirrels, who took a sudden liking to Hinch's great height and to the bell on his cap, and refused to climb down off his head when their master called.

"Nursemaiding doesn't suit me, my lady," Davie whispered, while Hinch was distracted. " 'Tis time

I got back to squiring for a true knight. If you know what I'm saying."

"I do know, Davie." She wanted to hug him, proud of this boy who tottered so compassionately on the edge of manhood. But he was fourteen and would surely object to her mothering, out here in the open. "You've been a great friend to Hinch."

They both watched Hinch raise his gangly arms above his head, watched as the squirrels spiraled even higher up his close-fitting sleeves, until they were clinging to his long fingers. He lowered his arms quickly and grinned as he presented the furry adventurers to their red-faced master.

"I do love him, Kailey." Davie's eyes were glistening wet.

She squeezed his hand then, and he squeezed back. "I think perhaps Lord Simon could use a good squire."

"Do you think so, my lady?" Davie's eyes glazed with hope and he puffed out his chest. "Me?"

"We'll ask him—when he's in a better temper." As though the man's temper could be predicted.

"Kailey, girl, do you think Lord Simon needs a jester?" Hinch had ambled over to them.

"More than any man I know, Hinch."

Ten minutes and two food stalls later, they were standing at the open gates of Chester Castle. Somewhere beyond the ramparts and the sturdy guard towers, Simon de Marchand was keeping the king's court in motion.

A spectacle that she definitely wanted to observe.

But not before she found where he was keeping Julia. She left Hinch and Davie watching a boisterous drama about David and Goliath, and made her way into the great hall of the keep.

Above the milling sounds—the shuffling of

shoes and voices—she heard her husband's rich tones rising against the cool stones, hanging in the rays of morning sunlight slanting in from the tall, glazed windows.

She wanted to see him. Just a glance—to see if he'd gotten any sleep, to find those eyes on her again. But the crowd was thick and she needed to find Julia.

She kept to the perimeter and finally found the court clerks bent over their scripting in a chamber off the great hall. The cramped work space was lit like daylight with beeswax candles, furnished with a long, high table and tall stools, and surrounded by stacks of iron-bound chests.

A sandy-haired man looked up at her as he lifted his quill. He blinked away whatever passage had been in his head before he spoke. "Yes?"

"Your pardon, sir. I am Kailey—" She had been about to give the wrong name. "I am Kailey de Marchand and I'm looking for—"

"Ah, yes, my lady de Marchand. The lord sheriff's new bride. We've all heard." He smiled and stood, and the other clerks did the same, bobbing and nodding at her. "My name is Ranulf, chief officer of the clerks. What can I do for you?"

She hadn't thought that the man might know her husband. "I was wondering: where do you keep the prisoners?"

"The prisoners?" Little wonder Ranulf looked confused. The question sounded odd, even to Kailey. "My lady, with the royal court in session, prisoners are being held all over the castle grounds and in the cellars of each of the city gates."

She was willing to search them all, if need be. "I'm looking for a particular prisoner. A woman named Julia—from Wrexham."

"And the charge against her?"

"Theft." Just saying the word raised her hackles, made her stomach churn. "Though the charge is patently false."

"Of course." Ranulf's smile was patience itself, and so unlike the man he served so efficiently. He went back to the cluttered table with its bank of candles and leafed through a stack of vellum. "A moment, please, while I look."

"Yes, thank you." Kailey finally unwound enough to look around at the stone walls and all the iron chests stacked up against them. More than two dozen, each labeled cryptically.

"What do these strongboxes hold, Master Ranulf?"

"The court rolls of Chestershire." Ranulf seemed expansively proud as he looked around the room. "The king's judicial records, my lady. Lists of juries, writs, fees collected, names of petitioners and defendants, the full record of each suit preserved and laced onto the pipe rolls."

Pipe rolls? Marchand had spoken of them, and of Fletchard's confession. Here were trunks and trunks filled with the process and the aftermath of the king's justice.

"Are these records just from this session?"

"Heaven protect us clerks if that were true!" Ranulf's fellows shared his easy laughter. "The pipe rolls are normally kept at the court of the Exchequer at Westminster and are only brought to the shires on the justiciar's circuit, for reference to past suits and writs. These are all the Chestershire records since before the time of King Stephen."

"Since King Stephen?" A perilous chasm seemed to open just before her feet, made her dizzy. "*All* of the court records?"

"Those were troubled days, my lady, but most of the rolls have survived intact."

Father.

Kailey closed her eyes and it seemed she had stepped back to a time she had never lived, to a place she had only dared imagine in the quietest corners of her mind. A dormant longing rose up like a song inside her chest, leaving no room for a breath.

She spread her fingers across the lid of an iron box, startled at the chill of the metal seeping through her skin, sapping the heat from her pulse.

"Would the record of a trial for treason be here, too? Something that happened twenty years ago?"

"That would have been a plea of the Crown." Ranulf nodded emphatically. "It's most likely here, my lady."

Most likely. The full story of her father's crime, the whole of it laid bare. The answers to all the questions she had never dared ask, for she vividly recalled the crimson sensation of shame when she had asked FitzLandry about her father and been told she was never to ask again while she lived under his roof.

And so Kailey had kept silent for the sake of those fine men who had rescued her from a pauper's life, from starvation and misery. She had let her father's spirit rest undisturbed, but secretly and deeply loved, in a tiny corner of her heart, where his embers were still banked and warm beneath the airy thickness of ash.

How easily she could raise up that flame.

Father. He was here, and startlingly real in this dusty chamber of recorded memories—brushing up against her heart, whispering her name, calling her "daughter."

"My lady de Marchand?"

Kailey looked up, startled to find Ranulf waiting with his kind eyes.

"Yes?" she asked, as disoriented as if she'd just returned from some far away place.

"I found her: Julia of Wrexham. She is kept in the west tower. Alone, it seems."

"Thank you, Master Ranulf."

Kailey glanced again at the stack of black-iron trunks that looked too much like coffins. Her father was here somewhere, the last days of his life buried among the faded rolls of parchment.

So near to her she could touch him.

If she dared.

"Is there anything else I can help you with, my lady?"

"Nay, Ranulf. Not just yet." Kailey left the clerk's chamber in a blunt-edged hurry, praying that Neville Hewett's suddenly restive spirit would keep its peace while she decided what to do with him.

When Kailey gained the crowded, ghost-free bailey, she bought a honey wafer from a market stall, saw that Hinch and Davie were still caught up in the thrall of David's tale of the giant Goliath, then made her way to the westernmost tower in the castle wall.

She paid bribe money to the guard and was led through a fetid cellarway, imagining rats and fleas and slithery beasts, hearing whimpering and weeping from each side of the vaulted corridor. Too soon she could see the pearly flicker of fear-haunted eyes, prisoners awaiting their fleeting moments of justice.

And her father came to her again, nudging up

alongside her, as if he had followed her out of the daylight and into the darkness. He'd been hanged here in Chester, though exactly where, she didn't know—didn't want to know, for fear of stepping on his shadow. It was so long ago; out of mind to most. Only the pipe rolls could tell her of his last days.

Were you afraid, Father, and lonely? Did he wonder if his daughter would miss sharing her life with him?

Kailey refused to entertain her tears; she snuffled them away as the guard hurried her up the winding stairs to the windowed door of a small room near the top of the tower.

Julia was sitting against the stone wall opposite the door, her knees tucked up to her chin, her dark hair matted even darker, in need of brushing and a bright new ribbon. The only light in the room came from the sliver of daylight that spilled in from the arrow slit.

"Julia!" Kailey whispered.

The girl jumped to her feet and scrambled to the door.

"My lady, you shouldn't be here!" Julia gripped the thick iron bars in its window, her fingers surely thinner than they'd been the night before. "But I'm awfully glad to see you."

"I'm sorry I couldn't get here earlier—my husband has hidden you well. But I've brought you a sugar wafer."

Kailey slipped the wafer through the bars and Julia grabbed it.

"Dear, my lady!" She moaned as she stuffed a piece of the wafer into her mouth and swallowed it down with a whimper. " 'Tis wonderful sweet."

"You've not eaten since yesterday, have you?"

"No money for food." She took another bite of wafer and closed her eyes. "No family to bring it."

"No family, indeed! Mark me, Julia, you've just found yourself more family than you'll ever need." Food was the very simplest thing to remedy. Kailey offered the apple she'd been saving for later. "Here."

"You mustn't worry, my lady." But Julia took the apple anyway, her teeth chattering from the cold that clung to the walls like a lime wash.

"Do you imagine that Pegshaw's belly was empty last night? Or that his bed was naught but wooden planks? I'll be back shortly, with a blanket, a nightbucket, and a holiday feast."

"Why do this for me, my lady?" Julia gripped the iron bars with both hands, her voice ripe with a sob, tears about to slide down her grime-streaked face. "I am no one to you, nothing to anyone, and soon to be condemned to die. You are a lady—"

"Nay, Julia! Listen to me well." For some reason, despair had always made her boiling angry and steaming for a fight. "I am the daughter of a man who betrayed his king and died for his crime. I've lived my entire life in his shadow. I've had to take charity when I would rather have given it. I've been handed from one family to the next like a crazed old aunt, and now I'm married to a man whose life's work seems to be to punish men for their sins. But I found love in all that snaggle, Julia, and family and forgiveness, and even a bit of grace."

"Please, my lady." Julia leaned back against the door, sobbing out her desolation. "I don't want to even hope for such a thing."

"Then I shall do your hoping for you." Kailey had no intention of giving up on the girl. She had never given up on anyone, and she didn't plan to start now.

Aye, not even on that husband of hers.

"And how did your young cousin come by this virgate of land, Master Stenulf?"

Simon was standing below the judge's bench, had just asked his first question of the raw-boned man, when something in the gallery made him glance up, made his heart slam recklessly against the inside of his rib cage.

"Halwyn's father and mine were brothers," Stenulf said. "Their father owned the land."

Simon barely heard the man for the roaring in his ears.

Kailey.

She was sitting in the gallery above him, like an ill-informed angel come to bless him and to curse him in one sweet breath. Her arms were folded across the railing and her chin propped on her hands, making him wonder how long she had been watching. The fall of her hair ripened the carved oak of the screens, and even from this great distance its silkiness bound his senses, the irresistible feel of it against his throat, the tantalizing pressure of her backside against his groin.

"Shall I say again, my lord?"

"No," Simon snapped, righting his thoughts. He turned his back on the man and picked up Stenulf's writ from the judge's table. "So. Halwyn's father inherited from your grandfather, and then Halwyn from *his* father."

"Aye." Stenulf grunted the word.

"Did your cousin pay the death duty to his lord?" Simon felt his wife's eyes blazing on his back, but turned and leaned a hip against the table.

"Aye, my lord, Halwyn paid." Stenulf narrowed his eyes at the tight-lipped Halwyn, who stood opposite, as if faulting the boy for following the measure of the law.

"And why did your mutual grandfather assign the land to Halwyn's father?"

"Because he was the eldest son."

Simon had only meant to take a breath, but he raised his eyes to the gallery. His wife smiled boldly at him, wriggled her fingers in a greeting that struck him with all the ferocity of a kiss.

Simon felt his face flush crimson, as a surge of lust and guilt and wonder coursed through him.

"Damn the woman!" Not here in his court!

"What's that you say, Simon?" Wingate whispered from his chair behind him.

"Nothing."

But the man was looking too closely at him. "Are you all right, son? You seem flushed."

Simon rubbed at his jaw, at his wife's airborne kiss. "Not enough sleep, Wingate. It'll pass."

"She's quite lovely," the abbot said, nodding toward the gallery, flexing one of his gray caterpillar brows. "Your new wife?"

Wingate knew him too well. "Aye."

Cathmore was leaning forward on both elbows, staring up into the same gallery. "You're a lucky goat, Marchand."

Too lucky by half. She was stunning and gamin-faced, ripe and promising as a peach.

His need for her was a mountain-deep well, fed by ancient, underground springs. It had bubbled for years, and he'd always redirected its course. He would again.

Distance. Distance.

His pulse under tighter control, Simon disengaged himself from the blue-eyed woman and set his mind on the plea at hand.

"So far, Master Stenulf, you've presented nothing to me that would make me think you have been wronged."

"Not wronged, my lord." Stenulf began to stutter. "Halwyn is not of an age to hold a virgate of land. He is but fourteen, his mother widowed and enfeebled. The virgate should be mine."

"In wardship?"

"Aye, in wardship! I would see them cared for."

"Would you?" Simon turned to Halwyn. The boy had been standing quietly by, masking his fury by gripping his white-knuckled fists behind his back. He was young and needed guidance. Perhaps a wardship would be best.

Kailey hadn't realized that she was shaking her head until she noticed her husband glaring at her from beneath that slashing brow. His dark hair shone even darker in the spill of light from the clerestory windows. His forest tunic brushed at his calves, his boots rose to his knees, and he stood in them as if he owned the world. But he was about to make a terrible misjudgment against the boy.

"The Crown will hear your plea, Stenulf," Marchand said abruptly, as if to Kailey alone. "To be returned to this hall two days hence. See the clerk."

So, he hadn't decided against the boy, only postponed the inevitable. The poor always lost to the rich, the weak to the strong, and, in Halwyn's case, the young man would lose out to his much older cousin.

Kailey had seen too many pleas today that could have been more fairly judged. Claims against dowries, fines for raising the water level of a pond, for erecting fences, a man with six children made to abjure the realm for stealing a barrel of oats.

And Julia had been charged with theft.

Kailey stayed in the gallery through the course of the session, watching the turn of every cog and wheel in Marchand's legal millworks. And when it was done, she had only questions to ask of her husband.

Kailey hurried down the stairs, delayed by the crowds, and finally found Marchand standing with the abbot at the edge of the dais, his hand on the older man's shoulder.

"Wingate, this sort of thing is rarely as simple as it seems. I want to look into it."

The abbot's face had gone ashen, his hand to his chest. A failing heart? Sir Robert's illness had begun the same way.

Kailey's own heart pounded with the memory. "My lord?" She touched her husband's sleeve and he whirled on her.

"Yes?"

He seemed taller than ever, and exhausted. A dark beard stubbled the stark planes of his jaw with a sheen of glassy midnight. His fury seemed to settle when he saw her.

"Ah, good, madam." He raked his fingers through his hair. "I want a moment with you."

"What's happened here, my lord? Father Abbot, you don't look well." Out of habit and care, Kailey put her hand to the priest's brow. It was cold and clammy. "Do you feel light-headed?"

"He isn't ill, wife." Marchand's face had gone pale around the edges, his fine mouth a thin line. "He's just now learned that his son has been taken hostage by the Saracens."

"Merciful God." Kailey added a silent prayer for all fathers and sons. "You need to sit, sir."

"As I told him." Her husband's eyes were poorly shielded, those flecks of yellow now pierced clean through to his heart. "But the man has always been stubborn."

"I just need a moment, Simon." But the priest's voice was far from strong or steady. The letter he held trembled with the motion of his hand.

"I'm terribly sorry about your son, Father," Kailey said, taking up the abbot's hand. It was warm, but damp, his pulse quicker than it ought to be.

"His name is Nicholas. My son. And thank you," he said, quirking his head as though he just noticed Kailey. "Ah, you are Simon's wife—the one he rode so hard to collect."

"She is."

Kailey glanced up at her husband, who stood near enough to shade the fall of light from the high windows with his shoulders. She didn't know what to make of his fierce scowl, the very same one he'd been wearing last night when he'd fled their chamber.

"If I can help in any way, Father Abbot?"

"Your husband seems to think there is something not right here. But he sees the devil in most things." His color was better, and his breathing.

"I've made no such judgment, Wingate. It's too soon to know anything. Brother Claremont brought the message to you at the castle; now I want to find the man who first delivered it to St. Werburgh's."

"And all I want is my son back, Simon."

"Yes, I know." Marchand's voice had smoothed from impatience to silk in a single breath. "Are you up to a ride to the abbey?"

"By all the saints, Simon, I can walk. I wish you'd stop speaking as if I were your deaf old grandsire. God help me, were that true!" The abbot took in a chest of air and began gathering his papers into the cloth bag he had slung across his shoulder.

Marchand tried to disguise his smile in a thin line of mock irritation, but Kailey saw the relief in her husband's eyes; a softer kind of gray. Compassion. It was artless and compelling in this unapproachable man, made her wonder why he'd learned to hide it so well and offer it so sparingly.

An orphaned heart? So easily wounded.

She felt a great stirring in her chest, felt her husband's gaze on her and met it squarely.

"The abbot needs his rest, my lord. As you do."

He detached himself easily, hardened his jaw, and summoned that familiar chill. "And in case you don't think that I am made aware of your every step, wife, I know that you visited the thief today. Twice."

"Then you know that I took a sugared wafer to her."

"And a blanket and bread and cheese later in the day."

Of course, he would know that already: Hopton was the very best of spies. She'd even had the man carry the blanket for her.

"I told you, madam, to leave her to the law."

"Aye, it would save the court a world of trouble if she starves first, wouldn't it?" Kailey was about to give her opinion of the king's wicked prisons when she heard Davie's voice ringing out over the clamor.

"There she is! Kailey! My lady! And there's the sheriff."

Allan followed closely, and Kailey's heart was in her throat. Hinch wasn't with them.

Marchand met Allan in the center of the hall. "What is it?"

"They've found a body, my lord."

"Not Hinch!" Kailey took hold of Davie's arm and he patted her hand.

"Me and Hinch found him, my lady!" Davie said, eager but green-gilled. "I left Hinch to guard the body."

Marchand made a noise low in his throat and shook his head. "Christ on the Cross," he muttered. "Where, Allan?"

"Caught in the reeds upriver of the mills, near the Welshgate."

The abbot joined them, crossing himself. "A body, Simon? Such a plague of violence."

" 'Tis all we need, Wingate. We'll take him to the morgue in the abbey, if you don't mind."

The abbot nodded and Marchand turned back to Kailey. "This matter of my prisoner isn't finished between us, madam. I will see you at the inn."

"I'm coming with you," she said.

He studied her for a moment, looking too tired to argue. " 'Tis a grim business, wife."

"I'm sure of it, my lord. I've seen many a body and will see many more, the longer I am married to you."

That seemed a stunning revelation to him, and Kailey was sure that he was about to argue the fact when he nodded.

"Come, then," he said, leading them from the castle.

Chapter 6

❧

Kailey followed her husband through the streets to the riverbank, past the line of horrendously noisy mills, until they reached the edge of the river, where it seemed the entire city of Chester had gathered to gawk at the tragedy.

Hinch patrolled a six-foot circuit around the mud-mired site, brandishing his krummhorn as though it were blade-sharp and he were about to use it.

The body had been drawn halfway out of the water, the arms crossed against his chest. Marchand knelt down and peered at the bruises on the young man's face.

"When did you find him, boy?"

"Not ten minutes ago, sir," Davie said, looking everywhere but at the body, his face even greener than it had been a moment before. "Hinch and I noticed him from the walls, then came down to see for ourselves."

Kailey had expected to find the translucent blue-white of death, but this body seemed too pink and vital as it lay facing her. The young man's hair was a brilliant orange, no doubt a prize as well as a plague that would soon be only a memory for those who loved him. She bent over the smooth face and lifted his eyelids, felt the whisper of breath across the heel of her hand. Her heart skipped.

"I think he's still alive, my lord."

Marchand put his fingers to the man's throat. "There's an infirmary in the abbey."

"Davie! Someone! A litter, please! Or a cart!"

"Aye, my lady!" Kailey heard Davie's footsteps running toward the mill as the growing crowd muttered, leaned in, and stepped closer.

Marchand pulled the young man free of the brackish water and the clinging rushes, then settled the battered form gently on the grassy bank.

"Poor fool," he said, turning the young man's face toward them. "He's been beaten and stabbed and left for dead. The mark of a fist here, and here."

Kailey lifted aside the soggy tunic at the neck. "A drunken brawl gone bad, do you think?"

"More deliberate than that." He stood up, his brow creased and free of the mocking arrogance that came so easily to him. "I'll need to talk with Davie and Hinch. As first-finders, they must be presented to the court by the Chester Hundred to be cleared of the charge."

Kailey's heart stopped completely. "What charge?"

He glanced down at the too-still body. "Hopefully not murder."

"You can't mean it!" Was the man bent on incarcerating everyone she loved? "How can you believe that of Hinch and Davie? They are the gentlest of souls!"

"I don't believe either of them guilty of anything but eagerness to please. But it matters not, madam; I must keep the king's peace."

"And you gain the king's peace by frightening

two innocent men, who would be shattered if they thought you suspected them? Will you put them in jail, as you did Julia?"

"Not unless they give me cause." He rested his forehead in the crook of his fingers, then scrubbed at his brow. "Please, wife. I have to raise the hue and cry. A man has been assaulted and lies near to death. Someone is to blame—"

"Not Davie or Hinch!" She'd never heard anything so outrageous.

"They must come with me to court."

"Now? But I want to see this poor young man into the infirmary."

"Do that, madam. Resurrect him, please." Marchand lifted the limp body into his arms and started toward the handcart that Davie was pulling through an alleyway of spectators. Kailey followed on her husband's heels.

"But I want to be in the court to hear what Davie and Hinch say."

"You'll have to trust me, wife."

"Trust *you*?"

"And the law. I will take their statements, then I will let them go while my officers look into the matter. It's the most common of procedures."

He settled the body into the handcart as easily as if it had been a small sack of oats, and set the cart on its way.

"If you hurt either of them, Simon de Marchand—"

But Davie and Hinch were already eagerly following her husband up the embankment, a spellbinding piper leading her family away.

"Will he live, Lady de Marchand?"

"I can't say yet, Father Abbot. The wound from

the knife has stopped bleeding." Kailey wiped the red-caked mud off the young man's bludgeoned face. His skin was as cold and unresponsive as the stone floor of the vast infirmary. She put her hand on his heart and her mouth near his. The cool brush of his shallow breathing came lightly, haltingly, and still he clung tenaciously to his spirit.

"We thank you for lending a hand here."

"I am glad that I can." Kailey's thoughts were pulled tautly toward the castle, though, tugged by the inquisition Marchand was executing against her innocent family. And by Julia, so mournful and hope-lost in her cell.

"As you see, Lady Marchand, we are full up with broken limbs and bruised heads. 'Tis all too common at a market faire, with merchants here from all parts of the shire."

"Add the king's court to that brew, and tempers are sure to flare." Kailey made a quick scan of the harried monks who scurried through the long, candle-smoked hall with their bundles of herbs and trailing bandages.

"Someone wanted this one dead." The priest picked a glob of stinking algae and mossy reeds from their patient's bright hair.

"They've nearly succeeded; he's as cold as death. And if I'm to help him, I need to get him out of his clothes and under a blanket, else we'll be treating a well-healed corpse." Kailey expected Father Abbot to object when she picked up a pair of scissors and started to cut away at the sides of the man's torn tunic and sagging trews. Instead, the priest merely covered the body with a blanket as she proceeded—propriety and purpose made one. She liked the man immensely.

"Seeing this boy, I can't help but think of Nicholas," he said, dragging a brazier closer to the cot. "Both of them wrestling the devil. I've seen Saracen prisons—Christian prisons, too—and I'd wish neither on the very worst of my enemies."

"I'll pray for him, Father."

"As I do. He's my only child—I was a soldier on crusade when my young wife bore him. She died of her fever. Twenty-five years it's been since then."

"I am sorry, Father." Kailey reached beneath the blanket and tugged the clinging trews from the lifeless legs, hampered by this need for modesty. "Then you raised Nicholas alone?"

"I raised him not at all—to my utter shame. I was so much more interested in my holy cause than in my infant son that he was nearly five when I returned for him. I was a stranger to him, and he was thriving happily in his uncle's home. So I let him stay. I had a great emptiness inside of me to fill, and so I took this cowl." Abbot Wingate frowned as he struggled to lift the limp man to a sitting position, allowing Kailey to slide the remains of the ragged tunic from under the body.

"But you found your way back to each other, Father Abbot. That's a great miracle."

"The miracle was that Nicholas and I persevered through our estrangement and now we share a great love for each other." Tears shimmered in the abbot's eyes as he bundled the clothes and set them on the end of the cot. "Knowing now what I missed is my penance for leaving him to his uncle. I regret that I never fought for him."

Another father who sorrows for his lost son. "But you *are* fighting for Nicholas. As he would for you."

Father Abbot smiled ruefully. "You are wise in your kind counsel, my lady."

"A requirement to keep pace with my husband."
She touched the blueish water-puckered knife
wound on the young man's shoulder.

"Aye, you've married a man with enough en-
durance to swim upstream through a white-
foamed cataract." The abbot added another blanket
and tucked it close about the body. "I thought the
hounds of hell were after him when he received
the note that his father was dying. I had no idea
why he left the court so abruptly—he keeps his
heart silent. Then he returned last night with you."

The hounds of hell. They were still baying, still
nipping at her husband's heels. "Have you known
him long, Father?"

"Nearly ten years. We were together on an itinerant circuit three years past, and I remember him
even earlier at the Clarendon Assize when he
clerked for Leicester. Your husband is a brilliant
man, learned in legal matters, dedicated to the
king's peace and devout."

"And so difficult."

"Yes." Wingate smiled fondly at some memory
that animated his hoary brows. "I've known few
men as exacting on themselves as Simon de Marchand."

"Then how do I make a family of him?"

"Listen to your heart," he said softly.

She would try. But it was difficult when her
heart was forever running riot in her chest. "I'll
keep that in mind, Father Wingate. Especially
when the man is blustering."

"Which reminds me! He wants an accounting of
the messenger who delivered this hostage note to
the abbey. I'd best go investigate before Vespers.
Do send for me if you should need anything." The
abbot touched a prayer to the young man's fore-

head, smiled at Kailey, then scuffled away in his sandals.

A father who had found his son. Sir Robert had never been so blessed. And her own father had suddenly begun to wreath her thoughts.

But this moment was for the living.

The brothers brought her pots of green unguents, and bruise plasters and bitter-smelling lotions. They tsked over the near-corpse and shook their heads in doubt. Unwilling to give an inch in her cause to save the man, Kailey dressed his wounds, making notes in her head for the inquest Marchand would surely make, assessing every mark for its meaning: a stab to the shoulder and a slice against the inside of each forearm, as if he'd tried to defend himself from a knife blow before he was struck.

Hinch and Davie had nothing to do with this crime, and she did her best to preserve all the evidence so the truth would prevail.

And all the while Kailey whispered into the young man's torn ear, called him Carrotlocks as she tried to bring him back from wherever he was hiding from his pain.

"Did you keep his clothes, wife?"

The rumbling question came from the foot of the cot; the unreachable lord high sheriff had managed to arrive unannounced. Hinch and Davie had come with him, Hinch staring solemnly down the length of the still body and Davie's nose wrinkling as he came to peer at young man's bloodless face.

"Is he dead? I do pray not." Davie crossed himself in sudden horror and took Kailey's hand.

She squeezed it. "You found him just in time."

"Hinch saw him first." The boy's smile returned and he flashed it brightly at Marchand. "And that's what the lord sheriff wanted us to tell everyone at the court!"

Kailey slid her gaze toward her husband and found his assessing gray eyes already on her. "And did you tell everything to the court, Davie?" she asked pointedly.

"Oh, yes, my lady. Just as we saw it. *Where* we found the body; *when* we found the body; did we see anyone standing around, or find anything in the river? Aye, we told 'em *everything!*" Davie hitched his thumbs into his belt and raised himself up on his toes, looking very, very important. "Yes, my lady. Every detail we could remember. Right, Hinch?"

"They wouldn't let me play my horn," Hinch said, shaking his head sadly. "And me a court jester."

"I return your family to you, madam, unharmed, as promised." Marchand's irritation with his first-finders was palpable. Not that she cared a fig for his temper; he'd brought the problem on himself.

"Will you need Hinch and Davie again, my lord?"

"No!" he said, pinching his brow as though he were nursing a headache—perhaps two.

"Good. And there are the young man's clothes on the bench." Kailey covered a thin tongue of willow in fresh linen, dunked it into a cup of wine, then began gently to probe the depth of the knife wound. It wasn't as deep as she'd imagined, a half-inch, no more, and must have missed any of the greater vessels.

Marchand bent down to the pile of clothes. He lifted the young man's single shoe with the blade of his dagger, turning up the worn sole. "Did anyone come looking for him?"

"Not that I have heard. But someone is bound to miss him."

"Unless he's not expected home soon." Marchand watched her probing, grim-jawed and pale as she rattled off her observations.

"I pray that he lives here in Chester; then his family can bring him comfort. Though I do doubt he's a farmer, my lord. Else his face would be more ruddy. And his palms are uncallused, so he doesn't pull a plow. He also wasn't robbed." She left a tail of wine-soaked linen inside the wound and nodded to the young man's cloth belt-purse. "There are still two farthings and the tip of a water-wilted peacock feather inside."

Marchand inspected the purse and its contents, listened to the rest of her assessment, and carefully scrutinized the body as she described the bruising and the cuts.

"You've done well here, madam," he said.

"I'm not helpless, my lord." Kailey expected to see derision when she lifted her gaze, but her husband was nodding seriously as he took possession of the pile of clothes.

"I never thought you were." The darkness under his eyes had increased over the last hours. "Have you seen Wingate?"

"He went to find the messenger."

"Ah. Then good evening, wife." He left her without another word, striding purposefully down the center of the rows of cots, straightening his slumping shoulders.

He was a bewildering man. And dangerous—as a landslide is dangerous because it sweeps everything off the hillside without an ounce of prejudice.

Yet he had returned Davie and Hinch to her not

only unharmed, but also unaware that they had been the most natural suspects.

Davie couldn't have looked more proud if he'd been appointed to high office by the king himself.

And Hinch . . .

Hinch was sitting on his haunches, humming softly to the unconscious young man he'd rescued from the Dee.

A few hours later, as the abbey bells tolled Compline and the monks hastened off to their holy office, Kailey reluctantly left Carrotlocks in the care of God and St. Werburgh's infirmarian, regretting that she could do nothing now but wait.

Which was also all she could do with regard to her husband, who hadn't been at the inn when she and Hinch and Davie had arrived. Nor had he returned when she'd sent them off to sleep in the stables, or when she'd climbed the stairs to their chamber.

Not the right season for a wedding night, he'd said—whatever that meant. How the devil was she supposed to take him into her family if he stayed away?

Their room was less than homey; it was dusty and needed a good cleaning. Most telling of all, it was empty of her husband.

She went downstairs through the tangle of the tavern crowd to Odard's kitchen, got a broom and a bucket of soapy water, then carted them back upstairs.

Kailey piled the furniture on top of itself and onto the bed and had just begun to sweep along the wall base when she heard thunderous footsteps on the stairs. Then the door clicked open quietly.

"What the devil are you up to, wife?" Her husband stood in the doorway, blotting out all other things and making her feel like stammering and stuttering in the aftermath.

"I'm cleaning," she said, trying to sound crisp when her heart was fluttering absurdly in her chest.

"You're not asleep." It was an accusation. He gaped in disgust at the mess she'd made of his room and his bed. The place looked like a badger's nest.

"No, I'm not asleep, my lord. But you should be." And here in their bed, she wanted to add, but he already looked scandalized enough. "I'll be finished in moments, and then you can sleep."

"I can't." He turned away and yanked open the uppermost drawer of a tablechest and pulled out a flint box. "I've business in Blacon District."

Kailey's heart hadn't yet rested from his abrupt entrance, and now she realized that the man planned to desert her again.

"Tonight? But it's nearly ten." And he was near staggering with exhaustion. Seeing him so made Kailey feel intensely protective of the brute. She leaned the broom against the wall. "How far do you go from here, my lord?"

He gave her another of his quick assessments and then dropped the flint and a thick candle into his belt pouch. "An hour north."

"You've been days without proper rest and are nearly drunk with exhaustion. I say again that you need sleep, my lord."

"What I need, wife, is to pay a surprise visit on a man named Hadlow."

"Why?" Kailey asked, as sharply as she would have done to Davie had he planned to endanger himself.

"Sheriff's business." He pulled a long length of knotted ribbon from the same drawer and looped it into his belt.

"Is this something to do with the abbot's son?" She could excuse a mission for Abbot Wingate—as long as he had an escort.

"Nothing at all."

"Then I don't approve, my lord." Kailey placed herself between her husband and the door—a statement only, since she couldn't very well block his way. "Do you go alone to Blacon District? Because if you do, then I shall go with you."

He finally turned fully to her, peering at her as though she were a curiosity.

"You *won't* come with me, wife." He seemed maddeningly amused. "But if it will ease your mind, I am taking my usual cadre of men."

"Good." Kailey crossed her arms over her chest and planted her feet hard. "Then you'll have someone to lift you back into the saddle when you fall off."

"Exactly." His eyes were almost smiling as he turned from her to the washstand. He poured water from the ewer into a basin, filled his hands with it, then scrubbed his face.

He made satisfied noises and repeated the splashing until at last he drew his fingers through his hair. It stood randomly on end, and Kailey smiled when he looked at her.

"What?" he asked defensively, toweling off his hands and then his face.

It was a wife's duty to keep her husband's dignity well polished. No time like the present to begin training him to her touch. Kailey reached up and feathered her fingers through the dampness until his hair lay lightly across his forehead as it should. He was so very big: an oak planted in a pea patch.

She hadn't realized his closeness, nor that he had bent forward to accommodate her, until she let her gaze slide down his brow, and further to his thick lashes. His eyes were closed, and his breathing had gone disturbingly steady. His shoulders rose and fell and rose again.

"Are you asleep, my lord?"

His eyelids flew open wide and he straightened. "No! I was resting my eyes."

"You were sleeping on your feet!" Kailey went to the door and spread her arms. The man needed a nursemaid. "I'm not letting you out of this room."

"You lulled me, madam!" He balled the towel into a wad and left it on the table.

"I did what?"

"Your stroke was too pleasant. I was momentarily lulled."

She laughed because she couldn't help herself. "Well! Pardon *me*, my lord sheriff. I was only suggesting that perhaps if you sleep now, you'll wake in a better mood and be wiser in your judgements at court."

"Madam, I am a trained legalist!"

"Obviously."

Simon had meant to slip into the room and out again. Yet here was his wife, wide awake and tantalizing in her too-airy nightshift.

She grabbed the broom and started to sweep along the wallboards, the ribbon that ought to have secured the drape of her shift across her shadow-clung bosom, open too casually and trailing to her waist. He knew that ribbon, and it pleased him more than he could have imagined: the plainest, palest buttercup, one of a dozen he'd sent to her last Twelfth Night through his clandestine channel of observers.

"I watched you today, my lord, with that man Stenulf. You may know the law, sir, but you don't know people."

"Don't I?" Great God, either her nightshift was nearly transparent, or he was bewitched and able to see through linen.

"You certainly know nothing about young Halwyn and his greedy cousin." She swept the broom past him and then completely around the supporting post in the center of the room. She was bobbing shadows and scented mysteries.

"That's a matter for the court." His mouth had gone dry and his palms damp. He had to be away from here. "I will not discuss the merits of the suit with you."

"But did it come to your notice that Halwyn was well clothed and well fed, as was his mother? She was sitting in the second row of benches, my lord, wearing a lovely new red cap."

Simon wanted his wife to stand still, but she was determined in her sweeping and he could only follow on her heels.

"And how came you by the notion that this was Halwyn's mother?" He ducked as she lifted the broom to the beams overhead.

"The way she smiled at him when he spoke. The way he looked to her for affirmation." She batted at dust-heavy cobwebs that rained down on her.

"I saw no one like that."

"She was there." Giving up on the rafters, she swiped the broom bristles across Simon's boottops and he stepped out of her way. "And, my lord, if the young man wasn't able to take good care of himself and his mother, wouldn't they both be as thin-limbed and bedraggled as Stenulf and his son?''

"I saw no son."

She sighed and continued her sweeping as Simon followed her. "He was the angry-faced young fellow—about Halwyn's age—sitting in the row behind Halwyn's mother."

Simon had seen nothing of this part of the drama, but now that she had pointed out the particulars, he would have to consider them in his decision. His interest lay in the truth, not in the outcome of the suit. Aye, and just now it lay too much in the play of her breasts against her shift.

"My lord sheriff, you can't allow Stenulf a wardship over Halwyn's virgate. That lazy man would surely break both families." She put one hand on her hip and looked up at him impatiently. "Will you step one way or the other, my lord?"

Damn, the woman was more brash than a newly minted knight. " 'Tis my court, madam. I'll do as I see fit, without your permission, without your deceptions, and without consulting you first."

"I have no doubt of that, my lord. But you've trapped me here."

Simon glanced around. He'd followed his wife and her broom and her clinging nightshift right into the slope-ceilinged niche, and now she was nearly tucked up under his chin, her soft mouth barely a breath from his. His stomach felt giddy.

Her eyes were three shades of blue-violet and the summer sky. She stared earnestly up at him, fully expecting him to step aside when he would rather slide his hand along her throat to her nape and drag her mouth to his.

Would she taste of fire, of sugared mint? Would

she push him away for the cold man she thought him to be? And would he insist that she stay and bear his embrace as a wife should? He had a husband's right, could demand her obedience on the spot—

"I trust, my lord, that you'll do the honorable thing." Her breath floated past his ear, caught at his temple.

"Honorable?" Damn the woman! Would his husband's-kiss not be honorable?

"My lord, will you at least think on it before you act so heartlessly?"

Insulted to his very bones that she might think him capable of dishonoring her in any way, Simon cupped her jaw and lifted her chin, daring her to deny her disgust. "Do you so abhor the thought of my kissing you?"

"You were going to kiss me, just then?"

"Is that so vile a prospect, woman?"

A look of confusion settled on her brow, then she slid her hand over his at her throat, lacing her fingers between his as if she had to prove something to herself. A smile overtook her and she started to laugh quietly.

"Nay, my lord, I was talking of your judgment of Halwyn."

"Halwyn! Be damned!" Simon stepped too quickly backward out of the niche and banged the back of his head sharply on the crossbeam. "Damnation!"

Stars lit the edge of his sight and a reeling darkness claimed his focus. He closed his eyes, holding the clanging spot on his head with one hand. He heard furniture clattering and scraping against the planking and felt the insistent pressure of her hand on his shoulder, and then he was sitting down on the edge of the bed.

"Are you all right, husband?"

Simon carefully opened his eyes to find her kneeling in the crook between his knees. She was peering up into his face, her cheeks pinked, her gaze as soft as the silk of her hair that had again found its way between his fingers.

"I will live, madam." Tormented, with his blood boiled to death . . . but he would live.

"I'm glad of that."

He could only grunt at the truth she'd had to stretch to find that sentiment.

"And as for your kiss, my lord, I'm sorry I hadn't understood your intent. I've never been kissed before and didn't recognize the signs."

Simon's heart leaped to his throat, alongside an unvoiced shout of stolen triumph. Chaste and unkissed. She'd waited for him, though she couldn't have suspected he would come for her across the years. And now she was raised up on her knees, her eyes level with his, her hands clutched together as if she were prepared to become a blood sacrifice to his lusts.

If only she weren't so beautiful, weren't so free with her heart and determined in this crusade to make a family of him.

His nerves sizzled against the inside of his skin, the knot on his head forgotten for the rush of sensations that now raged elsewhere. Kissing her would only feed the fire, and he would take her badly. He was too exhausted to think.

He needed distance. And his night's work was not yet finished.

"Yes, well. Next time, wife, I shall warn you." He stood abruptly and left her at the bedside, glad for the weighted folds of his tunic and hauberk, and the passion they hid from her innocent eyes.

Yet the gaze that found him when he dared look her way was forthright and as protective as a mother bear's.

"You said last night that it wasn't the season. Is that truly why you did not take me to your bed?"

"To my *chair*, madam." Her brashness taxed his every nerve. "Consummating our marriage would have been awkward at best and an entertainment for hundreds at the very worst."

Her chin came up, her brows winged in surprise. "And where was this chair, my lord?"

Simon's heart slammed wildly, improbably against his chest. "The chair, wife, was on the judge's dais, in the great hall, at the castle. The very one I sat on all the day through."

"I see." He watched her chew at the corner of her smile. He wondered what the devil she was thinking, what she was planning for this marriage. "You're right, my lord, I think I would prefer a bed the first time."

Simon's heart skidded along his ribs. "And after that?"

Her shy grin made the air too hot to breathe. "Wherever you think best, husband."

Simon blew out a full chest of steam, his ears surely aflame. "Good. Yes. Well." He grabbed up his saddlebag and went to the door. "Good night, madam, and sleep well."

"Like a babe, my lord."

Kailey watched as her husband shut the door overloud, fanning the candles with the force of his leaving.

The lout! He would surely fall asleep in the saddle and drop like a rock to the roadbed. His head was so hard, he'd probably just sleep wherever he landed and wake in the morning wondering how he'd gotten the wagon ruts across his back.

Kailey decided that she wouldn't want that to happen. She spoke a quick but fervent prayer for his safety, then continued sweeping.

She had certainly felt the fool for not recognizing his kiss when it had been scribed there on his dazzling face, and in his thunderous breath, in the way he'd wet his mouth and seemed so intent upon her own. And her own sensation of ever falling toward him.

At least she knew where her husband was, where Hinch was, and Davie. And now Julia.

"Family," she whispered. She had always loved the sound of the word, loved the play of it on her lips—a whisper, then a kiss and then a smile. 'Twas a fine word, for a blessed state.

And now hers included Simon de Marchand—whether he liked it or not.

Simon heard the abbey bell ringing two in the morning as he led his men back across the drawbridge and beneath the portcullis of Chester's hulking Northgate. Bone-weary and bleary-eyed, he considered taking a pallet on the floor of the abbot's guest house as he passed St. Werburgh's.

But his wife was at the inn, asleep in his bed, and so he dragged himself through the city, too sleepy to crow at his success in Blacon District, too driven by the memory of her glorious fingers slipping through his hair.

He hadn't been lulled to sleep; he'd been staggered by her tenderness, by his need for her. He'd been a breath from carrying her against him.

He ought to stay away this night, and the next. And for all the other nights of the world, until he could tether his need for her. He hadn't expected the tightness in his gut when he gazed at her, when he touched her however accidently. He was afraid of this nearness and not certain why.

As he opened the door to his room, she stirred—a gentle rippling of moonlight across the counterpane as she straightened her knee.

Aye, he ought to run, far and fast.

Simon shed himself of his boots and belt, drew off his chausses and hauberk, listening carefully for signs that she had awakened—for her breathing to change, for dream-wrought words. But she slept on, even as he carefully stretched out across the counterpane and focused on the lath of rafters instead of on the strands of rich silk that curled beneath his ear.

He would find little sleep himself this night, lying abed in his braies and tunic. She was too near, and he had a guilty ache in his loins that increased with his every breath, made him long to be naked with her beneath these woman-scented sheets.

"My lord?" She turned her head toward him, dashed her minty breath against his ear. Every pulse and current in his body came to a halt for a moment only to surge through him like molten lead the next.

"I didn't mean to wake you," he managed, feeling altogether exposed and crossing his arms over his chest for good measure.

"I haven't been sleeping. I couldn't. I've been wondering if Julia can be hanged for theft." She was quiet, obviously waiting for him to ease her mind with a denial. He would rather not have answered, but she would learn the truth soon enough.

"A hanging is decreed sometimes for notorious thievery."

"Just for stealing?"

"But most likely, if the suit goes against her and she then fails her ordeal, she will lose only a hand—"

"*Only* a hand!" She rolled to her elbows and her words landed hard on his chin, her sudden fury just as startling as her nearness. "There is no such thing as *only* a hand, my lord! Do you realize what that would mean to a girl such as Julia? If she lives through the punishment, she couldn't possibly find work afterward, and without work she will starve! 'Tis a death sentence."

"And thereby the will of God, madam!" Simon craved the simplicity of her benevolence. But people were flawed, their judgment too easily shaped by selfish desires.

"The will of God! Is that what happened to Fletchard?" She sat up on her knees, her eyes bright, accusing pearls in the moonlight. Hewett's eyes.

"Fletchard helped himself to his fate. He had his chance to prove the innocence of his intent. But God had seen his heart, and so he failed his ordeal." Simon closed his eyes, hoping she would give up.

"Which ordeal was he given, Marchand?"

"He was a knight; battle was his due."

"An ordeal by battle? With whom?" Now she was the Furies themselves, her nose not an inch from his, her hair like a storm of lightning setting fire to his skin.

"With the king's champion swordsman."

"Damn you, Marchand!" She threw herself off the bed and paced away to the window and then back again to stand over him. "Fletchard's shoulder wasn't yet healed from last winter's fracture! He'd have been no match against the king's laundress, let alone an expert swordsman. You knew this!"

"Fletchard was pronounced well enough by the king's physician."

"Aye, by a man who would no doubt swear that a Christmas pig was the Archbishop of Canterbury, if the king so willed it."

Simon refused to be baited, closed his eyes to the moonlight and to the enticing curves so well outlined beneath her shift.

"You can do nothing for the girl. Go to sleep."

"I can advise her!"

"So now you're her lawyer." Simon yawned pointedly.

"Someone must stand for Julia!"

"The truth will stand as it always has." Simon turned away, rolled to his side. "The process of the law is sure and swift."

"So is the process of melting iron from ore. But people are not made of stone, my lord. They cry out when put to the torch."

"It works, woman."

He felt her crawling across the mattress, heard her just above his ear.

"I see great hope for Julia now, my lord. Armed with a stale crust of bread and paired in mortal combat against the king's champion swordsman."

"Not combat, wife. The ordeal by hot iron is the usual for women. Now go to sleep."

Kailey wanted to smack the man with a pillow, no matter that she had been grandly relieved when she'd heard him slip into the room. "I don't see how carrying a red-hot iron ball for a distance of nine feet and then waiting three days to see if the wounds fester is anything more than a lunatic's way of raising huge painful blisters."

"To sleep, wife."

The man was a stone.

So certain of himself and his laws; so dangerously cool-tempered and clear-voiced in his convictions. Today had been painfully instructive. She had watched as he'd quoted the king's laws from his formidable memory, cited provocative cases from the history of England as if he were spinning fantastical tales around a winter hearth, until every man, woman, and child in the court seemed convinced that God himself had handed down these common laws to Simon de Marchand.

Kailey knew better. And now she was terrified for Julia.

She'd seen nothing arbitrary about Marchand's ideology. He fervently, strictly, embraced the minutest precepts of his laws—which frightened her even more, because a man's beliefs were as difficult to change as the motion of the sun.

The truth was to be Julia's only defense, and now Kailey feared it would not be enough to save her.

Kailey slept badly, dreaming of sundered, bloodied hands, ragged bruises, and hangings. When she awoke, out of breath and drenched in a cold sweat, she dressed quietly, keeping watch on the giant form of her sleeping husband, then slipped from their room.

She left the inn with Julia and justice on her mind.

Chapter 7

~~~~~ ◯◯ ~~~~~

Simon woke at the sharp knock and the even sharper realization that he was in Chester, upstairs of an ale-sour tavern, that he was married, and that his wife had just kissed him.

"Wife?" he shouted, throwing an arm across the place in the bed where she ought to be. The bed was stone cold.

Gone. He found himself on his elbow, lifting the pillow and looking beneath it.

"Good morning, Lord Simon!"

Simon sat up and squinted through streaming sunlight toward the shadowed door that was creaking open by inches. "Who is it?"

"Me, my lord." The de Broase boy popped his head into the breach. "A word with you, if I may."

"Come."

The boy entered on his toes, followed by Hinch, who stooped to get through the passage, then folded himself into a chair directly across from Simon, the krummhorn thankfully nowhere to be seen.

"Good evening, my lord," he said, nodding.

" 'Tis morning, Hinch," David said, with a patience for the old man that he must have learned from his mistress.

"Ah, yes, then, 'Morning, Davie.'" The jester grinned at the boy as he corrected himself.

"Where's my wife?"

"Gone to the castle, she said." Davie had sped directly to the pile of clothes Simon had left on the floor last night and was now examining each piece. "Shall I see to your laundry, sir?"

"Why?" Simon hated people idling about in his chamber, couldn't imagine sharing the master's quarters with a half-dozen servants tending to his every whim.

"You've a hole here at the knee—"

"Never mind, boy," Simon snapped—not meaning to, but damnation, he'd expected to have a word with his wife before she went skittering off on her morning's crusading. He steadied his temper. "Why the devil should you see to my laundry?"

"You were Sir Robert's son, my lord; I was his squire. It stands to reason that I ought to be yours now."

Simon let the boy's comment about the lord of Stoneham pass. "I have a squire."

"Well, he isn't very good, is he?" Simon's spent clothes were now in a neat bundle on the end of the bed. "To leave your things lying around your chamber."

"My squire is at home in Northumberland."

"Ah, but my lady seems to think you need a squire here in Chester." Davie had retrieved Simon's boots and was brushing at them with his sleeve.

"Does she?"

"And she thinks I need the practice." The boy set the boots on the floor by the door, then smiled eagerly at Simon. "She thought you wouldn't mind, sir, if I practiced on you."

"She thought that, did she?" Simon hadn't even needed a clerk when he'd arrived alone in Chester two weeks ago; this simple room away from the clatter of court had been a vast paradise. But she had changed things, this fated wife of his; crowding him with her fancies, making him seek the blue of her eyes in everything.

"All right, then, boy. You'll find more of my clothes in my saddlebag."

"All right? You mean I can be your squire?" The boy's smile couldn't have grown any wider.

"Aye. Be off to the laundress with my clothes— the one across from the abbey church. And tell her to have them back to me tomorrow noon—at the latest."

"I will, my lord."

"Scrubbed well, squire, not boiled to rags."

"Not boiled, my lord. I'll tell her!" Davie was already on his way to the door, his arms loaded down with tunics and chausses wrapped up in a linen towel.

"And what do you know of saddlery, boy?"

Davie managed to turn at the door with the bundle. "Enough to repair my own, sir."

"Then see to the care of my girthing straps. A nearly cracked buckle, I believe."

"Aye, my lord." The door slammed behind him, and Simon was left staring at the old jester, who smiled and nodded, as though he wanted to speak but couldn't remember how.

"Good morning, Hinch," Simon offered in the silence, suffering an unaccustomed bout of indulgence for this aged man his wife seemed to adore.

"Your name is Simon."

"That's right."

More nodding. "You married our Kailey."

"Aye." Surely the man must have confirmed this before today. Simon scrubbed his fingers through his hair, then too easily remembered her fingers, and the touch of her breath on his chin.

"And did she marry you, my lord?"

"How's that?" He didn't need riddles this early in the morning.

"Did she want to marry you?"

"I didn't force her, if that's what you mean." Simon suddenly felt as if he were being questioned by the girl's father—but that thought reeled back on him.

Hinch was smiling. "Kailey's a stubborn little miss, don't I know. I doubt you could force her to do anything that she didn't approve of."

"Yes, I've been privy to her stubbornness."

"You were Sir Robert's son."

Simon wanted nothing to do with the rest of this conversation. He stood. "Look here, Hinch—"

"You were Sir Robert's *only* son." Hinch sat forward, his spindly elbows stuck into his knees, his pale eyes framed in pale, pointed lashes. "And he told me something before he died."

A chill swept across the room, lodged itself like a stone blade between his shoulders. He felt exposed, the memory and his guilt forced upon him like an indictment.

"He told you *what?*" Simon asked quietly, not wanting to spook the man. Deathbed confessions spilled into an addled mind weren't safe.

Hinch cocked his head, his grizzled brows nearly meeting. "But you know, don't you?"

His chest felt stuffed with hot ashes and fouled with hate for Robert of Stoneham. "Tell me again."

"Sir Robert told me the fault was his—"

"What else?" Simon wanted to yank the man to his feet.

"You didn't believe him."

"What *else* did he tell you?"

The old man peered up at him. "He told me he sent for you because he loved you—"

"Christ!"

"Because he loved Kailey."

"Loved her." Disgusted, Simon yanked his hauberk from the clothes peg. Robert of Stoneham didn't know the meaning of the word "love." Or "honor." Oh, but how the man knew the facets and finery of betrayal.

Hinch stood in front of the strong light of the window, his flyaway hair translucent. He fixed Simon with a gaze that drove to the center of him, catching him off guard.

"Do you love our Kailey too? Like Sir Robert did?"

Falsely? Bloodied and blinded by his own guilt? Simon hoped to God he would never love her in that way. She deserved purity and hope, not shadows.

"Or is it too soon to ask that, my lord? Too soon to love her, do you think?"

Too soon to love grace and forgiveness? To dare mix his dreams with his impossible longings? Simon forced the palsy from his hands and scrubbed his face with a cold rag to rid himself of her influence. But he found her scent there and drew it high in his nostrils.

"Fear not, my lord, if you don't love her. You haven't known Kailey as long as I."

A lifetime? Simon would have told Hinch to leave, but he hadn't control of his voice.

Hinch persisted, his hat jangling. "Oh, but I did love her the moment I first met her. Eight summers, she was then, and such a tiny, bright-haloed thing. And me still FitzLandry's jester. She came to us with huge eyes as blue as truth and a heart filled to overflowing with kindness for everyone. She thought I was the funniest creature in all of God's kingdom. And I thought she was the prettiest. I still do. She is pretty, isn't she?"

Simon nodded, his heart lodged in his throat, cutting off his air, threatening the indignity of scalding tears. He remembered her well on that frosty morn: her tiny newborn hand, silk-pale curls, and eyes that dazzled him.

"Don't worry yourself, my lord. If you don't love her now, you'll love her soon; everyone does." Hinch paused in his tribute, no doubt waiting for a response that Simon was incapable of giving. "Ah, and so now I'll leave you to your morning, sir."

Simon couldn't look at the old man as those long legs trod the noisy planks toward the door.

"One last thing, my lord. If you have no objection, Kailey thought you'd let me be jester to your household. May I?"

"Whatever you wish."

"Oh, I wish you and my lamb great happiness. Great happiness, my lord."

When Simon turned on the man to order him out of the chamber, he was gone, and the door closed.

"Too soon to love her, Hinch?" Simon whispered to the unremitting silence, his throat raw, his eyes hot-rimmed and watery. "When have I ever stopped?"

*   *   *

Kailey hurried first to the infirmary at St. Werburgh's Abbey and checked on Carrotlocks. She stayed to change his dressings, dismayed to see him still so silent, so closed in on his pain. She left him in the care of the brothers and promised to return in the afternoon.

The abbey gate opened onto the bustling, brightbannered market square and the warren of food stalls and craft wagons. Such a contrast to Julia's dark future.

Kailey bought bread and cheese and two apples for the girl, and a crock of fresh cider. Thinking to elevate Julia's spirits and the forbidding pall of prison with a rushlight, Kailey was about to step up to one of the merchant's wagons when she saw Pegshaw scurrying away from the drop-down counter, looking quite pleased with himself.

She wanted to trip the man and lay him flat in a soupy horse puddle, but instinct told her to keep to herself. It was better to watch and wait. She would return later to dog him, as soon as she made Julia comfortable for the day. She bought a rushlight holder, a half-dozen fatted rushes, and a tin cup for Julia's cider.

With a clean nightbucket in hand, Kailey climbed the stairs to the tower, paid her bribe to the yawning guard, and this time gained admittance to the cell.

The door shut behind her with a soul-blighting thud, the lock sounding like the rattle of dried bones. Julia was hunched in a dark corner, wrapped to her ears in a blanket.

"Well, jailer," the girl murmured, "is it finally time?"

Julia hadn't even bothered to look up in her misery, and Kailey's heart ached anew for the despair in her voice.

"Nay, Julia, it's me."

"My lady!" Julia got to her knees and wiped at her dark-ringed eyes with the corner of the blanket. "You come again like an everlasting angel!"

"I am far from an angel, Julia." Kailey replaced the offal bucket with the clean one and set the other by the door, grateful for its tight-fitting lid. Which reminded her. "I just saw Pegshaw beetle-bugging around in the market square."

Julia's eyes blazed with anger and she spat into the matted rushes. "May the little sot roast in hell!"

"Good, that's the kind of spirit that will bring the man to his knees." Mayhaps the girl was in the mood to talk. And they did need to talk—of severed hands and ordeals.

She'd never seen anyone put to the ordeal, hadn't the stomach for it. She knew only that these were the cruelest of tortures. Even if the victims lived, they were never whole again in mind or body.

Her father must have suffered such a trial—with sword or lance against the king's champion—and he must have failed in the eyes of his Lord God.

Dear Father, why? But she would have to see to him later—Julia was the one in great trouble at the moment.

"I've brought you bread and apples, Julia, and even some cider."

"You are kindness itself, my lady."

Julia's gratitude for such a meager offering fit uncomfortably, and Kailey dodged it with a change in subject as she gingerly handed her the thyme-scented loaf.

"I near-paralyzed my backside sitting through

my husband's court yesterday, learning points of the law, and noting which of the court's questions carry the most weight. When you are finished eating, we will get down to the business of Pegshaw's wicked suit against you. It will come to the court soon, so I must pluck your memory clean of clues that will lead to Pegshaw's motives."

"His motives are of the devil himself." Julia twisted the bread apart and stuffed a wad into her mouth, then picked up the cider jug and put her mouth to the lip.

"Wait, Julia! I've brought you a cup to drink from. You'll feel more civilized." Quite pleased with herself, Kailey presented her with the little tin cup.

"By Christ, my lady!" Julia howled in horror. Then she was on her feet and scrambling across the small room, her eyes huge and hollow. "How you devil me with your unkindness! Go away!"

"I only bring you cider! What have I done?"

But Julia wouldn't look at her, had turned to the wall in her wailing. "You befriend me with your lies," she cried miserably. "You make me want to trust you, when all the while you are in league with that monster Pegshaw."

"You think that? How, Julia?" Nothing riled Kailey's ire faster than a false accusation—whether it be lodged against herself or another. "And stop your howling, else you'll have every guard in the tower in here, and my husband besides. What is the matter?"

Julia finally turned to look at Kailey, wild-eyed and suspicious, hiccoughing out her sobs. She pointed a filthy finger at Kailey.

"You can hold that cup in your hand and still call me friend? Expect me to believe your sympathies, when it makes me ill to see it?"

Kailey looked closely at the cup for the first time. And then with a staggering flash, she understood. She dropped the offending vessel with a thunk and hurried to Julia. "Mother Mary! That's one of Pegshaw's cups, isn't it?"

"As if you didn't know." Julia wrenched away, doubled over in her grief. "Now, leave me! I don't want you here!"

"Julia! Don't you understand?" Kailey rescued the cup from the floor and slipped it into her purse, trying not to shout for joy. "This cup is your freedom!"

"Nay, my lady. 'Tis the damning evidence you will bring against me in your husband's court." Julia shrugged off the hand Kailey had settled on her shoulder. "It signifies my doom. I will hang."

"Nay, Julia, this evidence will hang Pegshaw in his own noose. It will, I promise!"

"How?" Hope was such a miserable state, and it looked wretched on Julia, streaking her face with grime, chipping away at her frown as she searched Kailey's face, and then the cup. "They'll think for sure I stole it. How else could it have come here, but with me?"

"Because I know where the others are."

Julia's sob subsided into a whimper. "The others?"

"I just saw Pegshaw leaving the very wagon I bought this from. And there were five other cups hanging from the rack, each one identical to this."

"That means nothing." She turned again to the wall.

Kailey wrenched her forward again, gritting her teeth in frustration. "Julia, it means that we have proof that Pegshaw lied about you stealing his precious cups—for how can they be missing when he knows where they are?" Kailey reached out and pushed the hair out of Julia's eyes. "I want to help you. But you've got to want to help yourself."

The tears came again, running down her face in a wide wash. "It doesn't matter, my lady. *I* don't matter."

"Bloody hell, you matter to me!" Kailey used the sleeve of her shift to scrub roughly at Julia's tears; there was no time for self-pity. "You mustn't think like that. Now what else can you tell me about Pegshaw and his family? Does he have a son, perhaps?"

Julia swallowed thickly and shoved the heel of her hand across her eyes. "Aye, he does. Riley is his name. He often brings goods to Chester on market days."

It was the very best news Kailey had heard all morning. "In a merchant's wagon?"

Julia nodded hesitantly, as if she thought her affirmation might be the wrong answer. "I don't know. Probably."

"Excellent! What does the son look like?"

"Not at all like Pegshaw. A very plain man. Twenty-five or so." She snuffled and shrugged. "Difficult to describe."

"We must be sure that the cups are actually in the hands of Pegshaw and his son; else he'll certainly claim that you sold them to another merchant. And if he actually *has* sold them himself to the unsuspecting man in the wagon, then the hapless merchant will be caught up in Pegshaw's falsehoods and charged as well. We can't allow one injustice to compound another."

"How will you do this, my lady?"

Kailey was stumped, but more determined than ever, despite the nettling thoughts of her husband.

"I didn't get a good look at the man who sold me the cup; you'll have to identify him yourself."

"Me? How?"

"The merchant's wagon backs to the abbey and stands beneath an enormous spreading hawthorn. Here, you must wear this." Charged with finger-numbing excitement, Kailey took off her own cloak and draped it across Julia's thin shoulders, then raised the hood over the girl's head.

"But, my lady, the cloak is yours. 'Tis cold today; you'll need it when you leave here."

Kailey draped Julia's thin blanket over her own shoulders and drew it over her ears as she sat down where Julia had been sitting. "Now come sit and block me from view of the door."

"Why?" Julia sat down hard in front of Kailey, her jaw limp and her dark-smudged eyes wide.

"Because you're to leave here, Julia, as *me*."

"As the high sheriff's wife? Oh, no!" Julia panicked like a crow caught in a net, trying to throw off the cloak, fighting Kailey for the clasp at the neck. "I cannot, my lady."

"You must." Kailey caught Julia's hands and held them tightly. "You will tell the guard that you're fetching the prisoner some medicine for her cough." Kailey coughed loudly for effect, then watched the window. "Then it's off to the merchant's wagon with you to identify Pegshaw's son. Do you understand?"

"But I'm frightened."

"So am I, Julia. But I've discovered that outrage is a very close kin to courage—only louder—so grab yourself a lungful of anger and leave here now. You're to see if the man in the wagon is Pegshaw's son. Then come back here immediately with a handful of weeds—"

"Weeds?"

"Herbals, Julia, to heal a cough. So the guard will let you in."

"But he'll know we're not the same person." Julia's fingers clutched at the neck of the cloak, pale gray against the rich wool.

"He won't notice, as long as your bribe to him is sizable. The corridor is dark, and with the hood pulled down—"

"But I'm taller than you—"

"Then stoop, damn it!" Kailey silently begged forgiveness for her blasphemy and calmed herself. "And whatever you do, Julia, don't let Pegshaw or his son see you."

"But—"

"Take these coins." Kailey dropped a dozen pennies into Julia's clammy hand. "You'll need a few of them to grease the guard's palm."

Julia stared down at the coins, then raised her tear-damp eyes to Kailey. "My lady, you'd trust me with all your money?"

"I'm trusting you with my liberty, Julia." And risking her husband's untested wrath. Kailey gave a racking good cough and looked again toward the door. "You must hurry."

Julia turned the coins in her hand. "I could run away with these—"

"But you won't. We're family now, remember?"

"Family?" Julia's eyes puddled, and Kailey's heart grew tight with hope for her.

"Now go! Go!" Kailey coughed again, even more wracking than the last time, then spoke in an overloud wail. "I beg of you, my lady. Bring me something to soothe my fever! I'll not last the night."

Julia's eyes were huge as she listened to Kailey's echoing voice.

"Take the dirty nightbucket," Kailey whispered. " 'Tis how I always leave here."

Julia stumbled to the door and picked up the bucket.

"Aye, Julia . . . poor lamb!" the girl shouted unevenly, looking to Kailey for approval. She received a wink in return. "I will bring medicaments, girl."

"Guard!" Kailey heard next, pleased at Julia's newfound confidence, and praying that it would hold long enough to trap Pegshaw. "Unbar the door, guard, and let me pass."

Kailey heard the door squealing open on its hinges, and Julia left the cell without a moment's suspicion from the guard. A dreadful finality settled over Kailey as the bar thunked into place against the door, and the lock clicked shut.

Merciful Mary, how could anyone live like this? To be locked for days and weeks in a lonely cell, at the whim of an unfeeling guard and an impartial justice, one that seemed always hungry for the most innocent flesh. A hand, a delicate neck, a father's love for his daughter: it didn't seem to matter.

Restless and yearning, Kailey went to the deep arrow slit and leaned her elbows on the sloping sill. Its few inches opened onto the dewy countryside, beautiful with its gold and green field crops and its low, smoke-distant hills.

Beautiful but distant. Too distant.

Kailey was very glad she would be locked in the cell for less than an hour; glad, too, that her husband would never know of her sleight of hand.

"Please hurry, Julia," Kailey whispered into the musty cocoon of her blanket. "I don't want him to find me here."

*   *   *

Simon stood on the edge of the dais searching the crowded hall and the gallery for the honest blue of his wife's eyes. She hadn't been at all pleased with him last night. But trial by ordeal wasn't a bedtime subject. He had done his best to assure her that the girl–thief wouldn't hang, and still the woman hadn't understood the necessity of the ordeal.

God's judgment: it was the only true test of innocence.

And yet Hewett hadn't been offered such a test. Simon had been too young to notice at the time, but he'd learned the reason quick enough. Neville Hewett had been the king's champion swordsman.

Simon scrubbed the memory from behind his eyes, looked again for his wife. The day was nearly spent and he'd had no word of her, but that she'd left the guard tower and had been heading for the market square. That was hours ago.

She was no doubt bent over the injured boy in the infirmary, cooling foreheads and healing bruises with her touch. She needed something to do besides cull the streets for abandoned hearts.

She needed a home. A place where she could keep her hands busy. Their room at the Cask and Coffer was miserably cramped; the noise of the tavern below didn't quiet until after midnight.

The king had promised him one of Earl Hugh's manor houses here in Chester, a house befitting the sheriff of the shire. He hadn't thought to claim it, had no use for this region of the realm, no use at all. But she deserved better than a rabbit warren. He would lay his claim to this manor—tonight, if possible.

If he could find her.

Frustrated to the very roots of his beard, Simon took his place in his stone-hard judge's chair, then threw himself into the oppressive flurry of paperwork that had already piled up during the court day.

The common pleas began, and he listened to each in turn: a writ of dower against a widow, rights of land, warranties of charters, debts, trespass.

And still his wife did not come to him, leaving his gut in turmoil and his heart thready.

As the day closed he saw that among the suits to be heard in the morning was the thatcher's charge of theft against one Julia of Wrexham.

He would have to remember to tell his wife.

It was the least he could do.

Kailey waited hours for Julia to return, listening for footsteps on the stairs, for the guard's voice to come climbing up the spiraling steps. But as the day darkened, the only sound came from the plaintive bells of the abbey church, tolling away the afternoon as efficiently as it did her hopes for Julia's return.

She had warned Julia to keep away from Pegshaw and his son, but she might have been discovered. Yet if she had been found out, why hadn't anyone come storming into the cell to return her?

That wouldn't be at all helpful to her marriage—if her husband was to find two Julias.

She preferred not to think of the alternative to Julia's having been caught: Julia having left her to rot in the cell while she took to the road and to safety in some faraway corner of the country. A warm cloak, enough money to serve her for a half year, and the freedom to fly. How tempting the notion must have been!

"She hasn't abandoned me!" Kailey whispered. Julia was family now; she knew desolation and understood belonging.

But as the twilight turned to full darkness and the Compline bell began to toll, gloom seeped through the arrow slit and entered her bones. Something awful had happened to Julia—that was the only explanation Kailey could live with.

And here she was, tucked up like a broken-winged sparrow in a stone tower, unable to help, unable to see that Davie and Hinch were well fed tonight and safely in their beds, or that Carrotlocks would be looked after kindly in the infirmary—if he was still alive.

And her husband? No matter what his feelings for her, he seemed forever bent on knowing where she was.

What would he do if he found her alone in Julia's cell, and his prisoner escaped?

Dear Julia, for both our sakes, please come back!

"I've come for my wife, Wingate." Simon stood outside the abbot's lodgings, out of breath and feeling as if he'd been chasing an invisible sprite all over the city. "I'll take her off your hands now."

Wingate peered at him as though he'd grown horns and a barbed tail. "Kailey isn't here, Simon. Come see for yourself."

"I'm out of patience, Wingate." Simon stepped inside the hall, rubbed at the headache that was sprouting from the back of his neck. "Tell her it's time to go. Wife!" he called.

Wingate waited pointedly for the echo to diminish.

"I haven't seen her since yesterday." The abbot's mouth was pinched, his brows knotted with what Simon damn well hoped was loyalty and not fear.

"It is nearly ten, Wingate, long past dark. Neither Hinch nor Davie has seen my wife since this morning."

"And what say the hounds you've had following her?"

"Hopton lost sight of her in the market square—for which he will pay dearly." Simon dragged his fingers through his hair to keep them from shaking. "You are my only hope, Wingate."

"Why would she come here?"

"You seemed to have her ear, Wingate." He hated to think that his wife would confess the convolutions of their marriage to anyone, but he would concede himself a hell-born ogre if it would bring him word of her. "I haven't been the best of husbands."

"Ah. Well, I'm not her confessor, if that's what you wonder."

Until that very moment, Simon had held out the hope that his wife might be holed up here, waiting for him to come find her. But now that he considered it, that wasn't her way. His guts knotted and doubled over on themselves, because now Wingate looked worried.

"Then she's missing, Wingate."

"Have you checked the infirmary?"

"She hasn't been there since this morning. And she had been expected to return."

Wingate's face paled and he sat hard on a bench. "I don't like it, Simon. Where else could she be?"

Simon resurrected a thought he had already dismissed, and now summoned only in his desperation.

"I know for certain that she's not with her little thief. She was there once today but left within the hour and has not been back. But the girl might know something."

"You've got me suddenly sick with worry, Simon. We've a young man lying in the infirmary, fighting for his life because someone decided to beat him near to death."

Simon was well aware of the threat, of the cold sweat prickling his back. "I'll find her, Wingate, if I have tear the town apart stone by timber."

Simon shoved himself up into the saddle and rode through the dark-pooled streets of Chester, into the torchlit castle bailey, and directly to the tower where he'd kept his wife's befriended thief safely alone in a cell and in some comfort without appearing prejudicial.

The guards righted themselves from their leaning and stood at attention as he approached.

"Welcome, my lord sheriff," the sergeant said, roughly clearing his throat.

"Has anyone been to visit the Wrexham thief since this afternoon?" He watched the man's rugged face for a flash of guilt.

"Nay, my lord." He shook his head so quickly, his jowls jounced. "I am posted here from noon till midnight. There's been no one let in at all since the abbey bell rang Sext. Cleaning the cellars, we were. As per your orders."

"And you did see my wife take her leave from here?"

"Oh, aye, my lord. Unmistakably. At one o'clock."

Simon had no choice but to confront the thief. "Take me to the girl in the tower."

"Right, my lord."

Chapter 8

The thunking of footsteps on the stairs were the sweetest sounds Kailey had heard since this miserable day had begun so many dark hours ago.

"Julia!" she whispered through teeth that chattered in the damp chill. She must have found a way back inside! "Blessed Mother, thank you!"

Kailey flew back to her nest against the opposite wall, gathering the blanket over her head and close around her ears.

Julia hadn't broken her promise! She'd never doubted it! Pegshaw was as good as defeated, and Julia would be free of this horrible place and the king's foul justice. And Simon would never know that she'd traded places with his prisoner—though it was getting late and he might well be worried that she wasn't at the inn. If he noticed such things.

The guard was on the other side of the door, rattling his keys. "Here she is, my lord."

My lord? A hot stone dropped into Kailey's empty stomach and sizzled there.

"Shall I unlock the door for you, sir?" the guard asked.

"Not necessary. Leave the lamp. This won't take long."

The voice was the low-rung echo of her doom. Simon de Marchand!

Mother Mary, he'd found her out! Julia must have been caught in the same shallow barrel; he'd come to pass sentence on them both.

Kailey shoved herself deeper into the pitch-dark corner, trying to think of what to do next, what kind of excuses she could dance past him for helping his prisoner escape, for defying him and flouting his justice.

"You there, girl!" The walls seemed to rattle. He was nothing but the soft rushlight that hovered behind the barred window, a halo inside the woolen blanket that she tugged tighter over her head.

"I am looking for the lady de Marchand. My wife. Where is she?"

His *wife?*

"Answer me, girl!"

Dear God, had he truly mistaken her for Julia?

"You'll tell me where she's gone, damn it!" His voice was harsh, wild.

He didn't know!

"My lord?" Kailey hissed the words through the blanket to disguise her voice and then coughed, hoping to keep him on the other side of the door.

"On your feet, girl! Come closer."

Nay, then he would see her face, even hidden beneath the blanket! She couldn't allow him to discover that his prisoner wasn't still locked up in his jail; Julia would be outlawed! If she had truly panicked and abandoned Kailey, then she couldn't have traveled far enough to escape the hue and cry from Marchand's sweep of soldiers.

He mustn't learn what had happened—not yet. Not if she was to give Julia a chance for her freedom, for her life.

Kailey stood awkwardly beneath the weight of the blanket and slid her hand over the pile of ash and soot that had gathered beneath the spent rush-light. She smeared the mess across her cheeks, ground it against her eyelids, and scrubbed it through her hairline.

"Come here!" he bellowed.

"Aye, my lord," she said roughening her voice and bowing as she sidled toward the door.

"My wife came to you today."

It was a statement of fact, not a question. Hopton would have told him—what else did he know? "Aye, she came here."

"Where did she go when she left?" He clipped off his words as if he feared they would spill from him too quickly. So unlike the stiff control of the inquisitor.

Kailey coughed to scour out the softer tones that might be too familiar to him. "Don't know."

"What were her plans, girl?"

"Didn't say."

"Then what kind of mood was she in?"

"Mood?" An odd question.

He bellowed and struck the door as he wrapped his invulnerable fingers around the bars, making Kailey flinch from the violence of his grasp.

"When my wife left here, girl, was she wrathful?" He was talking through his teeth.

"Nay."

"Bitter? Despairing?"

"Despairing?"

"Yes, damn it!" he rasped. His knuckles had gone white. "Did she say anything about me?"

Where was he going with this inquest? "She never talks of you, my lord."

He gave the door a shove, but his fingers stayed.

"Do you know if she was planning to leave the city? Did she mention High Stoneham?"

"No." Kailey shook her head and coughed.

"Damnation!" His voice shook the timbers. "Then where the hell has she gone?"

"Not far, I am certain."

"She has vanished off the face of the earth!"

Blessed Mary, her husband was worried about her! He had come here because he was worried!

Family *did* matter to him. *She* mattered!

Wildly happy inside her dank cell, Kailey turned away and leaned back against the door. She could hear him breathing roughly, felt the solid weight of him pressed against the panel, his fingers still clinging to the bars. She wished she could see his face; wished she could read him better and give him comfort.

"She wouldn't leave you, my lord." The gravel in Kailey's voice came easily, strewn there by tears of longing for a man she hardly knew. "She wouldn't ever."

"I take no comfort in that, woman."

Her heart had been soaring; now it fluttered to the ground. It seemed the man would confess to a stranger that he cared nothing that his wife might have left him.

"If you don't care that she is gone, lord sheriff, why bother in your chase?"

"I bother, damn it, because if she *hasn't* left me, then she has met with foul play." His mouth was near enough that she could feel his apple-scented breath through the crack between the oak boards.

Well, then, it was settled: the man *did* care.

Kailey turned her cheek to the cool panel, wishing she could somehow let him know she hadn't been assaulted, wasn't lying broken in an alley. But she was only Julia to him, and Julia couldn't very well change her story now without him tearing apart the door and discovering her deception.

"My lord, your wife is not fool enough to travel the dark streets unescorted."

He was still for a moment, breathing out his fury. "You're so sure of her?"

"You should be, too."

"Christ's bones!" The door shook on its sturdy iron hinges as he thrust himself from it and started away.

"Please, my lord!" she called.

"Yes?" He stopped and the lantern bobbed its bar-striped threat across the cell.

"The abbot at St. Werburgh's—if you see him . . ." Kailey coughed again and roughed out her whisper. "He counseled me wisely yesterday. He told me to listen to my heart. Do thank him for me, if you will!"

He was quiet for a long moment. "Aye, I'll tell him."

"Those very words."

"Aye."

At least Abbot Wingate would know she was all right, would know for certain that he'd counseled Kailey with his wisdom, not Julia. Hopefully he'd keep the knowledge to himself.

"Thank you, my lord."

Marchand left her then, taking his howling storms with him.

Kailey sank to her knees, her back against the door. He was afraid for her, and afraid that she would leave him.

"Hurry, Julia. Please, hurry."

*   *   *

Davie and Hinch were eagerly waiting for Simon as he rode into the innyard of the Cask and Coffer. Hope snagged him and sent him spinning. She'd been found!

He slid out of the saddle and met the boy on the run, grabbing his arms and holding tightly. "Is she here?"

Davie looked lost himself, undone. "You didn't find her, my lord?"

The boy might as well have punched him, for the cramping in his gut. His heart caught up with his pulse in a hollow rush.

Hinch took Simon's saddlebag off the horse. "Is someone missing, my lord?"

Davie shushed him. "Kailey is missing, Hinch."

Simon didn't know where to look next; he wanted to yank the sun up into the morning sky so he could scour the city.

"She isn't missing, Davie," Hinch said. "His lordship has just misplaced her."

Aye, he had misplaced her, all right. Misjudged her mood. For every day of nearly twenty years, Simon had known exactly where his wife was; now after only three confounding days of marriage, he'd lost her. And if he knew anything about her at all, he knew that she would never willingly set foot out of the city without Davie and Hinch.

Which left him with only one incomprehensible explanation.

Despairing of her life, he'd come back here looking for clues, for something that might have sent her running from him.

Damn it, woman!

"Abbot Wingate is here, my lord," Davie said, as he started for the stable with Simon's roan.

Wingate was waiting just outside the tavern, his

black monk's robes buffeted by all manner of revelers passing in and out of the establishment. The Cask and Coffer looked suddenly worn and seedy, and overrun with bawds and bandits.

Certainly no place to keep a wife.

"No word, Simon?" Wingate asked, looking as hellish as Simon felt.

"Nothing." Having a friend here with him, someone who knew Kailey, made Simon's fear seem sharper, gave it the power to wound deeply.

"I tried the riverbank, Simon," Wingate said, his clasped hands buried in the folds of his robes. "By the mills where the boy was found. I thought perhaps she had gone looking for clues."

Simon stopped cold. The river. "And?"

"No sign of her, thank God. Did you see her thief?"

"Aye, and the girl might as well be mute for all the answers I was able to wring out of her."

"So she said nothing helpful?"

"Only that she wanted to thank you for some counseling you gave her."

"Me?"

"Have you been visiting the prisoners, Wingate?"

Wingate was frowning deeply. "What counsel was this?"

" 'Twas something about listening to her heart." Simon led the abbot through the press of bodies to the stairs and then up to the room.

Wingate was quietly pensive as he closed the door. "Simon."

"What?" Simon had already dashed the contents of Kailey's saddlebag onto the table, was chasing blindly through the pile, his fingers trembling.

"I've . . . heard from her, Simon."

Simon turned to stare, certain that he had created hope where nothing else existed. "You've heard from my wife?"

"Yes." Wingate seemed unsure of his words.

"What the hell are you saying, Wingate?" Simon reeled on the man, his pulse raging like the wind.

"I just realized that she . . . probably doesn't want to be found just now."

"Not found? Where the devil is she?"

"Safe. That's all I know."

"All?" Simon was a breath from squeezing the answers from the man. "She sent a message?"

Wingate pondered that simple question for a tellingly long moment. "Yes."

Simon expelled a furious breath, his heart caught somewhere in his throat. "By Christ, if you knew this earlier, Wingate, and kept it from me—"

"I didn't. It just suddenly . . . came to me."

Simon filled his lungs with the air that his wife had brewed for him in their chamber, apples and lavender and hearthfire.

He'd been denounced and dismissed. She didn't want to be found—wanted nothing to do with the madman she'd married.

But Christ God, at least she was safe.

Safe. And at a distance. He should be pleased.

"When?" Simon nearly lost the word down his throat. "When will she be back?"

"I suspect sometime tomorrow."

"There's little comfort to be scraped from that, Wingate." Simon leaned his fists against the table, the contents of his wife's saddlebags strewn out in front of him like artifacts from a pagan ritual: a fall of dried rose petals, a small green-flecked stone, a braid of ribbon she'd tied to a delicate iron key. *His* ribbon.

"Bloody hell!"

Now Wingate seemed amused. "Call off your search, Simon, and get yourself some sleep."

Simon snorted and started throwing Kailey's things back into the bags. "I haven't slept since I met the woman."

He doubted he would ever again.

The morning sun sliced through the arrow slit and cut a line of fire across the ceiling of the tower.

But it wasn't the sun that had awakened Kailey, it was the plodding footsteps on the stairs, and the ominous jangle of keys. She prayed that Julia had come but knew this would be an emissary sent from her husband to punish her for trying to cozen him.

Kailey kept her eyes averted to the floor as the guard thunked the bar from its housing. She pulled the musty blanket tighter over her head when the door squealed open.

A pair of unfamiliar boots slipped beneath her gaze. "Stand up, woman. 'Tis your time."

Kailey froze. Today? Nay, not yet!

Julia, where are you?

"On your feet, girl!"

But Kailey's knees weren't working as well as they should. Her mind stumbled over itself trying to find excuses that would send the guard from her cell. "Where are you taking me?"

"To stand before the judges."

"No! I can't go yet, sir! I'm not ready." And Julia was still on the run! Kailey scrambled away on her hands and knees, giving another of the wracking coughs that had begun to scrape her throat raw. "I'm not well. Tell them I can't come."

The guard grunted, and slapped a lash of leather

against his thigh. "Right, miss. I'll go tell the king's justices that you're a wee bit under the weather today, and can they wait a few days."

"Would you, please?"

"And find myself hung by my thumbs from that gibbet out there? Not likely!" The guard wrenched Kailey up off the floor.

She stood wordlessly and unrecognized beneath the cowl of her blanket while he wrapped her wrists in the stinging cinch of the leather lash, watching every detail as if it were happening to someone else. She was a prisoner, bound and trussed, and on her way to the king's court of justice.

Reality and riveting terror struck her simultaneously as he yanked her toward the door. She fought at the binding, trapped by her panic.

"You needn't drag me, sir!"

"I'm not above clouting a woman!"

And Kailey was not above stomping on a man's heel to protect herself, which she did as he hauled her down the stairs, past thicker doors and danker, more crowded cells.

Kailey scanned every face as she was hurried from the tower and into the morning-bright bailey. *Dear God, where is Julia?* Was she languishing in some other cell, held under suspicion of escaping the king's justice—soon to be outlawed, no matter how innocent she'd been as an accused thief? Perhaps it was best if she *had* stolen away with Kailey's money, if she'd just disappeared and were never to show herself again.

Kailey, too, had broken the king's law, and now she must pay.

Blessed Lady of all mercies, protect me.

Because at that moment, the king's law was Simon de Marchand.

Chapter 9

Her husband was sitting back in his chair, one knee drawn up against the edge of the table, his elbows planted into the arms. He was watching with murderous intensity as the hapless man in front of him stammered on about the plight of his pregnant wife and sickly children.

At an abrupt nod from Marchand, Father Abbot stood. Just as quickly, the frightened petitioner fell to his knees sobbing.

"Mercy, please, my lords!"

"Master Rogum, we have found the testimony of the jury from the Wrexham Hundred to be sound." Father Abbot looked drawn and weary, and she wondered if he had gotten word of Nicholas, or if Marchand hadn't delivered her message. "You are charged with the theft of a horse from your master's house. Yours shall be an ordeal by water. Let the Almighty determine the intent of your heart. It shall be done on the morrow, in the abbey churchyard. God's mercy on you. Take him, bailiff. And bring the next."

"That's you, thief," Kailey's guard whispered, as he hauled her through the crowd by her wrists.

She stumbled along behind him, cloaked and hooded in a blanket that was far too thin, weighed down by the enormity of what was about to happen. Marchand would have her head and would send for Julia's in the next stroke.

She was let go of abruptly, left to stand on her own, facing the judge's bench. All she could see was the hem of the blue woolen cloth that covered the long table.

If only Julia hadn't run from her fears—the evidence against Pegshaw was hanging heavily in Kailey's belt-purse. She would try to mitigate the charge against Julia with the proof that Pegshaw had lied. Her husband claimed he was a champion of the truth; she would tell the truth as she knew it: she had released the king's prisoner in a search for evidence and Julia had never returned.

He'd be more likely to believe them transported by demons.

Kailey lifted her chin enough to peek from beneath the edge of the blanket. Her stomach folded on itself.

Marchand was sitting directly in front of her, his thunderous sleet-gray eyes shifted to her left.

He didn't know. Father Abbot hadn't told him.

Mother Mary, let him not kill me in front of Hinch and Davie. She prayed they were elsewhere and that they would never see her body.

"You are Pegshaw of Wrexham?" Father Abbot asked of the stinking ball of nervous energy who stood a dozen feet from her.

"That I am, my lords." He tittered when he laughed.

Kailey kept her head bowed and her eyes downcast for as long as she dared, terrified of that stark moment when Marchand recognized her. That would be quite soon.

"And you, woman," Father Abbot said too

kindly from his perch upon the dais. "You are named ... Julia?"

She could hear the amusement in his voice, and it gave her no comfort at all.

At the moment she wished she were anyone else but Kailey de Marchand, wife of the lord high sheriff. But she could delay no longer. She would tell the story against Pegshaw; the truth would have to serve.

I'll do my very best for you, Julia!

"In all truth, my lord abbot ..." Her wrists still bound together, Kailey tugged on the blanket and let it slip from her hair to gather at her shoulders. "I am called Kailey."

"Christ's teeth, woman!" Marchand rose up on his feet, every inch the ferocious beast, poised to leap the table in a single bound. She would be eaten alive.

"My lord sheriff," Kailey began, trying to smile, though her lips trembled. "When you hear what—"

"Silence!" The world and all its burgeoning sounds went deathly still.

Her husband seemed to gather his astonished rage into the center of his chest, his eyes now glittering shards of ice. He came round the end of the table and stepped to the floor, came toward her like a stalking wolf ... a winter-starved wolf who bent his shining teeth to the very soft part of her cheek before he spoke.

"What is the meaning of this farce, madam?"

Kailey wished he had roared out the question, instead of smothering it under his breath and letting it break against her lashes. She could see little else but him. A very private inquisition played out between them. His angry disappointment, his shock; how could she begin to make him understand?

"Not a farce, Simon. It's—"

"Where the hell have you been?" His eyes were eagle-bright and piercing. "I looked the world for you!"

"I was—" Kailey opened her mouth to speak more of her excuse, but she was transfixed on the flare of his nostrils and his too-familiar snarl.

His breath puffed at her lashes and he whispered again through his teeth, "That was you last night, wasn't it, madam? In the cell?"

She nodded slowly, raking her thoughts for what incriminating remark she might have made to him. Her heart remembered only that he had been worried.

"I told you then that I'd never leave you, my lord."

"Guard!" He said it quietly, yet sharply enough to stop the departing man in his tracks.

Mother Mary, protect me from my husband's wrath! And tell Julia to run!

"Aye, my lord sheriff?" The guard who had brought her here sounded thunderstruck as he came forward out of the crowd.

"Where is the prisoner, Julia of Wrexham?" Marchand's teeth were shiny white as he glared down at her, muscles flexed where his powerful jaw met his pulsing temples. She couldn't bring herself to look directly into his eyes for fear of being burned and blinded.

"She stands there beside you, my lord sheriff."

"Nay, Master Cluny, where is the thief I put into your care?"

Kailey heard the guard swallow, heard his feet

shuffle. "She is there, my lord. I just now took her from the tower."

"The very same?"

"Aye, my lord. And I held fast to her all the way here."

"Did you?" Marchand split his gaze from Kailey and advanced on the guard in his terrifyingly steady stride, passing Pegshaw on his way, sending the man scrambling. "And is that the same woman you've been guarding on your watch for the last three days?"

Cluny nodded, though with very little certainty.

"Look again, boy. Closer." Marchand shoved the man in Kailey's direction, and they met nearly nose to nose. Confusion turned to horror in the man's close-set eyes.

"Dear God, protect me." The guard crossed himself as he shook his head furiously. " 'Tis not, my lord."

"Then where did this one come from?"

"I—" The man's eyes searched for an answer in the heavens. "I don't know."

He hadn't been the kindest of guards, but Kailey knew the man wasn't completely at fault.

"My lord sheriff, he's not to blame here. The idea was mine—"

"Yours?" Her husband rounded on her like an eagle diving on a sparrow. "You thought that by spiriting the king's prisoner out of her cell to escape the jurisdiction of the court, you could save her?"

"That's not the way it happened."

"But that is the result. She is gone and you are here." He looked furious, her enemy and her husband. A stranger.

"My lord, Julia is innocent."

His eyes gleamed dangerously. "That is for the law to decide, madam, not you. Now where have you put her?"

"Put her?" But of course . . . he thought that she'd somehow sneaked Julia out of the cell for safekeeping, that she could produce her if she had a mind to.

Run, Julia!

"Is she in the castle, madam? In the abbot's guest quarters?" He leaned even closer, this final threat again for her ears alone. "By God, wife, if you've stashed her at the inn you shall regret it."

"I wouldn't, Simon." But that wasn't true; she'd have stashed Julia into the chest at the foot of their unused marriage bed if it would keep her safe. But Kailey couldn't confess that the girl had spooked and run in fear for her life. She would have to stall, make him think that she knew where Julia was. To somehow shift all the blame to herself, accept his anger, and pray that he would forgive her.

"My lord, Julia is not at . . ."

"I am here, my lord sheriff."

"Julia?" Kailey whirled toward the sound, her heart running wild as she sought the voice in the thick wall of people.

"Here, my lady!"

A fluttering hand and then she found her. Kailey shrugged off the scratchy blanket and ran to her.

"Julia!"

"My lady, I'm sorry and so ashamed—"

"An outlaw, my lords!" Pegshaw had finally found his tongue, was sputtering and pointing. "First a thief and now an outlaw. Guilty as sin— they both are!"

But Julia seemed unafraid as she looked into

Kailey's face. "I did as you asked, but when I went back to the tower, the guards wouldn't let me in. I didn't know what to do!"

" 'Tis all right, Julia. I knew you wouldn't desert me. But did you find it? The evidence?"

Julia's grand smile was all that Kailey needed. She gathered her courage and turned resolutely to Marchand.

He was standing as she had left him, one hand clamped around the hilt of his dagger, and hellfire in his eyes.

Did he question the worth in keeping this wife, whose very existence shamed him and mocked his credo? Was he forming those words in his heart that would separate them forever? She was not yet his wife in body. Annulment was still possible . . . probable.

Blessed Mary, she hoped not. She was developing a great fondness for the man. *Forgive me, my lord.*

"My lords of the court, I've come with evidence that Pegshaw's charge of theft against Julia of Wrexham is false."

Simon couldn't hear past the humming, still couldn't see past the clear light of her eyes. He'd not seen her for more than a day, had convinced his darker self that she was lost to him irrevocably.

And then, by Christ, she lands on her feet in the middle of his court, leveling that fierce, soot-smudged gaze on him in direct challenge to the king's strictures, contradicting Simon's own ethics, her wrists bound with a thong that pinched her fair skin in streaks of pink and pale. She wasn't in pain, only safely harnessed for the moment while he decided what the hell to do with her.

"Madam, you have disrupted the process of the

law," he said, ticking off her other offenses in his head: breaking a thief out of jail, breaking into one, shattering the king's peace, and all for the sake of a girl she'd met on the road.

"I told your guard I wasn't ready to come, my lord. But did he listen?"

"You gain nothing by mocking the court, woman."

Did she know the danger she provoked? A writ drawn against her, a hearing, an ordeal by hot iron if matters fell out badly against her. Simon wouldn't allow it, would take the ordeal himself or go to the gallows before he let her suffer such pain, but she did try the limits of his jurisdiction with this charade.

"I only want justice to be heard."

"The Wrexham jurors will be duly sworn to tell the truth—"

"But they couldn't possibly know the truth, my lord, because it has only just now been discovered."

"Aye, from the mouth of an outlaw!" the thatcher bellowed. "My lords, I object to this—"

"*Silence!*" Simon despised the little man for his whining and would have liked nothing better than to toss him to the dogs. But this was the king's court; there was order to uphold, as his wife would soon discover.

He turned back to her but she had stretched her wrists toward him. "Will you untie me, my lord?"

"For what reason?"

"I have proof—on my person."

Not trusting his own bewitched hands, Simon jerked his head toward Cluny. The guard scrambled to untie the leather lashes and then disappeared into the hushed crowd.

She reached into the purse at her belt and produced a battered tin cup as though it were the treasure of King Solomon.

"Proof, my lord!"

Pegshaw blanched and seemed ready to bellow,
but only sputtered.

"And this is what?" Simon took the cup from his
wife, stunned for the instant that her fingertips met
his thumb, fired to the center of his gut by the sky-
blue of her gaze.

"Tell the sheriff, Julia," she said.

"My lord," the thief said from behind her
smugly smiling protector, "that is the cup that Pegshaw said I stole."

Simon turned from the lawyer and thief to the
thatcher. "Is this cup yours?"

"Mine?" Pegshaw's squinty eyes darted from the
cup to the thief, and back again, as though he were
weighing his response on the edge of a rust-bladed
razor: which answer would better serve?

"Is the cup yours, thatcher?" Simon asked again,
knowing with certainty that it was.

"Aye, it is!" Pegshaw thrust out his belly and
pointed his finger at the accused. "Ha! And the
proof of her crime! How else could she have come
by that cup, but to steal it?"

"If I may answer for Julia, my lord sheriff . . ."

As if she hadn't been. But he was as suspicious
now of the thatcher's story as he was intrigued by
his wife's unflagging belief in the young thief's innocence. And the truth was his standard.

"You may speak, madam, but you will be done
quickly—and without histrionics."

She scowled sharply, but nodded. "Aye, my
lord. As you have all read in his writ, Master Peg-

shaw claims that Julia stole six cups from his croft—"

"She did!"

"And that each of the other cups looked like the one in the lord sheriff's hand."

"Aye, they did!" Pegshaw chimed in again, nodding to his sureties, who nodded back intently because they were liable if he was proved wrong.

Simon stood on the dais, grudgingly admiring his wife's command of the moment, and stirred to an unseemly degree by the gilding of her hair as she passed through a pillar of morning sunlight.

"And there were only six cups, Master Pegshaw?" she asked, her fingers laced at the small of her back, which only drew Simon's gaze to the ripeness of her breasts, reminding him that she was his wife and that he had yet to make that particular claim; that he had spent an utterly sleepless night on a bed haunted by her dreams of family, too easily finding himself craving the same.

"That's right, missy. Only six." Pegshaw looked down his blade of a nose at Kailey, blithely unaware that Simon would give his life in defense of the woman he now challenged with his insolence.

"And how did you come by them?"

"The cups were crafted by my wife's father some twenty years ago. Fine family treasures to be passed down to my son. And now they are gone. Stolen! By *her*!" He flung his point at the accused.

"If these cups are so precious, Master Pegshaw, then why did your son sell this one to me at a booth here in the market square only yesterday?"

"How dare you spread such a rumor!" But Pegshaw had turned a chalky white even as he was bleating.

"Is that true, madam?" Simon stepped from the

dais. "You bought this cup here in Chester?"

"Aye, my lord. Yesterday afternoon."

That was all the story she offered. He would ask her later how the hell she had changed places with his prisoner. As for the thatcher, Simon had a few questions of his own.

"Have you brought a merchant's wagon from Wrexham, Pegshaw? And is your son selling tin cups from its counter?"

Pegshaw chewed on the truth again, a sour mash, by the looks of his grimace. "I'm a merchant, my lord, with more to sell than rushes. We have various items of interest. Knives and string and all sorts of cups: metal ones and some made of wood. And if you'll just excuse me, I'll go get the lot of them for you to see. My entire stock."

Pegshaw set off across the floor at a dead run.

But Simon was on him in a stride, catching him up by the belt. "Leading the way, thatcher?" Simon asked. "Or are you running to shield your guilt?"

"She is the guilty one, my lord." Pegshaw pointed vaguely behind him. "The lying little strumpet."

Simon yanked him closer. "By strumpet, I hope you mean the accused thief, thatcher. For the other woman is my wife."

"Your—" Pegshaw made a strangled squawk in his throat, which pleased Simon mightily.

"Simon de Marchand, Julia is not a strumpet!"

Simon dared not look in his wife's direction, else he might smile, and she would think him approving of her methods. They were dangerous and incorrect. "Our apologies to both of you, madam. Am I right, thatcher?"

"Aye, my lord," he squealed.

"And you wish me to release you to fetch all your cups from your cart?"

Pegshaw beamed and nodded. "Oh, yes, your lordship! I shall come right back with them." He tried to scramble away, but Simon held fast to the man's belt.

"I'm sure you would, thatcher. But I think I should like to accompany you."

"No!" The man stopped breathing, stopped moving.

"No?"

"On second thought, my lord, I have decided to withdraw my suit against the lying little thief." He seemed to collapse under Simon's glare, slid to one knee.

"Oh, but that isn't possible, thatcher."

"It isn't?"

The vile bastard; mocking the law, terrorizing innocent women.

"You've set the court in motion with your writ. Theft, Pegshaw, is the king's business. The mechanism of justice turns slowly, but it does turn, and you'll find that it eventually grinds us all to a fine meal." Simon lifted the man by the belt and carried him to the nearest guard. "Bind him and see that he follows closely."

Simon turned to his fellow justices. "Gentlemen, the court moves to the market square. Come, clerk."

Ranulf grabbed up his writing table. Cathmore was already on his feet, eagerly rubbing his palms together, and Wingate was standing, too.

The crowd parted as Simon led the justiciars through the vestibule and into the bailey. His wife was a half-dozen steps behind him, whispering with the fortunate young woman whose life she had just altered so dramatically.

By the time the movable court had reached the edge of market square, a sea of bodies had formed behind it, craving the high drama. In the market, banners flapped in the morning breeze and awnings fluttered; pasties were cooking in food stalls, and cider flowing; horns and lutes sent competing melodies into the festive mix; and Pegshaw looked like a boiled beet.

Disliking the commotion, Simon motioned to the court guards to keep the mob back, and they became an efficient wall.

"Which wagon is the thatcher's, madam?" Simon stood above his wife, kept his hands to himself when he'd rather have smoothed back her tangle of hair and kissed her. This enchantment of hers had become a plague.

" 'Tis there, my lord, beneath the hawthorn tree. My lord—" She caught his sleeve between her fingers and he felt the exquisite impact of it all the way to the bone. "I didn't mean to worry you."

"Nay, wife," he said, at last giving in to the bewitching glory of lifting her chin in the cradle of his fingers, "I didn't know you could."

She frowned and he left her.

Flanked by Cathmore and Wingate, Simon approached the wagon, the evidence tucked into the fall of his sleeve. The ruddy faced young man behind the counter leaned forward, eager-eyed.

"Good day, my lords."

Simon paid little attention to him; looked beyond him to the five cups sitting just where his wife had said they would be.

"Merchant, do you recognize this?" Simon set

the identical cup on the counter and watched for the man's reaction.

"Ah yes, my lord," the young merchant said, beaming. " 'Tis one of a set of six. I've the rest back there. But I sold that single one yesterday morning to a young woman."

"Yesterday? Are you sure?" Wingate asked, peering into the shadows of the wagon.

"Oh, aye, my lord. And a right, rare beauty, the woman was." He winked. "Nearly closed my shutters and took payment in kind, if you know what I—"

Simon had the man by his tunic, dragging him and his goods over the counter. "And if you had, merchant, my hand would be around your throat and you'd be breathing your last."

"Easy, Simon." It was Cathmore, his fingers digging sharply into Simon's shoulder. "He's not worth it. Save your high passions for your wife."

Simon let go of the bastard roughly, his anger still blazing, his question spat from behind his teeth. "And you acquired these other cups how?"

"They belong to my family," the man said, gingerly straightening his tunic, as if he spoke to a wealthy madman whose purse he coveted, but whose violence he feared. "Fashioned by my own grandfather. My father—"

"Pegshaw."

"Aye, sir—"

"Enough! Guards!" Simon bellowed, pleased at the merchant's start of terror. "Bring me the thatcher! And the girl. Bring my wife as well."

Three guards and the castle bailiff arrived in a flurry of clanging swords and Pegshaw's blustering.

"Damn you, boy!" the thatcher shouted, throw-

ing his fists forward against the counter, sending
rush wands and cups and bowls flying.

"But Father, I—"

Simon shoved himself between father and son to
glare down at Pegshaw. "Your sins against that
girl, thatcher, have cost you your wagon, your
goods, and, if he has wisdom at all, your son. May
you rot in hell." Simon turned to the king's constable. "Guard the wagon, sir."

"Yes, my lord."

Simon saw his wife and the Wrexham girl standing just beyond Wingate, their elbows hooked in
comradery. Somewhere in all the confusion she had
picked up Davie and Hinch. She'd made a spectacle of his court, a vast entertainment that would
grow legendary in the retelling, and would surely
come to the ear of the king.

Damn the woman for her meddling! He would
teach her. But he had fines to levy, an innocently
charged woman to release, and a man caught red-
handed in a falsehood.

A mockery of truth. Pegshaw would pay dearly.

"Come forward, Julia of Wrexham."

Simon watched as the girl detached herself from
his wife, who nudged her forward and followed
closely.

"Yes, my lord sheriff." She stood almost in profile, ready to bolt if he should bark.

"A crime of false appeal has been committed
against you, and the king's peace broken in the
process." Simon lifted the tin cup from the counter
and held it out to her. She backed away as though
it were a viper.

"Please, my lord. I'm sorry."

He felt suddenly like an ogre, seeing the same
fear on her face that he'd seen when Pegshaw had

thrown her against the table at the inn. " 'Tis the thatcher who will be sorry for his disregard for the law. His wagon and its chattel now belong to you."

"To *me?*" She touched the front of her stained kirtle, quirked her brows, but did look past him to the wagon.

And Simon's wife was smiling in her quiet triumph, thinking herself in the right from the first, the ends justifying the means. He would set her straight the very next chance he got.

"The wagon is yours, girl," Simon continued, though watching his wife, "after the king's clerk has taken inventory of the contents and determined the amercement for the king's peace."

His wife gave a breathy little snort. "A costly thing, the king's peace."

"The wagon will be in mercy for no more than a tenth part of its worth," he said, wondering why he was justifying his judgments when she had been so vastly in the wrong.

"You can't sell my wagon, sheriff!" Pegshaw had found his vile tongue again.

"Oh, but I can." Simon turned to the constable. "Lock up the thatcher in one of your darker cess holes, Balford. He'll keep better that way. A year maybe—perhaps two."

Simon heard Pegshaw sputtering, but soon the thatcher and his groveling son and all that fusty noise faded into the breeze.

The Sext bell began to ring in St. Werburgh's tower just behind them, drawing Wingate to his holy office.

"Imagine it, Julia!" his wife was saying, "this entire wagon and everything in it is yours!" She had hold of the girl's wrist, was leading her toward the counter.

"Yes, but what'll I do with it?" Julia peered inside.

"You're a merchant now. You buy three of something at a low price and sell at a higher."

The pair of them looked like urchins sizing up a house to burgle. His wife's clothes were strewn with the same bits of filth as her friend; her face was streaked with soot, and Julia's with teary grime. Somehow his wife's hair had escaped Julia's matting, though, and still hung loose and silky.

"Julia, look!" Davie was inside the wagon already, dangling dangerously out the window, a new blue cap hooding his eyes. Hinch was picking up the scattered bowls. "There's all sorts of amazing things in here! Can I help you, Julia?"

The girl's teary smile fell into sobs and laughter. "Oh, I'd like that, Davie."

Before his wife could climb inside with the crowd of them, Simon took hold of her wrist and tugged her away.

"A word with you, madam, if you please." He met her startled resistance with a gentle yank that eased her arm through the crook of his elbow and fit her hip against his thigh.

"Where are you taking me?"

"To paddle your backside."

"You wouldn't!" It pleased him to see her eyes grow wide in horror.

"I assume you prefer to suffer your ordeal in private."

"I'll suffer it nowhere!"

"Ah! This footstreet will suffice." He caught her around the waist and swung her into a recessed doorway.

"Simon de Marchand! You can't paddle me!"

She looked so unbridled in her well-exercised out-rage, so very lovely.

"I am sheriff of this county, and I am your hus-band. I can do as I wish." He backed her to the door itself, spread his hands on either side of her head, and pinned her against the panel. "What were you after in my court today?"

She wore her indignation high on her cheeks, bit the word off her damp lips. "Justice and truth. The same as you."

"And last night, when I came looking for some word of you?" He leaned as closely as he dared, his nose near enough to brush hers. She smelled of rush-smoke and cinnamon, as she had in the dark of her cell. He should have known her. "Were you looking to bait me?"

"No!"

"Did you think to test my convictions by releas-ing my prisoners, wife? Were you trying to punish me?"

"None of that, my lord. I only sent Julia out to identify Pegshaw's son. She was to come back im-mediately. I didn't want you ever to know. I was miserable for Julia when she disappeared."

"And when I showed up?" He scrubbed his thumb across the smudge on the fine-boned ridge of her brow, the momentum of his anger spent and no longer protecting him.

"I was frightened to death."

"As you should have been. A bit of prudent fear never hurt anyone." *Prudence*, he reminded him-self.

"I was defending my innocent friend."

"By sneaking into the king's prison, releasing his prisoner, bribing his guards, threatening his peace! These are high crimes. Madam, I ought to throw your precious little backside into that cell where you'd not see the light of day for years."

"Why don't you, then?"

She looked like a hearth-lass, wild haired and sooted, leaning back against the shadowed door.

"You're my wife."

She drew in the softest breath, a start of triumph that shaded her eyes with undisguised approval. "So the sheriff's wife gets special treatment, above scullions and nightmen? Where is the justice in that, my lord justiciar? And think of the money the king has lost."

"I'll settle with Henry later." His heart had begun to beat madly, and his need for her strained at every seam. He wasn't keeping his distance. "As for now, my lady, I have arranged for a house while we are in Chester."

"A home for our entire family?"

That's not what he had said, but he wouldn't argue the point.

"For the five of us?" she persisted.

"Five?"

"Julia, of course."

Next it would be the red-headed boy in the infirmary, and then Blind Humphrey, who dangled his feet from the Northgate and dropped walnuts on the heads of passersby.

"Of course," he said.

Chapter 10

〜⌒○○⌒〜

66 9"Tis commodious, my lord." His wife smiled crookedly as she stood beside Simon in the small eating hall of Middle Crookston Manor. "But from the drifts of chaff and the stalks of straw scattered about, it looks to me as though it's most recently been a tithe barn."

Damn the woman for being amused! Simon had hoped to present her with a comfortable home—however fleeting their use of it. She could at least be as outraged as he to find it little more than a double-storied barn.

"Madam, 'tis an affront to my sworn office." He held the lamp aloft and strode toward the boxed-in stairwell that dropped down from the upper story. It stood like a room of its own in the center of the building. The rest of the ground floor was open to the stone outer walls, save for its solid support posts and a few isolated walls. Its windows were shuttered fast against the harsh midday light.

"How did you find this place, my lord?" She had gone with him to the stairway and was now tucked against his shoulder as she leaned back to peer up into the dimness. Her hair was soft wisps of sprigged lavender, reminding him of the moonlight.

152

He cleared his throat. " 'Twas offered to me by the king as the sheriff's residence."

"I doubt Lord Fletchard ever lived here." She took two more steps up the stairs, a distance that tugged at him.

"And neither shall I. Come." Furious that Henry should have offered him so little, and that he had shown this barn to his bride in such a ruined state, Simon turned to leave. But her warm hand came around his wrist and drew him back to her, his lamp still hanging between them.

"My lord, it isn't so very unlivable. It smells only of hay, not animals. The roof seems sound, the walls, too."

"Aye, but it's no kind of home for you." She was making too much of this folly, trying too hard to make a home of it.

"We haven't looked up here." She gave a gentle tug on his wrist. "The lantern, please, my lord."

Simon gave up the lantern helplessly, as though she'd momentarily mastered his will. She failed at hiding her suspiciously indulgent smile as she started up the stairs in a whisper of soft slippers and a flash of trim ankle.

He stayed below, breathing unsteadily, and mistrusting these ripples of tranquility that bumped against him, as if he were an oarless boat. It must be exhaustion—after a night spent staring at the beams above his cold-sheeted bed, spinning thick cobwebs of discontent and worry.

"I need a place to sleep tonight, madam," he bellowed after her.

He heard her indulgent smile break into bits of even more indulgent laughter. "You shall have a place to sleep, my lord. Come see for yourself."

Knowing that he would regret it, yet beyond denying her anything in his present state, Simon trudged up the stairs and through the doorway at the landing. He found her in a cloud of lamplight at the rear of the house.

"See, my lord?" She was peering into a deep storage chamber, piled to the rafters with furniture fit together every which way, like a giant's toy puzzle. "Chairs, chests, and tables, and surely that is a bedstead beyond."

"Earl Hugh must have thought he'd be back soon and successfully from his campaign against the king in France." Simon lifted a leather-slung chair out of the mess and sat it on the floor. "But then the earls of Chester have never lacked for arrogance."

His wife hung the lantern on a peg, then settled herself into the chair and looked up at him through her lashes. "Comfortable. Would you like to try?"

She rose and motioned to the chair, her eyes gleaming in a kind of mischief that made Simon want to bend and kiss her. He blinked away the thought. Not now, not while he fought to stand upright against his exhaustion. How could he keep his distance when she only tugged gently and he fell toward her?

Because she was his wife.

"If I sit, madam, I'll not rise again until morning."

As unconscious of her actions as a child, she cradled his forearms in her hands, as if she would guide him to his rest. "It's plain that you need your sleep."

It was plain that he needed *her*. If she were more experienced, she would notice the telling changes her touch had wrought in the shape of his hauberk.

"Nay, madam, I have a session at the court." *And I'm not prepared for this.*

"Then you must leave me here to make sense of this shambles while you're gone. Send me Hinch and Davie, and the cartful of our belongings, and I'll have a bed for you when you return."

"And my pillow?"

She laughed softly at that, and he wondered what was so amusing. He was near stumbling with the doubled need for sleep and for her, his senses muddled by her scent.

"Aye, my lord, your pillow. We'll make a home of Crookston Hall. A fine beginning to our family, don't you think?"

And there it was, like a treacherous old dream, that unmercifully vulnerable feeling of belonging to someone.

Family. Lost to him in the same shattering stroke that had taken her father. Could she hear his heart flailing around inside his empty chest?

She was so free with the words "home" and "family"—as though she truly understood what such things were. She couldn't possibly understand. He had stolen both from her a very long time ago, and he'd left her with nothing but shadows. He was trying to make it right for her, though he wanted no part of it himself.

He understood what she wanted of him, but he couldn't give it. He didn't need a home . . . or a family. He'd done fine without either for all these years.

"My lord?" She peered up into his face and tucked a shock of hair behind his ear—the simplest of acts, yet one that built a closely banked flame where her fingers brushed his neck.

His arms ached with emptiness, ached to be

filled up with her goodness. Christ, but if he embraced her, he'd quite likely never let her go.

Kailey thought her husband looked wary of her. Her nerves were split and jangling. Julia was safe from Pegshaw now, and well provided for in the future, thanks to this handsome justiciar whose jaw was stubbled, whose lips were so well defined that she wanted to explore them for their texture and taste.

Sir Robert had been right: his son was a good man. He would be a good husband, a good father.

If that was still his plan. If it had ever been. He still hadn't even kissed her, though he'd been close enough and simmering on a dozen occasions.

"My lord, when you wed me, you never said what sort of marriage we would have."

He pulled away from her to the center of the empty room, his eyes averted to the farthest, most shadow-ridden corner. "What do you mean?"

How could she show him what was in her heart? "I mean to ask if you and I are to have a *real* marriage."

He made a gruff noise in his throat, derisive, expertly distancing. "What is it you expect of a real marriage?"

Here was her chance, her very short list of wishes. "I expect a home."

He snorted, tossed away a crinkled stalk of straw, and watched it whirl to the floor. "And so I bring you to this barn. I see I have provided well for you so far in your life."

"Crookston Hall will do nicely, husband. So would your room at the Cask and Coffer."

"A room above a tavern? Hardly fitting for a bride."

"The place is not the point, my lord." Kailey

counterstepped the man's broad back, preferring to speak to a face, even one as well masked in its shadows.

"Then what *is* your point?"

"Where did you go when you left your father's house?"

"Why, madam?" His eyes were unrelenting, his voice deadly, as though she'd just stirred a basket of vipers with her bare hand.

"Is it a secret, then?"

He shrugged, narrowed his eyes. "I went from High Stoneham to live in the household of the earl of Leicester. He was Henry's chief justiciar."

"But not a father?"

He paused before he shook his head.

"Never a family, my lord?"

He said nothing to that either, only tracked her eyes and her mouth. His coolness stung, saddened her, crowded tears into her throat. He was an achingly good man with a heart full of sorrow. A lonely man who needed family more than anyone she'd ever known.

She'd made a promise to Sir Robert to make a family of his son; it was time she made the same promise to Simon—though she couldn't very well tell him that.

"Home is family, my lord, and family is those you carry around in your heart. Simple to move, always warm, ever accessible. Tucked right inside here."

She flattened her palm against his chest, felt the marvelous pounding of his heart through the thickness of leather and wool.

"What else would you have in this marriage?" he asked quietly, his eyes soft and seeking, though

he looked as though he would spook if she should
raise up on her toes and kiss him.

"Children. If God wills it."

His heart thrummed even harder, matched the
pulse in her fingertips. He swallowed. "And?"

Kailey smiled to herself.

"And, my lord: a bed."

Kailey watched her husband gallop out of the
forecourt of Crookston Hall less than a minute
later, her chest so stuffed with love for the irascible
man that she couldn't even cry.

She dug into her work like a woman possessed,
inspecting every wall and corner, every pillar and
window, throwing open the shutters as she went.

An hour later, she had finished the sweeping and
was just beginning to disentangle the furniture
from the storage room when she heard the cart in
the forecourt, Davie shouting her name and Hinch
blowing a sour-noted fanfare. Her husband had
sent not only the cart with their bags, but four of
his men to help with the moving.

In no time at all, Middle Crookston Hall began
to look like a home where her family might live
comfortably for a while. She found a workbench
for the kitchen, and pots and spoons, a table for the
eating hall, and a half-dozen chairs to set about the
house. Sleeping quarters downstairs for Julia, for
Hinch and Davie. And a bedchamber upstairs, with
a comfortable bed where his lordship could finally
sleep the night through.

Where their marriage might finally begin.

She yearned for her mother, for the advice she
would give to a new-married daughter, and that
yearning came again even stronger while Kailey
tugged at the leggy herbs in the neglected kitchen
garden. Her father's spirit was there too, in the sun-

light on her cheek, riding the warm breeze that buffeted the roses.

She spanned a treacherous chasm between her father and her husband. Between the law and the outlaw; between honor and betrayal. She would have to bridge it somehow, though her husband wouldn't approve. He would surely damn her for her interest.

It was plain that she would have to go to the source—to Ranulf and his clerks. To the pipe rolls.

Aye, and she would go tomorrow morning.

Simon stayed away from Middle Crookston Hall as long as he could. He'd left there aching for her and ridden just as hard by his guilt, had spent the court session in the same state.

The shadows had always been enough for him, and he had expected them to deepen with their marriage. He'd even once considered sending this wife to his estate in the north. But her sunlight beckoned, and her forgiveness. And for the first time in his life, he felt a yearning for something more—for family, for the home that she offered inside her heart.

Ah, but what insidious poison he would bring with him! He carried his father's betrayal around in his heart as unconditionally as Kailey carried her own father's love.

Nay, he would keep his distance, would remain her unworthy guardian, well hidden in the shifting shadows, where he could watch as he had always done, and keep her safe.

It was full dark by the time he arrived home and dropped from his horse.

"I'll take him to the stable, my lord!" The de Broase lad came bursting from the house with his usual windmill of limbs, and in a single flying motion had grabbed up the reins without startling the horse.

Simon nodded and looked toward the hall. "Fine. Thank you. Oh, and, boy?"

"Yes, my lord?"

He was about to ask if his wife was at home, but she was standing in the doorway, her hand against the jamb. His stomach lurched as she paused on the threshold in the torchlight and studied him.

Perhaps he should sleep in the stable.

But she was holding out her hand for him, walking toward him as if from out of one of his most recent dreams.

"Welcome home, my lord."

Her hand was warm in his, her fingertips firebrands as they brushed across his palm. He couldn't think of a thing to say as she led him by the hand across the stone threshold and into the wide entry hall. He could see the door open on the landing above, and a light warming the upper story.

"Your bed is ready for you, sir," she said, unclasping his cloak at the neck, stunning him with the graze of her knuckles in the hollow of his throat.

His bed. Not *theirs*. He suddenly didn't like that notion, wondered what he'd said that day to make her think he wanted to sleep alone.

"You'll sleep with *me*, wife."

She raised her placid, approving gaze. "Of course." Then she left to hook his cloak on a peg in the stair wall.

He realized then that he'd spoken only those five words to her since he had arrived—a bellowed command that she share his bed.

"What I meant, madam, is that I expect you to share a chamber with me."

"Which is the reason I set aside only one chamber between us, my lord. I am your wife, after all."

A surge of white fire shot through him, stirring his loins and making his hands burn to hold her. He took a step toward her, but he wobbled and her face swam. She took his arm and steadied him.

"You've slept but twelve hours in the last four days. Now to your bed, my lord."

Simon hadn't remembered climbing the stairs, but here was their chamber. He hadn't seen or smelled anything so welcoming in years: the furniture storage room turned to wedding bower, swept clean and scented with summer, and the shutters opened to the evening wind.

"This way, my lord sheriff."

Her warm hand was in the middle of his back and he was drifting effortlessly toward the bed, and then there came the resounding but satisfying crackle of freshly stuffed straw as he nosed into the mattress.

Simon knew he had some unfinished business with her, some of it sweet, tinged with a guilty longing, some of it dark and bitter and stinking of another time. He needed to apologize for being a beast and a bastard. He had to keep his distance.

Forgive me, Kailey. Nay, he couldn't ask that. Forgiveness required truth telling, and there was danger there.

"Your pillow, my lord." She cradled his forehead with her hands, slipped something soft beneath his cheek. Then all his cares melted into lavender-flavored honey.

"Sleep well, husband." The lightness of her voice

was against his ear, the fantasy of her kiss against his temple.

Simon's dreams came dear to him that night.

He awoke face down on his own flattened pillow, drooling, he was certain. Rushing, watery sounds came from nearby. He groaned and lifted himself onto his forearms.

"Ah, good, my lord. You're awake!"

Simon turned sharply to sit on the edge of the bed and found his wife smiling at him from behind the expanse of a steaming tub of bath water. Both seemed a shimmering vision to him, and he scrubbed his face with his hand.

"What is this?" he asked, unsure what he meant by the question.

" 'Tis a bath, my lord." She held out a towel to him.

"Yes, I'm well aware that this is a bath—"

"I've had mine—"

"In here?" He felt utterly drunk as he looked out at his wife from under his sleep-heavy brow, and wondered how he could have slept through the sounds of this stunning woman standing naked just feet from his bedside. The image made his skin ache. He took a huge breath of her.

"Nay, my lord. I didn't want to wake you, so I took mine in the kitchen."

She was as fresh as a field of clover in her plain gown of green-trimmed burgundy. There was lavender everywhere, and he couldn't shake the thought of his wife—his still unclaimed, untouched bride—lounging unguarded in any part of this barn but his locked chamber.

"You bathed in the kitchen, wife? And where were those men of yours at the time? And mine?"

Hell, he had her watched from day to night.

"Davie and Hinch?" The question seemed to confound her. "You'll be pleased to see the work they've all done to make sense of the stables and the house. And Julia is already gone to the market square to tend her new wagon."

Simon gave a grunt, not at all satisfied with such an innocent sounding evasion.

"I have errands to attend to myself. But if you wish it, my lord, I will bathe you. 'Tis a wife's duty."

Simon swallowed hard against his imaginings. "That won't be necessary, wife."

Her cheeks flushed like late summer roses, yet she didn't shy from his gaze. "Enjoy your bath, my lord."

"Wife?" he said, stopping her at the door.

"Yes?"

"Do you recall the man Stenulf and his plea to gain wardship over his young cousin Halwyn?"

"Of course."

"The plea was turned down last eve in favor of the boy."

Her smile was roundly absolving. "As I knew it would be."

Then she was gone, leaving his skin afire.

And his heart too fond.

Chapter 11

66**M**y lady de Marchand!" Ranulf met Kailey at the door of the clerk's chamber. "Welcome again."

She hadn't meant to rouse the entire room, but his fellows rose like stick puppets from their scribing and grinned at her. She had wanted to come and go unnoticed, to take the pipe rolls to a private corner and read about her father.

"I'm sorry to interrupt. Please continue; I know you're all busy. But Master Ranulf . . ." The other clerks settled back into their chairs and bent to their swift scripting. "I've come about the pipe roll for a particular trial."

"Ah, yes. Wonderful. Please sit." He pulled out a chair for her at the long table. "You may study the roll in question for as long as you wish."

"I'd rather to take it with me to read."

Ranulf shook his head firmly, and put his hand tenderly on top of the nearest trunk. "I'm sorry, my lady, but I can't let the king's property out of this room."

Kailey's heart sank; she gulped back a sob that seemed to rise out of nowhere. Her father had seemed so close.

"But as I said, you may sit here and read all the day long if you wish."

With all of these curious clerks wondering why she wept so loudly? With her husband presiding over his court not a hundred feet away, ready to condemn her for her interest in her father's crime?

"Perhaps another time," she said finally, guiltily relieved that her decision had been so irrevocably made for her. She would find another way . . . someday.

"Or, my lady, I could have one of my clerks make a copy for you."

Kailey stopped at the door, hardly able to breathe. A copy. How very simple that sounded. "You could do that for me?"

"We are holding ground here against the current court session. We could have something ready for you tonight."

"Tonight?"

"I need only a name and a year." Ranulf had been a convenient obstacle, and now he offered her an invitation to meet her father face to face.

"I don't know the date—but it was early in the year 1155." It shamed her not to even know that much.

"The year 1155. Ah, then the pipe roll ought to be—" He followed along the stacks of trunks, then tapped the lid of the one nearest the end of the row "—in this chest."

The sound was dull and thudding. Her father's tomb; a daughter's buried dreams. And yet the trunk looked like all the others: iron bound, plain, a date stamped into the face near the handle: 1155.

The year she was born; the year she was orphaned.

She had nothing left of her mother's: the blue of

her eyes, someone had once said, but nothing more. Here was a chance to know her father, and his last days, to fill in a corner of her heart—though that corner might then be shadowed with his crime and no longer with her childish, merciful wondering.

Would she have the courage to still and truly love the man, no matter what she found?

Ranulf lifted a ring of chattering keys from his belt, and in an instant the lock was open, the hasp hanging loose on his finger. Inside, the trunk looked like the honeycomb of an underworld bee: two dozen or more metal cylinders, capped and labeled.

"I'm afraid these rolls aren't as neatly organized as the more recent years." Ranulf lifted the cylinders one at a time, squinting at the rusted labels. "They shift as they travel, and God only knows when this trunk was last opened. What name would I be looking for?"

Hewett. But she hadn't said it aloud.

"The name, my lady?"

Kailey swallowed.

"Hewett." She breathed her father's name, then spoke it louder. "Neville Hewett."

A terrible weight lifted from her shoulders, and a darkness from her eyes. Yes, this was right. This was the best thing to do.

" 'Tis what the court records are for, my lady: the past made present. And a bit of local history thrown into the pot. 'Tis what I find the most satisfying about my job."

The past. Oh, to keep it from the present, and from her husband. He wouldn't understand.

"Ah, yes, my lady. The name you seek is listed

here. Late January, the year of our Lord, 1155. I will take care of the matter promptly."

"Thank you, Ranulf."

"So, wife," came that always-astonishing thunder from the doorway. "Are you here to pester my clerk with your everlasting questions?"

Kailey turned in his direction; her heart stuttering, her face flaming. There wasn't a door in all the shire that Simon de Marchand couldn't fill with his shoulders, and nearly eclipse with his height.

"Good morning, my lord." Excuses clogged her throat.

"Yes, good morning." He wore that tethered calm which had so frightened her when he'd first come for her at his father's home.

"Your wife has an exceptional interest in the court rolls, my lord."

Please Ranulf! Say nothing more! He doesn't need to know.

"The court rolls, madam?" Her husband stalked into the room, giving it a careful study as though he'd never been here before. But of course he must come a dozen times a day.

"Aye, my lord," she said, her ears heating quickly beneath the fall of her hair. "The confession we spoke of."

"Fletchard?" he asked evenly.

No more questions!

"Ranulf has been very helpful." Kailey's balance left her when her husband's hand stole around her elbow and he bent to her slightly.

"Then I must thank him."

" 'Tis of no moment, my lord," Ranulf said, as he slammed the lid of the trunk and locked it. "Just showing your lady the old county rolls."

Her husband's casual smile hardened in that single instant, his eyes turned to slate.

"Old?" he asked.

"Aye, my lord," Ranulf said pridefully, "our records go all the way back to King Stephen. But surely you know that, sir."

The pipe rolls.

Simon had forgotten them. The evidence of taint and decay, dormant and lying in wait, to be resurrected from the ashes of the dead.

He'd been startled when he'd found his wife here. He'd only come to ask his clerk about a writ. But her eyes had glistened with welcome, and in that moment he'd been paralyzed with desire for her, his hand aching to caress her cheek, to ride the perfect slope of her breasts.

Now his limbs were leaden, his mouth tasted of stone chips. Ranulf had been digging around in the iron strongbox, stirring up foulness and pain; he could smell it in the cooling air. He dropped his wife's elbow before she could feel the cold sliding down his arm.

He reined in his irrational anger, spoke steadily for fear of shouting. "You waste my clerk's time here, madam. This is a court. We are busy."

He couldn't read her at all, not the stormy blue of her eyes nor the pull of her frown. Dislike? Disgust?

So much the better.

"As you wish, my lord." And now she wouldn't look at him. She turned stubbornly beneath his gaze and looked to the clerk instead. "My thanks to you for your kindness, Ranulf."

Then she left the chamber.

Simon felt a hundred years old, as dead as the others who had helped to bring about this curse.

The court records. The truth of Hewett's plea, his trial and execution preserved for the ages. A crooked finger pointed at his heart. And he had even arrogantly told her about the pipe rolls, had dared her to read Fletchard's confession in order to prove the righteousness of his justice.

She might well be curious enough to read of Fletchard's trial, but would she then think to look for her father's? He couldn't very well demand that Ranulf not show her, nor could he remove the rolls from the chamber. Ranulf's seal of the exchequer was required, and that seal was a commission from the king himself.

Don't do this, wife.

She would find only grief and betrayal.

St. Brigid's day. The first of February, 1155.

Leafless trees, and ice-bent grass, the frosty breath that had burst forth from the dying man in billowing grunts, then in soft curling clouds until finally there was nothing at all. An innocent man's spirit dissipated to nothingness.

Simon had stood beside his father on that foul morning, terrified and green-sick, and proud.

And he had watched Neville Hewett hang.

Kailey left the clerk's chamber and the great hall, blushed crimson with a shame that she had not earned, muttering curses against her husband.

"He's *my* father!" she said, stopping to collect herself in a corner of the long vestibule that led out to the bailey. She couldn't help that the sheriff thought his own sire so loathsome that he couldn't bear to breathe the same air.

He was probably even now asking Ranulf what she'd been doing. And of course, Ranulf would tell him: it was his job to keep the justiciars informed.

Then her husband would know that she had lied about wanting to see Fletchard's confession. He had probably guessed her intention already, and Ranulf would only confirm that she'd been searching out her father's trial.

And why shouldn't she? She had every right! The matter of her father's past was between herself and her father, no one else. She didn't need her husband's permission.

So much for peace between them.

But peace had little to do with seduction. And if this marriage was ever to begin, she would have to give her husband a good, solid shove toward the marriage bed.

Chapter 12

He'd been a grand fool—displayed his suspicions and fear like a peacock's tailfeathers. During the day he had constructed a dozen reasons that would excuse his having thrown her out of the clerk's chamber—but none of them would serve. And never in his long career had Simon been so entirely distracted from his duties. When the interminable court session finally ended, he was quickly gathering the day's notes, still wondering what to say to the woman, when his new squire appeared at his side, brimming over with exuberance.

"Yes, Davie. What is it?"

The lad thrust a small scroll at Simon, tied neatly with a leather thong. "A message for you, sir, from my lady, your wife."

Not wanting to appear overeager, Simon refrained from snatching the scroll from the boy's hand, and instead continued to sort through the day's notes.

"You've seen her?" Simon asked evenly.

"I just left her at home."

"At home?" That word again. The boy bandied it as freely as his wife did. Home wasn't a tithe

171

barn. And they were not a family. And this missive probably said just that.

"As I said, my lady sent me to find you."

"You may leave the message there." Simon indicated the table with a nod, and Davie dropped the missive beside the inkhorn, then stood there smiling. He couldn't want money; Simon had given him plenty only that morning.

"Is there something else, squire?"

"Ah, yes—that's what I'm wondering, my lord. About squiring . . . I was wondering when I would be able to start training with your men."

"Training for what?"

"For the sword, my lord. Tomorrow, maybe?"

Simon could see his wife now, lightning bolts flying from her eyes if he dared allow the boy within a mile of the lists. "No swords, boy."

Davie's grin fell.

Then Simon remembered himself as a new squire, longing to wield the tremendous weight of a sword against anything that didn't move.

"No swords, but you can watch."

"Can I?" Davie jumped like a drunken coney.

"Report in the morning to the marshal at arms."

"Oh, yes, my lord! And a good evening to you." The boy left on the run, dodging those in the great hall who hadn't his youth-braced energy.

Finally alone with his elusive wife's missive, Simon slid the thong off the scroll, his gut made raw with apprehension.

Her script was neat and precise:

If you please, sir, bring a quarter peck of fresh peas, a noggin of honey, a gill of dried currants, and a bundle of candles to Crookston Hall.

"Peas?" Simon read the message again, just to be sure there wasn't something deeper to be read between the lines.

But her words were as clear as any he'd ever seen.

His wife had penned him a market list!

"And *this*, madam, is your message to me?" Simon didn't quite know what to make of its meaning: he could hope it was an indication of her ease with him, hinting that he was nothing to her but a foul-tempered errand boy.

Damn and blast the woman!

He was still puzzling it out when he arrived at Crookston Hall, toting his wife's market goods in his saddlebag, and having decided that the talent for haggling over the price of dried fruit must be a woman-born trait.

"Your peas, madam!" Simon shouted, as he slammed the front door shut and strode into the eating hall.

She emerged from the kitchen passage, her hair bound into a loose rope behind her; her hands and her apron covered in flour. She was as simply dressed as ever in her rough-russet kirtle, more compelling to him than any silk and broidery.

"My what, sir?"

She looked roundly perplexed, even as he walked toward her holding out the bag of pea pods.

"Your peas, madam! And your dried currants, your candles, and your honey." Simon had put each item on the table in turn. "Did I miss anything?"

Her blue eyes had grown wider than the noon-day sky, her mouth round and wet from the tip of her tongue. Simon had an overwhelming urge to kiss her, and might have crossed the distance and done so, but just then she started laughing softly.

"What, madam?" Simon asked, pinched by the tight fit of her jest.

"My lord, did Brother Claremont give these goods to you to carry home to me?" She tried to hide the throaty sounds of her laughter with her floured fingers, but only managed to dust the white stuff across her upper lip.

"Nay, madam, I purchased the lot myself, as you requested." Simon felt vastly unappreciated.

"Oh, my!" She raised up on her toes and left a kiss on his chin. "What a very sweet thing to do."

She'd kissed him! Left him feeling as confused and flustered as an untried youth 'neath an apple tree. And that made Simon angry—blazingly so— because he felt a ripe blush growing dead center of both cheeks and he couldn't seem to stop it.

"What do you mean, madam? Didn't you ask me, in this very blunt-quilled note, to bring you these?"

"That note wasn't meant for you, my lord." She was laughing low in her throat as she opened the bag and sniffed at the peas. "But I thank you. There were two missives and they must have been swapped."

"Swapped how?"

"And if *you* got the market list . . ." She turned her bright eyes on him in rueful wonder. "Then what do you suppose Brother Claremont thought of the note *he* got?"

"Brother Claremont?" Now she was sending her inscrutable missives all over the city. "Why and what did you write to Brother Claremont?"

"When I was busy at the infirmary today, he told me that he'd be happy to go to the market for me when he went for the abbey, if only I'd send word of my needs. So I sent Davie with two notes—one was the market list and the other . . . !" She was laughing still, hard enough now to have to sit down on the lid of the plate chest. "Dear Brother Claremont!"

Simon resented not knowing the source of all this humor, especially when it came at his expense. "And the other note, madam? What was the subject?"

Now she was blushing, from her brow, down the length of her neck, and well into the front of her gown.

"Dear my lord, I'd written that I hoped you would come home tonight, for a fine cooked supper—prepared by me."

A harmless enough sentiment, but now she was stammering, squirming on her perch, still trying to stifle her giggling, but failing miserably.

"Go on."

"And . . . oh, my lord sheriff, what will you think of me?"

"Let me be the judge, madam," he said calmly. "What did this note say?"

She paused overlong, and her amusement faded swiftly to a shyness. "I . . . intimated in my note to you that after our supper together—"

"Yes? After . . ." Simon leaned over her, tilted her chin so that he could look into her bright eyes, wanting to kiss the flour from her mouth, yet knowing he'd be lost for hours. And damned to ruin.

"Simon, I wanted you to understand that . . . uhm, that it was acceptable to me if, well, if we acquainted ourselves more intimately with . . ."

Simon couldn't imagine what she was reaching

for, and wasn't sure he cared beyond the riot of spices that clung to her hair.

"More intimately with what, wife?"

Her eyes were enormous. "With our marriage bed—my lord," she said quickly.

Simon was stunned enough to stop breathing. He'd expected anything—a declaration of war, a dismissal for his incivility, a sermon on the black art of justice—but an intimate invitation to join with her in their bed!

"And you put that down in ink, wife? In a missive?"

"To my husband."

"To be read by a monk!"

"It wasn't meant for Brother Claremont's eyes."

"Damn his eyes! That note was for *me*!" Simon had never felt so madly jealous in all his life. The thought of another man's fingers touching such private words writ by his wife's own hand made him quake with anger.

"I fear he'll think me brazen, my lord."

"Brazen!" Simon bellowed, knowing how quickly the unfounded rumors of his wife's light skirts and roaming eye would spread like a pestilence along the abbey cloisters and through the city. "He'll think you more than that!"

"I'm sorry, my lord!" She looked suddenly wary, and scooted out from under him to the opposite side of the table, the high pink of her cheeks turned pale. "I meant only to . . . to make something of this union between us. I'd hoped that we could finally begin it tonight. We are family now—no matter what you say. You're my husband. And I wanted you to know that . . . that I am willing."

"Willing?" Simon realized the full intent of this beautiful, lunatic wife of his: she was bent on seduction, and *he* was her target. The keen-edged yearning for her grew, prickled the backs of his eyes even as it spread from his chest into his loins.

"What shall we do, my lord?"

Such honest concern on her brow, such conviction in her eyes to put things right.

"Do?" It took every shred of his reserve not to shove aside the table that stood between them and take her right there on the floor of the tidy little eating hall. Already his arms ached and his blood tore at his joints.

"Aye, my lord, what shall we do about Brother Claremont?"

Simon suddenly pitied the cleric, as he pitied any man who would never know the bliss of coming home to a stunningly flour-dusted wife whose mouth drew him like honey, whose eyes caught the last rays of the dying day and thawed his ice-clogged veins.

She wanted a husband. Not castles or casks of jewels or richly crafted gowns.

She wanted a family.

And he wanted *her*.

"Wife," he said, clutching her gaze to his heart like a miser as he moved round the table toward her, praying that he wouldn't spook her. "If that monk should come knocking at our door, looking for you to cook him the fine supper you promised him—"

"Nay, but I didn't—"

"Shh." He put two fingers to her warm lips and nearly undid his resolve. Her mouth was velvet moist and powdered, and the breathtaking sweetness of that haven dizzied him. "If he does knock, make no mistake, wife, I shall throw him out on his backside. You'll cook for me alone."

"Yes, my lord." Her breath rushed between his fingers and blew like a hot, holy wind across his palm, scouring every thought but her from his mind.

Family. She would have it, though his bliss would surely damn them both.

Kailey had been waiting for Simon's wrath to rain down upon her like ice stones in a hailstorm; she'd nearly made a stumbling run for the kitchen when he'd advanced on her. But he'd been smiling oddly by then, and his eyes had shown the colors of sunlight on an eagle's wing. And his touch on her mouth had nearly taken her to her knees.

She didn't know what else to say to this powerful warrior who bent so low to her; the king's stiff-necked justiciar who had dutifully combed his way through a naggingly noisy market to bring home fresh peas and dried currants.

He was breathing swift and low, like a hunted stag run to earth. Just like he had the other day— right before he was going to kiss her. Kailey could hardly move for the press of his gaze.

"If you'd like to clean up, my lord, there is time before we eat. And a ewer of water in our chamber."

He looked at her for a long time before he answered, and then so softly his words might have been the evening breeze that lifted over the sill. "I'll only be a moment, madam. Whatever you do, don't answer the door."

He hoisted his saddlebag over his shoulder and left her alone in the eating hall. Kailey stood quietly, listened to him on the stairs and then to his solid footfalls across the ceiling as he entered their bedchamber above.

Her pulse quickened with each of his steps, and

she imagined him stripped down to his skin, his stone-muscled chest—that massive wall of heat she'd only felt through his shirt and tunic—pressed against hers; the feel of his kiss on her mouth.

He'd come home shouting like a lunatic. She was certain Ranulf had told Simon everything, and that he had forbidden her the copy of her father's record. But that hadn't happened. He either didn't know, or he didn't care.

And he'd brought her a sack of peas! *Peas, Sir Robert!*

While he was thumping around upstairs, she shelled the sun-sugared peas and put the currants to soak in a fragrant bowl of mead. A fat, succulent goose had already been roasting for two hours on the spit, and a plump loaf of bread sat on a platter.

Then Simon was at the kitchen door. His hair was dark with damp, raked back off his forehead by his fingers. He must have shaved again, for the shadowed stubble was gone from his jaw.

He leaned against the jamb in a fresh green tunic, hip-girded with a loose leather belt, and not a sign of his sword. His trews were long to his ankles and his indoor shoes so doeskin-supple, she knew for certain that he had no plans to venture outside this night.

"So you cook, madam, as well as consult on matters of law?"

Kailey found breath enough to speak. "Roasting a goose is simple, my lord high sheriff, as you must have learned as the king's justiciar."

He laughed. "My dear, most geese end up roasting themselves. As I did in the clerk's office this morning. I"—he cleared his throat—"have a temper." He approached the worktable, watching her uneasily. "Did you read Fletchard's confession?"

"Not yet." She could say that truthfully. To divert his questions, Kailey plucked a currant from the bowl of mead and offered it to him between her fingers. "A sample, my lord?"

He lifted his solemn gaze to her eyes, seemed startled to see her standing so close. Not a good omen for a husband.

"Would you care to taste?" Kailey held up her offering, and a trickle of mead ran down her thumb and collected in her palm.

He seemed quite interested in that trail, touched his tongue to his upper lip as if he were ready to savor the delicacy.

Kailey could almost feel his mouth sliding down her wrist. His nostrils flared, and she was sure she saw him swallow hard before he spoke in a husky, very unsteady voice,

"I'll wait, wife. Else I won't be hungry when you are."

"But it's only a currant, my lord. Not even a mouthful."

"Don't tempt me, madam." There was a secret humor in his wry smile that made Kailey's knees go weak and her heart go warm, though she couldn't figure out what sort of amusement he could have found in a simple currant. When he stepped away to the fruit bowl and took an enormous bite from an apple, Kailey bristled and huffed. Afraid of her cooking, was he?

"Will you help me with the spit, my lord? Lay the goose here on the platter, if you please."

He moved quickly to lift the rod and its goose from the uprights, then he settled the bird on the platter, spit and all.

"Am I your first wife, my lord?"

"My first?" He burned his thumb on one of the

spit prongs and grunted sharply. "Damnation, woman, of course you are! Why would you think otherwise?"

He muddied the last of his words with the end of his thumb stuck between his teeth.

"After all, sir, you're well past the marrying age." Kailey unstuck his thumb and gave it a quick inspection. "Well past."

Certain that her husband wasn't hurt, she picked up the weighty platter and hurried past him through the passage that connected the kitchen to the rest of the manor. She sat the goose on the table and turned to find Simon bearing down on her, the end of his thumb still stuck between his teeth.

"I'm in my dotage at thirty-three, am I?" The lamp that hung from the ceiling so near his head picked out the telling strands of silver in his hair.

"As *I* am at nearly twenty. Most women have at least three children by my age." Unsure why she had started out on this very rocky path, Kailey ducked around her husband's sudden fury and headed back to the kitchen. She found a bowl and began to spoon the peas into it.

He had followed. "And how many of those children never lived through their first night because their mother was a child bride?"

"Many, my lord." At least three of her girlhood friends had married young and been taken in childbirth. She'd never known a man to think of a woman's plight on any scale, and here her husband had made a study of it.

"An absurd waste," he said, pinching one of the peas from the bowl and dropping it into his mouth. And yet he'd been so afraid of spoiling his appetite with her currants. "I've heard a thousand or more suits against the dowries of children who'd borne children to their husbands and then died. My daughters won't marry until they are twenty."

"Yours?" Kailey looked up at him then, moved by his mention of children, almost afraid to ask. "Have you daughters, my lord?"

He gave a snort as if she'd not been listening. "I've just told you I've never been married."

"That counts for nothing, as you well know."

"I have no daughters, madam, no sons, and you are my first wife."

"Almost." Feeling selfishly relieved that he was entirely unencumbered, Kailey picked up the bowl of peas and the platter of bread, then left for the eating hall.

"Almost?" she heard him shout as she put the platter and the peas on the table. Then he was beside her, turning her. "You are my wife now, have been for days."

"Then I shall be even more so before the night is over."

His eyes brightened as he slipped his warm fingers through her hair. He cradled the back of her head with one hand as he tilted her chin with the other. There wasn't a spot on her face where his gaze didn't light, and all the while he brought his mouth closer, until the sound and the scent of him were all that mattered.

"They told me you were beautiful, wife."

"They?" What a strange thing to say. Ah, but now he was going to kiss her—she was certain of it this time. His breath was warm and clean, and he was bending ever closer. And his mouth so nearly touching hers—

And then it was, and he was wonderful—

Then there came a furious pounding on the front door. A hollow hammering that caused Kailey to pull back from his embrace and her husband to snarl.

Simon had thought at first the hammering had been his heart, or the rich roar of his blood in his ears in that delicious moment when he could at last taste her lips. But then the accursed sound had caused her to desert him, and his anger fused with his frustration and he felt the urge to murder whoever was on the other side of the door.

"Simon, could it be Brother Claremont?"

He snarled as he started toward the door. "The monk will think he has pounded on the very portal of hell if it is!"

The hammering came again, louder this time.

"Don't hurt him, my lord."

"I'm not promising anything."

"Please!" She raced him to the hall, then blocked his way when he finally yanked the door open.

"Move, madam—"

"Davie!" she trilled.

"Oh, my lady, my lord!" The boy's face hung long and as white as death, his knobbly knees caved in on each other. "I beseech you to forgive me."

Simon doubted that was possible, especially if his wife should learn that tomorrow the boy would be joining his men at the lists—however peripherally. He should have asked her.

"Come, Davie!" She pulled the boy inside, hurrying him to the settle near the cold hearth. She tried to make him sit, but the lad was too bent on pacing out his misery. "What's happened?"

He whirled on Simon, his chin raised and prepared for the worst. "I've failed you, my lord."

"More than you could ever imagine, boy."

"It can't be as bad as all that, Davie. Tell us, please."

She stroked the pale hair of Davie's forehead, cooing her indulgent encouragements, when those soft hands ought to be stroking another, much, *much* more needy brow.

"Tell us, lad." Simon leaned between his wife and the boy, his patience nearly spent. "Now."

"Well," he said, with his dramatic, half-moon frown. "After I left you, my lady, I went straight away to the court, as you said to do, and I gave his lordship your message. But I was too late getting to the abbey: Brother Claremont was already gone to the market. Abbot Wingate asked to see the note." The boy started digging around in his leather pouch, speaking faster. "I don't know what the words said, but he started to laugh and then told me to find Lord Simon and give the note to him. But you were gone from the great hall by then, my lord, so I came to Crookston! Here it is."

Davie extended the much-wrinkled scroll to Simon.

Simon took it with a yank. "Thank you."

His wife was grinning. "Davie, I believe you've just saved Brother Claremont's life."

"Have I?" Davie's face brightened.

"Aye, but you'd best not let on to him that you did."

"My lips are stitched, my lady." He was clearly confused at the turn of his fortune. "Oh, yum. Is that goose I smell?"

"Here, boy." Simon grabbed up Davie's hand and settled a pile of coins into his palm. "You and Hinch go have yourselves a fine supper."

"But, Lord Simon," Davie said, as Simon gripped

his shoulder and steered him toward the door, "I still have your coins from before."

"Spend them all, boy!"

"All of them? On what?"

Simon threw open the door and spread his arms wide enough to include all things that a callow youth might find intriguing. "Use your imagination, son! Spend them on wine, women, and song."

"David de Broase, you'll do nothing of the sort. And you, my lord . . ." She frowned up at Simon. "He's just a boy. A song or two and a bit of watered mead is all he's to purchase."

"And some sugared wafers, Kailey?"

Her gaze had warmed to honey in that brief moment of searing contact, and in the very next she had turned it all on Simon's skylarking squire.

"No later than midnight, Davie."

"Yes, my lady. Thank you, my lord." Davie bowed his way off the threshold, stumbled into the forecourt, then waved and ran off toward the town, as free as any forest buck.

She sighed heavily, her back just touching his chest. "The goose has probably cooled, my lord."

"This one hasn't cooled at all, wife," Simon muttered to himself. "Not at all."

Chapter 13

S imon watched his wife through supper, com-
plimenting her on her cooking, sharing his
wine with her, and his trencher, but nothing of his
heart.

When she finally left the table and shyly climbed
the stairs to their chamber to prepare for him,
Simon sat back in his chair, exhausted with his long
unspent passion.

For so many years she had been only that little
bit of goodness that lived inside him. The part of
him he could look to for a glimpse of his salvation
whenever his guilt weighed more than he could
carry, when his judgment went awry.

Whenever a man had gone to the gallows.

He'd done it all for her: this quest for justice, for
the certainty of truth. Always and ever, for the orphaned daughter of Neville Hewett—that had been
his credo and the only tribute he could pay to a
man he had sent to his death.

He had waited nearly twenty years to claim her,
never certain when fate would bring them together,
yet assured that she would be no other man's bride.
That had been decided long ago. He had outlasted
the other men who had sent Hewett to his execution, and now Hewett's daughter was upstairs and

he was about to complete the cycle, to bind them in body as he had already bound her soul.

If she knew, if she had any suspicion at all of who he was—of who Sir Robert had been, and the others—she would leave him to the wolves.

And in the darkest part of him, he sometimes wished for that. The release—justice finally done. No longer a need to dodge behind the hypocrisy of the laws that he admired.

He took a deep breath. This was not the mood he needed in order to charm his bride on her wedding night.

Simon set his wine cup soundly on the table and rose from his chair, feeling every one of his thirty-three years as he mounted the stairs. His heart pounded with terror, his blood raged in giddy wonder at what was about to happen.

He'd given her plenty of time to have dressed in her nightshift and combed out her hair. And now, as he stood lamely in front of the closed door, ready to enter into this new bond with her, he wondered what state he'd find her in.

He knocked lightly and strained to hear her welcome. She didn't answer. She didn't seem the type to cower beneath the covers, and her invitation had been overwhelmingly clear, ink-drawn and pronounced to the world.

"Easy, old man," he murmured. Simon took a breath of the night air and opened the door.

The chamber glowed richly with candlelight and a summer garden. Her touch was everywhere: flowers on the sill, her day gown and her shift hanging on a clothes peg, her shoes and pattens tucked neatly beside the door.

Perfect, except that she wasn't in the room.

"Madam?"

Ah, but there she was, already bunched in the center of the bed, the counterpane pulled over her head.

So her boldness had deserted her. He smiled to himself, feeling the rogue. Now what? How to coax her out of her fears?

"If you're cold, wife, I can stir the fire in the hearth."

Still she didn't answer, and so he fit another split of wood into the grate and gave it a moment to flame.

"And if you're frightened of me, I can assure you that I will not hurt you. God be my witness, I would never hurt you."

When she still didn't answer or move, Simon approached the bed, thoroughly confused by her sudden shyness, but marking it down to unavoidable nerves, the reality of her enchantingly brazen invitation.

"Wife?" He felt a bit ridiculous lifting a corner of counterpane to peer into her hiding place. "If you've changed your mind, my lady—"

"Oh, I haven't changed my mind, Simon." Her silky voice came magically from the doorway.

She stood in the portal, a cloud of honey-dark hair falling loosely from her shoulders, draped in her pale gown of lemon-shadowed linen that hid all but the unsubtle outline of her small breasts and their showy peaks. She carried a handful of roses.

"I thought you were abed, wife!"

"In there? On my wedding night?" The melody of her unabashed laughter set his head to spinning and his heart ramming upward into his throat as she came toward him. "My lord, I'm not the sort to cringe in a corner or hide under the bedclothes. Though I'm not sure what's going to happen here."

And the burden was on him to guide her—as if he knew where to begin. He'd bedded many a woman in his time, but never a virgin, and never a wife. And truth be told, in the last few years he'd lived as chaste as a common monk.

"Where were you just now?" Simon closed the door and latched it against one of her misfits breaking in on them.

"I was outside in the forecourt, gathering flowers from the garden hedge."

"You were outside, in the open—wearing only a thin veil of linen?" He pointed to her gown, the one that now seemed no more substantial than heated air.

"We have neither servants nor close neighbors, Simon." She carried the tankard to the table at the bedside and set it down. "I assure you, I was alone."

He could think of nothing more to say that wouldn't stumble from his throat like a dried clod dropped from a hoof, so he just stood there, a prisoner of her unstudied seduction.

"I've never been a bride, Simon. Am I dressed properly?" She lifted her arms and turned in place.

She'd called him Simon, not Marchand or my lord. And then he realized that she'd been doing so since the moment he'd come home. He wanted her to speak his name again, to hear that obvious concession to the moment.

"Well, Simon?"

"I've never been a husband, my dear," he said, dizzied by the way her mouth formed the last of his name in a half-kiss. "But I do know that any woman who wears a sleeping gown as beautifully as you will soon find it entirely extraneous."

She was frowning. "Have you been with other women?"

"Yes." He waited for her condemnation, but she looked oddly relieved.

"Well, then—what happens now, husband?"

"I'm here at your invitation, madam, if you recall. What had you planned for me?"

"Planned?" She finally looked flustered, her eyes darting from his face to his hands and then stunning him when she looked to where his arousal bowed his hip-belt. "Well, nothing—in particular."

"Nothing?" This game was difficult to play.

"I'm new to this, Simon. I can't begin to imagine where to go from here."

Simon felt the tug of the tide and the motion of the stars when she looked at him with those pleading eyes. The urge to pull her to him right then and spend the next several hours showing her all he knew of rousing a woman's passions grew more overwhelming with each throb of his heart, but he stayed rooted beside the table, even managed to steady his grip enough to pour himself a cup of wine.

"Hmm," he said evenly, "I can imagine all sorts of things."

"Can you, Simon?"

Her innocent eagerness was as impossible to ignore as the erotic image of her that ran riot behind his eyes: the velvet curve of her litheness bent backward and bare over his arm, her cascading hair brushing his knees, his tongue tantalizing the daring tips that even now had grown darker and strained at her gown.

"What is it you're able to imagine, Simon?"

He'd apparently been staring and she apparently had been waiting for him to prompt her. He couldn't very well explain what he'd been thinking. Simplicity would carry the night—at least, as a beginning.

"Well, for one, I had assumed you would kiss me." He nearly laughed out loud when he heard her gulp from clear across the room. "Which shouldn't be too much of a stretch for you, since you've already kissed me once tonight."

That brought her brows together in a genuine frown. "I did?"

"You don't remember?" Simon waited patiently while she searched her memory.

She shook her head quite earnestly. "When, Simon?"

"When I brought you the peas."

"I kissed you then?"

"Right here." Simon pointed defensively to his chin.

"Oh, yes!" She cocked her head and smiled fondly at him, as if she were a doting aunt. "Now I remember."

"You had truly forgotten?" Simon felt sorely neglected and overly defensive. "Our first kiss?"

She shrugged away the notion as she approached him in her bare feet, her hands clasped behind her back. A dark peak broke from the shallows of her soft gown to become a taut guidepost for his hand, for his tongue.

"That wasn't a kiss, Simon. Not a lover's kiss, at all."

"Then what kind would you call it?" Simon had felt quite kissed at the time, could still feel the glowing outline of her mouth on his chin; and now the sensation burned anew, like a healed-over brand come back to mark him.

"That was a family kiss, Simon." She stopped a

few short steps from him, and looked up at him through her lashes.

"What the devil is a family kiss?"

"You don't know the difference?"

"It's been a long time since I had a family."

"There you see, and now you have one again."

His heart swelled.

She smiled as she rose on her toes to kiss his lucky chin again. "A family kiss."

Then she was tugging gently downward on his earlobes, and he was a willow, bending to a brook. Her words were heavenly warm against the underside of his jaw,

"And since I now have a lover—"

"You have a husband," he corrected, shuddering with a delicious agony as she briefly brushed past his mouth with her downy cheek.

"I pray you will always be one and the same, Simon." She threaded her fingers through his hair and drew him closer, her eyes bright-hued moons as she whispered, "This plan is coming to me of its own will, husband. Is it a good one?"

"Oh, more than good, wife."

And then she kissed him. Sweetly, earnestly. A gentle but determined explorer, pressing her lips to his at one corner, then moving to the other side, and then to everywhere in between, as if she would memorize the exquisite fit. And in the space of those heart-stealing kisses she would lift her gaze to his, searching for something he prayed she would find in abundance—for he would have her understand that he could be, yearned to be, all things to her.

"Oh, Simon, you taste of wine, and currants and mint."

And she tasted of the rare goodness in his life.

Simon kept himself rigid as a marble column for fear of coming undone completely. To have arrived so softly at this moment seemed a blazing miracle to him, and his life had been so lacking in them until now.

She kissed his mouth; grazed his lips with her fiery fingers and touched her kisses to his temples and to the corners of his eyes; and still he stayed his quaking limbs, because he was spinning out of control.

But when she cupped Simon's chin with her soft hand and moistened her parted lips with her sweet tongue, then slanted her kiss full across his mouth, a feral howl clawed its way up from his chest, and he seized her into his arms and held her against him, not sure that he could ever let her go.

Kailey was lost to everything but her husband and his wild embrace. She had always imagined him a coldly distant eagle and now she gladly soared with him, tucked safely against his chest and under his soft gray wings. She clung to him and to his thick mane, pulling herself closer to his kiss, yesterday's fears turned to wonder, and tomorrow a distant riddle.

His mouth was everywhere in its relentless quest, parting her lips with his searing tongue, steaming at her temples and in her hair; his hands were broad across her bottom, his arms a breath-catching prison; and at the front of him, at the juncture of his thighs, his singular male hardness found shelter against her belly and made her want to hold him tighter, made her willfully wrap her legs around his hips.

He whispered her name with every ragged-breathed kiss, the sweetest sound that she'd ever heard. And his kisses came like soft, summer rain on a parched meadow. She absorbed them as they fell, treasured them; her limbs grew leaden with his enchantment.

He reared up from his love-making. "Slow me, Kailey!" His smile was loose and his chest heaved as a race-winded horse, making Kailey feel as if she rode him face-on along a rocky course.

"Simon, whyever would I slow you?"

He swept the top of the tablechest clear of its noisy clutter and he lifted her backward until her thighs met the edge and her bare bottom met with the cool wooden surface, her gown rucked up to her waist.

"Because I want you under me now, my lovely wife." He spanned his huge hands across her naked thighs, making Kailey want to open shamelessly to him.

"And aren't you supposed to?"

He sucked in his breath and steamed it out again, blazing a long, chaotic trail of kisses beneath her ear and along the ridge of her shoulder. He dropped his sweat-slick forehead against hers and clutched the edge of the high tablechest on either side of her bare knees until his knuckles whitened, and his arm muscles thickened to fat ropes.

"A moment of grace, please."

"As you wish, my lord." She stroked through his silk-curled hair, loving the tug of the strands between her fingers, disappointed to her bones that he'd stopped his kissing. He caught her hand abruptly and took it to his mouth, then formed it against his clean-shaved cheek.

He'd built a restless fire in her that seemed to radiate from her chest and coursed through her like a syrup of pure sunlight.

"I have a grand curiosity, Simon."

"About?"

"About you." Kailey reached down the length of his tunic toward the hardness she'd felt against her, but an instant later found her fingers imprisoned by her husband's huge hand, his gray eyes narrowed and fixed on hers in something approaching alarm.

"Where do you think you're going?" His frown was as furious as the rise and fall of his chest.

"I wasn't quite sure, husband."

"You seemed well on your way." He pinned her hand to her knee with a very warm palm. "On what errand?"

Kailey mastered the heat that tipped her ears.

"I want to touch you. I've seen stallions in full rut, and dogs and bulls—"

"And?"

"And I've seen men—"

"In full rut, madam? And just when did you do all this looking?" He shoved away from the table-chest, looking thoroughly scandalized.

"Not in rut, Simon! But on occasion otherwise."

"Otherwise? When and how?"

Kailey found his outrage nearly as endearing as his kisses had been.

"You well know that the job of a castle woman includes tending to the care and healing of the sick and wounded, and it seems the ill luck of some men to occasionally need tending in regions where they least appreciate it."

"Only healing?"

"Believe me, Simon, lust was never the object. Quite the opposite. I've seen boils and scrapes and stabbings and one poor woodcutter who once sat down on a—"

"Enough!" Simon looked pained.

"And so that part of the human male is not unknown to me." Kailey swept a lock of hair off his brow. "I've just never seen one that was so . . . formidable and warm and firm, as yours was when you were kissing me. And so I thought I would—"

"Please don't think that again anytime soon. Your curiosity would make this wedding night disappointingly quick. We'd never have made it to the bed."

"And you promised me the bed for the first time."

The growling breath he expelled lasted long seconds, and his eyes went darkly gray and half-masted.

Then she heard a knocking. "Do you hear that, Simon?"

Simon heard only the thudding of his own heart and the crashing of his pulse against his ears.

"There it came again, Simon." She wriggled forward as if to slip off the tablechest, as if she thought he might let her free when now she was closer to him than he'd ever dreamed, her knees spread around his waist.

And then Simon heard the sound, too.

"Lord Sheriff!"

"That's Abbot Wingate!" she said, her fingers wrapped around his forearms as though she would leap off the tablechest.

But Simon didn't want to let her go. She was too precious now.

" 'Twas Wingate's choice to live as a monk. Let him pound all he pleases. He'll go away."

"Come, Marchand!" It was Cathmore, the blackguard, pelting the shutters with pebbles. "We know you're in there."

The abbot's voice came again, "Please, Simon. I wouldn't have come but for the urgency."

"Ha!" Simon wrapped his wife's hair in his fist and kissed her soundly. He had a wife to love and a family to make. Wingate obviously had forgotten the true meaning of urgent.

But she pushed insistently at his chest, her sweet brow furrowed. "Please go to them, Simon. The abbot might have word of his son!"

Simon knew she would be unrelenting until she knew that Wingate was well. "I'll give them five minutes."

"Tell them they have three."

Casting her a smile that must have seemed demonic, Simon donned his hauberk to disguise his unspent ardor. The image of her perched on the edge of the tablechest, draped in her cascade of linen and curls, followed him down the stairs.

He threw open the front door, prepared to do battle. "Christ's bones, Cathmore, what the hell are you doing here at this hour?"

"On the devil's business, it seems." Cathmore stood on the porch, his brows high and a smile ticking the corner of his mouth.

"Your pardon, Simon," Wingate said as he came to stand, winded, alongside Cathmore.

"Unless morning has come again and shire court has been moved here to Crookston Hall, I am otherwise engaged, gentlemen. Good night!" Simon started to close the door.

But Wingate wasn't to be stopped. "May we please come in, Simon?"

" 'Tis truly important, man," Cathmore said, his expression changed to match his words.

Simon cast a longing glance up the stairwell, his

mind still clouded by his wife's intoxicating fragrance. "Yes, yes, if you make it quick."

He led the two men to the hearthroom. Cathmore leaned against the cold stonework; Wingate paced across the room, then turned his aged eyes on Simon.

"A note just arrived at the abbey, Simon. About the ransom. I'm to meet with an emissary tonight. Just after Compline, in the great hall."

"To do what?" This scheme had an illicit stench about it.

"To learn the terms of the ransom, I suppose."

"It's too soon for that, Wingate. Months will pass before you hear."

" 'Tis why I came to you, seeking your advice."

"Then don't go. That is my advice." Satisfied that he'd offered the best of his counsel, Simon went to the open door, grabbed the latch. "And now if you will all leave me, I will get back to my—"

"But I must meet with him, Simon. I can't risk angering the people who hold Nicholas. I'd never forgive myself if something happened to him."

"If this is truly the emissary of the hostage-taker, he won't leave without arranging the ransom."

"Will you come with me, Simon?"

Simon looked to the ceiling, imagining his wife drifting to sleep in his bed as she waited for him to come home. Home to his family. "You don't need me. You've plenty of legal force behind you with Cathmore. Find the rest of my men-at-arms and take them with my blessing."

Cathmore shifted, fixed Simon with an unusually pointed stare. "You are the sheriff, Marchand. You've experience in the matter and carry the power of the king's laws. And if the man isn't what he says he is, you will be in place to apprehend him."

"Please, Simon." Wingate clasped his hands together, white-knuckled in his pleading.

Simon looked over Wingate's head at Cathmore. "You, sir, have no idea what you're asking me to—"

He stopped as he heard the familiar and bare footfalls hurrying down the stairs.

"Simon, you must help Father Abbot and his son."

At least the woman had the sense to tie back her tousled hair and fit herself into a decent robe. He was the only man in the room who needed to know that he'd left a tiny heart-shaped mark on the smooth curve between her shoulder and her neck, and that she'd been whimpering at the time, and that it had only happened moments ago.

"Go back upstairs, wife," he said over the thrumming that came again to his ears when he imagined coming home to her each day.

But she was already in Wingate's beneficent arms, her bright cheek tilted to accept his kiss, her generous mouth ready with one of her own.

"I'm so sorry to disturb your evening, my lady," Wingate said. The abbot was a man of the world, and by the embarrassed flush on his face and the shuffling of his feet, he must certainly have read the high passion in her eyes and now knew exactly what he'd interrupted.

Good Christ, the man had read his wife's note stating exactly her intention for the evening!

"Nay, I'm very glad you came with your news," she said, smiling at Cathmore and taking Wingate's hand. "I'm sure my husband will help you. Won't you, Simon?"

Simon couldn't possibly have misread the urgent frown she shot to him, this woman who seemed forever bent upon defending every living soul from every injustice.

"Will you come with me to meet this man, Simon? I'd be grateful beyond measure."

Simon saw his wife open her mouth, and commended her with a nod when she closed it again. He knew exactly what was in her charitable little mind, and was weary of the assault on his nerves. He scrubbed the languor from his face, and his fingers through his hair, feeling as if he'd just condemned himself to a life of celibacy and loneliness.

"Yes, yes, Wingate. Of course, I'll go with you."

Wingate clapped him on the shoulder and murmured low, "Thank you, Simon. I know what you're sacrificing tonight."

"My Lord Abbot, you couldn't possibly imagine."

Cathmore chuckled as he caught Wingate's elbow and started toward the door. "We'll wait outside, Marchand."

The door closed softly behind them as Simon buckled on his sword belt. He turned to find his wife holding out his cloak. She'd hadn't said a word.

"Thank you, madam."

"I do this for Father Abbot. And for his son."

For all the sons of the earth.

"So do I. I should only be an hour. You'll wait for me?"

She caressed his jaw with the palm of her hand, traced his mouth with the pad of her thumb.

"Forever."

Chapter 14

"What did this messenger look like?" Simon asked, as the group strode through the still-bustling castle bailey toward the great hall.

Cathmore had just rejoined them with a handful of sugared plums. "The note was handed to Brother Claremont at the gate by the court clerk himself."

"Ranulf delivered the note? Now that's damned odd." Simon slowed as they approached the keep. "May I see it?"

"Of course." Wingate handed the folded parchment to Simon. "It says that my contact would find me if I stand near the clerk's hall."

Simon stopped beneath a torch outside the great hall, and read the note quickly in the light. "Why not come himself and take care of the arrangements at the abbey? Surely it would have been simpler."

"Perhaps the fellow can't resist a market faire?" Cathmore said.

It seemed a shell game to Simon. "When the note that arrived at St. Werburgh's abbey four days ago was delivered, the messenger was never seen. The outer seal was damaged, but hinted that it had come from the Templar's holding at Cressing. If that was so, why didn't the messenger show himself? And tonight's message is marked similarly but delivered to the abbey by my own clerk! Why?"

"Possibly because," Cathmore began, spitting out a bit of plum stem, "the emissary is one of the Young King's men and wants to avoid detection by the enemy on this side of the Channel."

"Possibly, Cathmore. But there are other reasons not to show one's stripes in the bright light of day."

Wingate's face paled. "But Simon, the identity of this emissary isn't important. I care only that he is in communication with those who hold my son."

"I don't like the smell of it." Simon had heard the pleading panic in Wingate's voice but could say nothing that would soothe him. "Until we know the color of his underbelly, we'll play this emissary like a viper—at a pole's length."

"Play him, Simon? But I only wish to learn the price on my son's head so that I might pay it."

"Wingate, you've been out of the world far too long. I'm protecting your interests."

"And I'm protecting my son!"

"If you leave money lying on the table, Wingate, you'll look to be a fool whose pockets can be picked further."

"Is that possible? Who would—"

"Hell's teeth, Wingate. You begged my advice and my aid. I deserted my wife to come here for you. Now tell me, sir, have I wasted my time?"

Tears shimmered in Wingate's eyes, and Simon found himself as sorry for the man as he was envious of the son. His teeth hurt from grinding them.

"Nay, Simon, I just want to see my son again on this side of Heaven." Wingate swallowed back his sorrow, dabbed at his eyes. "I'll do as you say. Tell me what I need to do."

Feeling as though he'd just kicked a puppy, Simon handed the note back to Wingate. "First of all, you'll see this emissary alone."

"Alone?"

"I'll be near enough to hear every word, and to act if it becomes necessary."

"Then what shall I do, Simon? What do I say?"

"Just listen to him, let him talk, and we'll see what he's made of. I'll join you when I think it'll best serve our purpose. Cathmore, you keep to the gallery where you can see all."

"Ah, the catbird's seat. It'll be a pleasure, Marchand." He laughed with good nature, brushed his palms together. "And here I was beginning to think this justiciar business was one large bore."

"I'll keep my eye on you and on the abbot, Cathmore, and you keep yours on the crowd. Let me know if you see anything odd. And if Wingate leaves the clerk's chamber without me, follow him."

Wingate looked baffled by it all. "I hadn't meant this to be a sheriff's inquest, Simon. But if you think it best—"

"I do. And there sounds the Compline bell from the abbey. 'Tis time, my friends, to take our stations."

Simon watched them leave, pulled up the hood of his cloak, then bought a tankard of bitter-smelling ale from a vendor just inside the keep.

The stone walls of the great hall rang out with voices and music and pinched his nostrils with a noxious cloud of sweaty bodies, overspiced food, and overused spirits.

Without the Earl of Chester's thumb to press

down upon the shire, the king had sent his own marshal to manage the fortification while he decided the earl's fate and dealt with the rebellious garrison that had held the castle against Henry's forces. Putting it to rights again wouldn't be easy.

Adding a court to a market week was nearly too much for the walls of Chester, its castle, and the abbey infirmary. The surprise was that just one nearly dead body had washed up in the river.

Simon worked his way through the throng, keeping his mind fixed on Wingate, only allowing his bride to flit around the corners of his thoughts. Pushing her away didn't work at all.

It never had, because she had always been family to him. He'd just been too much a coward to admit it. Now she was his wife, would mother his children, and forgive him for all but his dark trespasses against her.

A miracle—and she was waiting for him at home.

He took his place on the edge of the crowd, near the clerk's chamber, finding a bench to slide back on, tipping his head to the wall, his brow obscured by the hood of his cloak.

Wingate's sandals slapped into view.

"Nothing yet, Simon," Wingate murmured through a cough into his fist, his toes tapping.

"Patience, Wingate." Simon lifted his tankard and pretended to drink the vile liquid. He ought to set the bailiff on whoever had made the swill.

Only moments later, Ranulf appeared.

"Ah, Father Abbot, you've come. There's a man here to see you. He wanted privacy so I put him in the cellar just below."

"In the cellar?"

"Aye, 'tis an extra copy room for my clerks. He

seems rather impatient. Shall I take you there?"

From under his hood, Simon could see the hesitance in Wingate's shifting stance, the tapping toes.

Go with him, priest.

"If you please, Ranulf."

"Follow me, Father Abbot." Ranulf disappeared into the passageway and Wingate followed. Simon gave him a few moments before he rose and glanced up at the gallery. Cathmore was leaning against the screen rail as if he hadn't a care in the world, except that his fist was clenched and his thumb was sticking up.

When Simon reached the cellar corridor, only Ranulf was visible, closing the door to the first room. Simon raised a hand to keep him from shutting it entirely, then caught the clerk's arm.

"Wait here," Simon whispered. Ranulf nodded and sat himself down on a cask.

The voice that came from inside the chamber was pleasant and overly serene.

"I'm sorry to bring you out of the cloister of St. Werburgh's so late this night, Lord Abbot. But I have other business in town as well, and much to do before I return to Essex."

"You have word of my son, that is all that matters to me." Wingate's confidence had soared in the moments he'd been gone from Simon's view.

The other voice continued in its compelling kindness. "I fear it's become the lot of our Order to deal in ransoms in these days of warfare. Though we will ransom none of our own."

His Order? Was this emissary another member of the clergy? Simon shifted closer to the door.

"You've been to the Holy Land, Brother Josten?"

Brother?

"I know the area far too well. But I am now clois-
tered in the monastery at Cressing in Essex."

Cressing? A Templar after all! Hell's teeth!

Irritated beyond measure at being hauled from
his wife's loveliness to referee a pair of holy men,
Simon rapped once on the door, then shoved it
open.

"Good evening, gentlemen!"

The knight–priest stepped back from the table
and put a gloved hand on the hilt of his sword.

"Who are you, sir?"

"Ah, Simon, good!" Wingate came forward and
clutched at Simon's arm, looking wild-eyed in his
relief. "My concern was unnecessary. All is well
here. Brother Josten is a Templar. And from Cressing."

"So he is." The blood red crosses stood out on
the knight's broad shoulders. His dark hair was
pulled back into a thong and his straggling beard
spilled to the top of his white tabard. "And so I
am gone from here, Wingate. To see my wife."

"Nay, wait, Simon! I want you to hear his news."

"Who is this man?" Josten came around the bare
table and pointed his snarl at Simon, his sword
now drawn a hand's breadth from its sheath.

The hackles rose on Simon's neck, and instinct
wrapped his hand around the hilt of his dagger. "I
am Simon de Marchand, the lord sheriff of Chestershire."

"*You* are sheriff?" the knight spat. "What of
Fletchard?"

"The man was hanged last week." Simon
watched the Templar's Adam's apple bob the
length of his throat.

"Ah, then my apologies, sir, for my suspicions.
We knights often carry great sums of money and

I've grown oversensitive to unexpected entrances."

"Understandable." Now Simon was intrigued by this wary knight who seemed to travel without escort. "What news do you bring of the abbot's son?"

Josten looked reluctant to deal with Simon, but Wingate insisted. "Please, brother, your news."

The Templar finally produced a folded document from the pouch at his belt. "From my brothers at the Temple in Paris, delivered to them last month, and to us at Cressing a week ago. I came as quickly as I could, hoping to overtake our original messenger."

"May I see the ransom demand?" Wingate took the page with quaking hands, squinting as he read silently. "He was taken three months ago. Ambushed."

Josten shook his head and leaned his gloved hands on the table top. "The roads are treacherous these days, Father Abbot, and the countryside rife with the wicked."

"And the ransom demand, Wingate?" Simon asked, wanting to be done with this and return to his wife. "How much?"

The abbot lifted weary eyes. "Five hundred pounds."

"Five hundred!" Simon took the parchment and scanned the preposterous figure. "Do they think your son a king, Wingate?

"It matters not to me, Simon." Wingate's eyes were afire with indignation. "I'll not bargain my son's life. There is no price I will not pay."

"And what is the Templar's guarantee that this king's ransom will arrive safely?"

"There are no guarantees on this earth, Simon, save the love that I bear my son, and my Lord God." The foolish priest turned those damp, devoted eyes to Josten. "I'll pay the ransom, sir."

"That always seems the wisest measure in these cases." Josten had the practiced cadence of a skilled merchant in a crowded marketplace, the sort of placating commerce that turned Simon away as easily as it drew others to buy.

"So you do this kind of thing often, Templar?" Simon asked evenly. "Play mercenary?"

"We are God's soldiers, sheriff. His peace is our creed." Josten stood upright. "I bear this news with great regret."

"Simon, please." Wingate put himself between Simon and the knight. "How much time do I have to raise this ransom, Brother Josten?"

"Every day is another risk." The Templar shook his head sadly and slipped into that solicitous tone like a foot into a worn shoe. "Tomorrow would be best."

"Yes, as soon as I can." Wingate looked broken and stumbling, making Simon's heart ache for the man. "Where do you stay, Brother?"

The Templar shifted slightly. "I have a room nearby."

"You're most welcome to lodge at St. Werburgh's. Indeed, I would be grateful for your company."

"Perhaps on my next journey to your fair city." Josten sliced a belligerent glance at Simon. "But I will walk with you to the abbey."

"That would please me." Wingate touched Simon on the arm as he passed him, the cold, translucent hand of a dead man. "Thank you, Simon. God be with you."

Simon kept his opinions silent.

Josten gave Simon a final glare before he stalked out of the cellar room and followed Wingate up the stairs. Simon prayed that Cathmore would see them as they entered the great hall.

Ranulf was waiting in the corridor where Simon had left him, perched on the cask. The clerk was staring after the Templar, a pursed frown on his mouth.

"I didn't much like the fellow, lord sheriff. Reminds me of a pet ferret I once kept. Bit me when I least expected it."

"My sense exactly." Simon motioned him to follow and they started up the stairs. "Did you notice what time the Templar arrived?"

"Do you mean in the clerk's chamber?" Ranulf's soft soles scuffed the stone steps as he followed behind with his shorter stride. "I'd say two hours ago."

Two hours? Simon gained the floor of the hall and waited for Ranulf while he watched Cathmore leaving the gallery. The man must have seen Wingate. "Did he ask you to deliver his message? Or did you offer?"

Ranulf smiled wanly. "He offered me a pence for the errand. I couldn't pass it up."

"And did he wait in the clerk's room while you ran your errand?"

"Definitely not, my lord." Now he looked roundly offended. "I'm an officer of the exchequer. Those are the county pipe rolls, and therefore the king's. Unless I'm there in the room, I keep the door locked and the key on my person." He lifted a cord from the neck of his tunic and jangled the ring of keys.

"Did Josten by chance say why he couldn't go to the abbey himself?"

Ranulf shook his head. "Said he was going to look for a room, and I assumed he used the time between to do so. Beyond that I didn't pay him any mind, my lord." Ranulf's eyes twinkled as he leaned forward in a confidence. "The king's wage to me isn't enough to question the occasional honest pence."

"There's another shilling in it from me if you can discover where our Templar is lodging."

"A shilling! Thank you, my lord." Ranulf hurried off to the clerk's chamber where his scribes would be working until well after midnight.

There was trouble brewing here between the arrogant Templar and the improvident, credulous monk. But Simon couldn't quite separate the details of the case, for the unexpected mist in his eyes. That a man would be such a fool for the love of his son—it blinded Simon with outrage and envy.

And left him aching with regret.

Kailey did battle with the goose's legs and finally freed them from the carcass. There were peas left, and even currants. A fine gift for Julia while the girl stayed the night in her wagon. Though Simon's sergeants patrolled the market square, and Allan seemed especially interested in Julia's well-being, Kailey had insisted that Davie stay with her—and Hinch as well.

A bath awaited her upstairs; two kettles of hot water steaming on the small hearth in the bedchamber, and a cistern on the roof, newly freshened and primed with rinse water. Simon might even find her there in the bath when he returned, if her timing was right—

Davie came whistling into the kitchen as she wrapped the wooden platter in a cloth.

"This just came for you, my lady." He was holding a bundle of folded paper, neatly sealed.

A note from Simon, telling her that he'd not be back till morning, or next week? This wedding night had been a near disaster. She took the papers, disappointed already, and prepared to sleep alone and cold in their vast bed.

"The fellow said to tell you that it was from Master Ranulf, of the clerk's chamber." Davie sniffed at the cloth that covered the platter.

"Ranulf!" Kailey's heart thudded with a dreadful awakening. *Her father!*

"What is it?"

The boy wouldn't understand; and her husband certainly wouldn't. "Just some information. Off with you now, Davie. See that Julia gets some of that goose. And take care of Hinch."

"Aye, my lady." Davie left in a clatter, leaving Kailey alone and unsettled with the copy of the pipe roll.

She had often imagined a noisy family of spirited brothers and enterprising sisters, a father she could have run to with her fears, and a mother who would have combed her hair and kissed away her tears.

But that wasn't her life. Wishing it so would mean forgetting Davie and Hinch, and Julia. And she would never have met Simon, if she hadn't been fostered to Sir Robert. That would have been a tragedy.

She was blessed by love in great abundance, and the past mattered only because of its mystery.

Her hands shook as she broke Ranulf's wax seal and unfolded the crisp copies from the tight cradle they made of each other.

There were three pages of tightly written Latin. On the topmost was the Crown's charge and summons:

Henry, by the grace of God, King of England,
Duke of Normandy, of Aquitaine, and count of
Anjou, demands the sheriff in the county of Ches-
ter to bring Neville Hewett, baron of Aldehurst,
to stand trial for treason against the king. Witness,
myself, at Bermondsey, 3 January, in the 1ˢᵗ year
of our reign.

"Treason." She sighed for the waste of it all. "Father, why?" What would she find here in these
pages that could explain such a crime and all its
tentacles?

Your heart's peace, my daughter.

A chill swept across her shoulders, tugged at her
fingers.

'Tis yours for the asking.

She might never know the truth of Neville Hewett's heart, but the court records would tell her of
his deeds.

And she would love him still.

Neville Hewett, charged with conspiracy against
the life of the Duke of Normandy before said
Duke came to the Crown of England, did make
off and is suspected, so he is to be exacted and
outlawed . . .

Outlawed and reviled.

Kailey took a rushlight up the stairs to the bedchamber and added fire to the grate to bring her
bathwater to a boil again. Then she sat down on
the edge of the bed and began to read in earnest.

Chapter 15

‿‿‿‿‿ ⟩⟩⟩ ‿‿‿‿‿

Simon left Ranulf and joined Cathmore just as the man got to the vestibule. They easily followed Wingate and the Templar to the abbey, watched Wingate enter the curia, and saw the Templar return in the direction of the castle.

All seemed too peaceful.

"I'll see Wingate safely all the way to his cot," Cathmore said from the cover of the moon-shadowed hawthorn. "Go back to your wife, Marchand."

There was nothing more he could do here at the moment. And, praise be to a merciful God, he had Kailey to go home to.

Kailey and all his hopes for her.

Propelled by the force of his pulse and the stunning thought of his wife, he blindly passed dicing soldiers and dancing couples, seeing only the haze of his imagination.

She would be lying in the middle of his bed, her lush hair tangled like a storm in the bedclothes, and then between his fingers, and he was ravishing her mouth with his. This time when she sought to satisfy her curiosity about the shape of his arousal, he'd damn well let her find out.

It was intoxicating, this feeling of belonging to a

woman who gave her "family kisses" so blithely that she could forget the first one she'd given to him.

By the time Simon arrived at Crookston Hall, he was as eager as a stag, and praying that Kailey was still awake and waiting for him. No matter, he would awaken her as she had never been awakened. He would make her his own.

He threw off his cloak and mounted the stairs to their chamber, then opened the door to a compelling outline that stood against the hearth. He could get very used to this.

"Good evening, wife." Her hair hung loose at her shoulders, her nightshift folded around her legs.

She was staring numbly at him, her quaking hand and the papers she held lit by a faltering rushlight resting on a table at the bedside, dropping its ashes in a soft pile at its base.

"You knew him, Simon." Her voice trembled on the verge of breaking, her breath short and shallow.

"Who, madam?" In his muddled state, Simon could remember only that damn Templar. She wasn't making sense; he'd never seen the man before. And he damn well didn't care if he ever did again. He shut the door against the rest of the world, ready to begin their lives together.

"You were there, Simon! And you didn't tell me." Her eyes were intense with a harrowing emotion that he couldn't identify.

"And where is it that you think I was, madam?" She looked small and wanting, made him ache to hold her. "I think you've awakened from a beastly nightmare."

He went toward her, reached for her, but she backed away.

"No, Simon." She raised her hand with its pale flag of crumpled parchment and hurried to put the half-filled bathtub between them, as if she thought to defend herself from him.

"Damn it, woman, what is it? What hornet's nest have you got there?" But even as he asked the question, the hair on the back of his neck prickled and time seemed to slip backward through his fingers.

"My father's trial, Simon." Bright amber stars hung firelight from her damp lashes. She held out the trembling sheaf of paper, fury and shame blended to make her voice ruffle from her throat. "Every wicked word of it."

A cold dread crept out of Simon's heart and oozed into his limbs. "Where did you get that, madam?"

"It doesn't matter. Because I understand now."

Christ, God, don't let this happen. But he was already lost, damned by her for his deeds, or would be soon. His stomach cinched itself up against his heart, his every defense caught in his throat.

"I know you were there at my father's trial, Simon. And I know you testified against him."

Ah, Kailey. You should have let it rest. We could have survived without the past rising up between us. Family, remember?

"And Sir Robert was there too, Simon, with his awful testament to my father's treason. And Lord Telford and FitzLandry. Why didn't you tell me the truth of it?"

The truth? Oh, how the lies and the truth mixed like oil and water, leaving a sallow-rainbowed slick across everything it touched. He hadn't expected this moment to come so quickly, hadn't expected it to make his heart ache. She had been too much like the sunlight, she'd slipped into his veins, turned his face to her warmth. He'd felt whole for the first time since he could remember. Amazing how quickly he could be torn apart again.

"Please, wife." He swallowed hard against all his memories. "Let the matter rest."

"But it can't rest. You knew the wicked truth about my father because you were there, and yet you didn't tell me! You made me dance in my blindness, Simon, you let me stumble and look the fool. You knew!"

"Aye, I knew, wife. But you never were a fool to me. I never thought that. I couldn't possibly." One of the logs on the fire shifted, and he watched the red showers dance across the embers, a fitting vision of his future, what was left of it. What more could he possibly say to her?

We lied, Kailey. We killed your father because he was in the way.

"I'm not afraid of the truth, Simon. That would have been easier." She came bravely from behind the settle to stand so near him.

"Not this kind of truth, madam." She was so close to it; if she shifted her gaze, looked at him in the right light, she would see it plain on his face.

"Simon, there is but one truth! God's truth, as you are ever preaching in your court. You above all men in this kingdom should know that. Better to confront me in the open with all that you know, than to let me unearth your disgust at every turn. I am not afraid of anything but your loathing."

How could she even think it, how could he let her? "I do not loathe you, wife. I never have."

"Please look at me, Simon!"

She caught his arm with her warm hand and tried to turn him. He felt like one of those ancient standing stones, ponderously anchored in the earth. But he did as she wished, as he would always do. Whatever she wanted from this day forward. He would set it right for her.

He turned and found her honest, water-blue eyes pleading with him when she should have been embittered.

"I have the right to know everything, Simon. Someone should have told me when I was grown. Why didn't they?"

" 'Tis long past; just let it be."

"But I can't, Simon. He is a part of me." She clutched the parchment to her chest. "He was my father, and this is all I have of him. For good or ill. And yet I find that it isn't enough—these are only words. But you knew him!" She touched the back of his hand with her fingertips. "Tell me, Simon, about the trial. All that you remember."

He'd been waiting for her accusations, for her to have stripped him of his mask. But now he realized that she believed all the lies: believed them because they were written there, copied from a book of shallow truths.

She believed him because her heart was brave and good.

And because he was an artful liar, sired by an artful devil. His guts were churning, lead melting lead.

"It was too long ago, wife. I remember little."

"But you must recall some of it, Simon." She thrust the crackling sheaf into his hands, pointed to lines of ink that had smeared with her tears. "You gave testimony against him at the trial. You saw everything. Was my mother there? Did you know her, too?"

"Damn it, wife." Simon took the pages and turned from her because she was frantic and she made his heart ache. Because his eyes stung and his chest was hollow.

"Did you see her there, Simon? Do you remember her?"

"No." He looked down at the ink and parchment, saw nothing more than a seeping void. Yet his head was full up with sharp memories. The soot-streaming banks of candles that blazed against the gloom of the winter's courtroom. A newly crowned king with favors to give to those whose greed raged the loudest. Examples to make of treachery.

And Simon so sure of his own loyalties that he had trusted without thought.

Aye, he had trusted like a son. *Damn you, Stoneham!* He bit now at the inside of his lip to keep from sobbing.

"Then what of my father, Simon?" She followed him, held his wrist still with her soft fingers as she scrutinized the top page in her relentless pursuit of his darkest memories. "It says there in the roll, Simon, that you saw him with the assassin Flemings; that you heard them all conspiring against Henry just before he came as king to the throne. Surely you remember!"

He remembered every moment, clearly remembered seeing Hewett with William Ypres's mercenaries. His beloved father had made certain that he had seen.

"Aye." Simon felt her gaze on him, eager and upturned, and he avoided her pleading, wondered if she saw the redness of his eyes.

"And here, Simon, you boarded my father's wool ship in Chester, with Sir Robert and King Stephen's marshal."

"Aye." He remembered that, too, remembered the excitement roiling in his gut as he stepped onto the fog-slick deck, feeling a grown man, at thirteen. On the king's business, though even then he hid his unfounded doubts from himself, and always from his father—that splendid warrior who had honored him with his secrets because Simon had been on the verge of manhood.

A father would never deceive a son, would never risk his son's immortal soul.

"And it says here, Simon, that in the ship's hold, they found damning evidence of a conspiracy against Henry, the king's heir—a plot against his life, to be carried out in Rouen."

Simon could still feel the salt-damp fog on his face, and that blushing need to share the thrill of this royal manhunt with his father. He remembered wanting desperately to cling to the man, to hold his hand and whisper his questions. But that would have made him look spineless and callow, so he had stood alone, observing it all.

"What happened then, Simon? It says nothing more here. The rest is of the trial." She slid the pages from his hands, brushed through them in a flurry, though he doubted she could see through the tears pouring from her eyes.

This was a dangerous, despicable game he made her play. The sinner on trial for his misspent soul, yet so easily leading his innocent judge along a rose-strewn path, treading the thorns with his own feet, trying desperately to leave the soft petals for her—for the woman he had come to love more than his life.

The truth would take her from him. An accusation of ancient perjury, a confession of his guilt, and then Simon would suffer his long-deserved punishment, would swing on the gallows as Hewett had done.

And then what would she do? Who would guard her against an evil world? Hewett's lands were scattered now. Simon had spent his life building a bride-price to give to Kailey. Safely wed, with the fortune entailed to their children so she would never suffer, she would be secure—but only if he was alive and untainted by this crime. Unless he could free a piece of Hewett's land for her to hold on her own—she wouldn't need him, then . . .

Unnerved by the possibility, he cleared his throat. "Neville Hewett was branded an outlaw before night had fallen. A writ was sent out through the kingdom for his capture."

"My father wasn't there on the ship?"

How could he have been, my dear?

"Nay, they caught him two months later." Simon felt as if he were spinning an epic tale for a child too tightly wound to settle into her bed. It was a tale of dragons and deception, but she was no child to be cajoled to sleep. He would have to work to remember it rightly, to skirt the truth and keep her believing in his falsehoods.

"Where was he caught?" She was making a careless scroll of the sheaf in her fist, twisting it around her finger.

"In London," he said quickly, picking up speed so that he could keep his voice steady. "He was held there through the advent of Christmas, through Henry's coronation, was brought before the king in those bone-cold days following Epiphany, and hanged on St. Brigid's day." There. It was done and he'd gotten through it.

"He was a coward, Simon. And it shames me." The truth was there in her hands, and she was twisting it with her goodness. The conspiracy ran so treacherously deep, had spanned so many years, inflicted such a great evil upon one innocent girl-child.

"Your father wasn't a coward. Far from it." He threw that to her as a bare comfort, something to distract her, but she shook her head.

"It is written here in the plainest of words: his cowardly denial of everything; the way he tried to shift blame away from himself. The way he professed his love for my mother, for me."

"He did love you."

"Are you so certain? These are words he spoke when he feared for his life. To love is to give honor, to care more for others than you do for yourself. He cared nothing for my mother's peace or happiness. He let my mother die alone and left me to the mercy of strangers." Her eyes were wide and her lip caught between her teeth when she turned to him. "He left me to Sir Robert, didn't he? To FitzLandry and Telford. Or did that happened afterward? After he died?"

Aye, afterward—after the truth had come to Simon, denied at first, yet so vast in its implications. If Hewett was innocent, and Simon's father and the others had conspired his downfall to rid the Midlands of his influence, then his father was a liar, a murderer. And Simon was just as guilty.

"Simon, they took me into their homes, these very men who had condemned my father." She looked at the parchment again, touching the words, searching for faces just as she had searched out names. "They fostered me through my life with far more generosity than the daughter of Neville Hewett deserved. Why? What did I matter to them?"

You mattered nothing to them, Kailey. Only to me. To me.

"Was this charity an act of friendship? Had my father been the one to go wrong among them?"

So near the truth, but she would never uncover the treachery because it wasn't in her heart to see it. How easily she took on the burden, added it to those fragile shoulders of hers. And how easily he let her.

"Aye, there had been some friendship before, alliances to keep."

Alliances shift, Simon, my son. 'Tis the way of the world.

And so an innocent man had died.

And in that same instant, a son's love for his father.

"Your father, Simon, and the other men—they kept a pledge made in memorial to a lost friendship! To my father through me." She seemed awestruck by such loyalty, her gaze distance-glazed with memories, seeking clues in the hedges and halls of her childhood. "How I wish I had known! How I would thank them if I could."

"You have done, wife."

"Dear, my God. Simon—" She touched her fingers to her lips, stepped closer to him, peered at him as though she had never seen him clearly before. "The elders fostered me. But you, Simon— you *married* me."

"So I did." But he'd never expected such wounding peace. Simon scrubbed away the sting at the back of his eyes, pushed aside his blinding loss that would surely come in some dark, unexpected hour.

A chance remark. A nightmare. And she would be gone from him.

"That was *your* pledge so long ago, Simon, wasn't it? To marry my father's daughter? And you kept that promise after all these years."

He was a fraud to the marrow, a great weaver of falsehoods.

"We pledged then to keep you safe, Kailey, to see you well cared for in your life. Each of us did. But it was my choice to wed you. *My* choice."

He hated the gratitude that came into her eyes, prayed that she didn't speak it.

"Then I will thank you, Simon—"

"No!" he blurted, unable to harness the sharpness in his voice. "Don't ever, *ever* say that to me."

She flinched only slightly, bearing his bellow with her agile defiance, catching him in her impossibly bright gaze and grounding him in his infamy.

"As you wish it, my lord."

He knew this was not the end of it. She would probe and probe again with her ill-founded gratitude.

" 'Tis time you go to bed," he said quietly, though his heart thudded hard in his chest, a leaden weight in a barrel.

"Do you join me, husband?" she asked forcefully, her every breath causing the dark peaks of her breasts to lift against her shift. "It is still our wedding night."

She was the richly furrowed earth asking for his seed and his sunlight. She wanted children and family. They were his to give, but his knees were locked down against legs that would no longer hold him up if he dared to move toward her.

Dread had settled into his joints like a grainy mortar of stone chips and lime. He wanted to shake the heaviness from his limbs, to lose himself in her forgiveness, but he needed to wash the taint of these ancient memories off him, else he would carry it with him to their bed.

He was still her shadow guardian, and shadows were made of nothingness.

"I would be no kind of a husband tonight, my dear." His mouth had never tasted so foul. His heart had never been so heavy or hollow. Leaving her when he would have stayed and loved her through the night, when the idea of family had felt so sublime, seemed a fitting punishment to him. He turned to go.

"In its season then, Simon?" There was no mercy at all in the rise and fall of her melodious voice. Her brow had paled and her cheeks blossomed apple-red.

Kailey knew her face flamed. She was righteously angry at him—at her father, at Sir Robert as well. She wasn't a child, hadn't been for years. Discovering only now that her fostering *and* her marriage had been an act of pity had only made her feel foolish. But there was more than pride at stake here. Her fear and her mortification came from this once-again adjourned marriage of hers, from her husband's painful retreat from her, when she could still feel the heat of his hours-old kiss on her mouth.

"You said that to me on our first night together—when I wondered about our wedding night. Do you remember?"

"Yes." His jaw had stiffened.

"I was frightened then, Simon, and shy of you—the man who had charged into your father's stronghold and demanded through anger-clenched teeth that I marry you." She had thought him mad at the time, and his father raving.

"I was never angry at you, wife." He stood in the recess of the door like an outsider, not quite in this world, and not a part of her.

"But you are angry now. You must be." She hadn't yet mastered her feelings between this outlawed father and her extraordinary husband, or sorted them so that they made sense. She knew only that Simon was here and now, and that she had disappointed him. "I've dredged this muck to the surface."

"I'm not angry," he said sharply. "I've told you, wife, it doesn't matter to me."

"But it must, Simon, else you wouldn't be so quick to leave me here when I need you most."

He slid his gaze from the floor, raking up the length of her to her eyes. "You don't need me in your life."

"I obviously do, Simon. You're my husband."

"I will always provide for you—"

"I don't need your house, my lord, or the protection that your titles bring." Blazes, the man was stone-headed! "I need *you*, the man who combed the market stalls for currants and candles."

"Kailey—"

"Whether you willed it or not, sir, you have persisted in making us a family. You could have married anyone in all that time, and not a soul in all Christendom would have faulted you for it. Not even I!"

He put his hand on the door latch, an isolating sound that chilled her. "I but kept my pledge, madam."

"Aye, you waited as few others would have." Kailey caught his sleeve beneath his wrist, fearing he would leave. "Patience, courage, or simple-mindedness, I don't know which quirk drove you to it. But you are here with me now, my outlawed father and all. And nothing has changed between us for my having learned the truth."

His jaw worked its tension beneath his skin, but his eyes were soft as clouds as they coursed her face.

"And yet you're suddenly not interested in me as a wife? Has my breath gone bad?"

"Hardly that." He frowned, and whether he knew it or not, his hand was hot and rounded over her hip.

Wiles. Perhaps they were working again.

"If I make unreasonable, unwifely demands on you, Simon, you need only tell me." She ran a finger along the edge of his shirt, where it met the down of curling hair below his throat.

"Please, wife." It was a whisper, puffed against her hairline.

"Nay, Simon we are married now—I think we have been for a very long time."

His chin came up then, and his defensive shoulders, as though she had accused him of some great crime. Hearth flames flickered in the slate of his eyes, but the man said nothing, only exhaled in a rush.

Suddenly weary and fresh out of wiles, Kailey left her husband, his reluctant half-embrace and his unattempted kiss, and snagged a towel from the clothes peg.

"But if you don't intend to be my husband anytime soon, then you'd best leave here, Simon. Because I plan to take a bath, whether you stand there watching or not." Fortifying her courage with a sniff of impatience, Kailey dipped a ewer into the iron kettle on the hearth grate, then turned and poured the near-boiling water into the tub to mix with the cold already waiting for her.

She would have fetched more water, but the shadows at the door moved and Simon came behind her in his utter silence, slipped his fingers around her waist, and breathed his words against the underside of her ear.

"Let me, wife." His voice was so low and heart-bindingly tender, Kailey dropped the ewer into the tub and melted against his chest, watched him brush his thumbs across the hard peaks of her breasts. The sensation was splintering, touched her everywhere.

She caught a gasp in her throat. "Simon!"

He turned her then in his rock-trembling arms and raked the hem of her shift to her thighs, spread his great, scalding hands wide, and rode the bunching linen up her belly, over her ribs and breasts.

A willing blade of river grass, Kailey moved with his fierce currents, stretching her arms to the sky to let him free her of her shift. He held her hands prisoner and she gasped when he caught the very tip of her breast with his mouth, tugging possessively. She rose up on her toes, clutching at his shoulders and winding her fingers in his hair.

He was the fevered cramping in her belly and the dampness between her legs, the singing in her blood. A blinding madness made her squirm against him, until he pulled away from the fury of his kiss and wrenched off his tunic and then his soft woolen shirt, until he was standing naked to his narrow waist in his braies and chausses and tall boots.

The man was feathered shadows and sleek planes. And there at the front of his braies was the rawness of his passion, so plainly, enduringly contoured, begging the fit of her palm.

And all the while his gaze was lightning-laced, teasing static into the ends of her hair, encircling her ankles.

"God save me, Kailey. You are glory."

Chapter 16

Simon had dizzied with the first sight of her standing naked—as elemental as the seasons, the breath of him, and the winds that drove and drove the seas to shore. He felt greedy and ungrateful, and so unworthy of such a gift that his throat closed over and he prayed for his dark soul to be healed.

Disaster had strayed so close this time. He'd nearly deserted her, forgotten his cause in his selfishness. But they were done with the secret, and it was buried like a cancer inside him. He would let her have her father and his memory. He would let her pry, if she must.

He would be her husband, her family, as long as she wanted him beside her. Just now he wanted to fit her against him, but the temptation to take her to the flame-warm carpet and enter her sweetness rode him like his practiced conscience. That urge to plunge and thrust and possess was the pounding in his veins, the throbbing in his lungs.

The room had grown hotter than blazes.

"Come, wife. I'll bathe you well." He gathered her into his arms and carried her to the tub.

He set her on her feet in the overgrown bucket, a white-hot pearl borne in a common oyster. And

God save him, she just stood there, uncovered and proud, so breathtakingly familiar with him. As though he were a long-loved husband. As long-loved as she.

"There's soap and a cloth on the dressing stand." Her crooked grin was as contagious as sin.

"I shall add 'demanding' to the long list of your charms, wife." He carefully poured the heated water into the tub.

"As I've added 'handsome' to yours."

"Me?" It made his blood rise that she had even spared a thought for him in that direction. Handsome? Not at his age, on the verge of succumbing to gravity, his skin sun-leathered, his hair beginning to thread with gray? But he would be a fool to lift the blinders from her eyes. Let her think it.

"I won't swell your chest with flattery, Simon, but I've seen the stares you invite from the women who pass through your court."

"Faulty vision on your part, madam." Simon found the chunk of lavender-scented soap wrapped inside a white raw-silk cloth, his fingers clumsy in anticipation of their destination.

"As for me, 'tis your kindness that attracts me most. Not just—" She regarded him steadfastly from her tub, flicked her glance downward to his braies, across his groin, as daringly as the moon at noontide. "But I have noticed that too, Simon. Indeed, I have."

The room rocked sideways, but Simon recovered his balance, quickly dipped the soap into the warm water, and then drew it out again, his hand slick and quaking at his side.

Christ's bones, she was beautiful. And he felt every inch the pagan pilgrim come to worship. His offering was only water, but this particular goddess was known for her forgiveness, honored for the absolution she granted to the unrighteous.

"Ah, Kailey." He'd never allowed her name to be more than an unsung melody in his head, and now it lingered in his throat like an ancient wine. He covered her mouth with a tarrying kiss, a carol dance shared by his tongue and hers, desire coursing through him like molten iron through a slip: pouring into his loins, heating and hardening him.

And she was his.

"Lady wife, how I've waited for this," he whispered, caressing her silky hip with his palm and his fingers.

"And me, Simon."

He wrapped his arm around her waist and drew her close—until her breasts were sizzling points against his bare chest and her belly was a cradle for his arousal, still captured inside his braies. And all the while his warrior-hearted wife was squirming to his melody, riding his hardness, and murmuring his name against his mouth.

"I like this, Simon."

"And this?" He kissed her shoulder and the lush hollow at the base of her throat, and then moved away until there was space enough between them for his soap-slick hand. The contact was a raging delight and loosed a gratifying catch of surprise from the back of her throat.

"Even better, husband."

"And tell me of this?" He wet the soap again, found the silk cloth clinging to it, then squeezed the water over her in a milky cascade.

"Simon!" She sighed his name inside his mouth and leaned her wetness full against him, sliding with him, measuring his arousal with rhythm of her hips, until she was his pulse and his heartbeat.

He filled his lungs with her lavender until he thought he would burst with the wanting.

Twenty years of watching her without seeing, of wonder and guilt. Never marrying, for his heart was already spoken for, and now she was his, and here in his arms. His wife.

His miracle.

"Kailey!" The lightning that ripped through him was white and hot, and far too intense. He righted himself and his world, struck by the dark past and the rainbow-hued present in equal force.

"Oh, sweet wife! This is folly. I cannot bathe you without breaking." He slopped the rag and the soap into her hand, then backed away three steps.

"I can't imagine you breaking, Simon." She looked so damned eager, her lips still damply parted from his kiss and the trail of his tongue, her blue eyes startled to violet. "You are the strongest man I've ever known. Ever."

"But I am only a man, wife."

She smiled at his confession, a no-quarter-given smile that ambushed him when he least expected it.

"Please." She held out the soap to him, a sensuously heavy weight trapped inside the silken rag and hanging like a talisman between her fingers.

"I warn you well, wife."

She shrugged one, glistening pale shoulder, raised a winged eyebrow. "Then I've only myself to blame."

Feeling as hesitant as a convent-sheltered virgin, Simon snagged the soap, then made a vigorous business of sudsing his wife from her stubbornly pointed chin to the bottom of her feet, separated from her soft flesh only by the wadded silk and a mountain of self-control.

"There! I am finished," he said, backing away from his grinning artistry, his hands aching for the want of her hot skin.

"And I am scrubbed, Simon. But I think I would rather have your hands on me. And the rest of you."

Simon dropped the soap into the tub, took a breath as if he were about to plunge a thousand feet into the dark sea, then slid his hands and arms around her until she was a part of him and she was sighing.

"Kailey!" He drew the hiss of his ecstasy through his teeth.

She laughed low in her chest, leaned into his hands. Her eyes glistened like brookwater beneath her lashes, flaring wider as he slid his palms over the fair places the cloth had been, lingering at her breasts—the bitter soap a barrier to his mouth, a boon to his senses, and an aching torment in his loins. She encouraged his hands to wander freely as she hummed and squirmed.

"Yes, Simon. Oh, there." Over her backside and her hips, across her flat stomach and to the very boundary of her soapy curls.

And with her indrawn breath he was sliding his fingers through soft hair to her cleaving, delving deeply to meet the tilt of her hips and then her richly tumid contours. Her eyes were glassy and as blue as the sky again.

"Wife." She was his life; he loved her. God, how he loved her.

She cried out and melted against him, and into his hand, clutched at his arms, her eyes round and pleading. "Dear Simon! What are you doing to me?"

"Preparing you for bed."

"Turning down the counterpane?" Her eyes fluttered shut and she sought him with her hips, trapped his hand between them.

He grinned. "If you will."

"Oh, yes, I will." Her brows dipped. "And soon, I think."

His pulse shoved against his groin and filled up his gut with too much yearning for her. She whimpered when he left that superbly heated place, but he captured the sound of her protest when he kissed her hard. He found the ewer blindly and poured the warm water between them, a cascading paradise that soaked his braies and his chausses to the skin and drained water all over the floor.

He made her stand still—a difficult task when she was forever touching him and dragging him to her for another of her kisses—while he rinsed the rest of her with buckets of half-warm water, until she gleamed golden and glossy.

"I think I'd like you to bathe me every night, Simon."

"I'd be dead inside a week." He lifted her out of the tub and wrapped her in a linen towel. "Stand here by the fire. I'll be done bathing in a moment." And before she could make the offer that he knew was perched upon her brazen lips, Simon stopped her with an outstretched hand. "No, Kailey, you can't."

"I can't?" She was blinking in her innocence.

"One touch from you and your soap, wife, and the night is finished." She didn't look like she believed him.

He shucked himself of his wet clothes with his back to her, and then sank into the tepid water.

"You forgot the soap, Simon." She was behind

him, and then her stunning hands were on his back, kneading his shoulders.

"Kailey, please." He knew he sounded like a wretched old soldier, crawling across his last battlefield, but her assault was as gentle as it was killing.

" 'Tis a wife's duty to bathe her husband." She was at his ear, whispering, tugging with her teeth. She dipped the cloth into the water and brought it out soapy, then scrubbed along his arm where it rested on the rim.

He managed to meet her with a frown as she scooted on her knees around the front of the tub. She'd lost her towel and whatever modesty she'd ever been born with. Her breasts were small and firm-fruited, but they had a wicked dance all their own, one that he would love to learn. He gripped the wooden slats instead.

"You are making this very difficult, wife."

"Good. I'm not at all sorry. You're very skittish for a grown-up justiciar."

She lifted his hand into the cloth and leaned over his bent knees, which stuck like desert islands out of the soap-milky water. And not far beneath that thin surface, his arousal was a standard that needed no more encouragement than the sight of her, and certainly none from her hand, if she should get one of her grand notions and go looking for it.

"And you are very forward for a chaste young bride."

Simon watched her carefully as she scrubbed at each of his fingers, so dangerously close to her bare and perfect breasts. The slightest move and he could have them cradled in his palms.

"Then good again, Simon." She avoided his eyes

as she leaned toward him and scrubbed across his chest with her efficient cloth. He'd never heard of a virtuous woman so bent upon being bedded.

"I would be no husband at all if I didn't take care with your pleasure."

"I was quite pleased while you were bathing me, Simon. Quite."

"Yes, I know. So was I. But making love is not a race, Kailey, nor a thing to be finished like the last of a sugared plum. 'Tis a time for exploration, and . . ." She had tilted her head and touched her very warm mouth to his jaw. "Ah, yes. But if you continue to pursue this seduction of yours, then I will win the race and we will both be the losers."

"Very well, Simon."

He closed his eyes and did his best to survive as she led her scrubbing cloth along the ridge of his shoulder and then down his arm to his palm. When he opened his eyes again, she was standing above the tub, his hands clutched between hers.

The firelight seemed to glow from inside her skin, touching her all over with shimmering gold, her passion-weighted breasts with their dark points, and the soft, curling shadows where her lean thighs met, where he ached to explore with every sense that a very generous God had given man.

"Will you stand, Simon?"

"Oh, no, no, no." He shook his head repeatedly.

"I'd like to soap the rest of you as you did me."

"No."

"Are you shy?"

"No, madam. I'm set to explode from wanting you. And if I do, there go all your plans for this night."

"Perhaps if you'd stop hinting around the subject and explain yourself—" She let go of his hands, and he welcomed her irritated frown and her impatient fist on her hip, as he would a gesture of peace in the midst of a siege.

"Kailey, once a man . . . performs his function . . ."

"Plants his seed."

"Yes, thank you. Once he's done that, he's usually not capable of . . . planting again for at least an hour, maybe all night."

She canted her head, shifted her hips. "But that can't happen unless he's inside a woman, can it?" At his silence, understanding dawned in her nod. "Ah. And unless we are fit together at the time, you'll miss your target. Which is *me*."

"Exactly." His knuckles were white where he gripped the edge of the tub.

"I see." She turned abruptly and left him to his bath for some place behind him, which only made him uneasy. He finished quickly, scrubbing where he hadn't allowed her, standing in the tub and drenching himself in cold water, letting the chill soak into his loins, hoping it would dissipate some of his desire for her.

But when he'd dried off and turned, his wife was standing at the bedside, plaiting a wine-and-gold patterned ribbon into a tendril of hair that disappeared above her ear.

Her smile was bewitching and damp, and when her gaze slid to his hips, he remembered that he was naked in his cravings.

"Ah," she said simply, completely. And then, "You're beautiful, Simon de Marchand."

"A man of great fortune, my lady." Simon tossed aside his towel and strode toward her compelling loveliness, every nerve in his body alive, sensing the cooling puddles of bathwater between his toes, the heated air from the hearth crisping every hair on his body, the smoke-tinted scent of lavender. He lifted her into his arms, wondering what dreadful justice he would suffer at the end of his days as miracle toppled miracle.

He tried to settle her into the pillows but she scrambled to her knees.

"You're not leaving, husband."

"To light a candle," he said, laughing as he trailed his mouth along her throat to an exquisite place beneath her breast, tugging gently at the straining peak he'd caught between a finger and his thumb. "I want to see you well."

Kailey felt dazed and heavy-limbed, unquenchably hungry for her husband. This guardian of hers who had pledged to take care of her, who had married her and would father her children.

He rose above her like a gloriously naked saint, kneeling on the bed, the candle lighting his sweat-glossed skin as he slotted the taper into the sconce above the bed. The tension in her hands was like an itching, and she eased them by slipping her arms around his waist, sliding her hands over the crisp hair on his chest.

"I want to touch you, Simon."

"And I do want your fingers around me, wife. But I want you trembling first, and ready for me." He spread his knees and sat back on his heels, dragging her forward with his remarkable strength to meet his hips, supporting her back with his unyielding arm.

Then he lifted her breast to his mouth and drank his kisses noisily, as if he'd found nourishment there. He made a steaming exploration, searing her with his splendid mouth, using his tongue and teeth on one nipple and driving her mad by toying at the other.

He clutched her backside with his fingers, hunching his shoulders as his muscles shuddered. He lowered her to the pillows, then lay beside her, one leg claiming both of hers, hovering on his elbow, kissing her mouth gently and then in all his fury. His staff radiated a heat all its own, thick and pulsing against her thigh. He was so near the source of her desire, she would have dragged him to her if she thought she could have lifted him. But he seemed wild with the need to claim every inch of her, and she encouraged him to be her husband in every way he pleased.

His touch was like moonlight; his hair brushed her neck and danced along her arms, following the trail of fire he was blazing along her belly with his tongue and his lips. And then he was at the core of her, a summer breeze between her thighs, teasing her with his hot breath, taking her curls between his lips, tugging, kissing.

He was so close and so very inflamed that his ragged breath caused its own firestorm as it parted her woman's down. Unable to abide another moment, Kailey arched her hips to meet his intimacies, as startled that such a kiss was possible as she was certain that she would die if he didn't do it quickly.

"Please, Simon!"

"Anything at all, sweet." He slipped his capable hands beneath her backside, lowered his magnificent head toward all that rioting and then he kissed her at her cleaving, a wickedly chaste kiss that struck the breath from her.

He nuzzled her with his nose, as if he were brushing a kiss across her brow at high noon in the market square.

But he wasn't anywhere near her brow; he was gazing up into her eyes from over the rise of her indelicately writhing hips. He stroked her tenderly with his fingers, plucked at her curls, playing her like a lute—an instrument that she would never again be able to look at without thinking of Simon and his kisses.

"Husband, is this regular?" She couldn't imagine that it was. He parted her with his gentle fingers and kissed her again.

"Highly irregular, wife." He bore his succulent words and then his ravenous mouth against her, and Kailey thought the stars had fallen from the heavens.

Nay, but that shimmering brightness was her husband.

Her guardian of the night.

Simon had never smelled a wilder perfume, had never tasted a more exotic delicacy than his wife. His bones ached and his muscles had long ago crimped themselves into thick, useless wads. He tantalized her with his tongue, found her core with his fingers, and reveled in her wanton sighs.

"Oh, Simon!" Now she had two fistfuls of his hair, was moaning and writhing, repeating his name over and over.

He wanted her like he wanted breath and blood, wanted to be inside her where her heart might wrap itself around him. He wanted to tell her that he loved her beyond reason, that all he'd done for the last twenty years had been for her. That truth was love, was faith. He would show her that he was worthy.

Tonight was hers, and tomorrow, and forever afterward.

Simon left the heat of her and laved his tongue

from her quivering belly to her luscious mouth. She
called him shy names and sultry ones until she fit
her heels into the hollows of his knees and the upward motion brought the tip of him to the slickness
of her.

"I want you here, Simon." She reached for him,
but he caught her straying hand, astounded by the
strength her fingers, bands of velvet-slipped steel
laced between his. "Please. I want to know you. All
of you."

"Oh, sweet Mother of God, you are a wife to be
reckoned with."

"Remember that." Her brow glistened, her
breathing was as quick and in time with his, as she
baptized him in her gaze. "Please."

"Be kind to me, Kailey." Simon released her, and
with a shudder of sweet anticipation he lifted up
on his arms. He closed his eyes and held his breath
and tried to think of writs and pleas and juries—
anything to hold back the onrushing tide—but
Kailey's progress was too precious not to watch,
not to celebrate.

Her exquisite touch at the root of him sent him
spinning out of time with the world and into the
skies. Ah, the view was spectacular and cleansing.
A stunning wife, her hair a cloud of spun honey,
passionate and inviting, and willing to love him
with every part of her.

" 'Tis wondrous here, Simon." She made little
sounds of approval and awe, grew bolder and
ringed him with her fingers, slid upward around
his shaft to the very center of his sharpest instinct.
"And here, sir, you are iron and silk."

"Enough, wife. Else I will split." Simon wrapped
his fingers through hers where she held him, then

shifted his hips lower. "Here, sweet. We'll begin and end together."

He guided her hand, feeling languorous and sunbathed for a precious instant, and then a breath later, Simon heard his own roar of stark, blinding pleasure when their flesh met.

"Forgive me, Kailey!" Like a man possessed, he drove upward through her sheath, broke through her maidenhead in a single, exquisite thrust, and joined himself to her with a ferocity that must have hurt, but that drew only a singing sigh from her.

She was as tight and pulsing as her hand, and slick-hot. He wanted to ride with her till they were lathered, to feel the stinging wind in his face, to feel her buck beneath him in her wildest pleasure. But she was rigid, her eyes grown large.

"Kailey?" He moved to withdraw, but she tilted her hips and gasped.

"No! Simon!" She held his head with her hands and clutched his backside with her heels. Tears welled in her eyes.

Kailey! Her gaze burned him, and he was lost to the moment. He propelled himself forward again, so stunned by the sense of utter possession he couldn't move, didn't want to move, for she was home to him, and life and sanctity. There was no other goodness in his life.

He kissed her madly, unable to hold her tightly enough. He would plant a seed for her, would grow her a strong, incorruptible family, child by child, year by year. And he would let her keep her strays, try to keep up with her lawless defenses— whatever she wanted. He had stolen one family from her, he would do his best to give her another.

"I love you, Simon."

His throat closed over, strangled him, her whispered confession making him quake with a guilty pleasure so heady it could have served as his release.

" 'Tis like I've always known you," she whispered, her eyes finding his.

His wife, his Kailey. She loved him, and love was forgiveness, was redemption, and promises kept.

For now, he was buried as far as his straining flesh and hers would allow, yet that would never be far enough. He was on the edge of his restraint, held there by nothing more substantial than the stroke of her hand across his brow.

Her eyes widened as she took up a quickening cadence with her hips, a rhythm that was the surging of his pulse and his every hope for her.

Determined not to steal this moment from her, Simon found her with his fingers and shared his mouth between her breasts and her lips, stroking and pulling and straining against her hips as she offered them. Never getting enough of her glinting eyes. She loved him.

Searing flame and the force of the earth tore at him, urged him toward his release, near bloodied him in his restraint. She trembled under him, straining toward that particularly precious part of the sky.

"My magnificent wife." Simon took up her bewitching rhythm, met her measure for delicious measure, read her quivering and her huffling sighs as easily as he had read her eloquent market list, until she was mewling and squirming, looking bewildered by her desire and begging his guidance.

"Please, Simon!" she breathed against his ear.

"At your pleasure, wife." He watched her bright eyes widen as he slipped his hand between them, found the ripe bud of her desire. Then she gasped, her hips suspended in their seeking.

"Oh, Simon, what—"

"Come with me, wife." At the moment of her joyous, throaty release, Simon teetered on the brink of his own, as she pulsed and trembled against his length, as she bucked again and arched against him.

"Closer, Simon!" Kailey abandoned the earth entirely, was caught up again in Simon's wings, soaring toward the farthest reaches of the sky—his sky—for he was all she could see, all she could ever desire. The urgent heat spread like splintered lighting through her limbs and out her fingertips, making her surge against him. She heard herself calling his name, saying wicked things to him against his mouth, and into his ear.

And in the midst of this dizzying explosion of unimaginable bliss, her husband suddenly, ferociously encircled her waist with his arms and lifted her hips, thrusting and pulsing ever upward reaching more profoundly into her, until he cried out her name and his every muscle turned to rock, his handsome face frozen in ecstasy as he pumped himself deep inside her, hot and streaming.

"Your family, my love," she thought he said, though his voice was harsh and stretched through the straining cords in his neck. "God give us a child."

He prayed for children. He called me "love." Tears ran down her temples and into her ears, though she could barely gather a breath. Why should such unheralded rapture make her weep?

"Sweet Kailey!" He seemed jubilantly distracted and dense-limbed, his eyes unable to focus, and still he pulsed and strained, nuzzled her neck with his mouth and his hot breath until he finally came to rest above her, his forehead to hers.

"Blazes, wife!" He collapsed like a great felled oak, kept from crushing her by the strength of his sturdy sweated limbs against the mattress. His breathing came in deep draughts as he scrubbed her damp hair off her brow and touched his mouth to hers.

He was her husband now, by every measure. And now Kailey couldn't stop the hiccoughing sob that rattled in her throat any more than she could stop her tears.

"What are these, Kailey?" He kissed the dampness away, tangled his fingers in her temples.

"You prayed for children, Simon."

"Lots of them, Kailey, if the blessing be ours." He lifted onto an elbow and kiss her cheek. "How could you think not?"

"Because . . ." She saw his suspicion clouding up his eyes and decided against pursuing that particular vein. "Never mind."

She glanced away to the hearthfire, but Simon caught her chin abruptly and made her look at him.

"I do mind, madam, despite my earlier boorishness. I want this marriage with you. I have always." His voice was unyielding. "I want its interfering householders, and its rose-trees and brood mares. I want feathers stuffing my pillows and a buttery full of May wine. And if children come of our union, then I will want them, too." He kissed her softly, slowly. "But most of all I want you, Kailey, however you came to me."

Blessed Mother, she loved him! This man who had lived so unselfishly near her heart through the whole of her life. He could never know how much he meant to her.

"Simon, thank y—" But he touched his fingers to her mouth before she could finish, tugged at the beribboned plait in her hair.

"Don't, Kailey." The depth of his fierceness rolled out of his chest and anchored her limbs to the bed. "I never want to hear those words from you again, wife, nor any others like them. They do not belong between us. Do you understand me?"

Kailey didn't at all, but she nodded for his sake.

"Good." He kissed her where he'd just been touching her lips—an affirmation or an apology, she wasn't sure which. But he watched her as he did, as if he thought she might ambush him with her gratitude.

The bullheaded man was her miracle. Aye, her guardian and savior, though he seemed unable to abide the idea. He was far from perfect, would probably always need her guidance when it came to tempering his legal opinions. But he had come back for her, had kept faith with whatever solemn pledge her father's friends had forged so long ago.

She couldn't possibly have been blessed with a more honorable man.

"Simon!"

"Aye, my sweet?" He had spoken around her nipple, and the sensation of his tugging teeth and the brush of his words made Kailey catch her breath and arch against him, made her lose the thread of her thought.

"I just wanted to say that I like that." She tensed her newly discovered muscles and drew a shuddered groan from her husband. "Do you see?"

"Aye! Your pity, please." His eyelids drooped over his soft gray eyes as if he'd been drowsing, though the man had been bent over her breast and his fingers priming the well where he was still joined to her in his fullness. " 'Tis the curse of the male and no doubt the boon of the female that we must let me rest for a while."

Yet he was grunting sharply now and grabbing at her hips, shoving himself deeper into her.

"You seem well rested to me, husband." He felt wonderful as he strained with her.

"Not yet." He held his breath, then seemed to gather his wits and pin her hips to the mattress. "Don't move, sweet."

But Kailey's own grip on the vines that held her to earth was slipping. "Oh, Simon, even when I want to move more that anything?"

"Especially then, wife."

But Kailey was already moving, matching the course of his tides, riding his urgent waves. He made cradles of his hands at the base of her breasts and firestorms of his fingertips on their peaks.

He kissed her as though he couldn't get enough of her, called her "wife" and "sweet" and "heart."

This time the driving ecstasy was deep and expected, and Kailey melted into his embrace as he shuddered and quaked and whispered his adorations into her ear. He held her tighter, and Kailey felt him tremble, heard something in the thundering of his chest that might have been a sob.

"Yes," he whispered, as his breathing and his muscles began to ease. He snuggled with her and nuzzled her neck. Kissed the palm of her left hand and then her fingers, and when he got to the wedding band that marked his hold on her, he lifted his gaze to her and kissed the band as well.

"Married," he said simply, inescapably.

Another "thank you" perched on her lips, but she held it back. There were other ways to his heart. She would honor him best by being the finest wife he could ever have married. She would nourish his soul and conserve his body, share his passion, challenge his opinions, and raise up his children to be as just and as good as he was.

Aye, she would show Simon her gratitude through all the seasons of his life, in all the things she did; simply telling him how much she treasured the blessings he had brought to her suddenly seemed inadequate. She would make sure that he never noticed a single moment of her thanksgiving, save for the peace she hoped to bring him.

His heart's peace.

Kailey yawned and stretched, joyously contented with this puzzle of a husband, and with her new plan. She wondered if anyone would guess what a wildly naked barbarian the staid justiciar became in the master's chamber. And would they guess that he was as kind as he was fierce?

"The court moves to Nottingham in three days, wife," he said, as he settled her against him.

"So soon?" She tried to sit up, but he caught her in his arms and drew her against his chest, tucked his knees behind hers. He cupped her breast so fondly that she sighed and settled into his possessive stroking, to the unsubtle pressure of his arousal against her hip.

"And after Nottingham, wife, to Yorkshire, and then to Lincoln, and finally home . . . to Northumberland." His breathing had already deepened, riffling the hair at her nape.

Home. He'd learn someday that home was right here.

Chapter 17

S imon awakened to a gnawing dread, his bed abandoned by his wife again and glacial-cold. A jagged emptiness filled him faster than he could fight it off, brought him to his feet even before his eyes had cleared of his unrelenting dream: a fiendish place where Kailey was an elusive sanctifying breeze and he was a solitary tumbledown grave-marker, rain-melted and unable to follow her. She came in summer to sear him and in winter to blanket him with blinding snow. But he was stone and couldn't touch her, couldn't feel her breath on his face or hear her speak his name, as she had last night.

He shook himself of the cold rigor that had set into his limbs and glanced around for proof that she hadn't left him with the dawn, that she hadn't reconsidered his barbarous behavior.

The effects of their lovemaking were everywhere, making his flesh rise and ache in memory. Her wispy shift and his clothes lying tangled where he had tossed them, the deeply fragrant roses, the wine-gold ribbon he'd loosed from her hair . . .

He was terrified again. Terrified of losing her.

But his heart steadied and his breathing eased as he accounted systematically for her presence: her pattens waiting by the door, her favorite girding belt hanging on a peg, her combs. She hadn't packed her belongings and set out for a less inconstant home.

He wanted her again, would spend the long day in court thinking of the night to come, when she would whisper again that she loved him.

Simon heard a single click and saw his wife standing at the door in a fresh green shift, with soft trailing ribbons at her neck, a tankard and two cups in her hand.

"Good morning, husband." Her gaze was a course of fire.

"Aye, wife, so it is."

Her sigh was as silky as the rose-dark peaks of her breasts, a comparison which he made again a very few minutes later when she was writhing in the wake of his tongue, and tugging at his hair.

And confessing her love for him.

The morning seemed worlds brighter to Simon as he strode through the streaming crowds into the castle bailey. Three days more here at Chester and then the circuit court processed to Nottingham, ever and ever closer to home. Perhaps he would give up this madness and stay in the north, where the streams ran clear and the lambs were fat, and the children he and Kailey would make together could grow straight and tall.

Great God, he was grinning at every butcher and spice merchant! Not a fit demeanor for the lord high sheriff.

But as Simon entered the great hall, he was reminded of Wingate and the Templar, and a noxious brew churned in his stomach—falsehoods mixed with deceit. The foolish priest was to deliver the ransom sometime today, an act that now seemed altogether wrongheaded. His wife's holy canon on the family seemed to color his every opinion lately. By her definition, anyone whom he kept in his heart was by rights family to him. And damn the man, he did feel a certain fondness for the abbot. Nay, a great fondness.

He would do something about this unease—he'd be there when Wingate gave his money to the Templar.

Cathmore was lazing back in his judge's chair, his thick bootheels dug into the table. He was sipping from a tankard, reading from a bound book of writs.

Simon dropped his saddlebag on the table, startling Cathmore into sitting upright.

"Well, good morning, Marchand." He leaned back again. "You look well rested."

"Where is Wingate?"

"On his way here." Cathmore wore his usual easy smile, deeply scribed into his face through forty-five years of a disposition that seemed able to pluck humor from the very dust motes. "He sends his apologies for his tardiness. He's to meet with the Templar."

Simon suffered an angry chill. "Already?"

Cathmore thunked his tankard down on the table, his humor flattened. "Yes. Why? What have you heard?"

"Hell's teeth!" He would stop the transaction cold, put the fear of the Almighty in Josten, and see the matter of the ransom taken care of himself. "Where is this meeting to happen?"

"In the guard tower at the Welshgate."

"Then I'll be back—"

"Wait, Marchand." Cathmore stood, looked contrite and concerned. "The deed has been done by now."

"Damnation!" Simon unbuckled his sword and sheath and shoved them across the table. "I don't like the feel of this, Cathmore."

"Nor do I. But Wingate obviously loves his son—blindly." He shrugged. "I would be the same fool in his place if my sons were threatened."

Sons. Kailey's sons, and his. Simon's blood surged, and a terrifying euphoria broke against his heart, made his hand ache for the flat of his wife's belly gone round and firm with their first child. He would walk through fire for this newborn family of his.

"Sons are not the subject, Cathmore," he said through a thickening in his throat. "Wingate is paying for this supposed treasure without opening the velvet bag to see what's inside."

"It's Wingate's decision."

"I should have insisted on being there! The damned fool."

"Well, there's Wingate now, Marchand." Cathmore raised his brows. "Be kind."

"I am kindness itself, Cathmore." Though Simon's jaw ached from wanting to shout, as he watched Wingate working his way through the court's petitioners.

The abbot's hair seemed thinner and grayer, and there was a droop to his eyelids that angered Simon, that incanted the face of Stoneham and made his eyes burn.

No. Not *that* man. *Not Stoneham. He'll never again be in my heart, Kailey.*

"Your pardon, my lords, for holding up the proceedings." Wingate took his seat without looking at Simon, and immediately began sifting through the stack of vellum in front of him.

"So you met with the Templar?" Simon asked, shrugging off Stoneham's clingy ghost. "You gave him money?"

"Five hundred pounds as the ransom demanded. I know you don't approve, Simon, but it is done." Wingate's brows were one, his cheeks slashed crimson as he dipped his quill in the inkhorn, then dipped it again. "The money is on its way to Cressing with Brother Josten. From there to the Knights' Temple in Paris, and then on to Acre and the release of my son."

His opinion roundly dismissed, Simon sat down. "I pray that your efforts are rewarded, Wingate, and that your money brings you back your son."

"Thank you, Simon. Now, oughtn't we continue the day's court? We've three days left to finish."

"So be it." Simon let the man alone in his thoughts and brought the court to order, turning his mind toward executing the pristine points of law.

He spurred the court schedule into an efficient gallop, pleased that the early morning and the writs passed quickly, only to have to break his gait for the very scoundrel who had given over his secrets to Kailey.

"My lord sheriff!" Ranulf hurried toward the dais, out of breath and carrying a swath of charred white cloth over his shoulder. "I found this, my lord. In the Templar's rooms."

Simon had forgotten that he'd asked Ranulf for the favor, else he might have reached across the table and rattled the man's teeth.

Ranulf wrestled with the wad of wool, then held it up in front of him for all to see.

The Templar's robe—or what was left of it from a scorching fire.

"Mother of God!" Wingate sat down hard in his chair. "Is it Josten's?"

Simon came around to Ranulf and fingered the singed edges. "Where did you find this?"

"In Josten's room at the Merrie Gate, my lord," he said between gasps for air. "Stuffed inside the hearth, but the peat was laid atop so the robe didn't catch."

Wingate leaned forward and lifted the robe, ran his quavering, blue-veined fingers down the cross of red on one of the shoulders. "Josten was wearing this when I met him at the Welshgate. He said he was leaving for Cressing as soon as I handed him the ransom. I saw him start across the bridge."

"The Merrie Gate," Ranulf wheezed, "is just the other side of the river."

"But why wouldn't Josten have worn his robe? 'Tis a precept of their Order to wear it always."

"Obviously because Josten was done with it, Wingate." Simon bit back his anger. Rancor would only bring the man more pain; enough was on the way. "Your money is gone."

"I won't believe it, Simon. I can't."

Cathmore settled a hand on Wingate's shoulder. "It might mean nothing, Father."

"Perhaps Josten met with foul play." Wingate's chalky face took on a sheen. "The roads are dangerous; Josten said so himself. Dear God—"

Wingate let out a long, despairing groan and brought the Templar's tabard closer, scraped his fingernail across the remains of the red cross, then muttered a curse as he wiped at his eyes with his gnarled hands. "This robe isn't from Cressing Manor in Essex!"

Cathmore took up the burned wool, squinting as he tried to make the same inspection. "How do you mean?"

"The fabric is too white and coarse, and the cross is too darkly red. This robe came from Kelstowe Grange, not twenty miles south of here. Dearest God, you were right, Simon."

More proof would only bring the man to his knees, yet there was little else to do but investigate. And no time at all to lose.

"Take me to this room, Ranulf. I'll find your Templar, Wingate. And he will long regret he ever set foot in my county."

"I can't go to Nottingham, my lady!" Julia leaned far over the counter of her wagon and handed a vial of lemon scent and a dried apple wedge to a bright-faced little girl. "Here you are, missy. And a bit of treat for you."

"Oh, thank you!" The child sped off, her black plaits flying, leaving Julia to rest her chin on her hands, frowning but looking grandly at home in this hard-bought rig that she had repainted in two shades of blue.

"Of course you'll go to Nottingham with us." Kailey hated to see Julia so near to despairing again—but gladness took some practice, as she was discovering about her husband. "Simon tells me that a whole caravan of crafter wagons and merchants follows the court, with special royal license to sell their goods."

Julia snorted then climbed out of the back of the wagon, her belt-purse a-jangle with coins. "How do I carry this wagon of mine—on my back? And please don't suggest to Hinch that he pull it, else he will try."

Kailey laughed. "I just happen to have a horse that will soon grow fat on oats if he isn't put to work."

"You do?" Julia looked skeptical, though she straightened a beaker of rushlight wands and smiled at a customer who came to poke at a small leather pouch hanging from the awning. "How far is Nottingham?"

"A week's drive from here." Kailey could almost see the wheels spinning in the young woman's head.

"Three days will be just enough time to collect the new wares that I've ordered, if I push my suppliers a bit."

"Good."

"And I'm only borrowing the horse, my lady." Julia's hair shone red-brown in the sunlight, curled round her face and honeyed her freckles.

"Of course. Though from the business you've done, you'll soon be buying your own. Now, where have you stowed Hinch and Davie, or did you send them packing for their snoring?"

"Davie was talking about visiting his lordship's marshal-at-arms, and Hinch has gone off to the infirmary again."

Julia's gaze had been fixed in the distance, but now it was fixed hard on Allan, who was standing at the abbey wall but looking their way. The girl was suddenly smiling shyly.

So was Allan.

"He'll be coming with us, Julia."

Julia's hands were twisted up so tightly in the sides of her new skirts, she had rucked the hem a half-foot off the ground.

"Who?" she asked.

"Allan."

"Hmmmm?"

Julia wasn't listening—at least, not to Kailey.

So she left as Allan started toward the wagon, a determined young man with courtship on his mind.

Kailey hurried through the abbey gate and into the curia, wondering what Simon would think of his guard and her acquitted thief. She hoped he wouldn't mind.

She had married a man of harsh grace and unshakeable honor. He had proved that in a hundred ways last night, had proved it through the years of her life. To think that she had worried about what he might learn of her father and her past, worried that he would send her away . . .

But Simon had married her not in spite of her father's crime, but because of a pledge he'd made to the man who had died in shame. Kailey still didn't know what to think of that, nor what to think of her father.

And so Neville Hewett seemed even more a presence now, his gentle whispering more insistent. His spirit was too kindly, like a rich meadow-wind, not the foul breath of a traitor.

He'd called her "daughter" in his final accounting, and "beloved."

Had he really loved her? Kailey sat down on a bench in the infirmary herbarium and pulled the crackling pages from her belt-purse.

The writ had been so precise and cold, the words of the inquest simple and chilling. Plotting with the Flemings to assassinate Henry, duke of Normandy; the evidence, the testimony, and her father's execution. She knew it all now.

But it was her father's statement to the court that still haunted her. The legal terms of the writ and

the inquest were clipped and without breath, but
his own words read like enchantments to her ears
and painted pictures before her eyes.

A broad-shouldered man, a steadfast gaze, his
arms outstretched, his face to the sky as he stood
on the gallows. Had it snowed that day? Had her
mother watched him die? Had she believed in him?

" 'Lord, my God, you know my heart as they do
not.' "

The ends of Kailey's fingers heated where she
touched his words. She could see him turn to her
mother. Had he stretched out his hand? Had his
voice spoken his heart?

" 'I shall wait for you, my wife, my love.' "

Kailey's tears came so easily when this man was
inside her head. He was buried with her mother at
a parish church called Eveside, but the location was
lacking on the page.

Their bones would be dust by now, finally made
one in the loam of the earth. She wondered at this
Eveside: where it was, and if its beauty brought
them peace. Were they laid to rest under the great
blue sky, or did they share a tomb inside a chapel?
Kailey wondered if they had worked through their
troubled marriage in heaven, if her father had finally confessed his sins to his cherished wife. She
loved them both so fiercely, the mother and father
she had never known.

Your heart's peace, little love.

God, how she missed them! Kailey wept quietly
into her hands until the late summer's heat min-
gled sage and rue and briar rose beneath her nose.
The sky was too blue for sorrow, and her life too
full. She had a family now, and they were beloved
to her, no matter how odd-fitting and perverse.

She wiped away her tears and set her chin for the infirmary.

The cavernous room was hushed but crowded. Hinch was sitting on a cot beside a sleeping figure, the lanky form curled up and turned away, and covered with a thin blanket.

Hinch was sewing bells onto his hat. Dozens of bells.

"Look here, my lamb!" Hinch clapped his sagging canvas hat onto his head and all the bells in Christendom seemed to ring out.

" 'Tis a magnificent marvel, Hinch." Kailey laughed and kissed his cheek. "May I see it?"

Hinch looked suddenly confused. "See what, lamb?"

"Your hat."

He cocked his head sharply. The hat jingled and chimed, and Hinch remembered with an enormous grin and handed Kailey the hat.

"You've done a beautiful job, Hinch." His stitches were huge but sturdily tied off, the bells of various types and sounds. She'd never have trouble finding the man again. "Where did you get these?"

"From the girl with the wagon." He shook the shoulder of the curled up figure on the cot. "What's her name, Davie?"

Kailey would have pulled Hinch away from the sleeping invalid and his confusion, but she suddenly recognized the berry-stained boots and heard a hissing *Shushh!* from under the blanket.

"David de Broase, what are you doing here?" Kailey jabbed her fingers into the boy's ribs. He sat up, as helplessly ticklish as ever.

"My lady, don't! Please!" he howled.

"And what is that on your forehead?"

"Nothing!" Davie clapped his hand over the sharp blue knot and scooted back on the high-side of the cot. "It's nothing."

"And he *didn't* get that lump sword fighting," Hinch said stoutly. "Did you, Davie?"

"Shh, Hinch!" Davie was shaking his head madly.

"Let me look at this great blue nothing!" Kailey knelt on the cot and pried at the boy's fingers. He gave way easily, wincing.

"I'm all right!"

The bulge was huge! "You got this sword fighting, Davie? Where?"

Hinch was overwinking at Davie. "Definitely *not* at his lordship's training lists!"

"Pleeease, Hinch!" Davie whined.

Kailey took Davie by the chin. "Do you mean to tell me that Simon de Marchand sent you to joust with his soldiers?" The man had no sense at all when it came to boys and their wildness.

"I am his squire!" Davie tried to look defiant even as he scooted off the cot and scurried out of Kailey's reach.

She let him go, because his head was rock hard and there was little she could do for a goose egg, but to ensure that it didn't happen again. "If that blow had been two inches lower, you might well have lost your eye."

Kailey stalked to the cot where Carrotlocks lay still and pale in his death-sleep.

Davie was fast on her heels, Hinch and his hat trailing them like a jingling cloud. "But I didn't lose my eye, Kailey! Or my arm, or a single toe."

"Nonetheless, Davie, you can forget about jousting and training." Kailey gave a quick inspection of Carrotlocks's bruises and cuts, relieved that the monks had taken such good care of him, yet imagining Davie lying as hopelessly still.

"I can't forget my sword training! 'Tis what a squire does for his lord and master! As his lordship will tell you himself."

"We'll see who tells whom. Now come, Davie, help me turn our friend here to his stomach, else we'll be treating bedsores on his backside."

They fussed over Carrotlocks to make him comfortable, but the young man's mind seemed unreachable.

And no one had missed him yet at all.

"Nay, my lord sheriff, the fellow you're talking about arrived here at the Merrie Gate six days ago." The landlady had nearly prostrated herself when Simon and his justices had stomped into her inn, and now she was standing in Josten's room, her shoulders pressed into a corner.

"And he left here early this morning?" Simon asked through his teeth, as he lifted the narrow nothing of a mattress off the wooden cot.

"Only two hours past, my lord," she whispered.

"He came back here, Wingate." Simon dropped the mattress, and the dust flew. "After you gave him the ransom."

"Blessed saints, Simon," Wingate said, staring into the ash-choked hearth. "I'm a great fool. And I pray that Nicholas will forgive me."

Josten's treachery had aged Wingate, narrowed his shoulders, had put an unbreachable distance between the man and his son that only Simon could close.

"Come. We've work to do."

* * *

Simon cantered into the forecourt of Crookston Hall, standing in the stirrups, praying that his wife was at home, as Davie had said. He had decided to take her with him on his inquest, but had refused to examine his reasons for fear of discovering flaws.

She was standing neck-deep in the herb garden, her pale blue kirtle and her bright face the only colors among the shades of green. She smiled and raised her hand to her brow.

"Home at noontide, husband?"

Aye, that was why he would chance her company on this ride—how could he possibly leave the sunlight that was her voice?

"Pack yourself, wife. We're leaving." They would have to hurry. He dropped from the saddle and looped the reins around a hitch pole.

"For Nottingham, Simon?" She came toward him at a run, her skirts held just off the ground. "Then I must find Julia. I've promised to let her—"

"Hold up, wife." She made to run past him toward the stable, but Simon caught her arms and turned her. Her plait was stuck through with bits of greenery, and he picked out the bits with his fingers, touching his mouth to her temple. "We travel south from here on sheriff's business."

"An inquest?" Her eyes grew dangerously bright, making Simon wonder at the wisdom of his judgment. "And you're taking *me*?"

She smelled too good.

"Aye, and we leave immediately." Simon propelled her toward the house, then up the stairs to their chamber. "And before you ask, wife, Hinch and Davie will stay with Cathmore. It's arranged."

That seemed to please her, made her smile at him

as he left her at the door. "Thank you for that. But where are *we* going?"

"Just pack." He flopped open the lid of a chest and dragged out a saddle bag, ignoring as best he could the intoxicating brew of herbs that followed after her like a cloud. "I've a half-dozen men waiting for us at the Welshgate."

"An army? What are we chasing, Simon?" She efficiently plucked her robe and nightshift from the clothes pegs, and added herself to his inquest all in one stroke.

"I am chasing Wingate's ransom payment," he said pointedly. "He delivered it to a thief."

"Father Abbot?" She stopped her folding and looked suddenly incensed. "Robbed in the streets? Is he all right?"

"Nay, I mean that the Templar was a fraud." Simon tossed the leather bag on the bed and started to rifle the drawer in the tablechest for his travel gear.

"This is not to be borne, Simon!" Now she was packing in a fury, throwing ribbons and candles and a bundle of clothes into a leather bag. "Father Abbot must be beside himself with worry. What will happen to Nicholas if the ransom isn't delivered?"

"Wingate's son is no doubt lodged safely among the ranks of the King of Jerusalem, and knows nothing of his father's foolish enterprise."

"The ransom note was a fake as well?"

"I don't know. But I plan to find out."

"Of course we will."

Simon caught up her chin between his thumb and a crooked knuckle, fought the urge to kiss her. "This is *my* inquest, wife. Remember that."

"Father Abbot is my friend." She was frowning

her fiercest. "I can't let this rest. And I am fully capable of helping you."

He grunted and left her unkissed while he still could. "That's what I'm afraid of. You'll stay out of it, wife."

She snorted lightly. "Then why take me with you?"

She might well doubt his motives, yet she was done with her packing and waiting at the chamber door with a saddlebag in each hand, her foot tapping out her impatience.

"I take you, wife, because I will be less distracted from my task if you're with me." He grabbed up his own bags and threw them over his shoulder. "I never know where you are, or what sort of trouble you're wading through."

"Trouble such as I stirred last night?"

"You stirred more than trouble, my dear."

Her smile held secrets. "I love you, Simon."

And, oh, my heart, I pray that you will always.

Chapter 18

Simon led his party south from Chester, traveling as fast as the horses could bear, until the sun painted branch and bracken a brilliant orange which faded to darkness even as it glinted on the edge of the world.

Then he slowed their pace and sent an outrider ahead with a lantern, a warrant against the hazards of the wagon-rutted road, and the shadowed understory that sometimes crowded the track.

"Why are we going to Kelstowe Grange, Simon, if you think this Templar is a fraud?" His wife returned from one of her missions to the rear of their column, having coddled his sergeants with her satchel of food. "He said he was from Cressing, and Cressing is in Essex, which is nearly a week's ride west of here."

"Josten isn't from Cressing." He took the chunk of bread she offered, but held her hand over-long and gained a smile from her, one that tossed his thoughts about in his head like a leaf-cluttered whirlwind. "Wingate recognized the Templar's robe as one of Kelstowe's."

"Ah, well, you hadn't said that."

"No."

"Perhaps Josten has stolen the identity of another. Here, Simon." She handed him a wedge of cheese. "He used the robe to make the good father think he was a fellow priest and could be trusted. The robe was taken from the grange at Kelstowe, therefore the thief must have passed through there recently, therefore—our destination. Excellent work, sheriff."

"Thank you, wife."

"What did this Templar's boots look like?" She rode easily beside him, plying a knife against the cheese, while she made her simple speculations.

"His boots?"

"Were they clean? Tall? Hard soled or soft?" The moon glinted off the dew of her smile.

Simon couldn't recall noticing them. "I didn't look."

"Were his hands tanned like a plowman's, or cracked and lined with grime like a blacksmith's?" She wrapped the food in a cloth and fiddled with her saddlebag.

"He was wearing gloves." Simon caught himself about to grunt a victorious "ha" at her because he'd had such a ready answer, but she'd think that as cocksure as it would have sounded. "And before you ask, they were gauntlets—buck brown, cuffed."

"And he was a young man? Younger than you?"

"Are you saying I'm old?"

"I think you are perfect, husband. But are you old in comparison to the false Templar?"

"I suspect we're of an age. Early thirties." He took a grinding bite of the cheese. "*Very* early."

"Bearded?"

"Yes."

"And the color of his hair?"

"Dark. Almost black. Parted at the center, shaggy to his shoulders."

"Excellent, my lord."

Then a memory came to him, the fall of rushlight on the man's forehead. "And he had a scar that sliced through his eyebrow."

"The mark of Cain, Simon. This false holy man's sins will tell. They always do."

The mark of Cain. Indelible and dark.

"Simon, what if this Josten is truly a knight–priest and he has lost his way?" She was squinting into the distance. "It happens even in the best of men. Do you ever wonder if a man's deeds can hide the true nature of his heart?"

She was thinking of her father. He could see her balancing it in the wings of her brow: all that she had learned of the man last night, against the kindly phantom she'd created in her innocence.

"The truth of the heart is in the intent, madam," he said quietly.

She made a long, incisive study of him, then a kind of peace settled over her and she lifted her chin. "I do believe that, Simon. As surely as I believe that one moment of evil cannot possibly negate a lifetime of good."

Oh, but it can, my love. It did. And yet he heard the hope in his own thoughts. He'd begun to watch the world through her merciful eyes: saw family where he had been militantly satisfied with a passing acquaintance, sought a more vibrant truth in his courtroom . . . and too often now he found himself confronted with Robert of Stoneham—the devil who had abandoned him, the father who had once meant the world to him.

"Simon, do you know of a place called Eveside?"

Aye, he knew it, though he'd never been there.

A parish church, and a graveyard—not an hour's ride from here. He had saved Hewett's corpse from being ax-split by the self-righteous wrath that blazed in the aftermath of hanging a traitor: an arm carried off to York, a leg shipped in salt to the Flemish Count, the head pike-mounted and sent to the Tower to be displayed.

Simon had seen to it that Hewett's body was shrouded in dignity and carted off in secret to be buried at Eveside.

And then he'd set about forgetting the sights and the sounds.

"I know of the place," he said evenly, as though each word might shift out from under the rest and give him away.

Unable to risk a glance at his wife, Simon watched the bobbing lantern playing at shadows and sticks along the roadside brambles, waited for Kailey to ask her favor.

I want my father, Simon. You have him and I want him back.

He waited, not breathing, hearing only the call of the nightbirds and the sigh of the dark wind.

But she didn't ask her favor, only smiled gently to herself—and surely to her father—when she said, "Good, my lord."

The late arrival of the sheriff and his party at Kelstowe Grange sent a dozen knight–monks scurrying through the small compound. Simon made his wife sit quietly on a bench near the door in the vestibule when she would have followed him, and left his men standing guard over her so she wouldn't traipse about and frighten the inhabitants with her inquisition.

In the briefest span of minutes, the sleepy-eyed

prior came rushing toward them in his spurs and boots and Templar's robe, fastening on his sword belt as if he had been rallied to a war.

"Good evening, Sheriff de Marchand." The man put out his hand and Simon took it. He was barely forty, still battle-strong and intense. "I am Prior Guillaume. What brings you to us? Trouble, I assume?"

"Your pardon for the lateness of our coming, Father, but I am here on inquest of a crime committed against Abbot Wingate of St. Werburgh's."

"Wingate?" Guillaume's concern seemed genuine. "A better man never drew breath. I knew him when I first took my orders. Has he been harmed?"

"Fortunately, only his pride and his purse."

"Simon! Tell the prior about the robe!" His wife was standing between her guards, speaking in a hush that could no doubt be heard in the nearby village.

"My wife, Father." Simon sent her a quieting glare. "She is concerned about Wingate."

"A commendable sentiment." Guillaume nodded at Kailey, then turned back to Simon. "What sort of crime was committed against the abbot?"

"Robbery. I think."

"You only think this?" Guillaume seemed roundly amused and easy with his laughter for one of the usually dour Templars. "And what has Kelstowe to do with this 'possible' robbery?"

Simon knew there was little they would learn tonight, but he wanted to wade through as much information as he could, and set the prior to thinking. "Have you a monk here named Josten?"

Guillaume shook his head, tugged at his lower lip. "No. And none of that name in the two years I've been here. We are a quiet grange-farm,

Marchand, a place for our brethren to come to live out their last years in peace. How can we help you?"

"You probably cannot. This ransom scheme is quite elaborate. Five days ago Abbot Wingate received word that his son was being held for ransom—"

"Ah, yes. A terrible business."

Simon cursed beneath his breath; he was hoping to learn different news. "Then Nicholas *is* being held by the Saracens?"

"Oh, yes, yes, the demand is quite real. Received here under seal, directly from our Temple in Paris a week ago tomorrow, and the note sent on to Wingate in Chester the very next morning. I saw to it myself. I sent no one else. We've yet to receive further instruction from Paris."

Damn, this puzzle was throwing off more pieces than a spent pinion gear.

"The ransom, Prior Guillaume, might be as real as rain, but Josten was a fake. The first note was written in the same script as the second. And I'm certain the second came directly from our false Templar."

"What gave you reason to believe he was sent by us?"

"Josten said he was from Cressing Manor, but Wingate noticed too late that the robe he wore came from here at Kelstowe. Someone had attempted to destroy the evidence."

Simon handed the prior the singed white robe. Guillaume took it to the better light beneath the sconce.

"Unmistakably ours. The red of the cross was woven and dyed here at the grange, and the carmine made from our blackberries and currants." Guillaume's face had gone the pinched pale of outrage. "It has been ill-used. And we shall learn where this abomination began. You have my word on it."

"Thank you, sir." Simon offered his hand, relieved that this much of the mystery had been solved, and that the prior seemed eager to cooperate. "I doubt much can be accomplished tonight. I'll return tomorrow at a better hour of the morning, after Terce, perhaps? In the meantime, we'd best keep this between ourselves."

"Though I am piqued enough to awaken the brothers of the grange and conduct an immediate inquiry of my own, I do understand the necessity of secrecy." He returned the robe to Simon's keeping. "We have comfortable lodgings in the hostel near the precinct gate, if you and your wife would care to use them."

Kailey. Like a moth to a candle, Simon looked past the knight–priest to where she frowned from her exile.

His wife and a bed. And a niggling sense of disaster that had nothing to do with false Templars and defrauded priests.

Kailey recognized the look in her husband's handsome face, even from across the spacious garret room: his gray eyes gone to heavy slate, a smile so sinfully irresistible it could be the devil's own. And she would most gladly give herself to this particular devil, her dark angel of justice. However—

"Simon, we're in a monastery!"

"Just outside." Simon unbuckled his sword belt with a triumphant flourish and held it outstretched for a brief moment before he tossed it onto the chest and closed the door. "I want you, wife."

Though she still wore her cloak and all her

clothes, Kailey felt entirely naked and freed from the earth in the updraft of Simon's regard.

"But is it a blasphemy, Simon? To satisfy our desire for each other under this roof?"

"Do you have a desire for me, then?" He seemed to grow larger of a sudden, more deliberate as he came toward her; not sheriff or beast or justiciar, but husband.

"Before I answer that, Simon, before you come any closer and make me forget, there's a matter between us that needs discussion."

He stopped abruptly, looked suddenly defensive. "What exactly, madam?"

"Davie, exactly. He has a huge knot on his forehead, my lord. And he got it training in your lists."

His great shoulders eased, and his smile returned full force, though he turned from her. "Did he?"

"I've watched knights in their training. It's dangerous."

"Quite so."

"He's too young for you to send him out with a sword." She followed Simon to the hearth, where he knelt and added a log to the newly made fire. "He could have been killed. You shouldn't have let him go."

"I merely gave the boy leave to watch today—perhaps learn a bit of fighting form." Simon rose and kissed her brow, then went to work unfastening the small clasp at her throat.

"Only to watch? Yet he managed to wield a sword anyway? Simon, he needs supervision."

"The boy walked into a rack of helmets. That knot is from a wooden peg, not a sword."

Kailey laughed as Simon threw off her cloak, feeling guilty for doubting him. "Poor Davie. He must have been shattered. He was so proud of being your squire."

"His pride remains wholly intact. The marshal picked him up off the ground, and we all pretended we hadn't seen."

"You were there, Simon?" Kailey watched his marvelous, kind-hearted eyes as he unlaced her kirtle, catching his glance when he lifted it.

"I went to check on the lad before court, early this morning—after I left you in our bed."

A father bear in the making? "You checked on Davie?"

"Aye, madam, I arrived just in time to see him do battle with the helmets." He guided her overgown down her hips to the floor, then lifted her into his embrace and started unsubtly toward the bed. "And I can truly say that I've never seen a body with arms and legs that could be in so many places at one time."

She was grinning like a fool when he sat her down on the edge of the overstuffed mattress and yanked off her slipper.

"You are a difficult man to know, Simon."

"Am I?" He pulled off her other shoe. "And you, my sweet, are a flayed flounder."

"A what?" Bristling at the insult, Kailey put her foot to his shoulder, gave a shove, and then scooted to the far side of the bed, well out of his reach.

But Simon had disappeared; not even a sound stole from him. She crept to the edge of the bed and found him sprawled out on the floor, facedown. Fearing that she'd hurt him somehow, she was off the bed in a moment, hunched over him, stroking his back.

"Simon, are you hurt? What have I done?"

"You have evicted me from your bed, madam!"

The brute had been lying in wait, and Kailey escaped only because she leaped over him and dodged his grasping hands.

"Because you called me a flounder!"

Now he was staggering to his feet, laughing. "I'm sorry, Kailey. I didn't mean—"

"So, I'm a bulb-eyed bottom fish!"

"I don't think that at all, wife." She loved the silk of his voice, and almost took his hand as he extended it. "And if you'll just settle in one spot—"

"Nay, Simon." Kailey put a wobble-legged table between them. "Not until you explain why you compare me so favorably to a flounder."

"A *flayed* flounder!"

"Oh, well, then I'm much relieved! *Flayed*, he says."

"Perhaps I should have compared you to a wild briar rose, or a carefully scribed book."

She loved his gentle laughter, too, a sound she hadn't heard often enough and vowed to cultivate. "What do books and flowers to do with me, or with the fact that you think I am a flounder?"

His shoulders sagged dramatically. "I am no good at poetry, madam, and meant only that you are as open to me as a flower is to the sun, as easy to decipher as a book. You tell me what's on your mind the very instant you think it, whether I am prepared to hear it or not."

"Ha! If that were so, then I'd ask you—"

She caught herself, but not in time.

"You'd ask me *what*?" He looked wary, as though he had just realized that the water was deep between them.

Why had she started this again? "Never mind."

"You'd ask me what, love?"

Her heart began to pound. He'd called her "love" again.

"I suppose, Simon, if you don't like my question, then you don't have to answer it. You are stubborn that way. But I warn you, it has to do with High Stoneham."

"Go on."

Easily said, but she could see him waiting to pounce on her next word.

Kailey took a deep breath, hoping she wouldn't have to fend off another of his tempers. "Did you ever live there with Sir Robert?"

"Yes." Simon waited for his dread to overtake him—the sharp twist low in his gut; that compelling sensation that he was standing on the rim of a bottomless chasm. But it didn't come, not even in the face of such a direct question. At least not that one.

"I lived there when I was a boy," he added, as a test. Again, nothing. He pulled off his boots.

"You never went back? Not even to see what I was like? Though you were pledged to marry me?"

"No." So there was her direction. He relaxed and let her wonder.

"A pig in a poke, husband?"

"Hardly that." Simon laughed as he imagined all the bacon that would go unsalted if every unopened poke contained pearls such as his wife.

"Simon, you didn't even know me."

"Ah, but I knew of you."

"How?" Now she was laughing low in her throat. She looked highly suspicious of him, but harmless, except that he wanted a taste of her. "Did you have spies at High Stoneham?"

"Yes."

"You planted spies in Sir Robert's house?"

Her feet were bare and she seemed cold to the tips of her breasts—or else she was keenly alert to his sudden arousal. Time to put his wife in bed again. He shrugged out of his hauberk.

"I was kept informed of the activities at High Stoneham." Simon lifted his willow-limbed wife into his arms. " 'Tis how I knew that you were as lovely as the first day of the world."

"Simon." Her smile was beautiful. "You are a terrible liar."

He was a practiced liar, but he never lied about his wife. "I knew you were well loved by everyone; that you were wise; and that your laughter made hearts sing. You see, I am a selfish man and I wanted you all for myself."

"Simon, who would say all this about me?" Her brows dipped fiercely as she scrambled to her knees on the mattress and peered at him as though she didn't believe him. "Who was this spy of yours? Did I know him?"

Who *hadn't* been a spy for him at some time or another, knowingly or not, in whatever household she'd been living? He'd known the day she had cut her first tooth; had discovered from the miller that she took great joy in sailing leaf-boats in the mill-race with the village children, and that she ran from her mentors, who would teach her to turn sheet hems in the solar. He'd known of her every fever, numbered the counterpanes on her bed and the hours of her study. He had closed his eyes and stood fast against the drifts of time when he learned that she'd begun her monthlies.

So soon a woman. The years had flown past. He had watched her grow, but only through the heart-blind eyes of strangers.

Now she was his bride, kneeling in his bed and

wriggling as she pulled her shift off over her head; so comfortable in her nakedness, so comfortable with him. And she had managed to remove his tunic, leaving him nearly as naked as she.

"Are you thinking of tomorrow, Simon?"

"And yesterday." He hadn't meant to say that.

"And your meeting with Prior Guillaume?"

His thoughts had ranged so far from the crimes of the shire, he almost laughed. But true to his wicked form, he lied expertly.

"Aye, sweet. Wingate's ills are heavy on my mind." Though she had managed to find a subject that truly vexed him. Wingate deserved his happiness and this son of his.

"Why did you come to the grange yourself, Simon, when you could have sent your sergeants to find the Templar?"

He drew in another breath of her before he gathered her into his arms. "I'm feeling roundly responsible for the incident. I should have stopped the old fool; should have had the Templar followed—done something. But Wingate was so determined to rescue his son, so blinded by his love."

She was gazing at him intently, as though she'd just accounted for something she hadn't known was missing. "He must have hurt you terribly."

Her touch was amazingly soft as she grazed the edge of his ear.

"Who?"

"Sir Robert." She was shaking her head. " 'Tis your business, Simon, but I am sorry."

He steadied his breathing. "The matter died with him, Kailey."

"Nay, Simon. You love him fiercely, else you couldn't still hate him so."

Tears clotted in his throat.

Rot in hell, old man. Aye, the incantation worked as it always did, walled up the man and his taint.

"I need *you* fiercely, wife."

Simon carried her back against the pillows and kissed her, lost himself in her surety, let her weave her enchantment as she had on that long ago morning when he'd lost his heart to her.

Chapter 19

~~~

Kailey felt more than a little odd sitting beside her husband at a table in the center of the grange's small chapter house, surrounded by Templar-robed knights. Most of the monks were older than Sir Robert, older than Father Abbot, and frail enough to blow over in a breeze; two were sound asleep and snoring loudly.

"This matter grieves us deeply, my lord sheriff," Father Guillaume said. "As I told you, I slept little last night, and I have determined that this robe belonged to our venerable Brother Kenward."

"Is he here?"

"He has recently gone to join our Lord in Heaven." Father Guillaume had hung the singed white garment with a stick threaded through the sleeve openings and across the shoulders, which gave it a decidedly ghostly appearance.

Simon left Kailey to stand beside Father Guillaume, the inquisitor once more, no longer the sweat-seared lover of the night before. Kailey commanded herself to stop such unseemly daydreaming. If she was going to be any help at all to her husband, she would have to pay close attention. And keep her questions to herself, as Simon had warned. He'd granted her a place in the audience only when she'd threatened to go in search of her own answers.

"Brother Kenward died how long ago?" Simon asked.

"A week today, just after the ringing of Vespers, if I recall." Guillaume studied his fellows. "He passed on in his sleep at the age of ninety-one. May the Lord grant us all the same peace."

Simon was frowning fiercely. "Where was Brother Kenward's robe kept upon his death?"

"He was to be buried in it, Lord Simon." A monk stood and scratched at his balding head. "Interment is one of my duties here at Kelstowe. But it was a curious thing about Kenward."

"What was?" Simon met the man in front of his chair.

"When the time came to dress him in his burial vestments, I couldn't find his robe in his cell."

"You didn't tell me of this, Brother Jared." Father Guillaume joined Simon.

"It didn't seem important at the time. Nothing terribly unusual in it." The monk shrugged. "I had another, and so I dressed him in it."

"But the robe would have been left in Brother Kenward's quarters?"

"Yes."

"And who would have known this?"

Another bone-sharp shrug from the monk. "It is common knowledge."

Kailey had a burning question to ask, but instead of blurting it out, she sat on her hands and chewed at the inside of her cheek, hoping Simon would ask it.

"Did Brother Kenward have any visitors just before his death?"

When her own question came out of Simon's

mouth, Kailey sighed overloud, drawing the barest flick of his long lashes—warning enough to make her settle back into her chair and clasp her hands together on her lap.

Prior Guillaume fitted his pointy chin between two of his tented fingers. "Our Order discourages visitors under normal circumstances, Lord Simon, but we welcome them when they will ease the last days of a dying man. Our seneschal will know if anyone came to see Brother Kenward."

"May I speak with him?"

"Unfortunately, he left early this morning to supervise the purchase of a milch cow and isn't expected to return until late afternoon."

If Simon was deterred, he didn't show it. "Brother Jared, was there anything else of Kenward's missing?"

"He had nothing else, my lord," Guillaume interrupted sharply. "Since our oath of poverty prohibits the possession of worldly goods, he would have had nothing in his cell of value."

"Value might not be a factor here. I'm looking for answers. Would he have had a rushlamp?"

"Light is a necessity for the safety of our more aged brothers."

"Writing materials?"

"Aye, for a book he was translating from the Greek."

"And the book itself?"

"Yes."

"And a chamber pot? Perhaps a dagger?"

"It was missing!" Brother Jared had popped up out of his seat, his finger in the air.

"Missing?" Simon gave the prior a satisfied smile and beckoned to the monk, who hurried over, his sandals slapping against the stone floor.

"I remember now thinking to bury him with it, since he hadn't held a sword for these twenty years, and this particular dagger was one he gained in the Holy Land. But it was gone."

Another monk stood. "My lord sheriff, I am the marshal here at Kelstowe. I know this dagger of Kenward's. It was not returned to the armory."

"I'll want a description of it, a drawing, perhaps. In the meantime, I would like to see his cell."

"I would, too!" Kailey stood up and every eye in the chapter house seemed to land on her, none more intently than those of her husband. She had thought of a dozen more questions, but it was obvious that she wasn't going to be able to ask them here, in front of all these frowning men.

"Never mind," she said, before her husband could chide her. "I think I'll go back to our quarters, my lord sheriff, where I can . . . nap."

Kailey left her husband scowling as if he knew she had no intention of napping. She wasn't at all surprised to find the youthful subhospitaler scurrying to escort her out of the chapter house and to the guest lodging.

"Brother Adrian, did you know that Abbot Wingate's son was being held for ransom?"

"Aye, mistress. The fact was made known to us all in chapter. And it was decided that the note must be forwarded to the abbey in Chester with all speed."

"And who was made responsible for delivery?"

"That I don't know. Father Guillaume would have made that assignment from those among us who were available for the duty."

"Someone from the grange?"

"Or from the village. Father Guillaume does on occasion employ a runner." Brother Adrian held open the hostel door for her. "These are questions I would have asked in chapter, but . . . well, you saw the way of it yourself."

"Indeed. And if you discover anything that might aid in my husband's search, Brother Adrian, please don't hesitate to come find me. A wife can ofttimes go where a sheriff cannot."

"My lady." The young man nodded a brief bow and hurried away.

The hostelry was a substantial building, two storied, L-shaped, and rambling. The warming room and a long eating hall that served as a tavern were deserted, but the kitchen was not.

Let Simon ask his official questions—they had their place. But if a Templar's grange was anything like a castle, the rivers of information ran deep beneath the surface, through the cellars, eddied past the buttery and the pantry, and bubbled up in the kitchen.

The cook's eyes narrowed when she saw Kailey; she stabbed an equally threatening glance at the two girls who were shelling peas.

"Does my lady need anything?" she said, puffing out a breath. "We are hours yet from supper." As if to prove her point, the woman yanked a haunch of dried beef out of a salt barrel and plopped it onto the workbench.

"Mistress cook, I am bored with my lot here." Kailey sighed and flipped her hair back over her shoulder, tried to look mindless. "At home in Northumberland, I have a household to run, but I left even my needlework behind in my husband's race to endow the grange, and I have nothing at all to do this day while he attends the prior. So I've come to offer my aid."

"But my lady, that isn't necessary."

"I saw a bountiful herb garden from the window of my chamber. May I harvest whatever you need for the supper? I promise to take my time."

"Yes, yes, certainly." The woman sighed and brushed salt off the edge of the table, obviously relieved to have discovered a simple task for the interfering milady.

"And might I borrow one of your assistants?" Kailey needed to start her investigation somewhere, and it didn't really matter who her first subject was.

The woman caught herself mid-huff and looked between the two kitchen helpers. She finally nodded at an ivory-cheeked young woman of no more than sixteen.

"Jemma, go with the lady and help her in the garden." The cook rattled off a half-dozen herbs for the night's meal, chervil and marjoram among them, and then Jemma led Kailey out of the heat of the kitchen and into the side yard.

"Thank you, my lady, for rescuing me!" Jemma lifted a cascade of hair off her neck as they walked along the shady track. " 'Tis a joy to be out here with the breezes, and away from my Aunt Aldyth, if only for a moment."

" 'Tis a beautiful day, not to be wasted indoors." Kailey felt a bit dishonest, taking advantage of the girl, but evidence wasn't going to just walk up and clamp itself onto her nose. "Your auntie seems a nice enough sort."

"Overworked, I'm afraid. She's not a very good cook even when she's at her leisure." Jemma plucked a shiny laurel leaf from the hedge. "But with my Uncle Clyde gone away, she must do all the work herself, and now she's even more sharp-tongued and careless than usual."

Jemma's uncle was gone? Kailey tried not to pounce on this random speck of information; it could well mean nothing. "Is your uncle gone long?"

"Five days now."

Kailey's heart was racing. "Gone where?"

"To Chester, my lady." Jemma shredded the edges of the leaf and Kailey heard every rend, rasping like sheets of parchment.

"Do you know the reason he went?"

"To pay a custom to the king's court on an inheritance of cattle, or something. Which I care not a whit about, because Rigney has gone as well." The girl looked suddenly beaten down, but Kailey needed to press on with her suspicions.

"He's gone with your uncle?" It was going to be difficult to unravel the comings and goings among these many players.

"Nay, Rigney left a day earlier than Uncle. The trip was of a sudden, and he wouldn't tell me the reason he went, or where. But he was very excited."

"Who is this Rigney?"

"Oh, my lady!" Jemma's eyes sparkled as she drew Kailey through the bent-willow trellis that arched over the opening in the garden wall. "Do you promise to keep my secret?"

"If I can. My husband can be quite persuasive."

"Aye, your husband is a most handsome man!" The heat of appreciation pinked the girl's brow; she covered her grin and her giggle with both hands.

Kailey felt vastly older than the girl, though they were no more than two years different in ages. "And may you be as happy as we are when you and your Rigney are married."

"Married to Rigney! How did you know?"

"That's your secret, isn't it, Jemma? 'Tis written in your eyes when you say his name."

"Oh, I do love him, and he loves me! But no one knows of our bond—especially not my auntie or my uncle! They would forbid us, because Rigney is naught but a scullion at the grange, scrubbing floors and emptying nightbuckets, collecting laundry. He lives in the hayloft in the stable. But he won't for much longer, not after he returns from his venture."

"How is that?" Kailey didn't want to hear this of the young man that Jemma loved. Could he be the false Templar?

"Whatever Rigney was sent away to do, he will be paid handsomely enough for us to marry when he returns. He plans to buy himself an apprenticeship with the carpenter in the village."

"From scullion to married carpenter, all on the strength of a single errand?" Oh, Simon! Where are you to hear this? Kailey pinched off a handful of parsley and tossed it into the basket. "And Rigney gave you no idea where this fortune was to come from?"

"Rigney is young and knows his mind. I trust him to do right by me."

Young? But the Templar had been Simon's age. "Has Rigney ever been messenger for the grange?"

"Oh, aye, he has. But I doubt he's gone for them. He's never gone more than two days, and would have been back by now. And I'd be sick with worry that he wasn't."

Kailey thought back on the young man they'd found so badly beaten and nearly drowned, and a chill crawled down her spine.

"What does your Rigney look like?"

"Oh, handsome as a day in June, my lady. Big

white teeth, and freckles. Hair as red as carrots—"

"Curly?"

Jemma giggled again. "Curly as a pig's tail, I like to tease him."

Dear God, Carrotlocks—the answer was so near! Kailey had to find Simon. "We'd best harvest the herbs for your auntie, else she'll wonder that we're gossiping instead of working."

Kailey tugged little else from Jemma's store of information, and soon they delivered an apron full of herbs to the kitchen. She needed more information about this Clyde fellow. He could so easily be their Templar.

Kailey's careful selection of herbs seemed to please Aunt Aldyth, and pleased her even more when Kailey set to work dismembering the stems from the leaves.

"Your niece tells me you are without your husband for days now." Kailey plucked the tiny marjoram leaves into a pile.

"My Clyde is ever underfoot when he is here, but bless the man, it seems now that I could use his help at every turn."

"Aye, and isn't that like a husband." Kailey shared the woman's reluctant laughter and tried to sound chatty, when all she wanted to do was to shake answers from her. "Will your Clyde be away long?"

"The devil knows. He was to return this morning with money from an inheritance, but he's one to be caught up with his ale at Penford and if that's the case, he'll not make it here till after Compline."

Compline, tonight! Then they must be ready for the man! When Kailey claimed exhaustion and a desire to take a nap, Jemma's aunt nodded as if she had once again affirmed to herself the uselessness of the noble class.

Kailey slipped out the back door.

First she would see if there were clues to be found in Rigney's sleeping loft. Then she would attract Simon's attention somehow, and tell him her news. And then they only had to wait until Jemma's uncle Clyde returned.

If he returned.

Simon crossed the tidy compound toward the hostel, relieved that the tower bell had rung for Nones, and that the brothers had left him to say their holy offices in the chapel. His wife was loose somewhere on the grounds, no more napping than he was, adventuring where she oughtn't be. He'd looked in their chamber, but she wasn't there—which was no doubt for the best. He burned for her, and would have lost the afternoon in her arms if he'd caught her alone in their bed.

He traced her from the kitchen to the vestibule of the small chapel to the deserted stable, and then he only noticed her because of the rain of straw from the hayloft, and the tumble of her soft giggles.

Had she been any other woman, he might have been tempted to jealousy, tempted to believe she had stolen away for an afternoon's play with another man. But Kailey was loyal and true, and he gloried that she held his heart so tenderly.

Not knowing what to expect, but anticipating her with a fever that instantly swelled his flesh against the front of his hip belt, Simon climbed halfway up the ladder and would have spoken to her then, but she was engaged.

"Careful little one!" she whispered through her sheltered laughter.

She had found a litter of kittens—or rather, they had found her. She was tumbled back against a ring of hay, valiantly battling an army of fur and tails, each kitten-soldier bent on gaining the top of her head or tucking itself beneath her hair, mewling impatiently when their claws lost purchase and they fell down the slope of her skirts. One intrepid scout had fit itself down the front of her sleeveless overdress, and now looked out from under Kailey's chin as if he'd claimed her for his own.

She's mine, little fellow. Go find your own family.

Simon's heart swelled to bursting in the shaded magic of the sun-striped loft; his pulse pounded in his temples. He wondered if he would be jealous of his baby sons who would someday suckle at her breast. They would have to learn to share.

"I thought you were napping," he said, forcing a growl.

She was surprised only for an instant. "No, you didn't. I don't take naps."

Bright-eyed and intense, she was on her knees but unable to move. Simon reached the loft while she lifted clinging, mewling balls of fur off her skirts.

"I looked all over the world for you again, madam." Simon took her into his arms and covered her mouth with his, dancing with her tongue, drowning in her lavender and sunlight, until he felt his scalp prickle and realized that a kitten was trying to climb the back of his head.

"Ouch! Easy, fellow," Simon managed between his wife's fierce kisses. He lifted the cat from his neck and set him on a nearby ring of hay. The lot of them began to howl and complain, then deserted Kailey's bower like a retreating vanguard gone off to raid the nearest town.

"Cowards!"

"Nay, Simon, look. There's mama; 'tis supper time." Kailey snuggled against him, pressed her cheek to his shoulder, and then her mouth to his neck, where she tugged at his earlobe. "She'll know what to do with her little family."

The heavy-bellied cat stretched out across a band of sunlight and closed her eyes as her babes tumbled and fought over her.

Christ Jesus, he wanted a family. Children—thundering hordes of them. And Kailey.

Though the woman was forever sticking her lovely bead-sweated nose into his business. He righted his thoughts and set her away from him. "What are you doing here in a hayloft, madam?"

"Inquesting for you. Successfully. I know who the messenger was!"

"One of the scullion lads. Yes, I know. Now, *shhh!*" Simon put his finger to her soft mouth, bit on his own lip to keep himself from supping there where his finger rested. "There may be ears below us."

She nodded and then whispered, "His name is Rigney. This is his sleeping loft. I thought to find something here, but I was waylaid."

And so had he been. "Kailey, the boy hasn't returned to the grange."

"I know."

"He has access to the sleeping chambers and all the linen. He's obviously not the false Templar himself—"

"Too young—"

"Yes, love, but he may very well be a conspirator."

"Nay, Simon." She shook her head fiercely. "Do you remember that boy back in Chester who'd been beaten nearly to death and left to drown?"

"I've not lost all my faculties, wife."

"That was Rigney, the real messenger from Kelstowe."

Simon expelled a bolt of air. "Right under my nose."

"Exactly. And someone other than Rigney delivered that message to the abbey."

"Substituting the first note entirely. Damnation. I need to know who came to visit Kenward before he died." He needed to find the seneschal.

"And Simon," she whispered. "I think the false Templar is Jemma's uncle."

"Whose uncle?"

"Jemma is one of the kitchen maids. Her Aunt Aldyth and Uncle Clyde run the hostel for the Templars."

"How do you know this Jemma?"

"I helped her gather herbs for supper."

He hadn't expected Kailey to nap, but he had bloody sure not expected her to plow headlong into the fray.

"Nay, woman, you sought her out and squeezed her dry. I told you this wasn't your inquest!"

She stuck her fists onto her bent knees and glowered at him. "Does it matter where the truth is found, Simon?"

"Yes." He'd never have thought to inquire of a kitchen maid. "But go on. The damage is done."

"Uncle Clyde has gone to Chester to collect an inheritance of cattle and to pay the king's death duty. Do you recall hearing the plea of a man named Clyde of the Kelstowe Hundred?"

"No, but court has not yet adjourned."

"And he was to be back this morning. And I tell you the next in strict confidence, Simon. You're not to listen with your sheriff's ear. Promise me."

"As much as I can promise anything."

"When Rigney left here with his message, he told Jemma that he would marry her upon his return, hinting that he would soon come into enough money to raise himself from a scullion to a carpenter's apprentice."

"Then this Rigney is surely implicated."

She shook her head. "I pray not. For Jemma's sake, and for his."

Next she'd have this calamitous pair living in the hearthroom at Crookston Hall. "Kailey—"

"As for now, Simon, you are the only one who can identify this false Templar. So what do we do next? Do we wait for Jemma's uncle to return? I could ask around in the village. It isn't far."

"*We?*" Simon had been distracted enough through the morning, wondering what tree she was climbing for a better view of the road. "This is my investigation, as I've told you countless times. You will return to our chamber and wait for me to return from the chapter house."

"I only want to help Father Abbot."

"And I merely ask, wife, that you refrain from pursuing this case at a full gallop."

" 'Tis difficult, Simon. I am most dangerous when my hands are idle and I know that something must be done." She looked roundly chastised, though entirely unrepentant, leaving him wanting to taste and tease her, here in the afternoon, in the crisp heat of the golden hay.

"You are dangerous anytime, wife."

"Remember that, husband." She scrabbled away from him to the edge of the loft.

Simon climbed down the ladder first and lifted Kailey from the last rung. She grabbed his arms as she landed, then clung to him with a gasp.

"Simon, look!"

"A good afternoon, children." Wingate was sitting on the edge of a short crib not a dozen feet from them, holding the reins of a long-legged mule.

"Father Abbot!" Kailey left Simon and embraced Wingate as if he were a long-lost friend instead of a lunatic cleric. "You are a welcome sight, Father!"

"And you, my girl!" Wingate gave Kailey a beaming kiss on her forehead.

Simon wasn't nearly as pleased; he saw the sleepless circles under the man's eyes, the unsteadiness of his hands. "Wingate, how the devil did you get here?"

The abbot stood up sharply, as if to prove Simon's theory wrong. "By the grace of God Almighty and a bit of help from Talley, here." He patted the mule's nose fondly.

"You traveled the road from Chester alone, Wingate, risking your scrawny neck while we ferret out your felon?"

"Mind your temper, husband." His wife was stroking the mule's neck, as she had his own backside not two minutes before.

"I left St. Werburgh's this morning just after Lauds, and here I am, unharmed."

And twenty years older, by the looks of him. "Because the Lord protects lunatics from themselves! Did you tell Cathmore where you were going?"

Wingate thought for a moment, no doubt judging the penance for telling a lie. "No."

"Because he would not have let you come. Why did you?"

"Because I caused you this trouble, Simon." Wingate looked suddenly chastened, wrapping and unwrapping the reins around his thumb. " 'Tis only right that I help solve it."

"That is *my* job."

"And Nicholas is my son. I couldn't bear another hour of idleness, waiting to hear if he is truly being held somewhere. I am no good to St. Werburgh's, no good to my God when I am in such a state. Do you know yet if he has truly been taken hostage?"

Simon felt as guilty as if he held Nicholas himself. "Prior Guillaume confirmed it, I am sorry to say."

Wingate remained steady on his feet for a moment, then sat down on the crib again. "As I feared."

Kailey dropped to her knees beside the man and took his hand to her cheek. "But your Nicholas is well, Father Abbot. I am sure of it."

"Nothing has changed, Wingate." A handsome lot of money in ransom made Wingate's son valuable to his captors, but only if he were alive when the exchange was made.

"You were right, Simon, I've been out of the world too long. I have become an ignorant fool."

"Nonsense; I would have set off for Cressing if you hadn't noticed that the robe came from here at Kelstowe. It belonged to an elderly knight named Kenward. The robe went missing when he died just a week ago."

Wingate's brows arched. "Brother Kenward is just now dead? I'm surprised that he lived to this age. He was ancient when I took the cowl twenty-five years ago; a fine man. So the robe was his?" Wingate seemed to take heart and sat taller, then creaked to his feet, suffering Kailey's guiding hand at his elbow. "I would like to speak with Prior Guillaume myself."

"Go where you will, Wingate, but keep that cowl upon your head." Simon untied the saddlebag from the back of the mule. "I don't want you to be identified here at the manor."

"But the prior knows me . . . why can't I been seen?"

"For the same reason that no one knows that I am sheriff of the shire. I am here to arrange an endowment for the grange, and nothing more."

"Utterly diabolical." Kailey was grinning, and Simon suddenly imagined her let loose on all the thieves in Nottinghamshire. He hid his smile as he led the mule toward a stall.

"My wife will no doubt tell you all about her theories. In the meantime, I'll see that your steed is tended, and tell the prior that you're here."

"I would like to see Brother Kenward's grave. Do you know if he was buried here?"

"Come, Father, I'll show you." Kailey started away.

"Where are you going, wife?"

She stopped and turned back to Simon. "Or I can sit in the hostel common and watch for Jemma's uncle, or I can walk to the village and ask a few questions—"

Simon locked the mule's stall. "Save me, Wingate."

The priest chuckled. "I had been about to request your company, my lady."

"I would be delighted, Father."

Kailey looked pleased with herself as she strode with the hooded priest from the dust-filtered shadows of the stable into the brightness of noon. The pair would either cancel each other's potential for mischief or increase it tenfold, and he'd end up pulling them out of a well.

Simon laughed in spite of himself. He found a stableman to look after Wingate's mule, and set off for the chapter house before he remembered that Nones was not yet over. He slipped into the back of the chapel and a guilty calm washed over him. He welcomed the coolness of the stone against his back and the oblivion of plainsong.

For his sins against Neville Hewett and his daughter, he had chosen a life of penance in the law. If not for Kailey, he would have offered himself to the church.

This marriage between them should have scraped his skin like a hair-shirt, should have made his gut ache in its emptiness and promise him only more numbness and pain.

But she was his miracle.

And now he wondered what unspeakable retribution he would suffer for his bliss. What hellish place awaited his eternity for having been loved by Kailey?

Chapter 20

"**D**o you mean to say that broken young man in our infirmary at St. Werburgh's is from here at Kelstowe? Remarkable."

"Aye, Father, 'tis becoming a twisted crime, growing more so as the hours progress. But ever and always, the evidence turns back toward the hostelry and Uncle Clyde." Feeling very much the spy and spied upon, Kailey glanced around the stable grounds as she unlatched the wicket gate that led into the narrow path behind the chapel and toward the cemetery.

"I am a dullard when it comes to intrigue, my girl. But if all you say is true of this Clyde fellow, then I've indeed sent us all into the adder's nest."

"But nearer the truth. I only hope that Rigney was deceived into his part in this conspiracy. Jemma thinks the sun rises in his eyes, and I would not have her disappointed if he's found to be guilty."

But Kailey felt her heart rise, called by the calming drone of plainsong that drifted from the choir to hang like a mist among the wildflowers on the verge of the footpath.

"Do you hear it, Kailey?" The abbot lifted his eyes to the crystal blue sky, and his cowl fell to his shoulders, exposing that undisguisable silver-white fringe of hair. " 'Tis a glorious sound that soars straight to God's forgiving ear."

"Oh, 'tis still Nones, Father! Shouldn't you be with your brother monks?" She hadn't given a moment's thought to the divine offices that he had missed because of his morning trek. "Will you not owe a great penance for skipping your prayers today?"

"For skipping them? Oh, my dear." He chuckled, and stood still as Kailey tugged his cowl back into place. "Believe me, I was in Holy Communion with my Lord God all the morning long. A lonely road and a bilious mule with a razor back brings one closer to heaven than a whole day spent prostrate in prayer. God forgive me, I've become a heretic in my old age, seeking blessings wherever they fall. And how easily I could have fallen on my backside—as your husband so rightly pointed out."

"Simon wasn't angry at you, Father." Kailey had seen the priest flinch at her husband's temper and planned to speak with him about it later. "He was worried."

"I know."

Aye, the man had known Simon far longer than she had.

"He doesn't seem to understand that the people we take to our hearts are sometimes quite wayward in their actions. And he doesn't yet know what to do with the great love he feels, especially the love he harbors for his own father." Kailey knew she shouldn't ask, that she should wait for Simon to tell her, but he was such a puzzle to her. "Do you know anything about their estrangement, Father?"

Abbot Wingate stopped beneath the rose-strewn

arbor, fishing around in his sleeve pouch.

"I don't, my dear. I'm sorry." He produced a short-bladed knife and sawed a pale pink blossom from the arching canes. "Simon has ever kept his own counsel. I've never heard the slightest talk of it—and we clerics are nothing if not Christendom's busiest hive of gossips."

"I've always suspected as much." Kailey laughed and accepted the purloined rose the abbot held out for her. "Thank you, sir."

"There, you see—I'm first a gossip and now a thief." He cut off another blossom and sheathed his little knife. "This one is for Brother Kenward. Though now that I think on it, roses set the man to sneezing. Ah, and there he is, daughter, where the earth is new-turned."

He pointed across the enclosure and led her under the fragrant arbor into the tidy and trimmed little cemetery, to the only fresh grave among the thirty or so simple markers.

He sighed and dropped the rose onto the hillock. His shoulders sank. "Ah, Kenward, we grew old, didn't we?"

Then he lowered himself easily to his knees, bent forward on his hands and touched his forehead to the crumbly earth.

Unsure what to do as Abbot Wingate whispered his prayers, Kailey stepped away and looked around at the other graves, at the rows of low-lying stones, and the gravel pathways that divided them from each other. It was a place of well-tended peace and Kailey felt its gentle touch, even as she felt the sun upon her face.

"Dear Sir Robert, I do miss you." And would always regret that she hadn't known the extent of his devotion to her, and to her father and mother.

What thanks she would have given, had she known!

The very gratitude that Sir Robert's son had so violently refused to hear from her. But maybe he was right, for how do you thank someone for loving you?

Forgive him, daughter.

The afternoon breeze and all its sun-warmed fragrances brushed up against Kailey's ear, made her fancy that she heard her father's voice in sweet plainsong. The sensation grew ever stronger and swept outward from the center of her chest, an exultation of love that stopped her breathing and dizzied her, slipped tears down her cheeks.

"Lord, my God, you know my heart as they do not." But God had found him guilty, and he'd been hanged for it.

"*You* forgave them, Father." Kailey heard the voice and looked around to find its source. But they were alone in the cemetery, Father Abbot still bent in prayer. She touched her mouth, and the bewildering words were still there.

Why would she say such a thing? And to whom? To her father? Nay, but of course it must have been a prayer to the Almighty Father.

She closed her eyes and offered other prayers: that she could bring peace to Simon's heart, that Father Abbot would find his son, and that Hinch and Davie and Julia were well.

She prayed for Sir Telford and his piety, for FitzLandry and his wisdom, for the extravagance of Sir Robert's spirit.

For her father, whose love for her mother had survived beyond the moment of his death; for his spirit that had become a haunting chanson that rang chaotically inside her chest, ringing change after change until she would soon hear nothing else. She needed to silence this too-persistent guardian, to put his spirit to rest again beside her mother.

At Eveside. But she couldn't very well ask Simon.

Abbot Wingate rose creakily from his murmuring, lifted his drooping cowl off his forehead, and caught Kailey's gaze as he brushed off his knees and his elbows. "Kenward was a font of Roman history, child. Spent years in study of this shire and never uncovered all that puzzled him. I prayed at the last that he had gained his answers."

This holy man was so comfortable in his skin, was so certain of his soul.

"Father Abbot, do you know of a parish church called Eveside?"

He nodded immediately. "Oh, yes. 'Tis one of St. Werburgh's. A small chapel and a graveyard. Not used often anymore, but the sanctuary and altar still stand."

A lonely spot, forgotten. It made her heart ache and her throat fill up with unshakeable sorrows.

" 'Tis where my father is buried. And my mother, too. I've never been there." Her mouth had gone salty and dry.

"Eveside is on the way home."

"So nearby?" Kailey's heart had leaped high, but then she realized that Simon hadn't told her.

"A side trip of less than a mile. I would be most happy to show you the way."

A chance to see them together. Her mother and father.

"I'd like that very much, Father Abbot."

"Ah, and there is your husband, my lady." He nodded toward the rose arbor and the broad-shouldered man who had to stoop beneath it to enter the enclosure. "Shall we tell him of this detour?"

"No, please." Kailey grabbed at the fullness of his coarse black sleeve. Simon wouldn't be pleased, but she needed to finish this. "I'll ask him when the moment is right."

"Right? He would object, daughter, when it would bring you such peace?"

"Simon never mentioned to you who my father was?"

"Should he have?"

Of course, he'd have kept the whole of the crime all to himself; he wasn't a man to unburden his heart. "My father was Neville Hewett; he was hanged for treason nearly twenty years ago."

"Executed?" A sheen of uneasiness moved across the priest's face so quickly it might have been only a scudding cloud. But he recovered in his next breath, and with one of his most beneficent smiles. "Well, child, we'll see that you get to Eveside."

"To my parents, Father. 'Tis all I want. To see them as one," she whispered as Simon joined them, his grin not hidden at all well.

"Has my wife told you of this theory of hers: Jemma, the herb girl, and her Uncle Clyde?" Simon fit his hand to the curve of Kailey's waist and she abandoned herself to the assurance of his possessively spread fingers, though she wanted to pinch him for his arrogance.

"I'm right about Uncle Clyde, Simon. You'll see tonight! I have a plan."

"Do you?"

Oh, the man had a wickedly skeptical eyebrow. "I do."

"We'll talk of this plan in private. In the meantime, Wingate, Prior Guillaume is expecting you."

"I am sorry for this intrigue, Simon," the abbot said, looking altogether grim when he had been so at peace. "Sorry you had to chase after my foolishness. You've been a good friend to an old man."

"You'll have your son back when this is over, Wingate." Kailey saw the redness come to her husband's eyes. "That I promise you."

Aye, he's a good man, Sir Robert.

Kailey sat beside her husband in the main room of the hostelry, with him straddling a bench, and her trying to watch the door over his wall of a shoulder. He looked dangerous tonight, over-wound and ready to spring, his eyes so hot they could char a man to cinders if he fixed them in anger.

The common room was bustling, salted with Simon's own men, noisy with villagers and those passing the night under the hostelry's substantial smoke-hung eaves.

Father Wingate sat beside the unshuttered window, his cowl drawn over his head, making him look as if he'd imbibed too much wine and would spend the next month fasting for his sins. Simon had tried to dissuade him from this venture, as he had tried with her. But Kailey and the abbot had stood fast, were integral to her plan, and so here they were. Waiting.

"I'm watching for a bearded man, Simon. And hair to his shoulders."

"All of which can be altered with a razor—"

"Yes, but he will have a ring, Simon! I'd forgotten!"

"I heard nothing about a ring." He was talking through his teeth, short tempered and snapping.

All of which made him vitally attractive at the moment.

"Whoever beat up poor Rigney was wearing a ring that tore up the boy's face wherever it struck him."

"The Templar was wearing gloves."

"Which can be altered by taking them off." Kailey did her best to hide the traitorous yawn that came over her, but Simon had seen and was frowning.

"It's after ten, Kailey. Go up to bed, and leave this to me and my men."

"You can't be the one who meets with the false Templar, Simon. He knows your face, and Abbot Wingate's. Therefore, the watching falls to me. I can see both doors perfectly from here."

The main door and the rear were opened against the warm night air; the drapes that closed off the kitchen doorway between were drawn open to let a breeze blow through from front to back.

Simon leaned forward and lifted her hand, put it to his lips, and looked at her from beneath his fierce brow.

"I have no intention of 'meeting' the bastard, Kailey. I plan to take him down mid-stride, plant his forehead against these planks, and put the point of my dagger to his miserable neck, all the while praying that he makes me use it."

Kailey didn't like the idea of Simon engaging in an exchange of blades with a dishonest thief, but she would have to trust him. A shimmer of movement at the door made her duck behind her husband and then peer around him.

"Simon, look!" she whispered. "No, don't look!" She grabbed the tip of his chin with her thumb when he would have turned, and then kissed him while she watched a large man tromp between the tables, meeting jibes and shaking hands. He was carrying a leather bag and a small coffer. "He looks like he belongs here, Simon."

"The hosteler?" he asked beside her ear.

"Can you see him, Simon?" Kailey watched for a nodding signal from Father Abbot, but his cowl was pulled too closely over his head.

"You are naught but curl, wife." He was parting his way through her hair with his fingers, a very sumptuous sensation that she would ask him to repeat at a more appropriate time.

"There, Simon. Aldyth, the cook, has come from the kitchen." The noise in the tavern rose as the man cut through the tables, swallowing up any words the woman might have spoken. "Aye, and that is definitely the glare of a wife who has been left to manage on her own for too long."

"Kailey, this is absurd."

"A moment more, Simon." Jemma was accepting a dutiful peck on her cheek from her uncle, but got a frown and a slap when she tried to take his bag from him. "It's him. I'm certain this is Uncle Clyde."

"Then it is time to see your plan in action."

"Be careful, Simon."

But her husband was already changing shape beneath her hands, becoming the lord high sheriff as his muscles gathered themselves to broaden his shoulders and harden his arms. She heard him fill his lungs, heard the faint click of his long-bladed dagger as he wrapped his hand around its hilt. He turned in deadly quiet to find each of his men, gave them signaled warnings to be ready, and when he stood, he looked twice his normal size.

He paused almost imperceptibly as he glanced

toward Jemma's uncle. He let out a slow breath, relaxed too much, then held out his hand to Kailey, his eyes wickedly disappointed.

"Time for us to retire, my sweet."

"Simon—" She nodded twice toward Jemma's uncle, but her husband only blinked and shook his head.

"We've a long ride in the morning, wife."

"Simon, what is it?" Kailey had no idea what he was up to as she took his hand, yet she would trust him with her life, the lives of all their children and grandchildren.

He seemed as wary and prowling as a stalking cat. He led her past the hosteler, through the tangle of tables and benches toward the stairs.

"My lady!" Jemma stopped them, and Kailey felt Simon drop back into the shadows of the overhead beams and the limewashed walls. "My uncle has come back. He was late home because he stopped to buy two horses. Imagine!"

"Two horses?" For a hosteler? What the devil was Simon doing? This was the Templar! His beard shaved, perhaps, but it must be him. And he was wearing a ring! "That's your Uncle Clyde?"

" 'Tis him. He's to start a livery with his new-found inheritance."

Why doesn't Simon arrest the man? She shot him a frown, though he had nearly disappeared into the timbers and ties of the tavern.

"A great good fortune for your family, Jemma." Stolen, of course, and bloodied. The abbot's son in danger for his life.

"No sign yet of Rigney, my lady." Jemma leaned into Kailey and whispered, "But I am not worried . . . not yet."

Having no comfort to give, Kailey glanced at the

abbot's corner in time to see him tipping back his cowl to his shoulders. He was watching intently as another man entered the inn from the outside.

The newcomer was well dressed, sharply shorn, and clean-shaved. Even from here, Kailey could see that his face was sun-browned only to the upper ridge of his cheeks and scarred at the brow.

He carried a heavy saddlebag under one arm and wore a broad smile that he cast about the tavern to the hailing and shouting.

He, too, had a gem-laden ring glinting from his middle finger.

The Templar? Now her plan had too many players.

Abbot Wingate's eyes were narrowed with angry amazement as he glanced toward Kailey. Then he looked past her to find Simon in the shadows. The priest nodded slowly and the air seemed to crackle a lighting-blue between the two men.

"Simon?" Kailey whispered.

Something was dreadfully wrong here. Simon's men were rising, moving at cold-honey speed, looking too casual, too lethal. She heard the hair-splitting rasp of Simon's dagger released again from its steely scabbard.

"Stand away, wife," he whispered beside her ear. The leather of his gloves dug into her wrist as he dragged her behind him.

Simon and Abbot Wingate had seen their false Templar! Not Jemma's uncle, who had slipped into the kitchen and drawn down the curtains across the door. But the man who now stood inside the suddenly close-fitting tavern!

"Who is that, Jemma?" Kailey asked quietly.

" 'Tis our bailiff, my lady, Master Sewell, though he looks an odd duck without his beard. I'd best get him his ale." Jemma started toward Sewell, but Kailey snagged her arm and the girl frowned.

"Take care, Jemma," she whispered, as Sewell came further into the room. He stepped over knees and around boots and bench legs as he wound his way through the tables, unwittingly through a gauntlet of Simon's guards.

Simon was moving like a wraith along the shadowed walls, communicating with his men as if by intent alone, until he was level with Sewell, the long blade of his dagger downturned but deadly.

Be careful, my love. She sent a prayer to all the saints, and to her father, who owed Simon so much. *Watch over him.*

But her husband was lethal grace as he stepped out of the darkness. With forbidding ease, and in the deadly silence that suddenly afflicted every tongue in the tavern, he raised his dagger and pressed the tip to the false Templar's throat, a move so startlingly unheralded that the man stopped still and wordless.

"Stand fast, Josten," he said evenly, "else you'll die here."

The man gasped, looked from the tip of the dagger into Simon's face. "You!" he said, as if Simon were indeed the Angel of Death.

Kailey wanted to watch the false Templar grovel at her husband's feet and beg mercy of Father Wingate, but she could see that Jemma was about to raise a ruckus and knew Simon would be safer without the distraction.

"To the kitchen, Jemma," she whispered. "My husband is the king's sheriff. He will do the man no harm if he is innocent."

"But, my lady—"

"Come!" Kailey grabbed Jemma by the skirts

and hauled her the three steps toward the kitchen. When they burst through the curtains, Jemma's uncle was bent over his small coffer on a table at the center of the room.

"Uncle?"

"Go away, damn you, girl!" He had been in the midst of pulling the ring off his finger, prepared to drop it into the coffer with a brace of silver coins.

"Uncle, the king's sheriff is here—"

It took no more than that to send Jemma's Uncle Clyde in a panic toward the rear door, the coffer tucked under his arm and now weighed down by the bag that he'd carried in.

Jemma's uncle, too?

"Damn the man!" Reaching for the nearest weapon, Kailey took off after the hosteler. She flew out into the kitchen yard and its stinking rubble, a landscape caltropped with sprung barrels and scraps of food. She righted her balance just as the hosteler stumbled out of sight and into the darkness around the side of the building. He would need a horse if he wanted to get far with his stolen treasure; would head for the stables.

She hoped that Simon was having better luck with the false Templar. At least her husband was better armed: she had managed to grab up only a serving spoon!

But she followed Uncle Clyde around the darkened corner and took heart that he was hemmed into a narrow lane by a shoulder-high fence and the wall of the building. Kailey followed him at a run as he hobbled with his burden toward the light at the front of the hostel.

Beyond him, a man stood in the forecourt, berobed and bent over, as if trying to find his breath. A monk! *Her* monk!

"Abbot Wingate!" she shouted. "Stop him!"

Clyde slowed to look back at her and dropped the bag, losing time to his greed as he stopped to snag it again.

"Damn it, wife!" Simon was behind her now in the darkness, his voice a roaring bellow. "Let him go!"

But Kailey was almost on top of the thief, and Abbot Wingate stood blocking the way, his arms and legs stretched out like the spokes of a wheel.

"Out of my way, monk!" Uncle Clyde ducked his head and plowed forward as if he planned to toss the abbot aside with a stunning blow from his shoulder, one that would surely shatter every bone in the old man's body.

"Move, Father Wingate!" she shouted. *"Move!"*

But at the last possible instant, Abbot Wingate fell to his knees in front of Uncle Clyde, caught the man's forward motion, and sailed him six feet into the air and twelve more across the compound.

Clyde landed with a groaning thud. The coffer exploded as it hit the ground, sending an arcing shower of clattering silver coins over the forecourt. Abbot Wingate staggered to his feet as Kailey caught his arms.

"Are you all right, Father?"

Blessed man! He was laughing. "We got him, Kailey girl! We got him!"

But Uncle Clyde had gathered himself and was crawling away to a hedge. Kailey made a leap and threw herself on the man's back. She jammed the spoon handle into the nape of his neck and growled.

"Move an inch, Clyde, and you'll be using this pig sticker for a tongue." Let him think it a dagger; let him think she would use it.

"That will be quite enough, wife." She knew that voice in all its moods, and didn't need to wonder at this one. Simon was breathing like he'd run here from Chester, furious and frightened.

"He was getting away!"

"Will you never listen to me, wife?" He scooped an arm though her waist, then lifted her against him. "You could have been killed!"

"He'd have escaped!"

"Not a chance in hell."

The forecourt was ringed by Simon's men, who kept the onlookers from the spray of fallen coins.

Clyde stumbled to stand and held his knee as he glared at Abbot Wingate, who glared back as he brushed at the dust on his robes. Sewell was shoved into the circle of torchlight and made to stand beside his fellow thief.

Simon set Kailey aside and she stood behind him, clear of the swing of his long-bladed dagger as he leveled it between the two men.

"Empty the bags," he said to them.

The men looked uneasily around the forecourt as they dumped the leather satchels into the light, no doubt searching for an escape.

The abbot's five hundred pounds of coin and treasure was divided neatly. There were brooches and cups, plate and folds of silk.

"Is this your ransom payment, Wingate?"

Kailey took the priest's arm as he approached and looked down at the two piles of treasure.

"Aye, Simon."

Prior Guillaume had been drawn from his cloister and into the fray, a group of gray-haired monks roosted behind him. He stepped into the circle and picked up a handsome dagger. He nodded as he looked at Simon.

"Brother Kenward's," he said simply.

"Well, then." Simon's voice rang out with the power of his office. "As sheriff of this shire, I charge you Sewell and you Clyde with theft, with conspiracy to disrupt the king's peace, and with deadly assault."

The men groveled and protested. Sewell spun on his heel to run, but found the faithful Allan too near and ready with his wrist cords.

Simon nodded and the pair were bound as he turned to the prior of Kelstowe Grange.

"Father Guillaume, these men were caught red-handed in their crimes, with chattel stolen from your priory and from the abbot of St. Werburgh's. According to ancient and current custom, it is your privilege to see them summarily executed. I would advise this action; they are men of notorious repute. But the choice is yours."

"No!" Kailey clutched at her throat, hoping her strangled cry hadn't escaped her. A capital crime, and she'd been the instrument of their capture. She waited, unbreathing, while the prior studied the two men. Surely a man of God would see them redeemable.

"You have broken faith with us in the most grievous manner, Sewell. You have injured one of our own, young Rigney, almost to the point of death."

"My Rigney! Oh, no!" Kailey heard Jemma's cry from the porch, but couldn't look away from the prior's face as he passed his sentence on these men.

"You have brought shame and ruin upon your household, Clyde of Kelstowe. And you, Master Sewell, a man we trusted as bailiff, haven't the conscience, nor even the sense, to flee your crimes."

The prior's face had lost its peace, was drawn

and claylike when he turned from the thieves to Simon.

"My lord sheriff—" His mouth worked, whether in prayer or in reluctance Kailey couldn't tell. "I will see them hanged."

Simon nodded solemnly, looked to Abbot Wingate. "In the king's name, my lords," he said.

Kailey's cry of helpless horror was masked by the wail that rose into the night from behind her.

"*Noo!* Not my Clyde!" Aldyth tried to wrench out of the tangle of arms that now held her. Jemma's eyes were drenched, but she held fast to the woman, and rightly fixed her hatred on the uncle who had betrayed her.

Simon took Kailey by the shoulders. His eyes were glassy and intense, his voice as ragged as his breathing. "Take the women from here, Kailey. Please."

She was suddenly horrified. "Now? You're going to hang them here?"

"As swiftly as possible, madam. Go." He turned from her fiercely and joined the prior.

Kailey wanted to protest, to rail against the certainty of her husband's convictions. This execution was Simon's uncompromising justice, whether decided by the prior or adjudged in his court. A man's life was worth far more than stolen plate or silver pennies—how could he possibly equate them? And yet Kailey's stomach churned in anger, with a need for satisfaction. These men had left Rigney to die, had defiled the Templars, and would have cheated Abbot Wingate of the son he had fought so hard to love.

She didn't understand the law or the men who lived outside it. But just now there was enough outrage in her heart to turn her back on the cowardly thieves and let justice be done.

Chapter 21

❧

Kailey was sleeping when Simon found her, bare-shouldered and innocent, so very fragile among the pillows and bolsters. Gone was the impetuous woman who had thrown herself at the center of his inquest, who had scouted for him and chased after his thieves, outmanned his sergeants. And, God shield her, she'd threatened a murderer with only a spoon handle to protect her.

She was always running a league ahead of him, granting indulgences to everyone in her path. She had protested the execution—the dense shadow of her father's life that dangled between them—but she had done his will, had taken Clyde's wife and the niece from the scene.

Ten minutes later the thieves were swinging heavily from the crossbeams of the tithe barn, their bodies gone still, their souls gone to hell—where he would meet them one day. He'd gotten little information from them in the meantime: word of a ransom note overheard in the hostelry; the well-timed death of Brother Kenward; commissioning the boy, Rigney, to carry the Templar's robe to Chester when he delivered the note; playing cat-and-mouse with the demand for money.

A grand conspiracy, and all for naught. He had

ordered the bodies cut down, had dispersed the crowd and the cowl-bent monks. Then when all was quiet, he'd found the nearest corner and disgorged his guts, a private indignity that he had never outgrown. He had sweated and suffered his way through every hanging since Hewett's, each one more raw than the one before.

And so it was finished. Wingate's ransom was tucked safely into his saddlebags, ready for the morning's journey back to Chester, where he would see it delivered under heavy guard to those who held Nicholas hostage. Guillaume's cloister was safe from its thieving bailiff and from a hosteler who preyed upon his guests.

He had cleansed his mouth with a willow brush and a cup of wine, and then he'd come here where the air was perfumed.

The world was a wicked place and his wife was too trusting. He would take her home when this judicial circuit was done—home to Northumberland, an isolated, mist-shrouded heathland that needed her sunlight.

And yet, with the door closed against a threatening world he was vastly content in this garret room, because his heart was here, tucked into his bed. He was home.

His eyes gone damp, he bent to her, touched his lips to her hair and then his fingers to her cheek.

"My love," he whispered.

She made a kitteny noise in her throat, yawned in her sleep, and rubbed her nose, then wrapped her slender fingers around one of his. His heart ran riot, dragged him to his knees and a growling sob to his chest.

Ah, love. Sweet love. The innocence of her touch caused the room to shimmer with a memory so real he could smell the frost of the bailey across twenty years.

Her hand had been so tiny then, no more than the length of his thumb, so remarkably strong and warm, still wrinkled from her birthing. And so very unsubtle when she gripped the end of his finger with the whole of her hand and tugged at him, tugged at his fourteen-year-old heart.

He hadn't known who she was at the time, so small and swaddled in rich green velvet, sheltered against her mother's breast. He'd never seen eyes the color of cornflowers, nor a gaze so filled with earnest wonder. He hadn't meant to linger, had only paused in his eager stride to smooth his knuckle along her downy cheek, stayed long enough to coax a smile from her rose-wrinkled mouth before he had disengaged her hand from his finger and left to find his father in the bailey, so impatient to watch his first hanging—to prove himself a man.

To watch her father hang.

He swallowed back the bile in his throat and looked down on his precious wife, at the white moonlight that had paled the curling sprigs of her hair to the fine gloss of a newborn's. He had lost his heart to her on that frosty morn, had become her champion, battled all the dragons of hell for her.

And if ever this deception went wrong, if the truth ever rose out of the grave to accuse him, he would find the means to see a portion of her fortune restored.

Hewett's lands had been long ago tossed to the ravaging pack and were now entailed so tightly to other men with grander titles that a declaration of Hewett's innocence, an exposure of the conspiracy against him, would gain his penniless daughter nothing. Simon would merely go to the gallows, and she would slip from his protection.

Perhaps it was time he acquired a parcel of her father's forfeited estate, to hold in trust to her against the unthinkable. A small manor and its rents; it wouldn't be much, but it would keep her and her family if his crime was ever uncovered.

But he loved her selfishly and would keep her while he could. He threw off his clothes and donned a light robe, went to the low window, and opened the shutter wide. Cool air poured in over the sill, carrying the ripe golden scents of the harvest. He took a long breath and let it scrub the dankness from his veins.

"So it's done, Simon?" She had come to stand behind him, rubbed her cheek against his arm, snuggled his bent elbow between her bare breasts.

"Aye." She was silent and he wanted to explain the inexplicable. "They were predators, love; they soon would have found others to violate."

"I know. An evil that touched so many lives. Still, it's hard to accept. So abrupt. Clyde's wife begged me to let her go to him—she wanted to hold him one more time." Kailey was weeping softly, dampening a patch on his sleeve. "But I couldn't. I knew what she'd find."

A vast barn, grain-dusted and heavy timbered, the thick oaken breastsummer creaking in rhythm with its two extra burdens. "She would have come upon a grisly sight."

" 'Tis why I held her back, and why we wept together with Jemma. And all the while, I couldn't help but think of . . ."

Had he frightened her so that she couldn't speak of her own father?

"You thought of your father," he said for her.

"Yes. And my mother." She slipped her hand into his, that precious and perfect fit forged between them so long ago. "I wondered if someone had kept her from running after my father, or if she had kissed him good-bye at the last. If their private words had been sweet and soft and forgiving, if she held him closely? Oh, Simon—"

"I don't know that, Kailey." Simon filled his aching arms with her softness, touched his kiss to her salty mouth, his heart on fire with guilt for this love that he had purloined.

"I can't even imagine my mother's pain—to know that my father was to die as soon as she let go of him! Leaving his arms for the last time, holding fast to his hands as they released hers, that final glancing spark from his fingertips." Candleborne glints gathered in her lashes. "I couldn't. I couldn't lose you that way."

He felt as if he were standing on a gallows trap, and Kailey was a ghost come to taunt him with her goodness. "I should have come to you sooner, love." Two-edged words, poised on a blade. "I didn't mean for you to suffer."

"Nay, husband." She was shaking her head, stroking her fingers through the hair at his temples, trying to smile through her tears. "You had your awful business to do. I understand. I told Jemma about Rigney, how we'd found him; she'll go to him in a day or two, when she's seen that her aunt is taken care of. Abbot Wingate stayed beside us and prayed. He's been such a great comfort. And he . . ."

She touched her forehead to his neck, gathering courage, it seemed. Simon raised her chin with his finger but couldn't coax her gaze from his mouth.

"And what else?" he asked.

She took a deep breath that caught before she spoke. "My father is buried at Eveside Church. My mother, too." She raised her eyes then, wary of him. "Father Abbot says that it's nearby."

"It is." Now she knew he'd kept this from her, too.

"Abbot Wingate said he'd take me there tomorrow, on our way home."

Neville Hewett had ever been a restless ghost, had lurked equally in the bright places and the dark. He had leaned over Simon's law books, breathed down his neck as he learned the fine art of the sword, coached him in his dealings with the king. He'd never feared Hewett's spirit, but he did fear the man's daughter. Feared most of all that he would lose her.

But Eveside was just a graveyard, not an unlocked coffer stuffed with secrets. A visit only. To honor her father, to touch her mother.

And then he would carry her home to Northumberland.

Home.

"I will take you Eveside myself, wife."

And then they would start anew.

"Would you, Simon?"

"Of course." *But that is the last of it, my love. To give you more would be to lose you.*

"I thank you, husband." She bit her lower lip. "But only in a companionable sense." There was too much irony in her voice. "No more than if you'd brought me peas from the market."

He couldn't help his smile as she blithely opened the front of his robe, fit herself against him and laced her arms around his waist. He was flagrantly hard against her belly, naked in his need for her.

"I remember that particular thank you, wife. I approved, if I recall."

"And this?" Her hair was a loose and clingy curtain, and her mouth a roving wonder across his shoulder, trailing fire and ice.

"Yes, absolutely." Her fingertips set flecks of lightning at his hips and streaked the front of his thighs, hardening him to steel, drawing a sizzling sigh through his teeth.

"I've kept my promise, Simon." Her lips brushed at his stomach.

"Your—" His breath caught in his throat.

"Until now." She touched a chaste kiss to the tip of his staff. "Until this," she whispered.

"Kailey!" Her mouth was slick and dizzying, made him catch at his own hips to keep from falling backward. "God's bells, woman!"

Then she was nibbling him between her teeth and tongue, fluting him with her fingers, breathing her magic, until he had no breath at all, and his skin was aflame.

"Enough!" Ready to burst and needing most of all to bury himself inside her, Simon grasped her by the wrists and kissed each palm. "Another time, wife, when I am not so fierce for you."

"A wake-up kiss, perhaps?"

He could manage only a groan before he straddled her thighs and carried her back gently to the bare floor. "You have me overripe."

"And sweating, husband." She was waiting for him and ready, as damp as the dew on a buttercup. Her fingers found him and pressed him home with the rise of her hips. He filled her fully, gloved himself inside her.

And prayed for children, lots of them.

And forgiveness.

"God, I love you, Kailey."

Her smile was earthy and wise. "I know, Simon. I've known all along. Forever, in fact."

"Aye, love. Forever more."

Kailey felt guiltily exuberant as she left Kelstowe. The dour-faced monks had buried the two thieves at dawn, somewhere distant from the churchyard, and Jemma's Aunt Aldyth had stayed weeping in her bed, leaving Jemma to comfort the woman and keep the hostelry by herself.

"I'll fetch my Rigney and bring him back here, my lady, as soon as I can get away," Jemma had said, holding fervently to Kailey's hand. "I'll heal him, and marry him, and then he and I will run the inn for my aunt."

"They are lucky to have you, Jemma. I promise to give Rigney special care when I return to Chester. God's peace to you!"

Kailey left the girl with a quick embrace and hurried to join Simon in the forecourt. He seemed pensive and deliberate in his movements, listening to the sky, as though he anticipated some far away thunder. She loved him everlastingly, as the earth loves the rain. He smiled resolutely when he saw her, and held out his hand, dark-gloved and steadfast.

"To Eveside, wife?"

Kailey was breathless to gather up this lost family of hers. Though blemished and blighted, they were hers, just as Simon was. She found it impossible to hide her joy, even from her husband. She only wished that she could share it with him.

"Aye, my lord."

Eveside.

Simon gave her the lead for most of the journey,

his mood silent and oddly indulgent, given her near-blithering gladness. And always his gaze lingered fondly on her, as close and ever-present as it had once been distant. Kailey tried to slow her pace, but a deep yearning pressed at her shoulder blades, let a cloud of butterflies loose in her chest. Abbot Wingate had tried his best to keep up with her, but Talley stuck to her own mulish gait, falling behind Simon, and the priest had finally taken refuge with Simon's patient guards.

When they at last left the main road for an overgrown track and were descending into the vale of the river Eve, a compelling happiness took hold of her.

She was a pilgrim come home.

And there it was.

"Eveside," she whispered.

Honey-stoned and slate roofed, the little church came into view above the scrub willows that suckled themselves against the grassy banks of the Eve. Not abandoned or lonely as she had feared, just simple and unassuming, and blessedly peaceful.

Her hopes soaring, Kailey glanced back at Simon, wanting to share the sight with him. But his unreadable gaze swept roughly across the sun-drenched hollow, and climbed the hills to the lead-dark heights of a gathering storm that seemed to have risen out of nowhere. His frown deepened with the rolling thunder.

Not just now! Please don't rain! Afraid that Simon would want to be away too quickly, Kailey gave a soft heel to her mare and forded the hoof-shallow stream, followed the stony track up the slope to the north side of the little church.

The cemetery was as humble as the sanctuary, tucked up against the eastern transept and bounded by a low stone enclosure, blunted by time and softened by colorful, clinging lichens. Starlings and wrens dithered overhead in the canopy of ancient oak and hornbeam as Father Abbot and the soldiers traversed beneath. Woodland scents rode the breezes, sharp and loamy. She could smell and hear the lyric rilling of the stream as it tumbled over its shallows.

Paradise.

"Simon, it's beautiful here." She dropped from the saddle and into the circle of her husband's stalwart arms.

"We're about to be rained on, wife." He'd caught her waist with both of his marvelous hands, seemed reluctant to let her go.

"I won't be long." She kissed him just below the corner of his mouth, wanting dearly to thank him for bringing her to this place, but knowing he would object.

"Do as you need to do, my love." He offered a brief smile, but it seemed to cost him.

Feeling as though he was stepping out of her life, she caught up his hand in a near panic. It was cold and trembled slightly. "Will you come, Simon?"

He shook his head kindly and kissed her fingertips even as he deliberately slipped his hand from hers.

"This is your time, love. See to your family. I'll give a look round the church."

He left her with his deep and unflagging stride, left his scent of woodsmoke and leather. She was ever asking too much of him. And yet each time he had granted her more. Today it was majestic old trees and scampering squirrels, and the rich scents of a sparkling afternoon that would always remind her of her father and her mother.

Aye, today he had granted Kailey her heart's peace. She would spend the rest of her days granting the same to him.

Abbot Wingate was inspecting the short cemetery wall, muttering to himself as he picked at bits of loose mortar. "Mmm, I'll have to report to Brother Claude that Eveside needs some careful attention."

"Perhaps I can return here with a planting of flowers before the court moves to Nottingham." Kailey was already through the gate and leaning over the wall where the abbot was wedging a fallen stone back into its niche. "Sweet woodruff would thrive here in the shade, don't you think? And bluebell."

Wingate straightened and swabbed a splotch of rain off his forehead with his sleeve. He studied her with a sigh that seemed too heavy for all this beauty. "First, let's see to your obligations, child."

Kailey waited for him to join her inside the enclosure, quashing the urge to race along the uneven rows of monuments. She felt as giddy as if she were a child at a fair, and these were food stalls instead of gravemarkers, and her parents were strolling through the crowd somewhere, waiting for her to find them so they could take her hand.

Haunted, made-up joys. But they would have to do.

Kailey trailed impatiently behind Abbot Wingate as he read the names in his steady voice. There was not a single freshly carved marker, and too many whose letters and loving ornament had been damaged by the rain and the tattering wind of the years.

She read each stone as Wingate did, worried suddenly that she wouldn't find the pair she was looking for—that her parents had lost her, had left without her. Nay, but they were here somewhere—

And then her heart came free of its moorings.

Margaret Hewett. Pax cordis. 1155.

The simplest of pale-yellow stone, and so beautiful.

" 'Heart's peace.' " Kailey had to whisper past the tears that clogged her throat and spilled down her cheeks. She was a child again, wanting to fold herself into her mother's embrace because the yearning hurt so deeply and she didn't understand. But her arms ached with emptiness, and she could only fall to her knees and spread her fingers across the cold stone. "Dear Mama, how I missed you."

The mossy ground was damp from an earlier shower and the rain soaked into Kailey's skirts. She welcomed the coolness against her knees and found comfort in tracing the sandy roughness of the carefully worked letters.

And as her terrible grief became wonder, Kailey found peace on the soft, sleepy bosom of land, with the wind soughing like a bedtime song through the trees.

Abbot Wingate helped her with a prayer, then let her babble to her mother about a flop-eared dog that she'd raised from a pup, and how she hated, *hated* sewing. She sang her favorite chanson—about a badger and a clever bee, recited how much she loved and admired the magnificent man she'd married.

And in the midst of telling her mother exactly how angry Simon had been when he'd discovered she'd changed places with one of his prisoners, fat raindrops began to fall.

"Come, child." Father Wingate put his hand on her shoulder.

"But I have so much more to tell her." Kailey wiped at her tears, dazed by a tender journey she hadn't meant to take. She touched a kiss to her hand and then to her mother's stone, and made promises to return.

Father Abbot was right: there was another grave to find before this summer-quick storm struck the valley. She had expected her father's to be close by, and she suffered a rolling wave of doubt not to see it here.

"Shouldn't they have been buried nearby each other?" It was the sustaining image she'd carried of her parents through all of her life, an even stronger image lately: resting side-by-side in a place as beautiful as Eveside.

But Father Wingate was leading her ever farther away from her mother, checking each marker as he moved among the rows. He turned to her when he reached the gate.

"I was hoping for better tidings, Kailey."

"Better? You mean he isn't here?"

The abbot had folded his hands into his sleeves, a gesture so monkish and so unlike him that Kailey began to fear in earnest that her father wasn't at Eveside after all.

She shook off the notion. The pipe rolls had said clearly that he was here. And the pipe rolls were the record of the unchangeable truth.

"Come follow me, my girl." He led her away from the cemetery, away from the church, toward a stand of giant gray-skinned beech trees.

Here were other gravemarkers resting in the heavy shade, and barren places where some stones had been removed. Lesser monuments, all of them: unadorned blocks, some merely misshapen boulders with crudely carved letters, or no name at all.

Lonely, forgotten souls.

"What is this place, Father?"

His eyes were sad and damp when he raised them from the landscape.

"Unconsecrated ground."

The whole of the world came to a standstill in that dark moment, the breeze and the birds. This was an unsanctified site, left for those who had died outside the sacraments, without confession, without absolution.

Abandoned by God.

"My father isn't here!" Outrage and horror crowded against Kailey's heart, made it difficult to breathe. "How dare you think that? He is in heaven with my mother."

Wingate's expression was aggrieved and acquitting.

"May we look for him, my child?"

"My father isn't here!" To prove the truth of it, Kailey walked blindly among the disorienting stones, reading off names and dates, not seeing anything clearly beyond the shadows. She stumbled over fallen branches and drifts of leaves. Her father was not among these neglected stones.

Browned bracken and last year's twisted berry canes clawed at the boundaries of the tract, had nearly smothered the largest of the markers.

It stood alone, a dozen yards from the others.

It was honey-colored, like her mother's, and as she approached the bramble-veiled stone, she could read the name perfectly. And it tore at her heart.

Neville Hewett.

Kailey caught back the frenzied sob in her throat.

"I am sorry, child."

The abbot's words were kind but meaningless.

She shrugged his hand off her shoulder.

"This is a villainous error! A blasphemy! And I will not suffer it!" Kailey dropped to her knees because they would not hold her, heard a strange keening sound and knew it had come from her throat. How dare they put her father so far from her mother, out here and alone, where the castings of worms would be his only hope of resurrection!

"Please, Kailey." The priest was on his knees beside her. "Your father died on the gallows—"

"That doesn't make him unredeemable," she cried out to the bleak sky.

"No. But he would have been denied the sacraments before he was executed."

"God does not abandon His children, not even the worst of them. Not my father!" Kailey yanked at the brambles, gasping at the biting sting as thorns dug into her fingers and sliced at her sleeves, sick to her stomach that they should embrace her father so fondly when she could not—when her arms had always been so empty.

"Stop now, Kailey." The abbot's voice was harsh, as cutting as the pain in her fingers. "You'll hurt yourself. Stop."

"No! Leave me, priest!" Kailey fought the stronger hands that tried to keep her away. "My father needs air and light! He needs *me!*"

"Not this way." No matter that she fought with every ounce of strength, Wingate dragged her by the waist from her father's hideous grave and into the rugged path where the gravel scraped at her knees.

"Please, let me go to my father!"

"Calm yourself, sweet child!" He took hold of her fists and clamped them together in front of her.

"You'll do no good to your father acting like a heathen."

"But that's what you think he was: an unredeemable heathen." Kailey's throat was raw with her sobbing. "He wasn't!"

"I didn't know your father, Kailey, but I live in the certainty that God Almighty knew his heart."

"I only want him to lie at peace near my mother. Just over there! 'Tis not far." She could hardly see him for her tears. Why didn't he understand? "I want my family to be together!"

"And I want to help you."

Nay, but this was just a priestly trick to distract her. She struggled to be away from him.

"There is great hope for him, Kailey."

"How? He is twenty years in hell, because no one cared to heal his soul. Why should you care now? What can you do?"

"Not me, child. You." He held both her hands between his, binding her prayers inside her own fists when she wanted to loose them for her father. "You have a great capacity for love, for absolution. 'Tis yours to give him. Yours."

Kailey stopped twisting then, grasping for this thread of hope that her father would find his peace beside her mother.

"Tell me how," she demanded. "Anything!"

He looked suddenly hesitant. "There will be a penance prescribed for the weight of the sin, masses said, a vigil here at his grave to commend his soul—"

"Then I will do it. Show me how."

He shook his head, grasped her shoulder. "Not just yet, child. I need to consult with the bishop—"

"My father's torment is everlasting. I will begin

my vigil now, Wingate; not tomorrow, or come St. Michael's Day."

The abbot looked as though he would argue, but then he nodded and let go her hands. "I will tell your husband that I shall stay with you."

Numb, yet sobbing still, Kailey watched Wingate skirt the dismal cemetery and disappear beyond the beeches. Surely Simon would understand that her father needed her now more than ever, that all she had left to give him was her love, her devotion.

Yet even as she thought it, she knew her husband wouldn't understand at all.

Chapter 22

⌒⌒⌒

Simon felt the private interdiction of his soul as strongly as though God's own heavy hand pressed against his chest. He rose from his outlawed prayers, certain that each of his sins had gone to live in his joints.

"You have cursed me well through the years, Neville Hewett," he said to the sun-smote mist that hung in the chapel vaulting. "And now you curse me still with this unheralded happiness, this false contentment—when I was so very good at loving her in my own way, from a distance."

The wind had risen, clattering leaves through the open doors of the transept. The rain would come any moment now, trapping them in the church for a time if his wife didn't hurry.

He'd seen her on her knees in the churchyard, her pale brown hair caught up by the wind. He was a coward for not standing beside her, for not holding her while she wept. But he couldn't have borne to see her in such pain. She would have her parents now, and then he would take her home.

"I love her more than my life, Hewett. I want children with her—your grandchildren. I want to grow old with her hand in mine. But you must stay away—quiet your soul, and let your daughter be content."

"Lord Simon."

Simon whirled around to find Wingate coming toward him through the church doorway, his dark sleeves flapping like the dusty wings of an errant angel.

"Is she finished?"

"'Tis what I've come to speak with you about." The priest's hands were hidden inside his sleeves, making him look far more clerical than judicial, unfamiliar somehow.

"Does she need more time?" Already it was closer to evening than to the afternoon, and Simon could see the lances of rain streaking through the low-slung rays of the nearly setting sun. She would be drenched soon if she didn't come inside.

"Aye, she does need more time, Simon, and I will stay with her."

"*You* will stay?" A fanciful notion: that Simon would leave Kailey behind. He nearly laughed. "What are you saying, Wingate? If she needs more time, we will wait."

But Wingate was shaking his head. The man was windblown, his robes flecked with bits of leaf and twig. "She will stand a vigil tonight. She wishes to begin her penance on behalf of her father's soul."

"What penance?" The question was sharp enough to sound like a hiss. "The man is long dead, Wingate."

"This vigil is for her comfort, Simon. And for her father's soul."

"Penance be damned. Where is she?" Simon started away from the altar, but Wingate caught his sleeve and held him with a remarkable strength.

"Leave her be, Simon. I'll watch over her."

The priest had gone mad. "You will not. I have watched over her, been her guardian since she was a babe; I don't intend to quit until I draw my last breath. What nonsense have you put into her head about a penance?"

Wingate's aged-mellowed eyes grew flinty. "I'll not have you speak that way in God's house, Simon."

"Then tell me what you mean. The man is well buried these twenty years. Why now?"

Wingate stepped in front of the altar, crossed himself, and then spoke in a hushed tone.

"Surely you realize that before Neville Hewett was executed, he was denied the sacraments."

Nay, Simon hadn't realized that; hadn't wanted to know what had happened. Another breach, another brink. "Was he?"

"Aye, and now his grave lies in unconsecrated ground."

This was a game of profits played by clerics, and Simon would play it gladly for Kailey. "Then consecrate it, Wingate."

"Simon, you know I cannot. It's not that simple. It means a trial before bishops, a request from Rome."

A trial. And the truth. No.

"Tell me what you want, priest, and I will buy it for your abbey. A new tower, a chapel?"

Wingate's priestly posture straightened. "This is a spiritual matter, Simon: between your wife and her father, and the God who judges the hearts of men."

A penance for Neville Hewett? For a man whose innocent heart was already known to God? "No. I forbid it."

"Husband, please!"

She was standing in the chapel doorway, a quavering silhouette, the opalescent blue of her kirtle caught in the gray wind of the coming storm.

"Please, Simon. He's my father, and he lies in defiled ground." Her voice wavered, the wail of sorrow and the shame of loving too much. "I want him at peace. I want him to abide with my mother. I must stay the night at my father's grave."

"Kailey, please." She didn't know what she was asking. Penance wasn't necessary. God had seen Hewett's heart, as he had seen Simon's own.

"They were buried apart, Simon." She left the light of the doorway, and the storm blew its darkness and a forest of leaves across the churchyard beyond.

His heart stopped as she reached out for him. Her hands were bloodied, as though she'd been scourging herself. He grasped them with his own and stared down at the abomination.

"Christ God! What is this, Kailey? What have you done to yourself?"

"He's covered in brambles and thorns, Simon." Her eyes were soggy with disbelief, her hands sticky with her own blood. "I tried to clear them."

"With your bare hands? Damn you, Wingate!" Simon shot his anger at the priest, directed the loathing at himself. "Did you think this a way to punish her?"

Wingate bristled, and Simon already regretted his outburst. "I pulled her away."

"I want to go back." Now his wife was tugging at him. "Penance for an abandoned soul is not punishment, Simon. 'Tis the greatest love a child can give a parent. And I do love my father—no matter what the world may say."

Penance for an innocent man. Blood on Kailey's hands, when it should be on his own.

"Please, Simon. This one last tribute, and then he will be at rest. So will my mother. I won't ask you again."

Wingate looked at him as though they were strangers. "Your wife will keep vigil at his grave from now until tomorrow at dawn."

"No," he said flatly.

"Later there will be fasts and intercessory prayers—"

"I said no, Wingate." How could he make them believe that he wanted only the best for her, and only honor for her father? He couldn't stand by and let Kailey take this punishment, not when it belong to him. "We leave for Chester immediately."

She gasped and cried out when he took her by the wrist, plucked at his fingers as he strode with her toward the door.

"Let me go to him, Simon!" She fought him madly, freed herself with a wrenching twist that must have burned her flesh. She backed away from him in all her wildness, tears and rain mixing with the crimson of her blood.

"Kailey, stop this—"

"He is my father. And he rests too far from my mother." The yearning madness of grief was in her eyes. "I will have them together in heaven as I could not have them on earth. Don't you understand? They are my family! I love them as surely as I love you."

She swung away from him and left him at a run, her skirts flying out behind her as she rounded the churchyard wall.

Her family—it had always been that, would ever

be. He had tried his best to atone for all the casualties of her life. He'd opened his coffers and allowed her every portion of his wealth; he had taken care of those who clung to her, had even tried to be a family to her.

But in the end he had betrayed her as surely as he had in the beginning. Allowed her to take him into her family, a reformed fox invited to live among the chickens. He had craved her love and had taken it falsely, just as his father had done. And now she would damn him for it—for the lies, for the deceptions, for stealing away her father and damning him to hell.

Her penance would be an obscenity to God, to a father who had done no wrong.

"Take yourself from here, Wingate," Simon snapped, as he watched his wife's iridescent shadow take flight through the misty rain. "Leave now with my men and return to Chester. Tell them this is my order."

"No, Simon." Wingate's hand was a vise around Simon's arm—the vestige of an old knight's crusade against the infidels. "You can order your men to your bidding, but not me. I am your wife's confessor."

"And I am her husband!" Simon watched as she passed through the glassy rays that pierced the clouds and stabbed into the earth, fearing she would be taken up and out of his reach. "She will have her father's soul at peace before the night is through. I will see to it."

"Simon, you know nothing of these matters—"

"Christ, Wingate." Simon whirled on the man, shrugged off his grasp. "She is my life—the very reason I breathe. And if it's her father she wants so badly, then I will give him back to her."

"How? What are you saying?"

A musty, unvoiced confession balanced on Simon's tongue, but it was hers to hear first, not Wingate's. "She will have her penance, Wingate. Let God be my witness."

Wingate's chest rose and fell with this unfamiliar anger that raged between them, their friendship on the brink. He nodded finally.

"Very well, Simon. I put a father's trust in you, for I do love the girl as I love you. God's speed." He left abruptly, his stubbornly protective shoulders slumped now, his cowl too heavy.

Aye, and the man was lodged quite stubbornly in Simon's heart, and that place was tattered and aching now as he left the church steps to find his wife and her father.

She was on her knees in the farthest reaches of the desolate tract. The plot of unconsecrated earth was dark and overhung with ancient beech trees, their great trunks bent as though they would rip their roots from the earth and wander down the valley.

A blighted place for Hewett's grave. Never once in all the years had he imagined that it lay in unholy ground.

Nor had he imagined that he could love so deeply, so completely. She was the part of him he'd always left unguarded, because no one else knew. His secret love, the bright angel who had carried him through his life. But angels never followed where he was bound.

"Your father was a good man, Kailey," Simon whispered, as he slipped to his knees behind her. He caught her hips between his thighs and held her against his chest, dragging every one of her shuddering sobs into his lungs, where his own penance for this man had begun to burn.

"But this is a grave for wicked, unredeemable men. My father wasn't wicked." She laced her fingers through his across her belly, and he wondered if a child quickened there, if his seed had taken root and if she would tell the babe that he had loved her.

Simon swallowed hard against the coming emptiness. "This is not your sin, Kailey, not your penance. I will make it right."

"But you can't, Simon. He was *my* father." She tried to reach out for the brambles, but he couldn't let her bloody her hands on any more thorns. He stood with her and turned her in his arms, haunted already by the despair he would find in her eyes.

"Kailey, listen to me."

"Why do you stop me, Simon? I want only to keep a night's vigil, to pray for him." Her tears were frightful and scalding. "It isn't fair that he is here. It isn't fair!"

"No, it isn't." His soul was lost, his heart drained. The back of his tongue was sticky with salt. "If there is a God, Kailey, if He truly sees the hearts of men who stand before His judgment, then your father already sits at His holy table."

"No! He died without sacrament! He lies here in unconsecrated earth, his soul damned unless I save it." She offered her forgiveness so freely to a father whom she thought had transgressed against the world and betrayed a little girl's hopes. There would be no such room in her heart for him.

"You've got it wrong, my love." He took another staggering breath, inhaled her lavender, and memorized its far-flung sweetness, for it would be gone with her sunlight in the next moment—gone with the stolen grace he felt as her water-soft eyes lit upon his mouth, as though she would trace his next words.

"Neville Hewett was murdered on the gallows," he said calmly, though his pulse surged like a storm tide, braking hard against his chest.

"What?" It was barely a sound, yet it struck him down.

"Your father was not a traitor to his king, my love."

Rain fell in spikes between them as he waited for outrage to spark in her eyes, relived the months and the years of his dread—years of loving her and longing for better endings.

But she was shaking her head, disbelieving and angry for it. "Why are you doing this to me, Simon?" she asked, too quietly. "I only want my father to find his peace. Will you give me that, Simon? Will you?"

Peace. *Oh, my love.*

He could keep silent now and she would stay beside him forever, his gift from God. He could let her fall to her knees at her father's grave and pray her way to the dawn. He could take her north then, give her children, and dance with her at Christmastide. His heart had stopped cold, suspended by his shame, by the impossible burden of justice.

He loved her. He had lived for her, would die for her as ordained so long ago.

"He'll have no rest this way, Kailey. Not for the stain of these ancient sins against him—against you, your family. 'Tis time, love, long past time."

Kailey heard a muffled roaring in her ears, a terrible, dark-smudged murmuring that told her to stop her wondering and silence this extraordinary husband of hers. He spoke in riddles that dazed her with foreboding; he smelled of altar smoke and the crackling storm that was building beyond the sheltering breadth of his shoulders. And she loved him for bringing her here to see her father, loved him for his wayward attempts to protect her from her father's thorns.

"You need to hear me out, Kailey." His voice was as intimate as their night whispers, and yet echoed off the distant hills and thundered lonely inside her chest.

"I am listening, husband," she whispered, suddenly frightened to her soul.

His smile seemed bruised and tender; he touched her cheek with a melancholy brush of his knuckles.

"My love, I give him back to you. Your father," he said, his breath coming tightly, the light in his eyes vanquished and strew with tears. "He was King Stephen's liege man, a powerful baron, loved and trusted, and so he fell hard to the lies that damned him."

"What are you saying, Simon?" She felt as though he was spinning a story for her, a parable of light and darkness that could only end in anguish.

"Others coveted Hewett's estates, and so they conspired and betrayed him, brought their falsehoods to the court and let your father hang."

Her tears came fresh, tasted sweet and tangy with hope. Her chest filled with a shout of joy, but she held it back. She wanted to believe that her father was innocent, that his soul wasn't damned and unredeemable, but feared it couldn't be so.

"Don't torment me with your kindness, Simon. Not this way. I couldn't bear it." Yet to doubt her husband seemed a blasphemy. He'd never lied to her; he was her measure of righteousness, as constant as the sea.

"No more lies between us, Kailey."

"Then my father was innocent! Oh, Simon!" She caught up Simon's hand, kissed his wrist and tugged on him. "Come then, we must tell someone—"

"Listen to me, love!" He yanked her against him, cradled the back of her head, and smoothed his hot mouth against her temple. "Your father was murdered! Do you understand that?" His voice was low and draped in awful mourning; his powerful arms quaked and made her tremble with their violence. "He was murdered in cold blood. He never had a chance."

"But he does now! Please, help me, Simon!"

He cursed and turned from her, setting her away as if she were plague-ridden.

"My God, woman, you make this difficult."

"I care only that my father was wrongly buried here. And that we can make it right." Yet there was something darkly harrowing about her joy, something that made her heart sag, made tears clog her throat. The truth was always costly, she knew that now. She'd known for years. There was a price.

And then the roaring came again, louder this time, Simon's disjointed tale knotting itself around her bliss, hobbling all her hopes.

These men—the ones who had betrayed her father, who had caused his death—they had brought their false testimony to the court. To give before the king.

The pipe rolls.

"No, Simon! You've got it wrong. That wasn't how it happened!" She didn't want to breathe, for the air had become thick and dangerous, and put incomprehensible pictures in her head. "I read the pipe rolls—the truth, sworn before God and carefully scribed, kept safe in those iron-bound boxes."

"Nothing but parchment and ink, Kailey."

"The truth told by honorable men."

"And twisted shapeless by those who are profane."

"Not Lord Telford!" Not the man who had been the first of her fathers. Impossible! "And Fitz-Landry?" He'd taught her Latin.

Then a brittle jab of fear splintered in her chest, made it hurt to swallow.

"No, Simon—Not Sir Robert! He loved me. He wouldn't!"

"You didn't know him, Kailey."

"I knew his heart; I knew his goodness. Sir Robert would *never* have betrayed anyone, let alone my father. You were there in the court, Simon! You testified yourself—knew the truth. You'd have known if the others had—" Her heart faltered and the world began to tilt.

"Oh, God, Simon—" Her terror caught in her throat with a naked cry.

He was tall and distant, cloaked in the blue-black of the storm, his jaw tight and working, his eyes hooded against her.

"Simon?" she asked in a tremulous whisper, "were you one of them? Did you know?"

Kailey held her breath and waited for his answer—would have waited till the stars burned cold and winked away, just to hear his denial.

"I knew, my love."

"*Nooo!*" She shoved at him and turned away, looking for something to hate besides the man who had claimed her love with such devilish devotion. Everywhere she looked she found desolation, the hulking gray beeches and the storm-shattered ground, the dry cross-hatching of canes and thorns that still barred her from her father.

What blasphemy they had practiced! Lord Telford's generosity; FitzLandry's attention to her studies; and, oh, God, Sir Robert! Her life had been a tangled skein of lies, made all the more beguiling because she had believed that they had loved her as she loved them. And all the while they had conspired to keep her from her father.

As Simon had conspired to love her.

"Damn you, Simon!" She swung round on him and grabbed his dagger from its sheath.

"Christ, Kailey, don't!" He reached for her hand and the dagger, but she thrust the blade between them sharply.

"You killed him, my lord, and you left him to this thorny grave."

His fingers were cold and stony around hers, his eyes half-mad. "Then let me—"

"No!" She shoved at him again and scrambled away, shaking herself of his webs. "I will clear his grave myself, and then I will stay the night and keep my faith with him."

"You needn't, madam." He stood away from her, an utter stranger. "This damnable vigil and this penance and all your prayers aren't necessary."

"Are you so arrogant that you think it matters to God? You of all people should understand the rigors of the law. Whether my father died of wounds in battle, or in his sleep, or on the gallows, he died without benefit of the sacraments. He needs me to free his soul, not you. Not anyone else. Or will you steal this peace from him as well?"

She saw him flinch, saw the pain in his eyes, and

a sob rolled up into her throat. But her anger and outrage were bits of nothing compared to the emptiness that overwhelmed her when he dropped his gauntlets at her feet.

The leather still held the shape of his able fingers, the doeskin cup of his palm. She loved his hands: fevered and wrapped in his fury round the iron bars of Julia's cell, the gentle passion of his touch as he breathed fire against her breast. As he loved her.

But he couldn't have loved her at all, not past the lies and the treachery, no matter this graveyard confession. This marriage had served him, and now it was done.

"Go away, sir. I don't need you here."

She deafened herself to the sound of him, and labored hard on her father's grave as the rain fell through the boughs of beech and landed in great splashes on her hands and on the ground. She threw aside the brambles as she cut them, and cleaned off the stone marker with her bare hands, trying not to think beyond the moment.

Nothing else mattered: not Simon, or lost children; not the sins that had brought them here, or the falsehoods that she had suckled as a babe.

The past was dead, and the future beyond her imagining.

Pax cordis, Papa. I love you.

And as darkness fell the rain came harder, rising up on the cutting wind and bringing the autumn with it, scraping yellow leaves from the branches and scattering them across the bleak landscape.

Kailey offered her prayers, but her father's voice had gone oddly silent here outside the churchyard, as though his spirit feared the place and wanted free.

And so she kept her vigil beside his grave, though she was cold and wet through to the bone, and so very weary. She knew Simon was nearby, heard his footfalls in the gravel, but slipped him from her thoughts, out of reach, out of her life.

But sometime during the impenetrable night, when the storm was seething at its wildest, and her prayers had begun to blend with her dreams, the battering rain halted abruptly and the wind took on a breath that whispered close against her ear. A softly embracing warmth had encircled her like a cocoon, asking nothing from her, giving only its heat.

Her shadow guardian. He'd come again, familiar and secure, flooding her with the unwelcome kindness of a man she didn't know.

"Please, go," she whispered, when she found her voice.

The warmth left her then.

And the storm came again in all its hellish fury, raging well into the night, until the dawn began to pink the sky and the birds sang out the day as though nothing in the world had changed.

Kailey was sore to the depths of her soul, and her heart turned inside out. When she rose from her knees, she found her husband standing a dozen feet behind her.

His mouth was grim and his eyes well shuttered against her. His cloak and hair were drenched; his dagger now hung gleaming on his belt.

What manner of man was he, bound tightly in his laws, wearing his venal truth and his change-able honor like a shield handed down to him from the angels of justice? He held up his code of morals as a strict standard for others, though his hands were bloodied with the lives of innocent men.

He had deceived her completely, this man who had married her out of guilt. It had felt so much like love. He had been home to her, and family. And now he was nothing.

The ride to Chester was unbearable and silent, and Kailey welcomed the emptiness. The city was nearly drained of its earlier vigor, the market stalls closed up and the court in its last hours, ready to move on to Nottingham in the morning.

Her husband saw her to the forecourt of Crookston Hall, and left her there without a word.

Because there were none left to be said between them.

Chapter 23

The court was already in session when Simon arrived. The great hall was less crowded now on the last day of the session, the rarefied psalm of truth a coarse echo of itself as the pleas for mercy and justice rang out in the near-empty gallery where his wife once sat in judgment of him.

She'd gathered her evidence now, and had passed sentence on him. Her justice had been swift and cruel and pre-ordained.

He tucked away his heart and made his way to the judge's bench, forcing himself to listen to the current petitioner's plea of dowry as he took his seat between Wingate and Cathmore.

Wingate's gaze was gentle and grievously forgiving, yet Simon held off speaking until the plea was finished.

"My wife performed her penance, Wingate, as you imposed."

"My trust in you has never been ill-spent, son."

"Now you must do the rest to see that her father lies in peace. Whatever she asks of you." Simon stared down at the pleas before him, weary of this judicial pretense and wanting to leave the city.

"And you, Simon? What may I do for you?"

Tears swam behind Simon's eyes, unshedable,

but fiery hot and blurring. He shook his head. "There is nothing, Wingate."

"Surely there is, Simon. When we are done here—"

"When we are done, Wingate, you'll have half-dozen of my men at your disposal, armed for travel to the Holy Land if you wish."

The priest reached out and wrapped Simon's wrist in his warm fingers. "How can I thank you, Simon?"

"Find your son. Bring him home. Don't lose him again." Simon swallowed hard against his regrets, and lifted his attention to the elderly woman who was pleading for her portion of her dead husband's estate.

He had waited the length of the journey from Eveside for his wife to call him down for his sins against her. He waited now for her to find him in his court, for her to denounce him as a murderer, as a fraudulent justice who played with laws and lives as others played with chessmen.

But she'd been silent. And in that silence had been his condemnation. Unspeakable and so very precise.

And as distant as the dark sea.

She deserved the life he'd stolen from her, her father's honor restored and land enough to secure her future.

And now he had the means to see it through.

Kailey had spent the day helping Julia with her wagon, rounding up Davie and Hinch and hearing their eager stories, seeing to her own wounds where the thorns had pierced and slashed, and seen to Rigney's—whispering to him how brave his Jemma was, and how much he was loved.

She tried to keep her balance in the bustle of the everyday, but every step she took seemed to land her on more unsettled ground. It had shaken with her father's innocence and made her proud; then that same ground had split wide and opened a chasm between her and Simon that she could never cross.

He'd murdered her father, and then he'd buried the crime in his law books and made her love him for his integrity and his goodness. He was wise and merciful, stood firmly on his principles, and yet he'd been willing to listen when he was wrong. He was an achingly tender lover and a magnificent husband. He'd made Davie his squire, and he'd let Hinch play his blasted horn.

The sour notes and the sweet.

How could the whole of her world have been such a great lie? So carefully, so expertly devised, kept secret for so long?

And if this secret was so well guarded, why did Simon tell her now? He could have let her keep her vigil and be done with it. Another quick lie and she would have been content in her penance, and her father would have gone to his peaceable rest.

And so the ground beneath her feet shifted and rocked, leaving her nowhere to turn, and light-headed with uncertainties.

She was tired to death as she opened the front door to Crookston Hall and stepped into a welling darkness that took its shadows from a bank of candles in the eating hall.

She followed the pale light like a moth.

It was Simon.

He was larger than life and leaning over the table, his broad shoulders hunched and his great hands gripping the back of chair as he studied a page of vellum in the amber light.

She hadn't seen him all day, and yet he'd been a part of everything she had done, every breath she had taken. Her throat ached from tears that had long ago dried up, and she wished as much for her tattered heart. But it still pounded roughly in her breast at the sight of him, too full up with love and loss.

He was justiciar and sheriff again—not husband and lover, but her pulse was caught by the soft murmur of his voice as he read something in the same whisper that had curled so often round her ear and confessed his love in so many ways. The pale flicker of his gentleness—that was all she'd been allowed, but the memories were haunting and dear. All the more wicked for the sweetness of his lies.

She followed his hand as he picked up a quill, then scribed a mark to the bottom of the page.

"Simon—"

He turned his head slightly, far enough for Kailey to see the dark planes and deeply hewn vales that had scored him overnight. His eyes were shadows, and his mouth set in some resolute decision. He turned his back to her then, and dropped the page onto the cluttered table as though he'd resigned something inside of himself.

"You'll find everything in order, madam." He put the wooden cap on the ink horn with an unsteady hand, spilling some of the blackness onto the iron holder and rattling its cache of quills.

"I think nothing is in order, Simon. Nor will it be again."

He ignored her, collecting the scattered vellum into a pile, one half-begun sheet at a time. He was cool, remorseless confidence, presiding over his villainy with his judicial efficiency.

"Damn you, Simon!" Full up with his pretense, she went to the opposite side of the table, putting the glare of the candles between them. "You conspired against an innocent man! What am I left to think? You told your lies and called it the truth. And you let me believe my father a traitor when I should have been celebrating him. And you dare call yourself a keeper of the king's law?"

He looked at her across all the brightness, his eyes gleaming darkly through the flames.

"I am a fraud, my dear wife," he said simply, an accusation thrown back at her in challenge.

"You betrayed a friend!" Her throat ached for his coldness, for all the warmth they had shared and lost.

"Worse, my love. A man that I admired for his honor and his courage."

That made her cheeks go crimson. Her father, so easily dismissed, and he'd called her "love" in the same breath! He was a master at falsehoods.

"Aye, Simon, betrayal takes friendship for granted, doesn't it? Assumes a measure of honesty between the parties involved—"

"And love, Kailey. Don't forget love. The knife pierces deeper then."

"As it pierced me."

He quirked his devilish brow, a rouge's jest turned back on himself in a snarl. "I'd ask your forgiveness, madam, but then again, I'd have better luck asking for the moon."

Kailey found herself wanting him to ask, to beg for it—wanting him to feel the measure of his life hanging in a delicate, deadly balance.

"What would you do with it, Simon?"

"The moon?" He tilted his head, so purposefully distant.

"My forgiveness, damn you!"

The devil's brow softened, kneaded by a tumble of emotions so quick that she couldn't read them.

"I would surely squander it, madam. I won't ask."

That made her angry, and her anger only confused her, pushed her to hear more of his confession.

"What did you gain in this conspiracy?"

"Nothing." He grabbed up the spent pile of vellum, tore it, and then tossed the lot into the cold brazier. "Crime is a capricious employer, wife. De Broase is the only one of us who gained even a penny—'twas an orchard of plums near his castle, I believe."

Kailey remembered the barrels of warm, fleshy plums collected late each summer while she lived with de Broase; she could smell the thickly sweet wine even now, the plum-butter for her bread that she had delighted in—but now the gorge rose in her throat.

"And that's all that was left of him? Plums and pits?"

"Aye. A sad lot, these conspirators. It was Henry's more favored barons who snatched up your father's lands even before his body was cold." Simon seemed calculating in his gestures as he dropped his saddlebag by the door beside his sword, as though he were idly telling his story to a stranger on the street.

"Then my father died for naught? And my mother, too?" Kailey swept around him to face him, her anger finally finding purchase where her heart wouldn't dare. "My family destroyed for the want of a plum orchard?"

"For want of honor, Kailey." He watched her too closely, watched her mouth and fought for an unsteady breath. "There was too little of that in my life."

"But more than enough guilt to last the years?"

"Cauldrons full of it."

"Enough to keep me fed and clothed and schooled."

"Yes, damn it." The words purled out in a hiss.

"Then why tell me now, Simon, after all these years of secrets? Why not let me love you and give you children? You didn't have to marry me."

"Fool that I was, my love, and selfish always in my need for you, I thought I could keep you for myself." His eyes were damp and angry, and her heart inexplicably hurt for him. He hooked her chin roughly with his thumb, brought his mouth close and his words closer. "But then, sweet, I never expected that you would love me for it and make me bleed."

He kissed her then, so tender in his fierceness, the whole of him quaking through his hand as he cradled her throat. She tasted salt and aleberry, and the soap that he shaved with.

"Ah, Kailey." His fingers were laced in her hair and his kiss had become a confession of love, hot words of sorrow and regret, and so hurtful in their longing.

And it all seemed so right and it all seemed so wrong, the world tilted and swirling out of focus. She needed clarity and distance. But before she could plead for a moment of it, Simon stepped backward, taking the air with him, leaving his emptiness between them.

"I'm sorry, love, sorry to my black soul." He swept the back of his hand across his mouth, as though he would rid himself of her taste, lifted his palm toward the table and the guttering candles. "You'll find your father's legacy there."

"What legacy?" He'd answered none of her questions, and now he threw new ones her way.

But he'd apparently finished with her; had picked up his sword by the door.

"It isn't much; a small manor in Lincoln and the rents there. And with those documents,"—he nodded again toward the table—"I've made certain that your claim is rightful and irrefutable if it comes before the court. Until then, you leave for my house in Northumberland on the morrow."

"Why?"

He rasped his sword into his scabbard with a terrible finality and bowed curtly toward her. "By your leave, madam."

Kailey grabbed for his hauberk, caught a handful of leather, dumbfounded at this leave-taking. "Simon, wait—"

He lifted her hand off his chest, brought her fingers to his cool forehead for a moment and then nestled them against his lips. He looked down at her wedding band, and then into her eyes with an anguish that nearly overwhelmed her.

"It was your mother's ring."

Kailey's heart took leave of her chest. "My . . . ?"

"From your father on their wedding day . . . or so I would care to believe, my love." He kissed her fingers once more, and then he left her to the hard clattering of the door on its hinges.

"Simon!" If she hadn't been so abused by her helpless anger, she'd have followed the blackguard to wherever he thought he would sleep tonight. He might very well be a man versed in debate, but he hadn't the slightest idea how to conduct an argument.

Kailey grabbed up the documents he'd left on the table and held them to the light. There were descriptions here of property and rents which had at one time been held by her father—dates, titles, tenants.

And on a second page, Simon's confession. The conspiracy laid bare to its rotted roots, and signed in his resolute script.

Oh, they had woven a tight plot, these clever, infamous men, men she had admired and loved.

Men.

Not boys.

And yet Simon had been little more than Davie's age at the time.

But she didn't want to think of that. Davie would never do such an evil thing, wouldn't allow himself to become embroiled in a plot against an innocent man, wouldn't take pride in his wicked falsehoods.

Nor could she imagine Simon, either.

Aye, but, damn the man, he *had*. She had read his testament against her father, his proud words spoken in the king's presence—in the presence of the clear and certain truth that must have been in his heart. There had been nothing vague or coerced in his statement; the devil's intent was found in the details: the time of day, the weather, the number and kinds of weapons hidden inside the wool ship among the bags of fleece.

And still Kailey tried to imagine what had brought Simon to betray a man, and then let him die. She tried to cast him into the huddling darkness of a tavern, sitting alongside the men he admired—his own father and FitzLandry—listening to those whispered conspiracies, plotting his strategy, his gray eyes banked with excitement.

What can I do, Father? How can I help bring down Neville Hewett? How can we make him bleed so that we may profit from his death?

Simon? Had it happened that way?

An innocent man's honor, Father? What matters honor, anyway? And his pregnant wife and his unborn child? Nay, they mean nothing to me.

No. It felt wrong and distorted. Only Simon knew the truth. And now she held his confession in her hands.

His death warrant! For surely this was a capital crime.

"My lady!" Kailey jumped when Davie came bursting through the door, his hair wildly askew and the knot on his head a dark purple. "I thought we were going to Nottingham with Julia and her wagon!"

"We are, Davie." Fearing that the walls had eyes, Kailey crumpled Simon's incriminating confession and looked around for a place to put it while she tried to make sense of its meaning.

"But his lordship just told me that we were leaving tomorrow for Northumberland."

"Did he?" Kailey didn't know where they were going next, but she was never again going to let Simon send her away for safekeeping.

"We must be!" Davie frowned at her and scratched at his bruise. "Lord Simon is never mistaken. He's a very wise man."

"Aye, and even wise men make mistakes. Grand ones. Unforgivable, hateful ones that change lives and batter hearts." She stuck the documents into her saddlebag.

"Now *you're* mistaken, my lady. But I'll go to

Northumberland as long as he's going, too. I'm his squire, after all." The boy's admiration for her husband rang clear and bright, made his eyes shine and her heart thump madly.

Tears swam in her eyes. "You'd do anything for him, wouldn't you?"

Davie pouted as though she'd insulted him. "Without question, madam!"

"Why?" She watched him carefully, looking for innocence, hoping to find it in abundance.

"Because Lord Simon would never lead me wrong. Never, my lady."

And there it was. A boy's devotion to a man he worshiped.

Kailey saw another boy then, dark haired and gray eyed, and so trusting, so willing to hand over his heart to his father.

Only to have it broken and betrayed.

But Simon had left Sir Robert then, estranged forever in the wake of this horror; he'd gone to live with the king's chief justiciar, to take on the law as his shield.

Not a shield for his crime, but to keep vigil against others.

"Kailey . . ." Davie was frowning, puzzling out another of a young man's mysteries. "I'm thinking that I do love the man—"

"Do you, Davie?"

"He's family now. Fits right here, I can feel him." Davie had put his hand in the middle of his chest, his fingers spread across his heart.

"So can I, Davie."

And the pain was nearly unbearable.

Simon stood on the top steps of the great hall and watched as the iron-bound pipe-roll chests were loaded into the wagons. The bailey looked like an army breaking camp in the path of an overwhelming enemy. Some of the court officials had already set out for Nottingham in the darkness, the merchants who traveled to the judicial fairs close behind.

But Simon would escort the Chestershire pipe rolls back to Westminster and then finally set justice in motion. If Henry was still in Normandy, wrestling his self-serving sons for his kingdom, he would join him there, confess in public the crimes he had so zealously concealed—and then the wait would finally be over.

"Ah, good, Simon. You're still here." Wingate hurried out of the great hall, his large leather bag overstuffed and sagging from his shoulder.

"Nearly finished." Simon took the bag from the priest and started down the steps toward a knot of horses.

"I am no longer abbot of St. Werburgh's, but off to the Holy Land. Such changes in the air." Wingate was out of breath as he followed, his sandals flapping on the stone. "We've left pleas unheard here in Chester. But I suppose you'll hear them in Nottingham in a week's time."

"Cathmore will, yes."

Wingate peered up at him from beneath his wiry brows, expertly finding his mark in Simon's regret. "But not you?"

"I'll be resigning my judicial commission as soon as I return to Westminster."

"You can't, Simon! There's no finer, fairer man in all the kingdom. No one more passionate or learned in matters of law. God knows I've seen miracles in your court."

Suffering his guilt ever more deeply, Simon

shifted his gaze from Wingate's undeserved tribute and handed the cumbersome bag to his sergeant. The world would know soon enough the sort of man who had barricaded his villainy behind the bastions of law and then sat in tainted judgment of others. Let Wingate be gone on his quest by then; let him not hear until it was too late.

"My reasons are complex, Wingate."

"You do it for Kailey, then?"

As he had always done, and ever would, until he could do no more. "Aye, for Kailey."

Wingate beamed, was no doubt seeing merry-hearted children and hearthfires in this doomed marriage.

"Then take care of yourself, son. You are a good friend, Simon, lending me the service of your knights to see Nicholas returned to me."

"You carry a king's ransom, Wingate. And my prayers."

Simon helped him into the saddle, gratified that the man had agreed to travel to Jerusalem on a horse and not upon that mule of his.

"God's peace, Simon, to you and to your lady wife." Wingate waved as he started away with one of Simon's sergeants on his flanks. "I shall miss her."

But you won't ache for her, priest, as I do.

Simon turned away from the disorderly scene in the bailey and went back into the clerk's chamber to see that the last of the legal documents were locked away and ready for transport.

The room smelled of rusted iron and the cave damp of a crypt, its echoes crisp and quick. He felt buried alive.

His saddlebags lay on the table at the center of the room, packed with what little he would need while he awaited his execution. There would be no trial. He'd made duplicates of the documents he'd left with Kailey. His confession would seal his fate even as it secured her future.

He was soul-weary and fresh out of time.

He had more than once imagined himself on the gallows, had felt the rough rasp of thick hemp against his throat as he stood above the trap, awaiting oblivion. He had lived beneath a gray sky for such a long time, it had been quite easy to imagine nothingness. But now his sky had become a wash of stunning hues and his whole world was Kailey: brilliant colors and vibrant fragrances, carol-songs and summer thunder. There would be no numbness at the end, only the gouging pain as she faded and slipped from his spirit, and he was dragged through the fires of hell.

"Do you pack away more falsehoods, Simon?"

His heart stopped still at the sound of her voice.

She stood at the door in her russet cloak and a pale green shift, so casually girdled she might have been at home and in their chamber, asking him when he was to join her in bed. He hadn't meant her to come again to him, not in his dreams or in his waking. He'd said good-bye once before—he couldn't do it again.

"Go home, wife. There's nothing more to say."

"I've decided that you're not a very good liar, Simon."

"Kailey, please—"

"No." She wore her burnished anger high on her cheeks, glaring at him as she swept into the room. "You told me that you were one of them, but you weren't, you couldn't have been."

"I was there."

"But you didn't learn of the conspiracy until too

late, did you? My father was already dead, wasn't he?"

"I knew well enough before then." He felt old eyes upon him even now, heard the adults whispering when they'd thought he wasn't listening. His skin prickled, rode his neck like a vulture.

"Nay, Simon, I read your confession." She came to stand across the table from him as he lit a candle of sealing wax with hands that shook, beguiled by the scent of her and unable to move quickly enough to escape the blackening tendril of smoke that sooted his finger. "You write like a lawyer, stating the barest truth but bending it to prove your guilty premise: that you were one of them and in the thick of it. But they were grown men, and they kept you in the dark purposely—enlightened you only when it served them."

"Go home, wife. I have work here."

"As I have, my stone-headed husband. The truth is buried deeply and well. You've not told me everything!"

"I've told you all you need to know—"

"Half-truths and twisted tales. They betrayed you, Simon—just as they betrayed my father! They used you because you could shinny into small, dark places where they could not . . . into ship's holds."

"Into a damned rat's hole, if they had asked me. And so I went. Willingly." And he'd felt the wrongness of it from the beginning—the furtive gestures, the glancing questions—and he'd held his tongue because of his pride.

"You thought you were collecting evidence in that wool ship, but they were planting it, weren't they? You left that out of your confession, Simon, but that's the truth of it, isn't it?"

The anger of betrayal burned as clean and hot as ever. "I was overeager to bring a man to justice, and too awed by this company of warrior–knights to risk being shunned. Too proud, Kailey."

"They were men to be proud of, Simon. But you were a just boy." Her voice had lost its outrage, but not its impatience, nor its caressing earthiness that made him want to believe in miracles. "You loved your father, worshiped him. Why should you have questioned him? Robert of Stoneham was a man of honor; he would never betray his son."

Simon knew what that admission had cost her, what she was forced to accept about the man she had adored. Her eyes were welled full of tears and made his breath fall short with longing.

Confused to the marrow by this truth she sought, he pinched out the candle, dropped it and his seal into a leather pouch, and threw them for last time into his saddlebag. If she wanted the truth, then it was hers.

"Robert of Stoneham was a man without a conscience, madam. He cared for no one. None of them did." He was there again, in the winter-heavy bailey, looking up at the creaking scaffold, his stomach churned to peat as he watched Hewett's body dangling half below the platform and half still above, in the pale sunlight. "They watched your father die without a moment's care that he was innocent. They would have walked away and let you starve but for—"

He'd said too much, and she was standing too near, listening too closely, to his pulse and to his breathing. He knew what she would do with his admission if he let on: she'd make too much of it, twist his motives.

"Tell me, Simon. They'd have walked away, but

for what?" And then, as though he had confessed it aloud, she took a small, telling breath and touched her fingers to her lips as though he had kissed her. "There was no heart-sworn pledge between friends to foster me when my father died. These men had no honor. It was *you*, Simon! *You* were my guardian from the start!"

"They gave me no choice." She was ready again with her gratitude, and he couldn't bear the weight of it. He turned back to his saddlebag, his hands unsteady as he tried to fit stubborn leather straps into rigid brass rings. "Your father's lands were already divided up; your mother was dead. The bastards would have walked away from their crimes and left you to the mercy of the court. I couldn't let that happen."

"And you stopped them?"

He hated the spiraling awe in her voice. He'd done as he'd had to, nothing more.

"How, Simon? You were but a boy. What kind of power could you wield against landed barons?"

"I threatened to expose them to the king. My soul was already damned for your father's death, so I cared not for my own neck. I made the devil's pact: that each man, starting with the eldest, would keep you in plenty and in happiness until his death, until at the last you would come to me."

He looked up at in her silence to find blue sky and wonder in her eyes.

"And so I did. You were my champion, Simon," she whispered as though he'd lit the stars and planted the forests. "You fought the dragons for me and you won."

"They were my dragons."

"And the ribbons! My Twelfth Night ribbons! They were from you!" She was smiling up at him, laughing gently through a sudden mist of tears. She raised up on her toes, planted one of her reeling "family" kisses half on his mouth, half on his chin, and held his face between her hands. "You were my own knight, and I carried your blazing banners. Oh, Simon, I love you. I think I always have."

Now her fingers were curled into the hair at his nape, and her mouth was soft and hotly accommodating. A growing sob had caught itself inside his chest, and he fell into the glory of her embrace, kissed her with the whole of his heart and his soul—for he would be an eternity without her. He held her against him, wishing for miracles and knowing there were none reserved for rogues like him.

None but Kailey. And he had stolen her . . . did love her everlastingly.

His pledge had been simple and noble when she was merely the essence of his guilt, walled up and easily forgotten. He could imagine her any way he liked. As bitter as gall, ungrateful, too prickly to handle or to love. But how could he scour away his corruption when she was silk and her eyes soft in wonder when she looked at him? When her kiss set him loose from the earth and let his dreams soar?

But her father was dead, and at Simon's hand. He was the survivor of this conspiracy, the very crucible of all the sins they had committed against her. The law was clear and dispassionate, and justice had to be done.

"Enough, Kailey." He set her from him with a sob, kissed her twice more, and then harrowed his fingers through her hair. He ached for her, wished that so much could have been different. But it was time. He could make Westminster in two days. "I must be away—"

"I forgive you, Simon."

Her eyes were clear and bright, and Christ, God, those were sweet words, said so simply that his throat clogged. He wanted to believe that she could, wanted to think that her dauntless forgiveness was sufficient to endure the years.

But even if it were, if she never lost her faith in him, he was a justiciar, had devoted his life to the laws of God and man, and must be held to a higher standard—else every man he had ever sent to the gallows had died without justice.

"I know your heart, Simon: fair and just and loving. I know it as God does. How could I not forgive you?"

He couldn't let her. "Forgiveness isn't the issue. You'll understand someday."

He stepped away from her while he could, shouldered his saddlebag, hefted the sealed coffer onto his hip, and left her for the vast emptiness of the great hall.

"Where are you going, Simon?" Her firm heels near-cracked against the stone floor as she followed him.

"To Westminster." He dropped the coffer onto the judge's table with the others.

"What's at Westminster?" There were few torches in the hall this late, but each had lit a flame in her eyes, indignity and anger, and always her abiding love.

"Justice."

"And the gallows?" she asked in fury.

"Yes." He didn't know how to leave her, so he merely walked away, hoping she would stay, praying she would follow.

"Damn you, Simon de Marchand, for an arrogant fool!" She caught his elbow in the shallow light of the chapel corridor and stunned him when she grabbed a fistful of his hauberk and shoved herself under his chin. "Your sin was against *me*! I'm the only one who *can* forgive you! Not even God can hold you to this crime as I can."

"Kailey, it's a matter of justice."

"Nay, Simon, it's your bull-headed pride! And I will fight to the death for you." Her fury made her strong of limb and compelling to his aching bones as she near-dragged him toward the soft light of the chapel. She kissed him soundly and sat him down on a deep bench in a niche near the thick door.

"Kailey, enough!" He tried to stand, but she knelt on the bench between his legs, trapping him, backed his shoulders against the wall, straddled his leg and then kissed him again.

" 'Tis my turn to be champion, Simon," she whispered harshly, her mouth bare inches from his, and her gaze as hot as her hands. "Champion of your heart and your soul and your children; champion to all those innocent thieves who will certainly lose their hands or even their lives if they come to stand in the court of some less honorable man."

"Nay, my judgment is tainted, Kailey." He spoke against her temple and the wreathing fragrance there.

"It was long ago blessed by God, by Julia, and by young men like Halwyn. Your heart is filled with His grace, Simon." She slipped to her knees on the stone floor, took his hands in hers and made him feel whole. "Never believe otherwise—never."

He was trembling, clutching at her hands. "I would have gone to the king, but for you, Kailey.

And for my father." A great, yearning sob tore out of him from across all those years. He was a boy again, his heart abandoned. "I couldn't let him die by my hand. I chose my father over yours. Oh, God, Kailey, how I loved him!"

"You love him still. He's your father, Simon." She pulled him into her arms and held him closer, as waves of fresh grief and ancient memories battered him and tore away at the darkness.

"My father." His chest tightened and he closed his eyes against the light of truth that had begun to filter through his impenetrable sorrow. "Damn the man, I do love him."

"And that's why you told me the truth about my father."

"You loved him, and wanted him back."

"Thank you, Simon."

He opened his eyes and the light was still there, brighter than before and the palest tear-spilled blue. He breathed through his sob-stuffed chest and cupped her face. She was love and hope and the milky wash of a moonless sky.

"You were to be a lifetime of penance, Kailey. A hellish burden to remind me of my sin and make me suffer it eternally. But I couldn't keep my distance, not even from the start. I never saw you, love, not in all those years. But I felt you—"

"You felt me here." Tears streamed from her eyes as she nestled his hand above her heart. "Because you made us a family, Simon. *You* did. All the years of wondering who I was and why I had always felt so untouchably loved. And all the time it was you, the keeper of my heart."

But it changed nothing, not his guilt or his fate. He tried to stand and be away, but she came up with him.

"Kailey—"

"The past is done, Simon." She held tightly to his hauberk, his furious defender once again. "My father's soul is at rest beside my mother. I can ask no more of you. But if you leave me, in your selfish quest for absolution, when I am standing here before you—if you make me watch you die on the gallows—and mark me, husband, I *will* watch and wail until they cut you down. If you leave me, Simon, I will never, *ever* forgive you."

That made his heart ache and sent him reeling with fear. "Never, my love?"

She took in a half-dozen great hiccoughing sobs and wailed to the vaulted ceiling. "Oh, damn it all, Simon, I *would* forgive you, because I love you more than my life. You'd find yourself with me in heaven and I would make eternity *miserable* for you!"

He had barely a breath to spare. "Would you, Kailey?"

She was snuffling loudly and so very wonderful, this wife of his. "I can be quite a nag."

"Can you?" He wanted to smile and shout his joy.

"I promise you, husband."

And suddenly all the cares of the world cleared away like a morning mist blown from the river. His heart grew and seemed to claim the whole of him, and he heard himself laugh.

"Then I'd best get some practice here on earth, my love—long years of it, I pray—if I'm to spend forever with you."

"I love you, Simon!" Kailey had watched in wonder as her magnificent husband let go his unwieldy guilt, watched as the warm light of peace came to his eyes and poured into his heart.

Peace, Sir Robert. He'll forgive you one day.

But just now, her husband's smile had grown huge, and seemed to take purchase in his chest alongside his laughter.

"My God, I'd given you up, wife!" He lifted her into his arms and stood her on the bench, where she was nearly as tall as he. "But now that you're mine again—"

"I have always been." He was close and dear, and his marvelous hands were cupped round her breasts.

"I have an unquenchable carnal craving for you, Kailey, that I can't seem to master." He kissed the underside of her chin, and then made love to her mouth, his fingers plucking at the ribbon that bound up the front of her shift. When the ribbons caught and wouldn't come, he yanked them off.

"Do you mean to satisfy me here, Simon? In the chapel?"

He looked up from his seduction and smiled. "I only wanted God to see enough to know that I was serious about staying."

"And what of my ribbon?"

His eyes grew bright with excitement. "I've another here."

Kailey watched him dig around his belt pouch, muttering into it and shaking it until he finally lifted out a crinkled length of green satin. The ends were frayed and a raisin had stuck itself on it midway.

Simon grimaced at it as if it were a wiggly worm. "They don't keep well, do they, love?"

Her Twelfth Night mystery. Her husband.

Kailey cupped his chin and would have given him a very carnal kiss of her own, when a great jangling of bells stopped her.

Hinch came through the open door, paused when he saw them, and grinned.

"I've come to tell you that Carrotlocks likes my hat!"

Simon laughed, a bountiful sound that clutched at Kailey's heart. "Oh, I like it, too, Hinch!" he said. "Indeed, I do."

"Carrotlocks?" Kailey jumped down from the bench and caught Hinch's hand, hoping that the man wasn't deep into one of his confusions. "Are you saying that Rigney woke up?"

"Woke up hungry, asking for a roasted Jemma. I had to tell him we were fresh out. But I promised to look for one."

"You can tell Carrotlocks that Jemma is on her way." Kailey grinned up at Simon, who had slipped behind her and wrapped her in his arms. He kissed her ear, murmured his wish for a bed and her company there. And children. Lots of them.

Oh, she liked this new husband of hers. Liked him just fine.

Hinch was staring at Simon, looking ferociously skeptical. "I see that it took you more than a week, Lord Simon!"

Kailey hadn't the slightest idea what Hinch meant, but Simon shook his head as if he understood.

"I should have told you earlier, Hinch," he said earnestly, almost confidentially. "It happened years ago."

"More than a hundred?" Hinch asked, wide-eyed, dragging the noisy hat from his head.

Kailey saw contentment and peace in her husband's eyes. She was in the dark as to this odd conversation, but she was proud of Simon and thought him magnificently grandhearted.

"In truth, Hinch," he said, turning her in his arms and kissing her brow, "I've loved our Kailey since before time began, and will forever and always."

Hinch winked broadly at Simon. "Very good, my lord." Then he was gone in a cloud of jangling.

They spoke in riddles, these men of hers.

"Simon?"

He put two fingers to her lips, replaced them with the feathery brush of his kiss, and then another.

"We've an eccentric family, wife."

She would have agreed aloud, but he was making love to her mouth again, humming as he was wont when his passion was high.

"Home?" she asked when she finally found her breath.

"Kailey, my love, my home is wherever you are."

Then he swept her up into his steadfast arms and carried her out of the chapel.

Your heart's peace, daughter.

"Aye, Father," she whispered, "and his name is Simon."

Dear Reader,

Coming next month from Avon Romance are terrific stories—historical and contemporary—beginning with *Perfect in My Sight*, the latest from bestselling author Tanya Anne Crosby. Sarah Woodard and her cousin Mary had vowed never to wed, but Mary breaks that vow. Now, she has died under mysterious circumstances, and Sarah travels to meet her dear cousin's husband for the first time. Sarah has no reason to trust Peter, but she begins to find it impossible to resist his charms . . .

If you like western settings, then don't miss Karen Kay's *White Eagle's Touch*, the next installment of the Blackfoot Warriors series. Katrina is a wealthy English socialite travelling west; White Eagle is the proud and powerful Blackfoot warrior who once saved her life. Together they find an unforgettable love that spans their two worlds.

For fans of Regency settings, don't miss Marlene Suson's *Kiss Me Goodnight*. The devilishly charming Marquess of Sherbourne never expected to be so entranced by radiant redhead Katherine McNamara, but her fiery kisses quickly ignite passion's flame in this seductive, sensuous love story.

And if you prefer a more modern setting, don't miss *Baby, I'm Yours* by Susan Andersen. The last place Catherine MacPherson ever expected to find herself was sitting on a bus, handcuffed to a sexy bounty hunter, with only a suitcase of her twin sister's shrink-wrap clothing to wear. Sam MacKade doesn't care how irresistible Catherine is, he doesn't believe for a minute that Catherine *isn't* her showgirl sister. Will Sam solve this case of mistaken identity and lose his heart at the same time?

Look to Avon for romance at its best! Until next month, enjoy.

Lucia Macro

Lucia Macro
Senior Editor

AEL 0498

Avon Romances—
the best in exceptional authors and unforgettable novels!